D0398078

My Heart Will Find You

JUDE DEVERAUX

My Heart Will Find You

mira

mira™

ISBN-13: 978-0-7783-3348-7

My Heart Will Find You

Mira
22 Adelaide St. West, 41st Floor
Toronto, Ontario M5H 4E3, Canada
BookClubbish.com

Printed in U.S.A.

My Heart Will Find You

1

March 2020

Henrietta Wilmont was sitting in the Kansas City airport when she first heard of the lockdown.

She had a while before her connecting flight, so she'd bought a couple of magazines, both about cooking, and she was absorbed in them. She was thinking she'd like to visit Portugal and find out how they make *pastel de nata*.

Since her phone was on airplane mode, the text didn't ding. By the time she looked, there were six texts from her sister, Alicia. Each was headed with all caps words like, "URGENT" and "VITAL."

Etta's heart started pounding. Something awful had happened. To Alicia? Her husband?

Please no, not their daughter, Nola. Etta took a breath. It had to be their father. She'd left him at home in rural Pennsylvania, alone in that huge house, and he'd fallen down the stairs. It was all her fault.

With shaking hands, she called Alicia's number. "What is it?" she whispered.

"California has been put on lockdown."

Etta had no idea what that meant. "Is Nola okay? Phillip? Is...?" She hesitated. "Is it Dad?"

"Everyone is fine," Alicia said. "Healthy. And we mean to stay that way."

"What does that mean?" Etta's voice was rising.

Alicia was a psychologist and was used to dealing with people in crisis. She turned on her calm-and-caring voice and explained that there was a virus running rampant throughout the world. It was attacking older people in particular and was said to be killing them almost instantly. People were being told to have no contact with anyone outside their immediate families. The lockdown would be in place for at least two weeks.

Etta was so relieved her family was okay that she couldn't be upset over a bit of isolation.

"We'll do it together," she told her sister. "I'll show you how to cook something besides pasta and—"

"You don't understand. You can't come here. The borders of the state are closed."

"But my plane—" With her phone to her ear, Etta went to the departures board. Her flight had been canceled. There were other flights available, but none to California. "I'll rent a car and drive. How far is it from KC to LA?"

"Etta." Alicia went into her therapist voice. "You can't come here and you can't go home. I don't want you on a plane with lots of other people. You need to stay there. In Kansas."

Etta looked around the airport. It wasn't very big, and she was seeing others who appeared to be as confused as she was. "I can't stay in the airport for two weeks!"

Alicia lost her professional tone and became the bossy younger sister. "Go to a hotel! Get one with a restaurant and stay there for as long as this lasts."

"Dad needs—"

"He's fine. I talked to him. I told him to go to the grocery store immediately and stock up on things, especially frozen foods."

"I filled the freezer before I left," Etta said. "There isn't room for more."

"Then he can get toothpaste and toilet paper. Whatever. The point is he can take care of himself. It's you I worry about. Who are you going to take care of?"

Etta laughed. "I'll find a hotel with a spa and get massages and facials. It'll be nice."

"I hope so. I'm going online now to try to find a place for you to stay. You do the same and call me."

"Sure," Etta said and they clicked off.

There was an older woman standing next to her, and she turned to Etta. "I didn't mean to eavesdrop, but you should know that all the cars have been rented. My granddaughter is picking me up and taking me home. I can give you a ride into Kansas City. You can get a hotel there."

"Thank you. I'll call for a reservation."

"Uh-oh. I have to go *now*." There was urgency in the woman's voice. She waved to a young, frowning woman who was hurrying toward them. "Sorry, but Rachel has never had any patience. Not even as a child." She straightened her shoulders as though preparing for a battle and faced her granddaughter. "We're going to give this woman a ride to a hotel."

"I'll just get my suitcase," Etta said.

The young woman looked Etta up and down as though she was the carrier of the disease. "We don't have room for another suitcase."

For the first time, Etta realized the seriousness of what was happening. If California had been shut down, how long before the other states followed? People around them were now moving quickly, and a sense of panic was filling the air. Was she going to miss an opportunity to get transportation because of a suitcase? She had her roller bag and her laptop so she'd be fine.

"Doesn't matter," Etta said. "I'm ready to go."

"We can't—" the young woman began.

"Rachel, please," her grandmother said.

Reluctantly, with a look of threat, Rachel gave a curt nod. "You'll sit in the back."

"Glad it's not in the trunk," Etta mumbled and followed them outside. She didn't say anything on the ride. She didn't even ask if where they were going had any hotels nearby.

As they drove, the buildings became taller. It looked like they were going into the city. Good. There'd be more places to stay.

A text came from Alicia.

Haven't found anything yet. Hotels are filling up. Grocery shelves are empty. Rent an apartment if you have to. Do whatever you must.

They were in a pretty residential area that was a combination of historical buildings and newer places.

Rachel pulled to the side and stopped the car. "This is as far as we go."

"Rachel," her grandmother said, "take her to a hotel. She's not from here. She—"

Rachel's eyes narrowed. "You haven't been listening to the news. This disease is killing everyone your age. You are in extreme danger. Every second that you're exposed to outsiders, your life is in further jeopardy." She looked in the rearview mirror at Etta with hard eyes.

"I'll get out here." Etta clutched the handle of her roller case, got out, then leaned back in. "Could you point me in the direction of a hotel? I—"

Rachel drove away so fast that Etta had to leap back to avoid being hit by the open door. It shut as the car sped away too quickly for the residential area.

Etta was standing on a sidewalk in a city she'd never seen before. So now what should she do?

She turned full circle. Not a hotel in sight. No signs for apartments for rent. There were a couple of little stores, but they were closed.

Worse was that there were no people anywhere. She thought it was like a sci-fi movie where a spaceship had invaded and taken away all the people.

She pulled out her phone, tapped the GPS and asked where the nearest hotel was. A mere mile away. She tried to make a reservation, but the site said it was full but maybe they weren't accepting guests online.

Etta walked toward where her phone said another hotel was, but she didn't find it. Her plan was to beg and plead. Midwesterners were known for being nice so maybe she'd succeed in getting them to give her a room.

But she saw no hotels, no open stores, and only a few cars. Twice she waved to get a driver to stop but no one did.

She called her father and asked how he was doing. He said he was fine, not worried about anything, and promised to eat well and not stay up late. He chuckled at her hovering. "You're the one who's the concern," he said. "You have no chicks to tend to so what will you do? Tell me when you're settled." She promised she would, then said goodbye. Introverts like her father were not scared by the idea of isolation. Actually, she doubted if he'd notice.

With a sigh, she looked around. Still, no people anywhere. She kept walking.

Maybe we should have listened to the news, she thought. When she was at home, after a long day with people, Etta was glad to spend quiet time with her father. They read or gardened and cooked. They both disliked network TV so if they watched something, it was an old movie. Thomas loved Westerns, and Etta liked black and whites from the forties.

Since Etta had been off work for weeks, they hadn't heard of the fear generated by the virus.

Again, Etta stopped and looked around. To her left was a pretty little street with mature trees and old houses. Maybe she could knock on a door and ask for directions. Maybe someone would give her a glass of water. She was hungry and thirsty and starting to get worried.

She passed four well-groomed residences, then she halted. Before her was the prettiest house she'd ever seen. Some people gushed over Victorians with their turrets and eyebrow windows, but Etta liked plainer, more simple. She knew this house was Italianate. It was two story, with a flat roof, and three tall, narrow windows on the second floor. The ground floor had a porch that wrapped around two sides, with thin columns with pretty headers. The front door was double wide and painted a deep marine blue.

Etta stood there looking at the house and admiring it. It was so simple yet so beautiful.

The front door opened and out came a man carrying a tray with a frosty pitcher. He was older, seventies, maybe more, but he had a face that was unlined, and he had a wonderful mustache. It was mostly gray but still had some dark in it.

It was a full minute before Etta realized he was watching her and she was staring. "Oh," she said. "Sorry." She turned away to keep rolling her case down the sidewalk.

"Will you join me?" he asked.

Etta hesitated. He had a nice voice. But from birth, females were indoctrinated about Stranger Danger.

He seemed to understand. "I'm here alone." He put the tray down on a table between two chairs. "The babysitter my son hired to look after me didn't show up. Do you know how to work a washing machine? I can't figure out where the wringer is. And the clothesline seems to be missing."

Etta laughed and thought what was more bonding than laughter? "You wouldn't know where a hotel is, would you?"

"I could look in the phone book."

This second anachronism made her laugh more.

He smiled. "I have chocolate chip cookies that I just took out of the oven and cold lemonade. I squeezed the lemons myself." He made a gesture of using one of those tall, old-fashioned presses.

Etta had one at home. He was a man of her own heart.

He held up a big fat cookie and took a bite out of it.

That was the last straw. She pulled her case down the short brick path, then up the few stairs to the porch. The man was taller than she'd thought and older. He looked pale. For all his joking about a "babysitter," she could see that he probably did need care.

He motioned for her to take the chair on the far side of the table, and he took the other one. "Help yourself," he said.

She drank deeply of the lemonade and was on her second cookie when he said, "I'm Henry Logan."

"Henrietta Wilmont," she answered. "But everyone calls me Etta."

"We are two Henrys." He nodded at her suitcase. "So what brings you to Kansas City? Or were you planning to fly somewhere else?"

"I was." She found herself telling him about her sister getting a job in Pasadena and moving there. "I miss them so much! I know it's no longer fashionable for extended families to live together, but we did. Dad and Alicia and her husband, Phillip, and their daughter, dear Nola. We all lived in one big old house and got along perfectly. I cooked and Phillip fixed things and Dad took care of anything with numbers. And Nola... Well, she kept us young. When they moved out six months ago, Dad and I..." Etta trailed off. "I'm sorry. I'm blabbing." She stood up. "Thank you so much for this. Could you point me toward a hotel?"

Henry didn't move. "Denver."

"What?"

"I grew up in this house. My great-great-grandfather built it in 1874. When I got married, Martha and I moved in here. Our son, Ben, spent his whole life here. When he married, his wife, Caroline, moved in. She's an architect and she converted the carriage barn in the back into a house for me." He looked up at Etta with eyes full of sadness. "But she got a job in Denver. A forever job. She's going to have a baby at any minute. A little girl."

Etta sat back down. "Oh." She took a breath. "And you're living here."

He nodded. "I'm afraid I'm not made for city high-rises, not physically or mentally."

She understood his deeper meaning. "Your granddaughter won't grow up in this glorious house. And you won't see her every day."

"No, I won't."

Etta's voice came out as a whisper. "Will they sell this house?" They both knew she meant after Henry was gone.

He started to speak but didn't. He just nodded.

For a moment they sat in silence. *Generations in one house*, she thought. *And all about to end.*

A wave of sadness and understanding seemed to pass between them. Both of them had recently had huge life changes. Neither of them believed they were for the better.

"Ben called me an hour ago," Henry said. "Everything all over the country is closing, even grocery stores. People are panicking. They're frightened. I don't think you're going to find a place to stay."

Etta had a vision of sleeping on a park bench. While the

weather today was nice, she doubted that a March night in Kansas was warm and cozy.

"Could I offer you a job?" he asked.

She looked at him. "Babysitting?"

"Exactly. The house is empty." There was a little hiccup of loneliness in his voice. "It would be yours. I stay in the house Caroline made for me. There are no stairs." He raised an eyebrow. "Did I hear you say you cook?"

She smiled. "I do. Not fancy, but it tastes good. For the last few years, I've worked with a man on a food truck. Lester loves change so we get creative." She frowned. "He tripped over his grandson's Lego set and broke his leg. He shut down the truck for the whole summer so I'm on my own."

"Which is why you were going to visit your sister."

"Yes." She sighed. "But now I can't get there."

"Stay and cook with me. I'll do the laundry if you help me rehang the clothesline."

She didn't know if he was kidding or not, but it didn't matter. She didn't have a lot of choices.

However, she dreaded telling Alicia what she was doing. Her sister would say, "You moved in with some man you don't even *know*?" For that, she'd use her how-could-you-do-something-so-stupid voice.

She looked at Henry. "Maybe I could…" She nodded to the house.

"Look around? Ascertain whether or not I'm a predator?"

She tried not to laugh, but didn't succeed. "For all you know, I could be one of the Benders."

At that Henry laughed loudly. In 1870s Kansas, there was an incestuous family of serial killers named Bender. They invited people in, murdered them in particularly nasty ways, then fertilized their garden with the bodies. After their treachery was discovered, they became known as the Bloody Benders. In spite of thousands of hunts, they escaped capture. Not one of them was ever found.

"You're a history lover like me," Henry said. His eyes were full of delight, as though he'd found his new best friend.

Smiling, Etta followed him inside. The interior wasn't what she'd expected. Maybe she'd seen too many historic houses where the owner tried to stay true to the time period. In Henry's house there were no hard, horsehair sofas, no lace curtains, no frilly porcelain ornaments.

The pretty entryway was painted a pale blue. To the right and left were two small living rooms. One was a comfy TV room with a chintz sofa. The one on the right was more formal. It had Japanese prints and pieces of Asian lacquerware.

"The rooms are lovely. I like everything." She nodded at a lacquer cabinet. "Caroline's touch?"

"Oh yes. She lived in Japan for a year and bought some nice pieces."

Farther down to the left was a more formal room. It was large, with a huge built-out bay window with a deep seat. It was done in blue and white, like a country estate.

On every surface were framed photos, drawings, and even paintings, of Henry's family. She picked up one. "You and your wife?" He nodded. Martha and Henry were laughing together. She was a big, strong-looking woman, more handsome than pretty. Ben was a cute boy, and he'd grown up to be a good-looking man. There were wedding photos of him and Caroline. She was very pretty, blonde, and her energy came through the picture. "Let me guess," Etta said. "He's quiet and she's fireworks on a stick."

"You got it perfectly."

When they left the room, Etta expected Henry to open the closed double doors that were across the hall, but he didn't. She followed him to the big stairs. To the left was Caroline's office, a well-lit room with big windows. All very neat and tidy. Very organized.

Henry stopped in the hall. "When Caroline redid the house, the only walls she tore out on this floor were back here. There were four rooms to the kitchen, with pantries and a staircase for the servants. My mother hated it all."

"What about Martha?"

"As far as I know, my wife had no idea where the kitchen was."

Etta laughed. "So Caroline redid the four rooms?"

"Oh, did she!"

When they reached the kitchen, Etta drew in her breath. It was the kind she'd dreamed of.

Along the back wall was a big sink, a wide fridge, and a six burner Wolf gas cooktop. Two ovens were separate. One could hold a thirty-pound turkey and the other was smaller and would heat up quickly. Open shelves were above.

In front of the long counter was a tall oak table. No fancy stone-topped island but a table that looked like it had seen a lot of use. A giant copper pot and baskets full of oils and wine were below. There was a door with windows that looked outside to a shaded area.

"This is beautiful." Etta was so in awe, she was whispering.

To the right was another table, but this one was lower, with white chairs around it. You could cook and serve in one room.

She ran her hand over the tall table. It made a true cook's island. "This is perfect."

"Ben and I liked it. After he got married, he and I did the cooking."

"Caroline's domesticity is like Martha's?"

"Softer, but in a lot of ways, yes." He nodded down the hall toward the big staircase. "You'll be staying upstairs, but I'm afraid..." He didn't finish, but she understood. No stairs for him.

She went up the stairs. There were four bedrooms, each with

a private bath. It was easy to see that at one time there'd been more bedrooms, and probably just one bath to be shared by both the family and the live-in servants.

One of the bedrooms was a nursery with a bassinet draped in white gauze. The sight made Etta think how sad Henry must be that his son and daughter-in-law and grandchild wouldn't be living there.

She knew too well the emptiness of when people you loved left your daily life.

There was a bedroom that she liked best. It was at the back of the house in what probably used to be the servants' quarters. There were windows in three walls, with a door to the bathroom in the fourth.

It was a moment before she saw the narrow door between the windows. It led out to a small, flat portion of the roof. An iron railing ran around the edges. The floor had been tiled, and Etta could imagine some old-fashioned teak furniture there. Like on a 1920s cruise ship.

Smiling, she went back into the room. The bed wasn't very big, but it was old and mahogany. There was a vintage trunk at the foot. The wallpaper was green-and-white stripes. The pictures on the walls were prints: David Roberts's sketches of Egypt, a black-and-white photo of Captain Sir Richard Francis Burton.

Between the windows on the far side were built-in shelves that were jammed full of books. David Attenborough's wildlife adventures were there, as well as books by Gerald Durrell. *Wonder if he's been to Corfu?* she thought as that's where the Durrells lived.

The room was quite male so she assumed it was Ben's. She'd ask Henry's permission, of course, and he could text Ben, but this was the room she wanted to stay in.

When Etta heard voices, she hurried downstairs. Henry was by the front door talking to a young woman holding a big box full of vegetables. She was very pretty, with auburn hair and a body that was big on top and bottom, and small in the middle. It was the kind of body women spent years in a gym trying to create. She wore tight jeans and a shirt with several buttons undone.

"This is Freddy," Henry said with obvious affection. "She feeds me."

"Just the raw ingredients." Freddy held out the box. "Kitchen?" It was as though she saw Etta as the mistress of the house.

"Sure. How did you get all that? I heard that the grocery stores are nearly empty."

Freddy put the box on the island. "I have a big garden, but it's too early for much so I go to the back of...well, to a few stores and ask the boys with the delivery trucks." As she said that, she leaned forward. It was obvious that she meant that her formfitting clothes helped her get first dibs on what came off the trucks.

"Whatever it takes."

Etta looked in the box. Berries, oranges, eggplant, onions, a bag of green beans and more. "This is wonderful. Thank you."

Freddy turned to Henry. "Everybody okay?"

"Yes. Caroline's just waiting to go into labor."

"Bet she's still working, though."

Henry smiled. "Of course. She'll be in the labor room and drawing between pushes."

"And Ben will be holding her drawing pad," Freddy said.

"Anything for her," Henry replied.

Freddy turned her back to him and gave Etta a serious look that let her know of Henry's sadness, his loneliness. "I gotta go. I have three other clients waiting for me. I'll see you next week."

Again, she looked at Etta, who nodded. Yes, she'd take care of Henry.

Freddy looked at her watch. "It's getting late if you plan to get it all done by six. Tell Sophie hi for me." With that Freddy left out the side door.

"What's at six?" Etta asked. "And who is Sophie?"

Henry started to answer but shook his head. "You'll see later. Right now I have something to show you."

She followed him down the hall to the room with the closed doors. When he opened them, she gasped. It was a library. A real, honest-to-heaven *library*. Three of the walls were covered with custom-made bookcases, honey colored from age and use. A brass bar ran across them so a ladder could roll around the shelves. They were packed with books and labeled files.

The center of the room had a huge green leather Chesterfield sofa, the kind with deep buttons in the back and big rolled arms. A leather armchair was to the side. A red-and-blue antique rug was on the floor. Scattered about were tables with lamps and more books.

On the fourth wall was a huge bay window that matched the one in the room across the hall.

The sides were draped with heavy green curtains. Facing the windows, its back to them, was a gigantic oak desk. It looked like it had come out of an Old West movie about some rancher who owned half of Texas.

Etta turned full circle as she looked around. "Now I see where Ben got his taste." When Henry looked puzzled, she said, "His room upstairs. I love the roof deck. Mind if I stay in there?"

"He would be honored." Turning, Henry nodded to the tall bookcase to the left of the double doors. "Those are mine."

"What do you mean?" she asked as she went to them. Every book in that section, some elegantly bound, some with beautifully illustrated covers, and all the file boxes, had the name H. F. Logan on them. "You?"

Henry smiled modestly. "The *F* is for Fredericks. There's a house in Mason that my ancestor built. It was restored a few years ago, and it's nice."

Etta went closer and began to pull out books. They were about history in the Midwest: Kansas, Missouri, Nebraska, Oklahoma. Drawings and paintings of cowboys, buffalo, Native Americans, and outlaws were all through the books. "My father would love these. He's an accountant with a passion for the Old West. I have to tell him."

She took her phone out of her pocket and texted her father.

I'm staying with a writer. H. F. Logan. Ever heard of him?

"It'll take him a while to answer. He——" Her phone dinged. "That was fast." Laughing, she held it up to show Henry. The return message was all emojis: exploding head, laughing to tears, thumbs-up, fireworks.

Autographed copy, please, came a second text.

Henry's face was pink with embarrassment but pleasure. "Tell him of course I'll send him a package of them as soon as possible. After this quarantine, that is."

"Or we'll let Freddy take it. She can flirt with the postmaster."

"Good idea." Henry waved his hand about the room. "So you like my study? It was my father's and his father's. I told Caroline she could redesign it so it's more modern."

"And she wisely said she wouldn't touch perfection."

"More or less. She did say she liked it. It's comfortable."

Etta nodded toward his giant desk. The back of it was carved with a cowboy on a horse lassoing a calf. "Where'd you get that?"

"Ben and I found it at an auction in Mason. He was hardly more than a toddler. I lifted him up and he stretched out on it. It fit him perfectly. We had to buy it." For a moment he was smiling in fond memory, then he looked up. "I bet you're hungry and besides, it's almost time. We need to cook. Mind eating outside?"

"I would love that." When they got back to the kitchen, she looked at the box Freddy had left. "Are you a vegetarian?"

Henry opened a tall cabinet door that she'd assumed was a

pantry. It held a freezer full of labeled packages and boxes. Beef, pork, chicken, seafood. "What would you like?"

"This is great. Um… I have a confession to make."

"You don't actually know how to cook." He sounded deflated.

"Not cook like other people. I learned from Lester. In a food truck."

Henry looked blank.

"Little space, hungry people waiting in the sun?"

Henry still didn't understand.

"Okay," she said. "Pull up that stool and sit there and give me this wonderful space to myself."

He did as he was told and Etta set to work. First, she hurried about the kitchen assembling what she needed. Henry raised his eyebrows at her speed. She slid a can of green chilies and an opener to Henry, then pulled a packet of trout from the freezer and put it in the microwave to thaw.

With lightning speed, she peeled and chopped a potato and an onion. She was chopping with one hand while she pulled the fish out of the microwave. She filled the two trout with onions, olives, green chilies, capers and olive oil, then wrapped them in parchment paper.

She put them in a hot skillet that Henry hadn't seen her put on the stove. Vegetables went into a pan. Then Etta used an immersion blender—something Henry didn't know was in the kitchen—to mix up eggs, milk, and sugar. He had no idea what she was making, but it smelled great.

In what seemed like minutes, Etta stepped back. "It's ready."

It took Henry a full minute to close his mouth. "I've never seen anything like that. It takes me ten minutes to chop an onion."

"You never worked for Lester. 'Fast' is the only word he really understands. He tells me I'm the tortoise."

"Who won the race."

"Exactly!" Etta said, laughing. "That's what I tell Lester. Shall we go outside?"

"You don't plan to toss the plates out, do you?"

Etta grimaced. "Don't say that out loud. Lester might hear you and tell me I have to learn how to do that."

Henry got the plates, glasses, and flatware, and led the way to the side yard. It was a beautiful place, house on one side, a tall fence painted white on the other. A mossy brick path ran down the middle, with flower beds on each side. A tree, just beginning to leaf, overhung it all.

Henry set the round iron table with the dishes, then helped carry out the food. "We don't have to eat at the speed of your cooking, do we?"

"Yes," Etta said without a smile.

Henry laughed. "I asked for that one."

As she sat down, he opened a wide panel in the fence. "What's that for?"

"A surprise."

"I look forward to it." They began to eat.

"This is utterly delicious." Henry looked at her in seriousness. "So why aren't you married and have three kids?"

Etta shrugged. "It just didn't happen."

"You're too young to speak in the past tense."

His look made her feel that she had to explain. "I was engaged when I was at university. As soon as we finished school, we were going to get married, then start producing those kids. It was all planned. I'd even picked out my wedding dress. Lots of lace." She shrugged as though that was the end of the story.

But Henry was still watching her. "So what changed? He cheated on you?"

"No. Worse." She took a breath. "My mother was very sick for a long time before she died. Dad had to work and Alicia had school. All of them needed me."

"So you left your own life plans and went home to take care of them."

"I did." She sounded defensive. "It was necessary. There was nothing else I could do."

"And the boyfriend?"

Etta gave a sigh. "He said that I had to choose between him or them. It wasn't a difficult choice."

Henry nodded. "I understand that. Family first. So what now? Are you meeting young men and planning for those kids?"

She shook her head. "I think it's past that. I'm thirty-four. In today's world, I'm practically a boomer. Any man interested in me has two ex-wives and three grown children who'd hate me for trying to take their mother's place. No thank you."

Henry was frowning. "You can't give up. There's—"

"Stop!" She was serious. "My life is good. I have a family and friends and a job I love. I don't ask for more."

"Maybe you should," Henry said softly.

Annoyed, Etta frowned. He wasn't the only person who'd said this, but it wasn't any of his business. Maybe it was a mistake staying here. She started to say that, but then the door to the house next to them opened.

Abruptly, Henry put down his fork, leaned back in the chair, and went quiet.

Etta was glad to drop the conversation about what-Etta-should-do-with-her-life. "What's going on?"

Henry made no answer, but then singing filled the air. It was a woman's voice but it was deep. "Rich" is the only word to describe it. The sound was ethereal. Divine. Jessye Norman come back to life.

Etta didn't realize that she'd halted with the fork to her mouth. When Henry reached out and touched her wrist, she put her hand down. Like Henry, she leaned back in her seat and listened.

The woman sang three songs, all church hymns. "Nearer My

God to Thee," "Holy, Holy, Holy," and "Just a Closer Walk with Thee."

When the third one ended, Henry got up, went into the kitchen, and returned with a fork, plate, and a tall glass of ice water. He put them on the table between them.

A minute later, a woman came out of the house. She was large but not fat, and she moved with her shoulders back, her head erect. She was an impressive-looking person.

Henry held out the chair for her and she sat down.

"This is Etta," he said. "She's staying here and looking after me."

"Someone has to." She was probably thirty years younger than Henry, but she gave him a flirty look. They'd obviously been friends for a long time.

"That was beautiful," Etta said. "Do you sing professionally?"

"Only in church," she said quickly.

"Oh but you should! You could—" Etta stopped at Henry's look. Uh-oh. Sore topic. "And for us," she said. "A private concert for Henry and me. We are blessed."

Henry smiled in approval. "This is Sophie."

Etta snuggled down in the bed. It was barely 10:00 p.m., but she was very sleepy. *Probably Henry's influence*, she thought. At nine thirty he said he hadn't stayed up so late since he was a youthful sixty.

As she looked about the room, deep in shadow from the bedside lamp, she was beginning to feel like there'd never been a time in her life when she didn't know him.

Sophie hadn't stayed long. She'd had a helping of Etta's custard with the burnt sugar crust, and said that she was a secretary at an insurance agency. Abruptly, she said she had choir practice and had to go.

As soon as they were alone, Etta gave Henry a hard stare. He knew what she was asking. Why wasn't Sophie singing professionally?

"Extreme stage fright," was his answer.

Etta cleaned up as fast as she cooked, then she told Henry she wanted to rummage in his library. "I want to see *your* books." She could see that he was pleased by her request.

They spent the rest of the evening in companionable silence. Etta pulled a chair and a table near Henry's books and began going through them. After he went to bed, she took a couple of books and went upstairs to shower and snuggle down. What was better than a comfortable bed with clean sheets and good books?

Yawning, she was about to turn out the light when a photo fell out of a book. It was of teenage boys playing soccer. She recognized Ben right away. He was running after the ball that was near the goalpost. *Bet he made it*, she thought.

She put the photo on the bedside table, then picked it up again. To the side was a young man, older than Ben, maybe early twenties, and he was smiling in what appeared to be pride. He looked a bit like Ben. A cousin? A nephew? she wondered. She put the picture down, turned out the light, and promptly went to sleep.

Two hours later, Henry made his way up the stairs. He had to pause twice to catch his breath. He'd had many years of nightly checking on people he cared about, and his faulty heart wasn't going to stop him now. The hall light was enough that he could see Etta was sleeping soundly. As he turned away, he saw the photo on the table. It was the day Ben won the game. That had been happy!

He picked the photo up and left the room, then struggled with the stairs. He was relieved when he made it down. Minutes later, he was in bed and his heart settled to an even pace. *I've done it!* he thought. *I've accomplished my goal. At least I pray I have.* He went to sleep.

2

When Etta woke up, her mind was fuzzy, unclear. It made no sense, but she seemed to be standing in a church. It was crudely built, looking like it had been slapped together in a weekend. There were rough pews to her right. When she had trouble turning her head, she realized that she wasn't fully awake, so she must be dreaming. There was something very tight around her middle. The bed covers?

She heard a voice she recognized and looked toward it. It was her father! He had on an old-fashioned dark suit with a black string tie. With her gone, had he started doing cosplay? He should have let her get the suit cleaned. It was wrinkled and dirty.

He was angrily glaring at Etta, not something he'd ever done before. "Do you or not?" he snapped.

"Do I what?" she asked. "I do think—"

"Those are the words," he said. "You're married. Now get out of here." He turned and walked away.

Bewildered, Etta watched him leave. *Married? What does that mean?* When someone took her left hand, she was startled, and looked down at it. A male hand was slipping a gold ring onto her finger. It seemed to go on very slowly. *I bet Henry's questions about why I'm not married made me dream this*, she thought.

When the ring was on, she looked up into the dark eyes of a gorgeous man. Not *Vogue* pretty, but rugged. Unshaved whiskers, square jaw, skin that showed he'd never used sunscreen. The hand holding hers was as rough as sandpaper, the palm one big callus. He too was wearing an old-fashioned suit.

"Congratulations, boss," said a man to the side. He was smaller, and he smelled like sweat and horses. Like her father, he was doing cosplay and wearing clothes from a Hollywood Western.

This dream is certainly realistic!

The taller man, the "boss," her so-called "husband," moved away from her. Three men, smelly and dirty, surrounded him. They were laughing and congratulating him as they took turns signing a piece of paper on a little table.

The boss stepped back, looked at Etta, and held up a pen. It was steel, and there was a bottle of ink she was to dip it into. "What? No rollerball?" she asked.

The four men stared at her in silent confusion.

I certainly dream authentically, she thought. When she took a step forward, she almost fell.

Heaven help her, but she had on a skirt that nearly touched the floor. How was she supposed to walk in the thing? The men were watching her, so she grabbed the front and walked with all the grace she could muster.

She made it to the table. The paper said Marriage License at the top. Henrietta Lily Wilmont to Maxwell James Lawton.

Etta started to refuse to sign, but it was a dream, so what did it matter?

She signed, then stepped back. "So now I'm a married woman?" She was beginning to think her dream was hilarious. She couldn't wait to tell Henry. Her unconscious had combined his books and questions into the most vivid dream anyone had ever had.

"Too late to change your mind now," one of the men said.

He really should take a shower, she thought. *And who dreams with smells?*

"You got the worst man," the second one said to Etta. "He'll put you to work at dawn. Won't let up until the moon shines bright."

"Then the *real* work begins," the third one said, and they all snickered like pubescent boys.

"Out!" the tall man ordered. "I want that fence repaired by sundown."

The men backed toward the open door with leering grins on their dirty faces. "Just sundown, boss? I could last longer than that."

"That's not what Freida says."

The three men fell into loud laugher, then scurried out the door as the man took a menacing step toward them.

"I apologize for them," he said.

Etta just blinked at him. What an odd dream. She would have put money on it that if she'd made up a marriage dream, it would be with a man who was madly, passionately, insanely in love with her. Except for when this man put the ring on her finger, he'd stayed several feet away. And now he was looking at her as though sizing her up. There was certainly no love in his eyes. There wasn't even familiarity. It was like he'd never met her before.

"Ready?" he asked as he picked up an old leather hat off a pew and put it on.

"Sure," she said. She was gradually becoming more awake. Or more… She wasn't sure "awake" was the right description for a dream. More aware of her surroundings.

When she again tripped, she looked down at what she was wearing. A long, heavy, dark skirt. The top was as tight as a sausage casing, but there was a little lace jacket over it. While the outfit was heavy and cumbersome, what was really awful was what she could feel under it. Only a corset could be that tight. Had someone used a tire iron to pull the laces together?

As she took a breath, she put her hands at her waist. To her astonishment, her hands weren't far from being able to encircle her waist, which was now teeny tiny. Yes, she was in pain, but the corset had achieved what years of going to a gym hadn't been able to do.

She looked up at the man, her eyes wide.

Maybe he saw some of what she was feeling because he gave a little half smile.

They left the church and at the door, Etta paused. In front of them was a wide street that was paved, if you could call it that, with horse manure, mud, corncobs, trampled rubbish, and she didn't want to think about what else. On each side were wooden buildings that looked like a fire waiting to happen. Barbershop, saloon, mercantile, saloon, livery stable, saloon, saloon, saloon.

"I guess people here like to drink," she said. He cocked his head toward her but didn't reply.

To the side was a beat-up old flatbed wagon harnessed to two horses. In the back were a couple of trunks. One of them looked like the one from the foot of Ben's bed. She was incorporating what she'd seen into her dream.

"All there?" he asked.

She guessed he meant those were her trunks. *Wonder what I packed?* She nodded.

They went down the steps, and Etta managed to not get entangled in her skirt as she walked to the wagon. She stood there looking at it. How in the world did she get up into it? Her foot went where? Hands where? As she prepared for the climb, she slipped out of the lace shrug. It was too pretty and fragile for wearing in a wooden wagon. The man was behind her. He took the little jacket, lifted the lid on one of the trunks, and carefully laid it inside.

Etta looked back at the wagon that seemed to be impossible to reach.

"Oooh!" she said as the man suddenly put his hands on her little waist, lifted her like she was a child, and set her into the front. "Usually a man won't even open a door for me," she muttered.

He must have heard her because as he got into the other side he gave a smile that was a tiny bit wider than before. He reached into the back and pulled out a roll of canvas. "This is a wedding gift from Alice."

She started to ask who Alice was but he seemed to think she knew. She unrolled the cloth. Inside was an umbrella. Correction, a parasol, that was so beautiful Etta could hardly get her breath. The panels on the wire frame were ivory silk, and the edges were embroidered with tiny blue flowers with green leaves. Cascading from the center were strings of matching flowers. Obviously, it had all been done by hand.

"It's beautiful," she whispered.

For a moment his face seemed to melt from tough to fragile.

"I'll tell my sister you think so."

His vulnerable look was gone, but it had been there long enough for her to see that he loved his sister. She liked that he had family he cared about.

She wrapped the parasol back up and put it in the foot trough.

His face went back to the inscrutable look he'd been wearing. He untied the reins and snapped them to make the horses go.

It took only a few feet before Etta realized that riding on a hard wooden seat down a rutted road wasn't like on TV. She was tossed to one side, then bounced up and down. If it weren't for what felt like half a dozen slips under her skirt, her backside would be one big bruise.

He looked at her. "Are you all right?"

"Comfy." Her teeth clicked together as they went over a pile of fresh horse manure that was on top of old manure. "Nothing like a sweet summer's day." She took a breath then coughed at the smell.

Again, he gave a bit of a smile.

Etta grinned broadly. Her family and Lester were so used to her jokes that they paid little attention to them, so it was nice to find someone who appreciated them. *This part of the dream makes sense,* she thought. Of course she would put in someone who liked her sense of humor.

Suddenly, a woman walked in front of the wagon. She didn't look at it, much less give the horse and wagon the right of way.

The man pulled back hard on the reins, and the horses did the best they could to halt. But their eight skinny legs twisted around together and they nearly went down. The man stood up, trying to calm the horses and guide them.

At the jolting, Etta started to fly forward, but the man grabbed her upper arm. He had reins in one hand, Etta held by the other one. When she came down, she hit the seat so hard her teeth rattled, and she thought she might have cracked her tailbone.

The woman in the road never so much as looked up.

"Damn you, Martha!" he yelled. "You could have been killed!"

She kept walking but turned her head to give him a look of disdain. "You should learn how to drive."

As the man sat back down, he turned to Etta. "Are you all right?"

She nodded as she stared at the woman. Etta had seen a dozen photos of her. "Martha Logan."

"No. It's Martha Garrett." He snapped the reins to go again. "Same name as this town."

"Does she own it?"

"Her husband did, but after they died, she didn't have much property left."

"'They'?"

"Her husband and son were killed in the war."

Etta wasn't sure which war he meant, but it couldn't be one of the two world wars. It must be… "North and South?"

"What other war is there?" he answered, giving her a look of shock.

"Henry and Ben," she said.

"Who are they?"

"Martha's husband and son."

"Her husband was Theodore. I don't know the boy's name."

As they slowly rode down the filthy, fragrant street, Etta looked at the buildings and the people.

Oh for a cell phone to photograph it all! If it were real, that is.

When he halted to let another wagon go by, Etta looked at one of the saloons. "'Girls and beer.'" She read the sign aloud. "That about covers the desires of the entire world." When he full-out grinned, she was pleased. Getting him to smile was becoming a goal for her.

The door to the saloon swung open, and two women came out. One had a broom, and the other had on a low-cut red dress and lots of rouge.

Etta's eyes widened. "That's Sophie and Freddy."

"Sally and Freida," the man corrected her. "Not your sort."

"You mean she's a sex worker so I'm supposed to snub her? Not in my dream! Freddy," she called out and waved. "And Sophie. It's good to see you two again."

The women looked at her in shock. Freddy raised her hand in a weak wave of hello, while Sophie just stared.

As the wagon started again, Etta turned in the seat. "Can you sing?" she asked Sophie and received a curt nod. She looked at Freddy. "And you like vegetables. And gardening."

Freddy's eyes widened as she too nodded.

Etta turned around, her smile broad. "It's always nice to see friends."

The man wasn't smiling. "I don't think those two can be your—"

"My what?" Even to herself she sounded aggressive. "Not my friends because they're not suitable? They're beneath my class?"

He gave her the oddest look, as though she were an alien being.

"Sorry," she muttered. "Where I come from, things are different. People are equal. We don't look down on how someone makes a living. I'm sure Freddy does what she has to do to survive."

"Your home must be a very different place," he muttered, frowning. They rode in silence, and the air between them was heavy.

It's my *dream*, Etta thought. *So why would I embarrass myself in my very own made-up dream?*

It was as they reached the end of the long street that a woman rode up on a truly magnificent horse. Big, black, shiny. The woman was also magnificent. Etta had begun to think that her dream consisted only of people who didn't know what "clean" meant. But then there was this woman. She was covered neck to feet in dark green wool. Had Etta read about such a garment in one of Henry's books, it would have sounded modest, but the way it fit was anything but. It was as sexy as lingerie in an underwear catalog.

When she halted her prancing horse on Etta's side of the wagon, she smiled in recognition. It was Ben's wife, Caroline, the firecracker, the woman who adored Henry and had designed a guesthouse for him. "Hello!" Etta said enthusiastically. "I'm—"

She ignored Etta. Her eyes were on the man. "Is it true?" she demanded.

His mouth was a hard line. "This is my wife, yes."

She gave a rather remarkable sneer. "Is *this* what you wanted? Old and plain?"

"That's not very nice," Etta said.

Caroline still didn't look at her. "You would do this to me? After all we've done together?" Her meaning was clear: bedroom antics. "You're a bastard, and I hope you get what you deserve. In fact, I'm going to see that you do."

Etta knew woman-scorned rage when she heard it, and she knew Caroline was going to lash out. She was going to strike at him with her long riding crop. But Etta was between them.

The man also knew what was about to happen. He pushed Etta down, out of striking range. Her head hit her knees. At her feet was the wrapped parasol, and she grabbed it. Unfortunately, the wrapping fell off.

Etta sat up, the closed parasol extended, and the whip hit it instead of him.

The looked of rage on Caroline's face was enough to cause thunder to crash. "This isn't over," she yelled as she rode away, causing manure and sawdust and mud to hit the wagon and its occupants.

When the air cleared, he was looking at Etta in disbelief. "Old girlfriend?" she asked with exaggerated calm.

He gave what was almost a laugh and set the horses to moving.

Etta looked at the parasol. One of the silk panels had a cut in it. "Oh no." Something so beautiful to be ruined was a catastrophe.

"Alice can fix it," he said softly.

Nodding, she wrapped it back up and put it down.

They left the stinking town and were on flat ground where the path was relatively clean. He stopped the wagon and took a moment before he spoke. "I know you want to meet Alice but maybe you and I could..."

"We could what?" she asked, while thinking, *Have I conjured a dream with a wedding night in it?*

She wasn't displeased at the idea.

"Thank you for what you did with Cornelia."

"She probably wouldn't have hit you."

He leaned forward and took off his hat. His dark hair was long. Not Wild Bill Hickok long but a little longer than dumb ole Custer's. He turned so she could see his left ear. His earlobe was crooked. It looked like it had been mostly torn off then sewn back on by a six-year-old.

"Was the doctor drunk?" she asked.

He gave a full-fledged smile. "As a matter of fact, he was."

"You should have let Martha do it."

"Martha Garrett?" he said in horror as he put his hat back on. "She would have yanked it all the way off and said it was a useless body part."

Etta didn't smile. "But if you became a pirate, you'd need it for an earring."

He grinned at her. "You're not like I thought you would be."

"Is that good or bad?"

"Very good." His eyes were sparkling.

When he looked at her like that, she thought, *Sex dream. Oh please. I want a sex dream.*

"I'd like to show you something, and explain a few things. Think you could stand my company for a few hours?"

"I do." They smiled together, and she thought, *Those are the two words that started all this.*

He picked up the reins and they rode in silence for a while. "Who was the pastor?"

"That's Tobias." He sounded grim.

"Is he a good minister?"

"The worst. His sermons are a misery to hear. We built him a church but that didn't help."

"Wonder why he became a pastor?"

"His father made him." She looked at him.

"Three shots of whiskey and he won't stop talking."

Etta understood. Her grandfather was a man who was sure he knew how everyone should live. He'd wanted Etta to be a lawyer. No one was less suited for that profession than she was. She wanted people to *like* her.

As they went across the undulating grassland, Etta felt sure they were in Kansas. She didn't want to question him and make herself seem stranger than he already thought she was. "Where are we?" or "What year is it?" were as bad as "What war was it?"

He halted near a narrow, shallow river. There were pretty cottonwood trees along the side. It was a beautiful site. "This is nice."

"I always thought so." He nodded toward a small hill nearby. There appeared to be a door in it. "That's where I grew up." He hesitated. "Would you like to see it?"

"Very much so."

He got down and Etta tried to figure out how to do the same, but the wagon was so high off the ground. Besides, she had on what felt like 150 pounds of clothing. But he came around to her side and held up his arms. *Great*, she thought and sort of fell forward, like a toddler playing Catch Me.

He swung her about, set her on the ground, then headed toward the door.

It was a house that was partially dug back into the hill, with extending walls made out of hard blocks of dirt. As she looked around, he told her about elephant grass and plowing under it and how the pioneers had made the sod houses.

She was more interested in the interior. It was one big room, with a bed in the back corner.

There was a fireplace and an iron stove with two burners on top. There was even a little oven.

The walls were coated in plaster that had been dyed pale blue. There was a nice oak table and chairs. As he talked, she opened a couple of wall cabinets. Inside were canned goods, rice and flour, and other food. Yes, she could make a meal with these.

The place was quite clean and looked like it was still being used. "Is this your man cave?"

He stopped his history lecture. "My what?"

"Your place to get away by yourself. To escape all things female."

He looked pleased at her perception. "It is. Not even Alice knows that I keep the old homestead up. Would you like some peaches?"

She'd seen the cans. "I'd love some." She watched as he opened two cans with a big knife, handed her one and a spoon.

"You want to go outside?"

She followed him to the river. They sat on the grass, looking toward the water. Etta loved the peaches. They weren't like twenty-first century canned fruit that was in a heavy syrup of sugar. These tasted more like peaches you'd pull off a tree.

"I guess I should explain about Cornelia."

"If you want to."

"My father came to America from Italy, and he was a good worker. He was ambitious and determined to succeed. He did without so he could buy more and more land. Maybe that's why he and my mother died so young."

"And left you in charge of property and your sister."

"Yes." He paused. "John Kecklin, Cornelia's father, owns the land on three sides of what my father left me. Mr. Kecklin wants to own all of Kansas, and he wants me to help him buy it. But most of all, he wants the land my father gave his life to get. The problem is that I refuse to sell to him."

She thought about what he was saying. "I see. It's like in the Middle Ages. If you marry his daughter, Mr. Kecklin gets all the land."

"Alice said you were smart." He paused for a moment. "She loved writing to you. I would have done some of it myself, but I have trouble with that. Sometimes letters look backward to me. I have less trouble with numbers, but there aren't as many of them." His eyes brightened. "But she read all your letters to me. I know about your father, your sister and her husband, and your niece. And I know you've had two years of university. Alice loves that. She reads all the time."

"And she sews. What else does she do?"

It was a simple question, but he took a while to answer. "It looks like she didn't tell you. Alice is crippled. She doesn't leave home much. Cornelia made a place for her, and Alice stays there."

"Made a place for her? What does that mean? No. I think I understand. Like Caroline. Cornelia designed it."

"Yes. Cornelia drew out a glass room for Alice so she can see the outside, then I built it."

Etta was putting this information together. If Cornelia knew his sister so well as to design a place for her, there must have been a strong connection. "How serious was it between you two? Just flirting or a ring and wedding plans?"

He ducked his head in a way that told her they were practically up the aisle. "You weren't, by chance, the one who broke it off, were you?"

"'Fraid so."

She nodded. "What made you do that?"

"One day I was doing the accounts so that meant I was thinking about something other than her, and she was horrible to me."

"What a crime! You deserved it."

He looked at her as though trying to figure out if she was serious, but then realized she was kidding. His laughter was a nice sound. "You know, I think I like you. I didn't think I would. An old spinster with all that schooling. I never thought you'd have a sense of humor."

Again with the old, she thought. Maybe this was her payback for telling Henry that her life was already set. "So you married an old woman just to spite Cornelia?" This was a dream, but really! A girl needed to have some pride.

He didn't seem to realize that he'd said something wrong. "I had to break my tie with her and her father. I couldn't have stood a life under the rule of John Kecklin."

"So you decided to get married to someone else."

"It seemed the best way to solve the problem." He again looked her up and down in that appraising way. "There were several other choices but I liked that you took care of your sick mother, and Alice wanted someone educated." He shrugged. "It all fit."

I'm a mail order bride! she thought. Romantic sounding but not in this case. He'd married her to be a nurse for his sister, and to protect himself from some medieval marriage. It was hard to believe, but she'd given herself a dream of a pity marriage. She had betrayed herself! "You could have hired someone."

"I tried that, but women are at a premium here. Old, young, dumb, smart, it doesn't matter. They get married as soon as they get off the train. I've hired four of them, and they never lasted longer than a few months. One of them married my head wrangler." He sounded outraged.

"Maybe my wedding gift should have been a mop and a bucket."

He seemed to understand that she was saying something bad, but he didn't get it. "The parasol was Alice's gift. Mine is this." He waved his hand to indicate the land around them. "I'll give you twenty acres of land, including part of the river, and if you stay for a year, I'll build you a house. Alice says that every woman needs a place that is just hers." He smiled. "It would be a woman cave for you."

The anger she'd started to feel left her. There was nothing malicious in what he'd done. He was a man who loved his incapacitated sister so much that he'd do whatever was necessary to help her. It's what Etta had done when her mother was ill. Those months of treatments and seeing that they weren't working had been the worst time of her life. After the funeral, she'd thought about returning to school, but Alicia and her father had needed her too much.

"A house of my own," Etta said. "How about something Italianate? Two stories, wraparound porch? Alice and I can sit on it and drink iced tea."

For a moment there was such gratitude in his eyes that it hurt her to see it.

"What about *you*?" she asked. "It seems rather drastic to marry someone just to get a housekeeper and a nursemaid. What about love and companionship? Children? And...?" She shrugged. "And affection."

"I'd be a terrible husband. I have a bad temper, and I never come home when I should. Alice says only a saint would marry me. But if I ever find a husband for her, she can have children. That's why I agreed to you."

"Right. As you and Cornelia said, I'm an old and plain spinster. Too educated for any man to want me. Fit only to be a cook and a cleaner." She wasn't angry. It was too much like what had been said to her many times before, but not so blatantly. Lester had introduced her to a few men, and Alicia had insisted she meet three unmarried doctors. But none of them had appealed to her.

"I didn't mean to upset you. I thought Alice explained things to you."

"She probably did," Etta said. "And I probably agreed. So you and I are to be friends with no benefits."

He looked affronted. "A home, meals, comfort. No one will mistreat you."

Or love me, she thought. She didn't say it, but it was in her eyes.

He gave her a hard look. "What about you? What's so good about your life that you agreed to marry a man you'd never met?"

That was much too good of a question. Suddenly, she'd had all of this dream she could bear.

She pinched herself inside her elbow where it would hurt the most. It wasn't easy to do through the long sleeve of the dress, but she managed.

He looked at her in surprise.

"Just trying to wake up. This isn't a dream I want to continue."

"Dream? What do you mean?"

She stood. "All of this. You, the mud house, even the peaches, are just in my dream. And right now I don't like it. I'm not an old, useless spinster. In my time that word isn't used. Besides, women like to postpone marriage and kids until their career is established."

She saw that she was making things worse. His face showed that he didn't understand what she was saying. He seemed to be drawing into himself. Wasn't this a time period when men could lock away wives for being "insane"? With the way her dream was going, she could imagine being put in a straitjacket.

"This is Kansas," she said. "If it worked for Dorothy, maybe it'll work for me." She closed her eyes and clicked the heels of the high-topped leather shoes she had on. "There is no place like home. There is no place like home." She opened one eye. He was looking at her like she was crazy. She closed her eyes. "There's no place like home." When nothing happened, she sat down. "Okay, I got it. This dream ends when it's supposed to, and there's nothing I can do about it." She turned to him and thought, *This is a marriage of necessity. There's no love, no kids. Freddy and her compatriots get all the fun while old me gets the work. This is a job. Like with Lester. This man is younger and a great deal better looking than Lester, but he's off-limits.*

She held out her hand to shake his. "I guess we have a deal. I take care of your life, and you give me food and shelter."

He looked perplexed, obviously not understanding why she didn't seem happy with that. He took her hand, shook it once, then dropped it. "Henrietta," he said. "I—"

"It's Etta. And should I call you Mr. Lawton?"

She saw anger flash in his eyes. It looked like she'd pushed him too far.

"Yeah, sure. That would be good." He stood up. "Let's go to Alice, and I can turn you over to her."

Etta wished she hadn't made him angry, but at the same time he'd hurt her, and she was glad to get back at him.

He lifted her onto the wagon, but this time it was more of a toss. He drove faster, seemed to hit all the rocks and holes, but never once asked how she was doing.

As for Etta, she would have died before she asked him to slow down. She held on to the sides of the seat and repressed grunts and groans while being slammed about.

They rode, not speaking to each other. Etta kept telling herself she was actually at Henry's beautiful house in a warm, cozy bed and none of this was happening. But right now the bruises and the muscle aches seemed very real.

A house came into view. There was a barn nearby, and men with horses stopped to stare at them. Etta would like to meet them. Maybe there were people she knew in real life.

But he pulled to the front of the house. It was a nice place: two stories with a steep roof, two chimneys and three dormers. The front had a long porch with five square columns. The yard in front of the house was messy and weedy. Although the house looked to be in good repair, it had an air of abandonment that Etta thought was rather sad.

To the left was a low addition with big windows, and she could see pretty floral curtains inside.

Was this the part that was designed by Cornelia? Alice's prison?

He swung her down from the wagon, but he didn't look at her. "Alice is in there," he said, then led the horses and wagon away.

At the end of the lower part of the house was a door. Etta

picked up her heavy skirt and the underlying petticoats and made her way through knee-deep weeds to the door. When it stuck, she knew it wasn't used very often.

She pushed it open and went inside. To her right was a bedroom and inside was a very pretty bed. It was a French design with wooden carvings of swags of vines and a bow in the middle. In the corner was an easel with a very nice watercolor landscape on it.

"At least it's a beautiful prison," she muttered.

There were other rooms, but she wasn't interested in them because at the end of the hall was a wide, glassed-in area. Tropical plants were along the edges: palms, orchids, bromeliads. It was like a botanical garden that a person would pay to see.

To the side was a young woman. She had on a ruffled dress of light blue, the square neck quite low. Her dark hair was piled prettily on top of her head. She was bent over a wooden embroidery frame and sewing on a sampler. *I need not sell my soul to buy bliss*, it read. Below that was the author's name *Charlotte Brontë*, but the final *ë* hadn't yet been sewn.

She looked up and saw Etta. "You've come at last." She stood up. She was Alicia. It was Etta's sister's face, body, voice.

The young woman took a step and Etta saw her limp. She picked up a silver-topped cane and took a few more steps.

"Alicia," Etta whispered, and her eyes filled with tears. Her sister was always ready to listen to people's problems, always had a solution. "I've had the most awful dream. I got married, but he says I'm old and ugly and your parasol was cut and—"

The woman let her cane fall to the floor, and she opened her arms. "Come talk to me." Gratefully, Etta took a step forward, then...

She woke up.

3

When Etta woke, she wasn't sure where she was. *This is becoming a habit*, she thought. Sunlight was peeping around the curtains. The fabric was a print of Western American animals: buffalo, prairie dogs, eagles. *Teddy Roosevelt's delight*, she thought. The name made her think of Martha's deceased husband, Theodore.

But wait, no, that wasn't real. All that had been a dream. By noon, she knew she'd have forgotten the whole thing. It was just that right now, this minute, her long dream was very clear. Sights, smells, voices, people. There was Alice who was Alicia, and Sophie and Freddy, two women she hardly knew but who had seemed like long-lost friends.

And her father was there. As a preacher! She'd have to call him and tell him. Her introverted, crowd-hating father as a pastor! It was a funny idea. His loves were numbers ("something a person can *depend* on") and the Old West ("where men were Men"). So what kind of sermons did Reverend Tobias give? How to balance accounts? Or did he give history lectures on what really happened at the O.K. Corral? Maybe he'd do a show-and-tell about his favorite, Wyatt Earp. He'd tell how he was six feet tall and that he never drank but ate a lot of ice cream.

The thoughts were making her smile. She heard a clatter downstairs and realized she had to quit reminiscing and get up. She had to earn her keep. *Just like Freddy does*, she thought, then laughed.

It was when she threw back the covers and put her feet on the floor that she felt pain. "What in the world?" When she moved, she hurt. From head to toe, she ached. "What did I do last night?" she muttered. She twisted her upper body. Everything was sore.

When she stood up, she closed her eyes in pain. She felt like that time she and Lester had loaded three dozen fifty-pound boxes into his pickup. She'd lifted, pulled, pushed, and dragged those boxes. The next morning, she could hardly move. Worse was that she'd had to listen to one of Lester's lectures of "You kids today are too soft."

Etta limped across the room. There was a tall mirror, the old-fashioned kind on a stand, in the corner. She had on a long T-shirt she'd found in a drawer, and she saw a bruise on her leg. When she lifted the shirt, she saw huge dark bruises on her backside. "Damned wagon!" she said.

But that couldn't be. She hadn't really been on a wagon. She was sore because… She took a moment to come up with a reason. Obviously, during the night she'd been sleepwalking. That made sense. Scary lockdown, surrounded by strangers, separated from the people she loved. It had all upset her more than she thought it would. The stress, the uncertainly, had caused her to have a dream so vivid that she'd left the bed and enacted it.

She started to turn away but then looked back at the mirror. The man in her dream—*her husband!*—had injured her ego badly.

No, she wasn't flamboyantly beautiful like Caroline-Cornelia, but Etta had always been called pretty. Not "plain" at all. Good skin, bright blue eyes, thick, dark hair. One time a boy told her she had the most beautiful lips he'd ever seen. Of course a boy making a pass couldn't be trusted, but still...

She looked about the room. There didn't appear to be anything that would give her bruises and muscle aches, but that didn't erase the fact that she had them.

Her eyes lit on the trunk at the foot of the bed. It was the one she'd seen in the back of Max's wagon.

She corrected herself. She had seen the trunk earlier, so she'd incorporated it into her dream. Wincing from pain, she knelt in front of the trunk and opened it. It was full of children's things: books about dangerous adventures, a pocketknife, a few X-men figures, and a lot of animals made by Scheich. She could imagine birthday and Christmas gifts. All in all, it was a time capsule of when Ben was a boy.

As she moved things around, she saw an old package at the bottom. It was in brown paper tied with jute string. It wasn't hers so she wasn't going to open it, but then she saw that a corner was torn. A piece of lace was sticking out.

Etta pulled out the package. The paper was so old it was disintegrating. As it cracked and fell away in her hands, the lace cascaded out. It was the little shrug she'd worn at her wedding. The one her husband had so carefully placed inside the trunk.

She sat back on her heels and ran her hand over her eyes. There had to be a rational explanation for this. Her body was sore and bruised, so it was clear that during the night she'd not stayed in bed. She'd moved about. In her sleepwalking, had she opened Ben's old trunk, seen the lace jacket, and incorporated it in her dream?

Yes, of course. That had to be what happened.

She got up, took a shower in the hottest water she could bear, put on light makeup so she was less "plain," then straightened the room. She told herself that she'd buy some acid free, archival paper, rewrap the lace jacket, and put it back in the trunk. How odd that the package seemed to have never been opened.

By the time she got down the stairs, groaning at every step, it was almost 9:00 a.m, late for her.

She found Henry in his library on his big leather couch, half a dozen books around him, bamboo lap desk and pens nearby. He had on reading glasses that he removed as soon as he saw her.

"Good morning. Sleep well?"

As she sat down on the chair across from him, she gave a groan. "Sorry. I seem to have done some sleepwalking last night."

He was concerned. "Is that usual?"

"Never happened before that I know of. I'll call Dad today and ask. Maybe I did it as a child. But anyway, I want to ask him how he'd like being a preacher."

"He's going to change careers?"

"No." She smiled. "I had the most extraordinary dream last night."

"Do you remember any of it?"

"I remember every minute. Even how bad the cowboys smelled."

"Please tell me. I do love stories."

She took a deep breath, then let go. "Well… I got married but he thinks I'm too old to, you know, be a real wife, so I'm to take care of his sister who looks just like my sister and run his household. I guess that means cooking and cleaning. I told him I should get a mop and a bucket as a wedding present, but he gave me twenty acres and said that if I last a year he'll build me a house. I said I wanted one just like yours, but I guess I won't get it because I'm here now. With my lace shrug. I always wanted to wear lace at my wedding." She stopped talking.

Henry was looking at her with a combination of interest and confusion.

He set aside his little nest of books, papers, and pens. "How about if I cook us breakfast? Since I don't cook at warp speed, you'll have time to tell me every word of this dream. Where was it? And when? It sounds almost historical."

"It was. It was just after the North and South War. In Garrett, Kansas."

"Never heard of it." He went to his shelves, pulled out a thick book, *Ghost Towns of Kansas*, and flipped through it. It seemed that there were many small towns that no longer existed. "Oh yes. It's here. Garrett, Kansas. Short-lived town. It died when the train line went to Wichita. Happened to a lot of towns."

"What else does it say?"

"Just dates. And a photo."

Etta nearly grabbed the book from his hands. The picture showed a flat piece of land with tall grasses. No church, no saloons, nothing.

She handed the book back to him. "I must have read the name somewhere. You ever hear of a man named John Kecklin? He tried to buy Kansas."

"So did a lot of people, but I haven't heard of him specifically."

Etta shook her head as though to clear it. "It was just a dream, but I can't seem to get rid of it. My father and sister were there, and Freddy, and Sophie from next door. I barely know them."

"Was I there?" Henry asked.

"No. Sorry. But Martha was. She—"

Henry's face drained of color, and he looked like he was going to pass out. She led him to a chair. "I'm sorry. I should keep my mouth shut."

He was breathing slowly, but color was returning to him. "That Martha was there without me isn't something I want to imagine."

"No," Etta said softly. "Martha wasn't a happy person. She'd lost her husband and son in the war. That's when I found out that it was the Civil War."

"Ah," Henry said. "So Ben and I were dead."

"No! Her husband's name was Theodore. I don't know the son's name."

Henry's eyes widened. "When I met Martha, she was a widow. Her husband's name was Theodore. How did you know that?"

Etta took a step back. "I don't know. Why is my lace shrug in Ben's trunk?"

Henry was staring at her. "It's wrapped up in old paper?"
She nodded.

"We bought that trunk the same time we got the desk. They were from an old house that had been in the same family for over a hundred years. The woman selling it all said the trunk had belonged to her late husband's great-great-grandmother. Her name was Amelia. No. It was Alice something."

Etta leaned against the bookcase. "Alice, Alicia. My sister. His sister. And maybe someone's great-great-grandmother. This is all very strange."

When Henry started to stand up, Etta went to help him, but he waved her away. "I'm all right. I just need some good Kansas beef and I'll be fine. How about a breakfast of steak and eggs? And you can tell me why you move like you're in pain. Did you sleepwalk straight into the walls?"

Etta smiled. "The truth is, I had to get in and out of a wagon that was about four feet off the ground. Then he got mad at me for being sarcastic so he drove over all the holes, not to mention the piles of horse manure, and I got beaten up. By the wagon, not him. Although he was driving. Martha said he should learn how to drive, so maybe she was right."

Henry stopped in the doorway. "Who is 'he'?"

"Oh yeah. Him. My husband. Maxwell James Lawton."

"The one who thinks you're old." That concept amused Henry.

"'Old and plain.' Cornelia called me that. She was Caroline, Ben's wife."

"*My* Ben?" Henry's eyes twinkled. "My wife, my friends, and my daughter-in-law were there, but I wasn't? I am wounded to my core."

Etta laughed. "I really tried to control the dream, but I couldn't. I even clicked my heels and made like Dorothy, but I stayed in old time Kansas right outside his sod house."

"Sod house?" Like a true historian, Henry was in awe. "I want to hear every word of this dream. Every syllable. All of it."

"Gladly," Etta said. "Maybe telling it will get it out of my mind."

Henry was right: Kansas beef cured a lot of problems. By the time she'd eaten a steak with eggs that came from Freddy's chickens, she felt much better. Pretend wagon riding had made her ravenous.

Etta had never been a good storyteller as her family had told her many times and as evidenced by her first rendition of it. Henry, a pro, helped her organize it.

"Start at the beginning," he said. "First day, first hour."

"It was only one day. We went to the sod house where I met Alicia, I mean Alice, then I returned here."

Henry gave her the look of a writer: impatience and a command of *do it right*. All he said was, "Chronological, please."

When they got to the library, he took the couch while she sat on the leather chair. As Henry directed, she started at the beginning, going through the hours she was there. The wedding, the ride through town, who she saw. She told about Cornelia and how she used her little riding crop. Etta waited for him to comment. She was silently asking if this was like Caroline, but Henry said nothing. When she told about the trip to the sod house, he wanted lots of details. Finally, Etta came to the end, when she saw Alicia. "I mean Alice."

Etta stood up. "She was so very alone in that glass house. My sister, Alicia, has a great brain. She's good with *people*. She helps them and always has. But Alice was reduced to sitting alone, looking out at the world, all because of a limp. And her brother is ashamed of her. He may mean well, but he locks her up like she's a precious gem."

Henry put down his pen. "You keep mentioning 'he,' as in *he* did this and that, but you haven't really told me about him."

Etta shrugged. "He was all right. Until I made him angry, he was kind and generous. He was certainly lovely to look at."

"But...?"

"He sees me as a worthless old woman. It's a wonder he didn't ask me if I did windows. And he imprisoned his sister."

"I thought you said he expected her to have children. That implies that she'd get a husband. It doesn't sound like she was imprisoned."

Etta sat back down. "Maybe not. I only saw her for minutes. Only *dreamed* I saw her, that is. Anyway, he has a beautiful, bad-tempered, entitled girlfriend who still wants him. And he probably desires her. If it weren't for her father, I'm sure he would have married her and happily lost both his ears."

"What about his ears?"

She told him of seeing the badly repaired earlobe. "I said he should have gone to Martha." Etta told him his quip that Martha would have pulled the lobe off.

Henry nodded. "In that era, that's probably exactly what would have happened. He seems to have known her well." He closed his notebook. "I think I'd like to do some research now."

Etta thought he was dismissing her, but she very much wanted to look through some of his thousands of books. And check out the internet. If Garrett, Kansas, really existed, maybe there was some history somewhere.

Not that it matters, she told herself, *but still...* "Do you mind if I join you?"

"I'd be honored," he said. "Do you type? Maybe you could transcribe my notes. I've been told that my handwriting is legible."

She took the notebook he held out. "Very legible. And yes, I can type rather well." She grimaced. "Yet another ability that is useless in the nineteenth century."

"You can cook. They had lots of beef and beans back then."

"Ah. Right. Flatulent constipation."

Henry laughed. "Come on, let's see what we can find."

For the rest of the day, they burrowed into Henry's extensive library. Over the years, he'd collected many obscure pamphlets and locally published books. The kind of things people threw away so they disappeared forever.

"Ben and I used to do road trips together," he said as they ate roast beef sandwiches for lunch. He told how they drove to small towns, to places that no longer existed, and fantasized about what it had once been like. "We went to many cemeteries," he said. "The older the better."

"I'm going to check sites about who is buried where." By nightfall, she'd found no record of the people she'd met, alive or dead. She and Henry had eyes that seemed to go in circles. Etta asked about Sophie, but she wasn't singing that night. Henry knew her schedule and honored it.

Etta made dinner for them, tacos that she put on the table seemingly faster than the beef could cook. As they sat down, she said, "What if I dream again tonight?"

"Lucky you." His head came up. "Please include me. And set me up with my wife."

"The names are the same, but I don't think your wife and the past Martha are the same person. The Martha of my dream was a bit, uh…"

"Grumpy? Sullen? Angry?"

Etta grinned. "Actually, yes. She looked like someone who could drive a mule train."

"My Martha was no-nonsense."

"I bet she was glad you took over the house and Ben."

"Very glad. She liked that we were happy, and she loved hearing about our adventures around Kansas." He picked up a piece of tomato. "Vegetables! Did you know that a lot of Mexicans lived in Kansas? I'll bet you they planted gardens. You'd have something to cook besides beef and beans."

"What a good idea! Not that I'll go back. I mean, I won't dream of the place again, but I'd like vegetables. You have any cookbooks around here? Historic, maybe?"

"Funny you ask that. Martha loved reading cookbooks."

"This is the woman who never entered the kitchen?"

"The same. They're in my house."

"The one designed by Caroline-Cornelia with the whip? Has she ever, you know, struck out at Ben?"

"Ben is as quiet as Caroline is energetic. They complement each other. I have a feeling your husband is more like her. They would inflame one another."

"My husband?" Etta said. "He's not real! It was just a dream." She got up and took the plates away. "Whatever, he's not 'inflamed' by *me*." She put the utensils in the dishwasher and turned it on. "Mind if I get a few cookbooks, then go to bed?"

"I think that's a good idea." He led the way out the back door.

Etta hadn't seen the guesthouse. The one designed by the beauteous, flaming Cornelia.

She slowed down. *Stop it!* she told herself. *It was a dream.* Caroline was not Cornelia. And besides, Cornelia didn't really exist.

Etta went around a tree and there it was. "Cute" didn't begin to adequately describe it. She would have guessed that Caroline would make the guesthouse in the style of Henry's Italianate house. But no. It was short and white, with glass-paned doors in the front. No modern sliders for Caroline!

Henry held the door for her. Like the interior of the big house, the little one was furnished in timeless modern. Very clean, white and blue, with splashes of dark purple pillows.

"It's lovely," she said. "Really nice."

"It suits me. I don't need a full kitchen and all those rooms."

"As long as you have your library, you're fine."

He laughed. "You already know me well."

The guesthouse had only two rooms and a bath. The kitchen was at the end of the pretty living room, and the cabinets had been custom-made. "Caroline put all the pans I'd need on the dining table, then measured them. She had the cabinets made to fit them."

"Very clever," Etta said.

The bath was cream and blue, with a walk-in shower.

The door to the bedroom was closed and Henry hesitated. Politely, Etta stepped back toward the main room.

"No," he said. "It's all right, but you'll see." He opened the door.

His bedroom was full of pictures of his late wife. There was a professional portrait of Henry and her on one wall. He could lay in bed and look at it. There was a long chest of drawers on the far wall, and it was covered with framed photos of his family, with Martha at the center of each one. There were several of her receiving awards.

"She must have been a great doctor."

"Brilliant," he said as he picked up a framed photo and looked at it lovingly. "Martha was the most undomestic woman I ever met, and we didn't have a conventional marriage. When I met her, there was a young buck doctor who was going after her. Everyone told her she was a fool to choose an old man like me over him. But Martha knew that he'd want a traditional marriage. He'd expect her to run the household, cook dinner, that sort of thing. That wasn't her."

Etta picked up a photo of Ben. Henry was holding him and gleaming with pride. "So how long after you were married was your son born?"

"Nine months and a day." His eyes twinkled and Etta laughed.

The cookbooks were in shelving on the opposite wall. There were a couple hundred of them, some big and glossy, some as old as Henry's history books. There were four library box files with KANSAS REGIONAL COOKBOOKS. MARTHA M. LOGAN printed on the spine.

"You did that," Etta said. "Your divine organizational skills put to use."

Henry seemed to blush. "Not exactly divine, but handy. Oh dear, it fell down."

Etta was on the far side of Henry's queen-size bed with its blue-and-white duvet, so she didn't see what he was picking up. He hung it on the nail to the right of the bookcase, then stepped back.

When Etta saw it, she grew dizzy and sat down on the bed. "It's…"

"It's what?"

"That's what Alice was sewing. She hadn't finished the *ë* with the dots over it."

Henry took the old, framed needlework down and sat beside Etta. "When we first saw it, the last letter was missing. Martha used her surgical skills to sew it. See? The *ë* is newer than the rest."

Etta held it. *I need not sell my soul to buy bliss. Charlotte Brontë.* "Tell me about it."

"It's from the auction, where Ben and I bought the desk and the trunk. The trunk was locked, and the woman said no one could open it so she didn't know what was in it. She said a horrible thing. And I quote, 'It's just old stuff, so who cares?'"

"I assume you let her live and later you opened the trunk."

"Ben did. I had a box of old keys, and he spent hours with them until he got the trunk open. Inside was the wrapped package and this. Martha saw it and claimed it. She said it was her life and what I had made come true."

"You showed up with a house and a job that you could do at home. And a willingness to take care of your son. That meant she could keep her life. Yes, you were her bliss."

"I like to think so," he said.

Etta held up the frame and studied the letter at the end. She could see that it was different. "I wonder why Alice never finished it."

"You hadn't seen this, yet you put it in your dream."

When she looked at him, she saw that he was serious. She stood up. "Oh, no, you don't. What I dreamed wasn't real. Somehow, I saw this before. I bet it's in a photo in the house. I wasn't conscious of seeing it, but I did." She put the needlework on the bed and went to the bookcase. "Any books you recommend?"

"So you'll know what to cook when you go back?"

"So I can help you with your next book about old time Kansas food."

Henry chuckled. "Okay, I've been put in my place." He pulled out three books and tossed them on the bed. "Mid-1800s. That should do it. Chuck wagons, the original food truck, Mexican cuisine, and farmyard." He took out another book. "Fred Harvey was about then. Read about him."

"Who's he?"

Henry put his hand to his heart. "You've never heard of *The Harvey Girls*? You and I have movies to watch."

Etta picked up the books, gave one last look at the framed needlework, then followed Henry out.

It was later, when she was snuggled down in Ben's bed for the night and looking at the cookbooks, that she thought more of the dream. It hadn't faded in her mind at all. She could still see faces, and remember smells. Her body was still sore. From a rough wagon ride? Or sleepwalking?

As she looked at the historic cookbooks, she asked herself why she was bothering to read them.

Was she doing what Henry said and planning for when she returned?

But that was absurd. People didn't repeat dreams. On the other hand, the whole world seemed to have had the dream of showing up somewhere in their underwear.

She put the books on the bedside table and turned off the light. Would she dream again? Part of her wanted to, but another part thought of turning on her iPad and watching a movie. Stay awake!

When she realized that what she most wanted to watch was *Tombstone*, which was set about the time she'd dreamed of, she closed her eyes tight. *Sleep!* she commanded herself. *And no dreams.*

4

The next morning, the smell of frying bacon woke her, and she took a moment to orient herself.

Was she in the past in the Lawton house? No. She saw Ben's animal curtains. She was still in the present in Kansas City, still in Henry's old house, still in lockdown.

When Etta got downstairs, Henry had breakfast waiting. "So what's on for today?" he asked.

To her dismay, Etta felt a bit glum. Yesterday she'd awakened from The Dream. But nothing had happened last night. She had no new bruises, no increased soreness in her body.

Henry was watching her. "What time does your father get up?"

Etta was pushing scrambled eggs around on her plate. "He's an early bird. He likes to work when the household is asleep." He was staring at her so hard she could read his thoughts. "Oh!

Good idea. I'll call him." She quickly finished her meal, then went back upstairs to call.

Thirty minutes later, she went down to the library, her good mood restored. She rattled off all to Henry. "We had a really good laugh about him being a preacher. He said he'd hate the job. Talking to all those people and listening to their problems. He hates that as much as Alicia loves it. She's like a magnet for people's misery. It would drive me crazy."

"You'd feed them," Henry said. "That would solve most of their problems."

Etta laughed. "I would. If Alice is actually like Alicia, *she* should be the town's preacher. People would line up to tell her their woes."

"Alice? The young woman who sewed the sampler that's on my bedroom wall?"

Etta squinted her eyes at him. "Yes, I mean the made-up woman who isn't real."

"Did you ask your father if you ever sleepwalked?"

Etta hesitated. "Yes, and he said I was always a good sleeper. Alicia was restless but I was like a…"

"A what?"

"A concrete block."

Henry laughed. "We fathers pull no punches."

She nodded to the dozen or so books piled around him. "Have you found any evidence that the people in my dream existed?"

"Not so far. I bet your sister would love to hear from you."

Etta went to the door. "Yet another great idea." She started down the hall.

"Ask her why she limps," Henry called after her. "Was it an accident or something from birth?"

"How funny you are!" Etta called back to him.

After the two calls with her family, Etta felt better and she settled down near Henry to read. She went through a lot of the books he'd written. She could see why her father respected him so much.

Henry had written children's books, dramatic renditions of historic events, and some scholarly works that were a bit boring. Too many dates and places for her.

She put green beans on to slow cook to prove that she could do something besides fast food, and she put a big chunk of Kansas beef in the oven to roast.

"I think you're a wonderful woman," Henry said when the smell reached him in the library. "You wouldn't want to marry me, would you?"

"I'd be pleased to accept unless you think I'm too old and plain for you."

"Old, yes, but never plain." He gave her a flirty look.

Smiling, Etta went back to reading about sod houses. In the afternoon they watched *The Harvey Girls* on the TV in the big living room. Etta enjoyed it. "It was a more simple time."

"To us, maybe, but not to those people then." There was so much sadness in his voice that she changed the subject.

That night, if she dreamed, she didn't remember any of it. And yet again, she woke in a less than happy mood.

"Want to talk about it?" Henry asked at breakfast.

"That stupid dream haunts me. I wish I could forget it."

"How about if you think about it more?"

"More than every minute of every day?"

"That's exactly what I mean. What if it happened for a reason? Maybe there's something in your life here and now that relates to the story you made up in your dream."

"This isn't about get-Etta-married, is it?"

"Since the man you married seems to hold the least of your attention, no. What you talk about is Alice closeted away in her pretty glass room." Henry leaned forward. "How would you change things if you went back?"

"It's not real. I can't—"

Henry held up his hand. "Did you tell your therapist sister about your dream?"

"Heavens no! Alicia would start analyzing it. And me. I would have to—" She broke off. "I see. Maybe I was seeing a real life problem that I need to fix."

"Could be. Just think about what you'd like to change if you went back again."

"Freedom for Alice." Etta got up. "I think better in a kitchen. Those early strawberries Freddy brought aren't the best, but I think I can use them." Her head came up. "Freddy of the past needs to do something besides you-know-what. Men like youth, and when that's gone women are considered useless. Not worthy of love."

It was easy to see that she was yet again talking about what the man had said. Henry shook his head. "Your poor husband. He's going to pay for what he said. Want some company in the kitchen?"

"Love it!" she said.

Henry was sitting at the end of the table-island, his laptop open as he line edited what he'd been writing. Etta was trying to save the strawberries.

"We should have eaten these sooner," she was mumbling.

"Oh!" Henry said, sounding alarmed.

"What is it?"

"Caroline had the baby." He paused. "I'm a grandfather."

Immediately, Etta was awash in guilt and shame. "I didn't ask. It's been all about me. I should have—"

Henry turned the laptop to face her. "Could you read it aloud? My glasses are a bit blurry."

From tears of joy, she thought. "Of course."

Alexandra Martha Logan was born nine hours ago. She is six pounds, eight ounces, and truly beautiful.

Henry was wiping his tearstained glasses on his shirt. "That's all he wrote? Ben would tell more. Something is wrong."

Etta closed the email and saw that there was another one from Ben.

Dad, I'm scared. There are complications. Our daughter might not make it. Caro is a mess. Send a story that I can read to her. Distract her. Pray for us.

Etta didn't know them, but she felt she did. When she looked at Henry, there were tears in her eyes, and she hugged him. "I'm so sorry. Surely, they'll be all right."

Henry pulled away and looked back at the computer. "Caroline will be hysterical. She isn't good with things she can't control."

"We'll get a car and I can drive you to Denver. It's not that far. You'll be a comfort to both of them."

"No, no," he said. "Ben's calmness will be better. They don't need an old man interfering." His head came up. "I'll write your story of meeting Caro in your dream."

"With a whip?" Etta was shocked. "I don't think she'll want to hear that."

Henry stood up. "Caro's father was a monster. A shouting bully. She'd love hearing that her prototype wore a tight dress and used a whip." He paused at the doorway. "Tell me what the man you two women were fighting over looked like."

"We weren't fighting over him."

"Of course not." His tone was of not believing. "What actor would portray him?"

"William Holden," she said quickly.

Henry's eyes twinkled. "A very masculine look. And how does your young man compare?"

She began speaking as fast as she cooked. "Six feet or more, broad shoulders, not an ounce of fat on him, cleft chin, a bit dimpled in the cheeks, perfect teeth, lots of dark hair but the sun gave it highlights, dark blue eyes with gold flecks in them, hands strong enough to hold two horses that were going wild, muscular thighs, a scarred earlobe but no other marks on him, deep voice like molasses, skin the color of sunlit honey, and—" She stopped and her face turned as red as the strawberries.

"My goodness," Henry said. "So *that's* what is needed to get women to fight over a man."

"There was no girl fight. Cornelia went after *him* with the whip, not me."

"Did she? She stopped her horse next to you, not him, then struck out across *you* with a short whip. He pushed *you* down, but he didn't so much as duck out of the way. Sounds to me like she meant to remove your ears, not his."

For a moment Etta blinked at him. "Maybe I should tell my sister about that dream so she can figure out what it means."

As Henry started down the hall and back to his library, he said, "Perhaps so."

Etta got the strawberries into jars, sealed them, then went to Henry in his library. He was bent over his lap desk and writing in a notebook. She didn't disturb him.

At four, Henry's phone dinged for a text. He handed it to Etta without looking at it. His hands were trembling.

"'The baby has stabilized,'" she read aloud. "'But we are staying in the hospital for a while. The first installment of your story made Caro smile. She wants to know who the old, plain woman is. And am I the attractive husband?'"

Etta put the phone down. She was greatly relieved, and Henry looked faint. "How about a Belgian waffle with strawberry jam?"

"That sounds delicious. Mind if I wait here?"

"I would like to serve you." As she went back to the kitchen, Etta realized that she too was shaking. She still felt bad that in the days she'd been in Kansas City she'd almost forgotten why Henry was there. He was so ill that his beloved family had left him behind. She would put money on it that he hadn't told them that his nurse never showed up. Or that he'd invited a stranger to stay with him.

But then, Ben and Caro didn't need the added stress.

She made the waffles, slathered them in butter and freshly made jam, then carried them back to the library. He was still writing. It didn't take much to know that this was his way of coping with the world around him.

He quickly ate a waffle, and the sugar seemed to revive him a bit. "I thought I'd add more to your dream story and send it to them. Would you mind typing?"

"I would love to. Are you going to embellish my dream and make it more dramatic? Do all those writer-things to it?"

"You want a romance, don't you?"

"I wouldn't mind if he stopped telling me that I am 'old and plain.'"

"And here I was thinking of using that for the title."

"You wouldn't!"

He smiled. "How about *He Thought She Was Old and Plain but Discovered She Was a Raving Beauty*?"

"I like it! But do you think it's too long to fit on the best-seller list?"

"Four point font will do it." He looked back at his notebook. "Your marriage is only a beginning. I need a middle and an end. Let's go back to my question. If you could return, what would you change?"

"I'd outlaw carpetbaggers, set up integrated schools, add—"

"I don't mean things you can't do. What can you achieve within the constraints of the time period?"

"Well…" She thought. "I'd find my dream's version of Phillip. He's the husband my overeducated sister adores. He could give Alice freedom."

"That's more like it," Henry said. "But first, I want to go back over what you've already dreamed. Didn't you mention a tire iron?"

"Oh yeah. Corsets are hell. Except for what they achieve. My little waist was almost worth the stays."

"Good line. I'll use it. So let's go over it all one more time."

5

Etta was absolutely *sick* of the lockdown. It had been a week and a day, and she was ready to go out and *do* things. But it seemed that there was no end in sight. If the news was to be believed, the country might be shut down for months. But that was ridiculous. How could businesses survive?

The person who most agreed with her was Lester. His wife had told him to stop complaining to her and to call Etta. She and Lester had spent hours reminiscing about all the things they missed.

She talked to her family every day. Alicia had already started using something called Zoom, and her business was flourishing. "My introverts love this isolation," she said of her patients. "Now they have an acceptable excuse for staying home. But my extroverts like you are struggling to adjust. Etta," she said in her therapist voice that gave warning, "stay busy."

Glumly, she'd said she would.

Her brother-in-law, Phillip, agreed with Etta. He was an airplane mechanic and he had no work. "I'm learning to cook." He sounded disgusted.

Her father was like Henry. Neither of them noticed that there was anything different in the world. Her father was mostly retired, but he still did a few accounts on his computer. Most of the time, he read and made notes for his biography of Wyatt Earp. He'd been working on it for fifteen years.

Henry was quite happy. His only outside contact was via email. When Etta showed him how to text, he thought it was a marvel. He and Caroline started texting back and forth as she was the techie in their family.

Henry kept Etta informed of all that was going on with them. It was the baby's lungs that were having trouble. Little Alexandra was in the NICU, and Caro and Ben were in a nearby hotel. Caroline knew Henry well, so she kept him updated on all that was going on in the outside world. The news of empty shelves and panic-buying shocked them.

Etta couldn't go to the grocery, and she hadn't been able to get on any waiting list for food delivery. She was glad for Freddy, who delivered a small box of fresh produce every few days. But she left it on the front porch and didn't enter the house. When she rang the bell, Etta would run to the front window and mouth, *Are you okay?* Freddy would grimace, then reluctantly nod. Like Etta, Freddy hated being cooped up.

When she left, Etta would watch Freddy until she was in her truck and out of sight. It was funny how some people you could know for years but not know at all. Then there could be an instant bond between strangers. That's how she felt about Freddy. They were friends.

To occupy herself, Etta cleaned things. She did the whole kitchen, removing the contents of the cabinets, washing it all, then putting things back.

Henry shook his head at her. He was content to read and think. "Create," Etta said. "That's what you do."

Henry's reply had been, "You can tackle the attic."

Etta said, "No thanks," but three hours later she pulled down the ladder and went upstairs.

Maybe she'd find some things from 1874 when the house was built.

But no. Someone had cleared away the past. There wasn't anything before the 1950s. After a thorough vacuuming, she asked Henry why it had been purged.

"That would be my mother. If something was two years old, it was too old for her. She wanted a one-story, new ranch house, but my dad said, 'My old house and I are one. Take us both or neither.'"

"Harsh," Etta said, "but I'm glad he did it."

The truth behind Etta's restlessness was that The Dream never left her mind. It was still as clear as the day she'd awakened from it. When she saw Freddy through the window, sometimes Etta would envision her as having heavily rouged cheeks and a dress that showed her bare shoulders. Was Freddy now in that other reality doing what she did to survive? It was a shame since Freddy was good in a garden. Her produce was top-notch.

Etta had met the neighbor, Sophie, only once, but she felt she knew the woman. Certainly knew her voice! Etta asked Henry questions about her stage fright.

"She's all right in church but put her on a stage even in a high school and she chokes."

Sophie had gone to stay with her sister for the lockdown. As for the other neighbors, the houses were closed so tightly it was like a barricade.

"Besides," Henry said, "houses here are bought and sold so often I don't know any of the people in them. Sorry, but it's just us." He smiled at her. "And I'm very, very glad you're here."

She was pleased that Henry wasn't alone. He read all the

emails and texts from his son and daughter-in-law to her. And they sent photos. Caro was holding the baby and smiling in deep pleasure. The picture of Ben with the baby made Henry teary. "My grandchild," he whispered. "I never thought I'd live long enough to see one."

Etta put her arms around him. It was great that he loved his family so much.

Most of the time he spent in his library trying to complete his story about The Dream. "It could go several ways," he said. "Henrietta and the man could fall madly in love or they could part forever."

"Make it modern and have the heroine and Alice have an affair."

"Sounds good except that *I* am not modern. What did you come up with for Alice's future?"

"You're the creative one, not me. I'd just look for Phillip and invite him to dinner. When my sister met him, I thought she was going to rip his clothes off."

"I remember those days. Now I'd be exhausted after five minutes."

"Come on! You'd last at least eight minutes."

Henry laughed. It was evening and they were in his library, as always, and Etta had worked enough during the day to settle down. She'd read about a dozen history books by Henry and other authors. They both knew she was looking for any mention of Garrett, Kansas. Other than in the ghost town book, there was nothing.

"If I had a car," she said, "I'd defy this lockdown and go see it. It's just a few hours south of here."

"There's nothing there."

"I know, but maybe I'd find an old beer bottle or something. There were certainly enough saloons."

"Tombstone, Arizona, had a hundred and ten saloons." His mind was full of obscure facts that could win any trivia contest.

"Speaking of that," she said, "tonight let's watch *Tombstone*. It's one of my dad's favorite movies."

Henry didn't look up. He said movies were so historically inaccurate that he didn't watch many of them. "What's it about?"

"Wyatt Earp. There were other people in the movie, but that's the only person my dad cares about."

Henry looked up. "I've narrowed it down to about three years." She knew he meant her dream.

"It's been a challenge, but your mention of a train helped. I'd say it was 1871 or two. Maybe 1870. It could be three but I don't think so."

Etta smiled. "Eighteen seventy-one. That's my father's year of celebration. One time he had me bake him a chocolate cake for the third of May, but I'm sure you know about that."

Henry was looking at her with interest. "Your father studied that year?"

"Avidly. He's been trying to write the definitive bio of Marshal Earp. I don't think he'll finish it. He just wants an excuse to read all there is about him. Dad wanted to name me Urilla after Wyatt's wife, but Mom said no. They compromised with the old-fashioned Henrietta. Other kids got to watch cartoons, but I grew up watching DVDs of Marshal Earp."

Henry's eyebrows were going higher by the second. "Remind me of what happened on that date."

"Sorry. I forget that people don't know the details. That date is when Marshal Earp escaped jail. He was very young. Dad said he was falsely accused by some woman but then Dad is biased. Anyway, if Wyatt hadn't escaped, he probably wouldn't have become the legend that he is. Can you imagine American history without the O.K. Corral gunfight? What would Hollywood do? And where would his buddy Doc Holliday be without him?"

When Henry spoke, his voice was low. "I've heard of Doc Holliday. He was a dentist and a gambler. He died of TB."

"That's him. He and Marshal Earp were great friends."

"Etta," Henry said slowly, "I've written many books about the Old West, but I've never heard of anyone named Wyatt Earp."

"That's ridiculous. You mean you've never seen the movie *Tombstone*?"

"No. Never. And I've never heard of the O.K. Corral."

"Billy Clanton? He was killed and later his brother Ike filed a murder charge against Wyatt, Morgan, and Virgil. And against Doc too. They were all acquitted, but things didn't go well there for Marshal Earp so he moved to Dodge City."

"In Kansas."

"Yes, of course," she said impatiently. "Boot Hill and all that."

"Etta." Henry spoke so slowly it was a three syllable word. "Did you dream about this man? Was he part of your fantasy? Maybe you made your husband into a lawman."

Senile, Etta thought. *Henry has the beginnings of Alzheimer's.* She'd seen no sign of it before now, but it must have been here. He couldn't remember computer things, and he'd misplaced his reading glasses more than once. "Maybe I did," she said in that placating way youngsters used on seniors. "You want something to eat?"

"No. I'm fine." Henry's voice was a bit distant. Older people *never* got used to the way young people assumed their minds no longer worked. Hit sixty and you're considered incompetent. Of no worth to anyone.

Etta practically ran from the room. It was the closest she and Henry had come to a disagreement. But really! This man, a so-called historian, said he'd never heard of one of the most well-known men on earth. People in Antarctica had probably heard of Wyatt Earp. He was the main character in dozens of movies and books. In legends.

She went to the kitchen, turned on the electric kettle, and prepared to make tea. As she put out the cookies she'd baked that afternoon, she was making vows. She would not treat Henry any differently because… Well, because his mind was going. It happened. The mistake was that she'd forgotten that he was an old man. His father had fought in World War II. Henry went to high school in the sixties.

It looked like his health problems weren't just physical but also mental.

She vowed to be nicer to him, kinder. Poor man. All those books written, and he could no longer remember their content.

She started to pick up the tray but then set it down. She texted her father.

Mr. Logan has never heard of Wyatt Earp. I think you better finish your book fast and inform the world.

She took the tray into the library, pushed aside some books, and set it on the coffee table. "I apologize for earlier," she said. "I overstepped. It's just my dad's obsession with some obscure historical figure. It's made me think everyone knows about him." She paused. "Have you written any biographies?"

"One or two." He poured himself a cup of tea and said no more.

Etta tried not to sigh. She didn't want there to be tension between them. When her phone pinged for a text, she was relieved. Maybe her dad had answered. Surely, he'd be as shocked as she was. Someone who had never heard of Wyatt Earp? How could that be?

Smiling in anticipation, she picked up her phone. Never heard of him, her father's text read.

Henry, moving the fastest she'd ever seen him go, caught her before she went down. He practically pushed her into the chair, took her phone from her, and read the text.

He did a web search of the name of Wyatt Earp, then showed her that there was no such entry anywhere. The man didn't exist.

"I don't feel well," Etta said. "I'm going to lie down."

"I think that's a good idea." He supported her until they reached the stairs. He started to go up with her, but she said no.

Feeling dizzy and weak, she went up the stairs to Ben's bedroom. Spread out on top of the trunk was the little lace jacket. She picked it up and hugged it to her. Something was really, really *wrong*. She wasn't sure what it was, but she knew that it had something to do with that blasted dream.

She fell down onto the bed, curled up, holding the jacket. "I wish I'd never had that dream," she whispered. "I wish it had never happened. Wish I'd…" She fell asleep.

"I think she's coming around," Alice said. "Miss Wilmont, are you all right?"

"Her name's Lawton now," a man said.

"But she isn't used to that name yet," Alice snapped. "Max, go get her some water." Etta heard footsteps fading into the distance.

"He's gone now," Alice said, "so you can wake up."

Etta opened her eyes to see the house and one of the people of her dream. She had the strangest feeling that she was home.

6

As Etta looked into her sister's eyes, what she felt most strongly was a sense of urgency. Yes, these were dreams, but there was something odd about them. She hadn't told Henry, but she'd looked at every photo she could find in his house. None of them had a picture of the Brontë sampler. She hadn't seen it until he showed it to her. But yet, she had seen it.

Above all, she didn't want to think about Wyatt Earp who may or may not have existed.

Etta was beginning to believe there was a deeper reason for the dreams. She didn't know if the purpose was about her own life or someone she loved—and that had come to include Henry—but there was something she was supposed to achieve.

"Are you all right?" Alice asked.

Since the core of her body was encased in an Iron Lady torture device, Etta struggled to sit up. "I'm well. I guess today was a bit much for me."

"So the wedding did happen?" Alice sounded eager. She was very pretty even with no makeup and furry eyebrows. Her skin glowed with youth and good health. She was probably early twenties.

"Yes. Married, witnessed, signed."

Alice let out her breath exactly like Alicia did when she'd solved a problem. "We are now truly sisters."

"We are indeed. I feel like I've known you all my life."

Alice smiled. "Max said my letters to you were too long and told too much. But it was so nice to have someone to talk to."

Immediately, Etta's hair stood on end. "He doesn't allow you to have friends?"

"He? You mean Max? Of course I have friends. As many as I want." She got up from her chair, picked up her cane, and went to the doorway. "Esmeralda? Could we have some tea, please?" She looked back at Etta. "Are you hungry? I told Max to take some food but he didn't. It took you two a long while to get here."

Etta was trying not to stare, but she really wanted to know why Alice was limping. Was it a disease? Something that in the twenty-first century could be cured with a few pills? Or was it an injury?

Alice sat back down. "I see Max didn't tell you. I was born with a twisted foot. He has always made me comfortable. And now I have you."

Etta thought that it sounded like a lonely existence, but she just smiled.

Minutes later, an old woman came in bearing a tray loaded with a pretty teapot and cups. Etta realized that "old" was relative. The women was probably in her fifties. Young in modern times. She didn't smile or show any emotion.

"Thank you," Alice said, and they watched her shuffle out of

the room. "She may not show it, but she's very glad you're here."
As Alice poured the tea, she lowered her voice. "Esmeralda has
been with me since I was a baby. She cooks for us, but…"

"Not very well?"

Alice nodded. "She very much wants to go home."

"Where is that?"

"Mexican Town," Alice said. "All her family lives there and
a lot of Max's men."

Etta finished a cup of tea, then wrestled herself up off the
hard couch. "Would you show me around?" She paused as she
made a discovery. Having your insides compressed to the size
of a toddler's didn't allow you to store much. She had to pee.
"Could I use your…?"

"Of course. I should have thought."

Please don't let it be a chamber pot under the bed, she thought.
She followed Alice through the house to her beautiful glassed-
in room. Alice opened the door at the end. There was a little
path disappearing through the trees.

"It's just mine," Alice said proudly. "Max had it made for me."

Etta followed the path to an outhouse. It was, of course, hideous. There was a rudimentary seat around a hole above open
sewage. It took Etta a while to deal with her undergarments.
She couldn't pull them down but had to part the overlapping
fabric of the crotch. It wasn't easy. "Elastic," she murmured.
"How I miss you."

On the floor was a stack of newspapers. *Triple ply*, she thought.
The heading read April 10, 1870. It looked like Henry had been
accurate about the date.

Relieved, she went back to the house. Alice was eagerly await-
ing her. She had the same lonely, needy expression Alicia wore
when she'd been stuck in the house alone for a few days. It was
exactly how she looked after their mother died and Etta said she
was returning to university. Because of that look, Etta didn't go.

She ran her hand over a palm in a big pot. "Your brother

said Cornelia designed this room for you. I guess you two were friends."

"We were." Alice sighed. "She's very entertaining, but she and Max fought all the time."

"He showed me his ear."

Alice smiled. "Cornelia does have a temper." She gave Etta a sideways look. "I doubt if she was nice to *you*."

"No, she wasn't. She needs a Ben to calm her down. Someone quiet like Henry."

Alice's eyes were wide. "You do talk strangely. I guess that's all your education. Why don't we get you some different clothes? Max likes pretty women."

"I could *never* look as good as Cornelia."

"None of us can."

They laughed together, then Etta spoke. "I'm more interested in you. You're so isolated here. I know you sew and read but what else?"

Alice went to a chair on the far side. In a frame was her sampler with the Brontë quote. "I'm almost done with this."

"Don't finish it," Etta said quickly. "It's when we met. Leave it as it is." *So Martha can do it*, she thought.

"All right." She hesitated. "May I show you a secret?"

"Of course."

The end of the glass house was so thick with foliage that the light was blocked. Alice slipped between two big palms and motioned for Etta to squeeze in beside her. Outside was the barn she'd seen earlier, and there was a horse trough.

"Nice view," Etta said and started to turn away.

"Just wait."

They stood in silence for a few minutes, then a couple of young cowboys led their horses out. They dipped their hats into the water and poured it over their bodies, wetting their shirts. They looked very, very good.

Etta gave a snort of laughter. "It's a wet shirt contest!"

"What a perfect name. They have no idea they're being watched."

One of the cowboys was exceptionally good-looking and muscular. For a brief second, he cut his eyes toward the house. *Like hell they don't know.* Etta pushed the palms aside and waited for Alice to leave the show and sit down.

"Your brother said someone who worked for you ran off with his head wrangler."

"That was Julie. Max was really angry."

"He liked her?"

"Oh no, that was when he and Cornelia were together. Max liked Joe. But Julie saw him at the horse trough, and that was the end of her. She was gone the next day. I got a letter from her, and they're in California in the mountains. It's a hard life."

And now pretty Alice was drooling over the wet cowboys. Etta couldn't imagine her with her limp trying to survive in the mountains. There was no electricity here. There wouldn't even be roads in the mountains. Or protection from bears and other predators.

Etta wondered if this was her purpose here. Was she to do what she'd told Henry and find a Phillip for Alice? Get her out of this pretty prison? "Between us, is there someone you like?"

Alice ducked her head shyly. "Well…there was a man. I went into town with Max. In the buggy. He let me off at the dressmaker and picked me up there."

Inadvertently, Etta glanced down at Alice's foot, hidden under yards of silk. It was Etta's guess that Alice wasn't to be seen limping down the dirty streets. Was that her preference or a decree by her brother? "And?" Etta said encouragingly.

"He was fixing a wagon hitch. He was very nice-looking and I…"

You wanted to rip his clothes off, Etta thought. *Just like my sister felt when she saw her future husband.* But Alice was too innocent to hear that. "Was he one of your brother's men? Or does he work for Cornelia's father?"

"Oh no! Max said he's a lawyer. He's new to town."

"A lawyer?" Etta thought about her brother-in-law, Phillip. He could talk and he was smart. Had he grown up in a more prosperous family, he could have been a lawyer. That this man was working with his hands was also like Phillip. "Dark hair? Tall? Shoulders…" She held out her hands wide.

"Oh yes," Alice said in a dreamy way.

"Your brother said women who came here get married quickly. What about eligible men?"

"It's worse with them. There isn't a lot of choice in men. I mean ones who are up to snuff. Women go after the good ones right away."

"I can understand that. This guy has a lucrative job, and he probably doesn't drink his whole paycheck every Saturday. And I suspect that he takes a bath in something besides a horse trough. Sounds top-notch to me."

Alice giggled. "You are funny. Now I see why Max kept you out so long. He promised to bring you straight home, but he didn't." She cocked her head. "Did he take you to the old homestead?"

"Yes, he did."

Alice was quiet for a moment. "He thinks no one knows about that place, but we all do. Everyone stays away from it and lets him have his peace."

"He said that if I stay here a year, he'll build me a house on that land."

Alice was so astonished she couldn't speak.

"I'm sure he would have said that to anyone he married." *Especially since the house and land were a substitute for the real marriage he wasn't going to give her.*

"That's not true," Alice said. "Max liked your letters best."

"Were there a lot of choices in women?"

Alice laughed. "Oh yes! I'm the one who put the advertisement in the Kansas City magazine. He wasn't happy that I did it, but if I hadn't done something drastic, he was going to end up married to Cornelia. They would have killed each other! So, as Max said, I offered him up like a prize bull with a ring of roses around his neck."

Etta laughed. "And he got a lot of bidders."

Alice was laughing in memory. "Many of them. Women from sixteen to forty-one."

"I was the compromise. The middle choice."

"None of them had been to school for as long as you," Alice said in a placating way.

"But that didn't matter because no one could compare to the divine Miss Cornelia. So he settled for me."

Alice looked puzzled. "I guess so." She changed the subject. "So what shall we do this afternoon? I can get Max to send someone for the dressmaker. I think you should wear green."

Etta stood up. "I need to talk to him. Where is he? Out wrestling cows? Branding them or whatever?"

"He's in his office."

"Of course he is. He'd want to be nearby in case you call for help."

"Did something bad happen between you and Max?"

"Nothing whatsoever happened between your brother and me. Didn't happen and never will. He made that clear. I have a purpose here, and I don't think it has anything to do with him. Or with me, for that matter. Point me in the right direction, please."

Alice didn't go with Etta to her brother's office. *Is she afraid of him?* Etta wondered. Or was she dreading what looked to be an argument? Alicia, the peacemaker, always intervened when harsh words were spoken.

When Etta got to his office, the first thing she saw was

Henry's giant desk, but there was no carving on the front of it. The sight of it threw her for a moment. Sampler, jacket, desk. All bought at an auction. Was it from a descendant of the man who was sitting behind the desk? Or from Alice? Did she marry some cowboy who looked good in a wet shirt? Or the new lawyer?

"Do you need something?" He was looking at her with a frown, as though she was a great bother to him.

My wedding day, she thought in sarcasm. *The way I've always imagined it. Ha ha.* The men were right that he'd work her hard. "I want you to invite the lawyer to dinner tonight."

"And who would that be?"

"I don't know his name. TDH. Tall, dark, and handsome. Arrived only recently. Are there many lawyers in town?"

His expression showed that he seemed to be wondering if she was insane or not. He looked back at the papers on the desk. "I can't go. I have work to do."

She went to stand on the other side of the desk. She thought that if she wanted him to do something for her, she should soften her tone. "Those are the accounts?"

He looked up at her. "You want to do them?"

"No. Sorry. I didn't inherit that ability. You should get Dad to do them. I mean Pastor Tobias."

He looked amused. "Get the preacher to add and subtract? The man can't even make people believe they should stop sinning. If his father hadn't—"

She didn't like hearing her father disparaged. "How would *you* be as a preacher?"

"The best," he shot back. "I'd serve beer."

She didn't want him to see her laugh so she turned away, recovered, then looked back at him. "I think you and I want the same thing. Alice can't spend her whole life locked away in a room, not even one as pretty as that one. She needs a life! Do you agree or do you like having her under your rule?"

"I got married for her, didn't I?"

His words were a metaphoric slap. At least it was out in the open. Deflated, she plopped down on a hard wooden chair. Did these people hate all things that were *soft*? "Alice saw a young lawyer in town and she was attracted to him."

He looked blank.

"The man who was fixing a wagon hitch?"

"Oh yeah. Bertram Lloyd. She asked me about him."

"And you didn't take the hint?" She didn't wait for him to answer. "You need to invite him to dinner. I want him and Alice to meet."

"All right. I'll come up with some legal work, hire him, get to know him, then maybe I'll let him meet her."

"Forget all that. You can get to know him at dinner. Tonight."

"You sure are bossy."

"If you'd wanted a submissive girl, you should have married the sixteen-year-old who applied for the job."

"At last we agree on something."

She felt like defending herself. "You wanted a woman with an education, and I'm what you got. Not that it matters, but I had to become bossy. I run everything so my father and sister can do what they need to with their lives."

"If you're so necessary to them, why are you here?"

"The lockdown. I mean…" She didn't know how to answer that in a believable way.

He gave a smug little smile. "They're doing fine without you, aren't they?"

She did *not* like that he'd turned the tables on her. She needed to go back to why she was there. She clenched her teeth. "Trust me on this—you don't have *time* to meet and judge the man. Before you even get started, he'll be swept up by some girl with rouged cheeks and Alice will end up in the California mountains."

"You make no sense. Could you leave now? I need to finish this."

Her frustration was taking over. She stood up. "With your dyslexia it'll take days. Hire the preacher. Test him. What do you have to lose?" She didn't know how to get him to do what was needed, then she thought, *How about showing him what I saw?*

His office was facing the back, as Alice's room was, but it wasn't in direct view of the stables.

She flung open the door. "I want to show you something."

"I don't have time for this," he said. "I have to—"

"Yeah, I know. Adding up numbers that sometimes look backward is more important than your sister's raging hormones. Are you afraid to see what your men are up to?"

"My men?" At last he left his chair and went to the door with her.

Etta led the way outside. There was a long stack of firewood at the back, and she directed him to look over it.

When he saw nothing, he turned back to her in annoyance.

"Just wait," she said, repeating Alice's words. She stayed back, but she saw by his expression when the men started doing their *Magic Mike* act.

He didn't watch for long. When he shouted, it was as loud as a dozen trumpets. He didn't say any words as he seemed too angry to enunciate them. But the men knew what the sound said: *Get back to work, and if you put on a show for my sister again, I'll feed you to the hogs.*

Or thereabouts, Etta thought. *Did a cattle rancher have pigs?*

When he turned around, he didn't look at her, but stomped back into his office.

Etta followed close behind him. "So who's the really handsome guy?" she asked. "The one with the muscles? Bet he makes the hearts of all the women flutter. He certainly does a number on Alice. Maybe she'll be like Julie and elope with him, and they can live in a tent high in the mountains. But I'm sure she'll send you letters. That'll be nice."

Turning, he glowered down at her with a scowl that looked like the wrath of Thor.

But he didn't scare Etta. She stood her ground, put her hands on her tightly bound waist, and glared right back up at him.

After a full minute, he turned away and went to sit behind his desk, his head bent over the papers.

"Dinner tonight?" she asked with exaggerated innocence. "The lawyer? Or should I invite the handsome cowboy?"

"Dinner," he growled.

Smiling, Etta left the room. She had a lot of work to do to prepare a nice meal. What was in the kitchen? She hoped she wouldn't have to cook over an open fire. She could, but it wasn't easy. And what food was available? Besides beef and beans, that is. If she had yeast, she could bake bread.

She hurried back to Alice's room. Who cooked for the cowboys? He'd know what was available.

7

Max took the wagon. He didn't plan to buy supplies, but he needed the challenge of the hard wood. The buggy was faster but it's what he drove when Alice was with him, so he tended to think of it as gentle.

He had to drive past the big horse trough. What he'd seen there was burned into his mind.

Knowing that the men did it in front of his sister on purpose sent waves of anger through him. That a stranger, the woman he'd married, had shown him what was going on under his nose further infuriated him.

Hank, the major source of the problem, was saddling a horse. In the year he'd worked there, no woman who'd seen him held back from making a comment on his looks. He was a hard worker, but Max was tempted to get rid of him out of sheer annoyance.

He was about to drive past when damned if he didn't see *her* talking to him. His wife!

She didn't see Max or pretended not to as she lifted her skirts up way too high and ran back to the house.

With his teeth clamped together, he yelled, "Hank!"

The man didn't have the courage to look Max in the eyes, but hid his face under his hat as he approached the wagon. It looked like he expected to be fired.

"Get in!" Max ordered. Hank looked up in surprise.

"Unless you want to stop and drown your clothes first."

Hank put his head back down. "No, sir," he managed to say then climbed in the back. He didn't dare sit on the seat beside his boss.

Max drove the wagon at a brisk pace, knowing he was tossing Hank around in the back. He already knew he'd made a mistake in all this. Alice had pushed him to get married. At that time, his anger at John Kecklin was inflaming him so much that he couldn't think clearly. And Cornelia was always angry at him. She never came out and said it, but she'd expected Max to marry her. Then what? He'd have a lifetime of her temper? Of dealing with the greed of her father? Max got to the point where he'd do *anything* to make it all stop.

Alice had agreed with her brother. "You cannot marry Cornelia. I couldn't live with all the arguing. And Mr. Kecklin is a dreadful man." She came up with a solution. Max was to marry another woman. She'd be someone nice. Competent. Someone who could run the house in an orderly way and spread joy and cheer to them all. If he did this, it would solve all the problems. Cornelia wouldn't be shouting at Max, and her father would quit demanding that Max merge his acreage with Kecklin's land.

At the time it had seemed like the perfect solution, and Max had imagined a life of peace.

Kecklin would stop pressuring him. And even better, Max

wouldn't be stuck with a woman who thought using a riding whip was the solution to every conversation she didn't like.

Alice had done everything. She'd placed the advertisement in the Kansas City magazine where it was one of hundreds. She'd read all the replies and compared them. At one of Esmeralda's bland meals, Alice said, "I like this one." She tapped one of the nine photos spread across the table.

Max liked the pretty girl on the end.

Alice removed that picture from the lineup. "She's younger than I am. She doesn't know how to cook or run a house. We need someone with experience."

Max looked at the picture of the woman Alice wanted. She looked too serious, well past her youth, and too weighed down by her long life. He certainly had no physical desire for her! *Oh well*, he thought, *there are lots of women in town available for that.* This woman's purpose was to put peace and quiet in his and Alice's lives. Max was beginning to realize that his little sister was going to be with him forever, which was fine with him.

All he needed in life was someone to look after the domestics, and he'd take care of everything else. It was a perfect plan.

Until *she* showed up, that was. He'd expected her to be grateful. After all, he was her rescuer. He'd saved her from a life as an old spinster. Thirty-four years old! She was way past her prime. That no other man wanted her was evidence that something was wrong with her.

He'd never tell Alice, but before she was to arrive he was quite nervous. He told his sister he had to see about business, then left. He went to the old homestead and stayed there for days. He lived on beans and peaches and spent hours by the river. He thought about his parents a lot. His father had been a humorless man who denied his family any pleasures. He just wanted "more." More land, more livestock, more money. Sometimes Max thought his mother died of neglect.

Whatever the truth, Max knew he didn't want to be like

his father. That's why he lavished his sister with everything he could. That she tended to hide away from the world because of her foot wasn't his fault.

As Max sat by the water, he thought about his future. He'd be nice to the woman. Kind. Courteous at all times. At her age she wouldn't expect the intimate parts of marriage, so he'd have no obligations in that respect.

By the time she was to arrive, he felt he had it under control. He had his future planned out and he liked it. He'd have a peaceful household. He'd come home to good meals and a woman who was grateful to him. He'd smile at her gray hair and her stumbling gait. He would become fond of her.

Yes, it was all going to be good.

The problems started when he met her at the train. He had three men with him—not Hank!—who'd be witnesses at the wedding. The pastor was waiting.

Several women got off the train, most of them young, but one woman had gray hair piled into a wiry knot on top of her head. She had a waist as big as his horse's. She didn't look like her photo, but he wasn't surprised by that. She'd probably sent a picture of her younger self.

He walked toward her but then one of his men called out. "She's over here, boss." Turning, he saw a woman surrounded by his men and he froze in place. She was pretty! And the shape of her was slim but curvy. She had a mass of dark hair that was messily piled up, not slicked back, and big blue eyes. Her mouth was exceptional.

She smiled at him. He'd never seen such white and straight teeth. Or skin as soft looking as hers.

His men seemed to understand what he was feeling as they started mocking him. They discarded the idea of Max being their boss and treated him like another cowboy.

All the way to the church, the men had at him. "Fun times tonight," they said.

"The girls of the Red Dog will be crying in loneliness."

"Tomorrow I'm gonna put in my order for a bride."

"Hey boss! What happened to the old woman you told us to look for?"

Through all this, Max drove the wagon and said nothing. Nor did she. She just held on in a way that looked like she'd never been on a wagon before. But then, she was from a city so maybe she'd only ridden in fancy buggies on paved streets.

It wasn't until the preacher asked her if she took Max for her husband that she seemed to come alive. And then she'd seemed bewildered by it all. Afterward, she didn't even seem to know how to walk in a skirt. So what did she usually wear? Men's trousers and boots? What a ridiculous thought.

When they left the church, he saw that she didn't know how to get up into the wagon. He thought how useless she was, but he'd very much enjoyed putting his hands on her waist and lifting her up. From what he saw and felt, she seemed to have a good body under all those clothes.

The ride out of town had been an experience for him. He'd imagined a quiet, mousy little woman who would be full of gratitude. After all, he wasn't poor and he wasn't bad to look at, so she should have been shy and humble.

But she was far from it. No matter what happened, she was brave and…and funny.

Nothing had intimidated her. Not Martha nearly sending them crashing, not the abundant saloons with the gaudy women outside. He thought that an educated Eastern lady would have been shocked.

But no. His new wife waved and spoke to the women like they were her friends.

When Cornelia showed up, he knew he should have driven on, but part of him wanted to gloat. At their split, she'd said some really nasty things about his masculinity. They shouldn't have, but her words hurt.

When she struck at his new wife with her whip, he managed to save her. Afterward, he'd expected her to be frightened or angry, maybe. But her only concern had been the damage done to the parasol Alice had made for her.

To Max, anyone who appreciated his sister was his friend.

On impulse, he took her to the homestead, his private place, where he didn't even take Alice.

Max had surprised himself when he told her that he *liked* her. He'd never felt that way about a female before. To him, girls were either like Alice, delicate, fragile people who needed constant care and protection, or like Cornelia, who expected everything to be done for her.

But this woman was different, and he told her so—or thought he did. He said he'd give her land, and if she stayed he'd build her a house. That offer had been spur of the moment, unplanned. He'd thought that legally marrying her was enough, but after what he'd seen of her, he'd wanted to give more.

He couldn't figure out how or why, but it had all gone wrong. She said she wanted to return home, that she wished she hadn't married him. She made it clear that she didn't want anything from him.

He'd been hurt. Cornelia's temper and her whip had suddenly seemed more honest, and certainly easier to deal with.

Maybe it was wrong of him, but he made sure he gave her the roughest ride possible on the way to the house. When they got there, he pointed the way to Alice, then left her to fend for herself.

It was just minutes later that Alice was screaming that the woman had fainted. He carried her to the couch. She seemed to be all right, but she refused to even open her eyes while he was in the room.

He left, but he didn't go far. Alice might need him.

After that, he didn't want to think about all that had happened. He made up his mind that he was going to ignore her. He would never again allow her to get to him. And if she said she wanted to go home, he'd put her on the first train out of town.

But she'd come to his office, ordering him to go get some lawyer he didn't even know. When he told her no, he tried to make her understand that what she was saying had no logic. He was hoping to teach her something.

But she wouldn't listen or learn. Instead, she talked utter nonsense about the preacher, a man she'd never even spoken to. What she said was so absurd he quit listening.

However, when she complained about his men, he did listen. That was his territory, not hers.

So he went outside and looked. He'd show her she was wrong.

He didn't want to think about what he'd seen. His men were in front of Alice's windows. They were wetting their shirts and showing off like peacocks on parade. *His* men!

If he didn't need their work, he would have fired them on the spot.

Instead, he was now sitting on a wagon heading into town to invite some man he didn't know to come to dinner. To meet his innocent young sister.

He stopped the buckboard in front of the law office. It was upstairs, over his favorite saloon, the Red Dog. He didn't allow himself to look at the place. Nor did he look at the man in the back of the wagon. He was afraid that if he did, he'd remember the vision of him in his wet, transparent shirt. Max thought he might rip it off and strangle him.

Max dropped the reins, leaving them loose for Hank to take care of, then he went up the tall outside staircase and opened the door. BERTRAM LLOYD was painted on the glass. Max removed his hat.

A woman sat at a desk. He knew her. She was in her forties and had buried three husbands. At the death of the last one she said, "No more! I'm done." All the men in town had let out a sigh of relief.

Mrs. Ellis glanced up, then back down at the papers on her desk. "Thought you'd be busy today."

He wasn't going to reply to that. "I need to see him." He nodded to the closed door behind her.

"John Kecklin's already been at him. He won't take you on."

"This has nothing to do with land."

She looked up at him with interest. "What do you want with him on your wedding day? Town says you got a mail order prize."

Max clenched his fists at his sides. "The town can keep its mouth shut." He stepped past her and opened the door. The office was empty.

"He ain't here," she said.

"You could have told me that. When will he be back?"

"About an hour. Old man Tucker died. He has to take care of it. You gonna wait for him downstairs?" Her smirking insinuation was clear. Was Max going to visit one of the girls in the saloon?

He put his hat back on. "I'll come back in an hour. See that he stays here."

Max left and closed the door behind him. "Her husbands probably ran away," he muttered as he went down the stairs.

Out of habit, he headed toward the saloon. *Might as well have a drink*, he thought, but then he turned and went in the opposite direction. The Red Dog was his favorite, but it's where his wife's "friends" worked. It's where they knew him and would ask lots of questions. He walked down the street to the Blue Moon. It was a sleazy place with a filthy floor covered in straw caked with years of tobacco spit. It stunk, but right now it suited his mood.

He ordered a whiskey then looked about the place. There were three tables with lowlife cowboys playing cards. Max knew they'd all been fired from every job they'd had. Stealing, laziness, quick temper. They deserved what they got.

There were a couple of "girls," but they were leftovers. Worn out from years at the higher end places. They looked at Max with hope. He gave a polite headshake, and they turned away.

As his eyes adjusted to the dark, he saw a man in the far corner. It was the preacher. This morning he'd told Max to hurry up as he had a lot of things to do. Looked like getting drunk was at the head of the list.

In spite of his better judgment, the woman's words rang in his head. She'd said this man could do accounts. For a moment Max struggled between his pride and his absolute hatred of all forms of paperwork. The thought of getting rid of the numbers won.

He downed a shot of the rotgut whiskey then picked up a second one. "I got a problem," he said loud enough to be heard next door. When everyone in the place turned their attention to him, it felt good. After all, he was the second biggest landowner for miles around. Only old man Kecklin beat him. With the day Max was having, he liked being respected. "I'm having trouble with my accounts."

Half the men looked back at their cards. Accounts were of no interest to them.

"I can't figure them out," Max said. "I've got twelve pounds of peaches at three for a dime, eight pounds of coffee at twelve cents a pound, four calves, two fifty each, and six and a half yards of calico at ten cents a yard." He looked at each person, but they turned away. "Who can figure that out?"

Finally, he looked at the preacher, bent over a whiskey, being the gloomy man he always was.

He said nothing.

Max shot back the second whiskey, put on his hat, and started to leave.

"Twelve dollars and a penny."

Everyone turned toward the dark corner. The preacher didn't look up. "Is that right?" the bartender asked Max.

"How the hell would I know?" he snapped. "Bottle."

The bartender handed Max a bottle of whiskey and two glasses that were relatively clean.

He took them to the table in the back and sat down across from the preacher. "How come my new wife knows you can add and subtract?"

The preacher poured himself a large whiskey from Max's bottle. "Is this the woman I married you to this morning? Why are you here and not with her?"

"None of your business. Why are you getting drunk and not taking care of that church we built for you?"

"Nobody likes my sermons."

That was so true that Max nodded. "So how does she know about you?"

"I have no idea. I never met her before today. Maybe somebody told her."

"Who knows to tell?"

The preacher poured himself more whiskey. "How would I know that? This could go on all day, back and forth. Don't you want to get back to your bride?"

"She likes me as much as the town likes your sermons."

"Ah," the man said. "That's a problem. Good women want to *like* a man. You better stay with the girls at the Red Dog. I hear they like you a lot."

Max closed his eyes for a moment. *Does everyone in town know everything about me?* "Come work for me."

"Wrangling?" He held up his hands. "I'm old and soft. I can't—"

"Accounting. Add up things. Put it all in books. I had a man for a while but he ran off with—"

"Parmelia. I married them, remember?"

"I'm surprised you do. You were drunk."

The preacher grimaced. "You say the same words a hundred times and see if you don't need whiskey to fortify you."

"You can't drink at my house."

"Ah right. Your precious little sister, the one nobody sees. Except the dressmaker. Who does she wear all that silk for? I heard your men—" He cut off at the younger man's look.

Max stood up. "If you want the job, show up tomorrow morning at eight. Clean body, shaved, and sober. If I even smell beer on you, you're out."

"That church has a hold over me." He sighed. "Takes my time."

"Stay out of the bars and you can do both of them." Max snorted. "Or maybe my wife can fix it. She seems to have a plan for everybody." He put on his hat. "Clean and sober, got it?"

The preacher pushed his full glass away, then gave a nod. He looked serious. "I'll be there. Tell your wife that..." He didn't seem to know how to finish.

"You tell her. She doesn't like talking to me."

Max left the bar. Outside, he didn't have to pull out his pocket watch to know it hadn't been an hour yet. It was too early to go back to see the lawyer. The whiskey had elevated his mood a bit. Down the street was the Red Dog, and he knew that if he went there he'd be welcomed. There'd be laughter. He took four steps in that direction, then the sign for the dressmaker seemed to flash in his face. Hadn't Alice said something about her?

He was lying to himself. He knew exactly what his sister had said. She'd told him he had to get his wife some new clothes. "She dresses like a middle-aged schoolteacher," Alice said.

"She isn't a schoolteacher," Max shot back, and was given one of Alice's looks that made him shut up.

Max went into the dressmaker's shop. Thirty minutes later, he walked out feeling like he wanted more whiskey. How does a man answer questions about fabric and lace, and necklines and sizes? He kept telling her she had to go to his house, but she wouldn't stop asking questions. And then there was the tea and little pink cakes.

When Max began to think he was never going to escape, the woman shooed him out, saying she had to get to work. Relieved, he headed toward the lawyer's office.

Max was only steps away from the stairs leading up to the lawyer's office and thinking hard.

How did she know about the preacher and numbers? Did the man give some hint when he was marrying them?

Maybe because he was preoccupied with his thoughts he didn't see the danger lurking in the shadows of the alleyway. Before he could protect himself, he was ambushed. As he was pulled out of the light by two strong hands, he nearly fell.

In the next second, he was pushed up against the wall, hands placed firmly on his chest, and he was being kissed.

He pushed Cornelia away. "You can't do that."

"Because you're married now?" Her eyes filled with anger, something he was used to, but then they softened with tears. Cornelia was a woman so beautiful that she could silence a roomful of people when she entered. Cornelia with tears could melt stone.

When she saw that her tears changed his attitude, she put her hands back on his chest. "I'm sorry," she whispered. "I drove you to someone else, but I didn't mean to. You don't know how much I love you. It makes me do things I wouldn't normally do."

He put his hands on her shoulders and moved her to arm's length. "We can't do this. I have another life now."

"With her?" The tears were gone. "You already care for her that much? Alice said—"

"Leave her out of this." He took a breath to regain his composure. "You know you and I could never be together. We fight all the time. I never got any work done."

She gave him a look through her lashes. "When you were with me, you didn't have *time* for work."

"I was well aware of that." He wasn't referring to the same thing she was.

"Remember the rainstorm? We were trapped in Papa's barn for hours. We took off our clothes and—"

"That's done! It's over. In the past."

"It doesn't have to be. This marriage of yours could be annulled. There are lots of grounds. She's too—"

"Your father sent you to me, didn't he? He told you to say anything it takes to get me back."

"Yes!" She looked at him without the tears, without the anger. "You hurt me. Badly. I thought our lives would be spent together. You, me, and Alice. I've always loved your little sister."

"I know." Max could feel guilt seeping into him. "But I couldn't think when you were around. Alice said I should..." He couldn't reveal what was private. All he wanted was to get away from this.

"Alice was in on it?" Cornelia sounded genuinely hurt. "But she and I were friends. Has this woman won her over? Are you already in love with her?"

"Alice likes her. I need to go."

"Where? To that new lawyer? I saw you go up there. Papa owns him, so it's no use trying to get him to help you."

"I'm not hiring him." He started to turn away.

When she caught his arm, she had the look of her father. Max knew that under her feminine facade she was as ruthless as that man was. Cornelia got whatever she wanted. Most of the time, anyway. "If you're not hiring him, why are you going to see him?" Her eyes widened. "You want out of your revenge marriage, don't you? You want an annulment. Unless you've already been to bed with her. Then it'll have to be a divorce. But that can be arranged." She drew in her breath. "That's why you went to the preacher at the Blue Moon and bought him a bottle of whiskey. He can just tear up the papers. I bet that's already been done and you're free. The lawyer will do the paperwork, then you and I can—"

He stepped back from her. "Stop it! There will be no annulment, no divorce. Quit spying on me. What I said to the preacher had nothing to do with the marriage. Nor does seeing the lawyer."

"Then *why*?" she yelled. "You owe me that much. What is going on?"

He closed his eyes for a moment in surrender. "I hired the preacher to do my accounts, and I'm inviting the lawyer to dinner. Etta wants him to meet Alice."

Cornelia took a step back, her face showing her astonishment. "Etta?" she whispered. "The wife? You are obeying her? She runs everything now?"

"It's not like that."

Cornelia glanced down at his crotch, then up again. She wore a sneer of contempt. "She's made a gelding of you." The sneer strengthened. "Was she that good in bed? Did she do something I haven't done to you? Did she—"

Abruptly, Max left the alley. He took the stairs up to the lawyer's office two at a time, then flung the door open and slammed it behind him.

Mrs. Ellis didn't look up. "You break that glass and you pay for it."

"He here?"

She shrugged in answer.

Max thought that he'd had all he could take of women today, but wisely didn't say so. He strode to the man's office, went inside, and shut the door.

The lawyer looked up from his desk. "If it isn't the kissing prince. I hear you tossed aside the ruling princess for a commoner."

Max sat down so hard on the wooden chair he almost broke it. "Don't give me crap or I'll hit you."

"I am warned. However, my free advice is for you to not add Mrs. Ellis to your conquests. She devours husbands like candy."

Max glared at him.

Bert Lloyd leaned back in his chair. "Gossip is that you got married this morning, but I just saw you kissing a stunningly beautiful young woman in the alley. I don't think she's your mail-order bride. Kecklin's daughter is my guess."

"Cornelia came at me, not the other way around." Max waved his hand. "Forget that. I'm here to—"

"I know why you're here. You own a very large piece of land and you run a big herd."

"Yeah," Max said. "And John Kecklin wants it all."

"Actually, he wants me to sue you to get it. Seems that you were supposed to marry his daughter, who I've been told is a real hellion." He nodded toward the door to indicate Mrs. Ellis as his source. "Kecklin wants you to give him everything you own as a dowry for receiving his daughter. I explained that dowries are usually the other way around. They're given to the groom."

"Kecklin didn't shoot you for that?"

"No, but he wanted to. I turned down his case, which is why I can tell you about it. So what can I do for you, Mr. Lawton?"

"My wife wants you to come to dinner tonight."

He looked shocked. "This is the wife you married this morning? Don't you have other things to do tonight?"

Max gave him the look he used to get his men in line.

"My apologies. I would love to come to dinner. Seven?"

Max stood up. "Sure. Whenever you get there." He left the office.

When he got outside, he stopped on the landing. He'd done all that he was supposed to do. He felt like he'd accomplished feats of strength, endurance, and sheer horror. He was almost smiling until he saw what was sitting on the back of his buckboard. He had no doubt in the world that the woman who had taken over his life had done it. He clomped down the stairs with a frown so deep his eyebrows met in the middle.

Inside the office, Bert watched Max close the door so hard the glass rattled. "Why did Max Lawton ask me to dinner on his wedding night?" he asked Mrs. Ellis.

"He's got a little sister so hideous he hides her away. Looks like you've been chosen for her."

"If it gets me Lawton's business, I might do it."

"Then you'll make an enemy of John Kecklin."

"I've already done that," Bert said. "On second thought, maybe I'll move to Wichita tomorrow."

Mrs. Ellis snorted. "It'd be better if you chose one of the women sniffing around you instead of loving being the town catch."

With a roll of his eyes, Bert went back into his office. He could never win against that woman.

Sitting in the back of Max's wagon were three people. Hank, who he'd brought to get him away from Alice, was flanked by two women. One was Freida who worked at the Red Dog. Max didn't want to think about his relationship with her. The other woman was Sally who cleaned the saloon. Since they were the women his wife had called "friends," Max knew she was behind this.

He stood at the end of the wagon and said nothing, but his expression told all.

Hank shook his head. "It's not my fault. Your wife told me I was to find 'em and take 'em back to your place."

"To do what?" Max's meaning was clear. They knew what Freida did for a living.

"I don't do that," Sally said rather haughtily.

"I do!" Freida said happily, making Hank laugh.

"Not at my house, you don't." Max stepped back and made a sweep of his arm, meaning for them to get down.

Hank and Sally started to comply, but Freida didn't move. "Your *wife*—" she emphasized the word "—wants me to look after her garden."

"I don't have a garden."

"That's the point." Freida was glaring at him. "If you go back on this job, I'll tell."

She didn't have to explain who she would tell. Say it to one person and everyone would start saying Max Lawton wasn't to be trusted, that he went back on his word.

Sally scooted back into the wagon. "I guess your house needs cleaning."

It did, but he wouldn't admit that. Every housekeeper he'd hired had run off with a man, so only Esmeralda was left. It took her thirty minutes to put her shoes on.

Max looked at the three of them, all waiting for his decision. That was a joke! He hadn't made a decision since he got married. He didn't know how she'd done it, but within hours his new wife had taken control of his life. *Just as Cornelia said.*

"I didn't know marriage was like this." He didn't realize he'd said it aloud until they started laughing.

He climbed up to the seat and headed home, and frowned all the way there.

When he got to his house, the two women wisely jumped out before he fully stopped. He tossed the reins to Hank, then turned to the women. But they had disappeared. "Herding cats," he muttered.

He caught sight of Freida's purple skirt turning a corner and went after her. "Where do you think you're going?"

She put her hands on her hips in defiance. "I'm going to get some of the men I know." She wiggled her brows at him.

"To help me clear up the front. Since you're one of them, you wanna join us?"

Max opened his mouth to speak, closed it, then said, "Only three of them. And not Hank."

"Deal," she said, then hurried to the barn.

Inside the house, he was startled to see that it was already clean. It looked like an army had gone through it and straightened and washed everything.

"Isn't it lovely?" Alice asked from behind him.

"How did this happen?"

"Etta had the men do it. You should have seen her. A general leading an army can't command troops as well as she can."

When he turned, he saw that Sally was beside her. In her hand was some sheet music.

"Your wife wants me to sing." Sally's eyes were wide in wonder. "How did she know that I sing? Only my family knows."

"Don't ask me anything about her," Max said, then looked at his sister. "Where is she?"

"Max," Alice said, "if you start a fight with her and ruin tonight, I'll never forgive you. Is he coming?"

"Yes," Max said. "I got the lawyer, hired the preacher, fought off Cornelia, and made an enemy of John Kecklin. And now I'm here with a couple of saloon girls. I've done it *all*."

Alice was unperturbed by her brother's outburst. "That's good. Etta is in the back. She's trying for a cooking prize. I don't know what she gets if she wins."

Max had no reply to that. He stormed out of the house.

She was easy to find as all the men who were supposed to be working had abandoned their jobs and were crowded around the chuck wagon. It's what they used when they were away from the house and the men had to be fed. Why was it here now?

Suddenly, a shout went out from all the men, and they raised their arms in triumph.

Some of the men saw Max, but they didn't scurry back to

work as they should have. Rufus, a man who'd worked for him for years, was grinning. "She won!" He slapped his hat on his leg. "By golly, she *won!*"

Max had an idea who "she" was, but he hoped it wasn't true.

The men parted and sure enough, Max's wife came through. In her hand was a fan of greenbacks.

"I beat him," she said to Max.

"She did," three men said in pride.

The men were looking at him in anticipation, waiting for his response. "You won what?"

"Your cook smirked at me," Etta said. "He told me that no lady could cook in a wagon. He said he had to do things really fast and little ole me couldn't possibly do that. I told him he hadn't met Lester. Then I challenged him." She held up the money.

"So you showed him," Max said.

"I did." She waved the money about. "I'll spend this on a feast for all of you. One that *I* will cook."

Again, the men cheered.

"I think you better go back to work now," she said to them. "My husband needs you." The men gave a quick look at Max, then scattered.

He was left alone with his wife. "What were you doing? A lady doesn't—"

"Give me a break! I'm not going to be treated like some fragile princess who doesn't know how to use an iron skillet. I can't bear being thought of as *useless.*"

"You've been here less than a day. You don't have to do everything at once."

"Maybe not, but lockdown makes people crazy. Anyway, I need someone to take me to Esmeralda's house to buy vegetables. I can drive two hundred horses but not just two of them."

He was so puzzled by what she'd said that he hesitated. "She lives in the Mexican village. Tell me what you want, and I'll send one of the men."

She just looked up at him.

Max threw up his hands. "I have a painted cat cutting weeds in the front, a lickspittle singing in my parlor, and a wife gambling with my men. Why not go visit the Mexicans? Maybe I'll build a house there."

"After you eat one of my enchiladas you might want to," Etta said, then walked away, her long skirt swishing.

Unfortunately, a couple of men heard her and they laughed.

For a moment Max glared at them, but he couldn't sustain it. He laughed too. She'd made a good comeback.

Smiling, he followed her into the house. For all that she infuriated him, he was intrigued by her. And more than that, he desired her. Just flat out wanted to take her to bed, but first, he wanted her to feel the same way about him.

8

As soon as Etta reached the house, guilt flooded her. She shouldn't have wasted time on a cooking contest. Her excuse was that, from her observation, women here were wives, prostitutes, or unmarried, which meant she was a spinster or a widow. And it seemed that the last two were to be pitied. A woman without a man was sad, or in Martha's case, bitter.

When the cook told Etta she couldn't do what he did, she lost control. She could almost see Lester. If she'd ever turned down a challenge like that, he would have been ashamed of her. He would have walked away and probably not spoken to her for days.

She just looked at the grizzled old cook and said, "You wanna bet?"

Blazing hot skillets and lots of meat were her domain. The cook stuck his dirty hand into a jar of sourdough starter, preparing to make fried bread. Etta knew that would be too slow. When she reached for a bag of cornmeal, a cheer went up. About half of the men were from Mexico, and they knew a tortilla-in-the-making when they saw it.

Etta rolled out dough on top of a metal box then slapped it back and forth in her hands as she'd done a thousand times. Lester didn't believe in tortillas purchased from a supermarket.

Oddly shaped tomatoes appeared, and she had an idea they came from the men's home gardens.

When Etta's meal was ready quicker and tasted better, she was concerned that she'd made an enemy of the cook. But he was laughing hard. He even whispered that he wanted her to show him how to season the beans like she did.

It had all been wonderful until she saw her husband. It was still strange for her to think of him as such. The men were laughing, cheering, slapping each other on the back and Etta was the center of it all.

He was frowning, but underneath it, she saw curiosity and interest. When an older cowboy told him about Etta winning, for a split second, her husband looked pleased.

That glance gave her courage to be flippant with him. To make a smart aleck reply.

When she got in the house, all she knew for sure was that she needed to make up for lost time. She could wake up from the dream at any moment. She didn't want to read in some history book that Alice Lawton had died alone.

Not that any of this is real, she reminded herself.

When she entered the house, she heard Sally singing in the distance, probably in the glass room. Alice had taken care of her and the music. Etta was happily surprised to see Freida and Alice at the big dining table looking at a long sheet of paper. They were talking quietly, their heads almost touching, and planning what to plant in front of the house. She heard "elm trees" and "dogwoods." Etta was relieved. She knew her sister never

snubbed anyone, but this was a different time and place. She'd
been concerned that Alice might be put off by Freida's gaudy
dress and her heavily roughed cheeks. Etta added "makeup les-
son" to her mental list of things to do.

When Etta turned around, her husband was there, looking
out the window. He obviously wasn't approving.

"You don't want your sister consulting with a scarlet lady?"

She saw the way his mouth tightened. He nodded toward the
front of the house. "Now there are two men outside helping
her. In half an hour there'll be four men, then six."

"Her past customers?"

He blinked at Etta's nonchalance, then nodded yes.

"She seems to be well-liked," Etta said.

"She's happy and she makes us, uh, *them* feel good."

He'd answered her unasked question, if he'd been a client
of Freida. It appeared that he had. She wasn't sure, but his face
seemed to turn red.

"I'll take them with me when I go get the vegetables," she
said.

He turned to her. "And you need two hundred horses?"

It took her a second to know what he meant, then she smiled.
"Mechanical horses, yes. A big truck would be nice. I could—"

Suddenly, she felt dizzy. She put her hand to her forehead. *No,
no, no*, she thought. *I can't wake up now. I have things to do. I have
to match people together.* She looked up at him. "I have so much
more to do," she whispered. Then her knees gave way under her.

When Etta woke up, she didn't open her eyes. She knew she'd
see Ben's room, then she'd go downstairs to Henry. There'd be
days in his beautiful old house, and she'd probably never return
to the past. Never again see Alice. Nor her husband.

"Are you awake?" came a soft, male voice.

Henry. She didn't open her eyes. The bed was so very soft.

She hadn't experienced an 1870 bed, but it was probably made of wood.

"Want some water?"

That voice! Slowly, she opened her eyes. She was *not* in Ben's room. *Not* looking at Henry. "Max," she whispered.

He gave a one-sided smile. "Not calling me Mr. Lawton?"

She started to sit up, but you can't do a crunch when wearing a corset. She fell back down and looked around. It was a bedroom but one she'd not seen. His? It was as bare as a monk's cell. There was a tall pine wardrobe, a plain chest of drawers, and a wooden chair.

When she turned her head, she saw that he was stretched out beside her, fully dressed, not touching her. "I guess I fainted. Again."

"Women do." He put his hands behind his head and looked up at the ceiling. "Last time, I thought you'd died."

"I did, in a way."

He didn't look at her. "To get away from me?"

"No. I didn't want to leave. And I don't now." She ran her hand over the coverlet. "This bed is *soft*. I thought there was nothing in this state that wasn't as hard as iron."

"My mother plucked the bellies of geese and filled the mattresses. She said it helped her deal with my father. It spoiled me."

"So you kept it up." She needed to get up. She still had so much to do.

"I sent Alice and Freida with Rufus to get your vegetables."

She rolled to face him and lifted her head on one hand. "You let Alice leave the house? With a… What did you call her? A painted cat? And who is Rufus?"

"Old guy. Red shirt."

"Ah yes. I remember him. Nice man. Bet he's all of forty years old."

Her words were a challenge, but he didn't comment on them. "The preacher's coming tomorrow morning."

"How did you achieve that?"

With barely concealed pride, he told her that he'd hired the preacher, and had invited the lawyer to dinner. "I swear that I can herd a thousand cows but not be this exhausted." He looked at her. "How'd you know the preacher knew about numbers?"

Caught! Etta thought. So now what? She would tell Max that he's not real? That he's only part of her dream? Or did she tell him she was a time traveler, then describe cars and planes and computers?

Right now, all that seemed unreal. It was like that was the dream and this was the actual world.

Alice's letters! she thought. They would be her way out. "Did Alice read you the letters she wrote to me?"

"No, just your replies."

Etta sighed in relief. "She told me about people here and I put the bits together. I shouldn't have told you that. Swear you won't tell her that I betrayed her confidence."

"Alice knew about the preacher? She's never met him."

"I guess you told her more about him than you thought, then she told me." She spoke quickly, before he asked more questions. "When you had trouble with the accounts, I realized there might be a solution."

He took a moment to think about that. "But—"

Etta didn't want to answer more questions about how she knew things. She interrupted. "Do you isolate Alice or does she do it to herself?"

He didn't take offense at her words but thought about them. "She and I both tend to stay away from other people. We meet who we have to. We don't have parties. Cornelia used to…" He stopped.

"It's all right. You can talk about her."

"She gave parties and she made sure Alice went to them."

"And now with Cornelia gone, there is no more socializing, so you and Alice stay home. Alone, just the two of you." Etta thought how much that sounded like Alicia and her father. After her mother died, it was Etta who got them to move and do and go. When Phillip entered their lives, he took over a lot of Etta's job as the "social director" as her father called her.

"I didn't know she liked the lawyer," he said. "I would have…" He didn't seem able to come up with what he would have done.

"Invited him over for canned peaches?"

"Yeah, maybe I would have." He turned to look at her. They were facing each other, quite close. "I can't imagine my little sister married. It seems like yesterday when I was fishing her out of the river." He smiled. "She tried to catch fish with her hands and always fell in. I taught her how to swim."

"Did she talk to many people? Listen to them?"

"She always has. More than once I found her alone with some stranger and they were whispering."

"Telling her things they told no one else on earth."

"That's true. One time I got really angry when I saw her with some old man and he was crying. I thought… Never mind what I thought."

"He was telling her his life story."

"Yes. Later, she told me about it. He built a big house for the woman he was going to marry, but she died right after the wedding. He never went back to the house. It's in Mason, Kansas, not far from here."

Etta drew in her breath. Mason was where Henry and Ben bought the desk and the trunk. The desk that was now in Max's office. It was also where Henry's ancestor built a house. Was he the man of the tragic story?

She knew what he was feeling. Strangers on planes, in restaurants, everywhere, told her sister horrible stories. They poured out their hearts to Alicia. "It's a shame to hide away someone who has the superpower of empathy."

He chuckled at that. "'Superpower.' You say odd things. So what's your superpower?"

Dreaming! she thought, but he was waiting for her to answer. "I guess it's that I tend to take care of people. It makes me feel good. Needed."

"You've certainly turned Alice and me upside down." For a moment they looked into each other's eyes.

"I haven't meant to be abrasive," she said. "I just feel that I need to do some things. Once I get them done…" She had no idea what to say. He was such a good-looking man! The extreme masculinity of him surrounded her.

"I'm sorry I made you want to leave. Alice and I, and now even the men, want you to stay." He looked at her for a moment. "Sometimes I feel like I've known you for a long time. I just can't quite place where and when we met."

Instinctively, Etta moved her face a bit closer to his. Was it time for kissing? He didn't move away.

"Maybe we could—"

Noise and laughter and a slamming door interrupted him.

"They're back." Reluctantly, Etta started to get up, but when Max stayed where he was, she lay back down beside him, and they listened.

They heard female voices through the closed door. Freida's was lower and had a suggestion of something naughty in it, while Alice's laugh was higher, innocent. Sally sang a few notes.

Etta looked at Max. His eyes were closed, and he was smiling. "I haven't heard her laugh in a long time," he said softly.

As they lay there, side by side, the air filled with Sally's beautiful voice in song, "Listen to the Mocking Bird." Freddy and Alice joined her. It was a trio of female voices, and it was lovely.

On the bed, Max reached out and took Etta's hand in his and held it.

When they began to sing the mournful "Rock Me to Sleep, Mother," he tightened his grip on her hand. Even Etta, with

her limited knowledge of history, knew that old song was as-
sociated with a young, dying soldier in the War Between the
States. She didn't know Max's age, but he may have fought in
that horrible war.

When the song finished, they lay there, not moving, just
holding hands.

It was Alice who threw the door open. "Max! I can't find
Etta. Oh," she said when she saw them. "Oh."

Behind her, a laughing Freida pulled the door shut. Max got
off the bed, then reached out to help Etta up.

She took his hand and let him pull her up. "It's hard to move
when there are planks of wood strapped to the middle of me."

"I could help you remove that," he said so solemnly that she
was startled. Was he making a sex remark?

He gave no hint one way or the other before he left the bedroom.

When Etta followed him, she realized she was on the second
floor. She hadn't seen this part of the house. Besides Max's bedroom, there were two closed doors. She opened one and saw
it was full of wooden boxes, old saddles, half a dozen trunks.
Storage. She wondered if her trunk, the one that sat at the foot
of Ben's bed, had been put in there. Did *she* put her lace wedding jacket in there? The idea gave her a bit of the creeps. She
closed the door.

The third door was locked. *More junk?* she wondered.

For a moment she fantasized that it contained a bathroom:
tub, shower, two sinks, a toilet that flushed. Turn on a faucet
and hot water came out.

Etta, she thought, *you are old. You've got a drop-dead gorgeous
husband yet you fantasize about a hot water heater.*

Laughing at herself, she went down the stairs, and found everything was quiet. No more singing, no laughter, just silence.

She found Alice in the kitchen, staring at canvas bags and a
big basket of freshly picked vegetables.

"Where is everyone?"

"Freddy..." She paused. "She said that only her father ever called her that, and she wonders how you know."

"It just seemed natural," Etta said. She was searching for an apron. There was zucchini, yellow squash, new potatoes, early peas. Not the variety of later in the season, but good for April. "Tell me what you did today."

"It's been wonderful," Alice said dreamily. "Freddy told me all about herself."

Of course she did, Etta thought. "Tell me everything." She gave Alice some potatoes to peel, but she was so slow and awkward that Etta took them back.

Etta chopped and cooked while Alice told Freddy's story. Her mother died giving birth to her third daughter, then her father died when Freddy was fourteen.

Alice lowered her voice to a whisper. "She sold her body to feed her two younger sisters. But after they grew up and got married, they wanted nothing to do with a harlot. That wasn't fair, was it?"

Etta smiled in pride. "Not fair at all."

"Max is going to be angry at me. I hired Freddy. She's going to make a real garden here. We're going to grow food like this. Esmeralda's cousin can help us. She was crying."

"Esmeralda?"

"No. The cousin. We saw her today. She's had two marriage offers. One man is good for her, but the other one, well, she craves him. I told her..." Alice looked at Etta in embarrassment.

"You told her to go for the guy who turns her on."

"What an odd turn of phrase, but yes, I did." She and Etta looked at each other and laughed.

"It's what my sister did. She went for a man who could use his hands in lots of ways."

The two of them howled with laughter.

And Max thinks Alice is pure innocence. Ha!

★ ★ ★

By six thirty, everything was ready. Food was cooked and the table set. "I have to dress," Alice said. "Silk and my mother's pearls." She disappeared into her side of the house.

Etta looked down at herself. She had on the dress she'd been married in. She'd worn it while riding through dirty streets, while cooking at a chuck wagon, and now when preparing a "cupid's dinner" as she'd come to think of it. The one to unite Alice with the love of her life.

Max returned from wherever he'd been, and he was sparkling clean. He had on a white shirt and dark trousers. There wasn't a spot of dirt on him.

"You took a bath!" Her tone was an accusation. She held out her arms to indicate her sweaty self.

"Just in the river," he said defensively. "You have other clothes?"

She had no idea what she'd brought with her. She didn't even know where her trunk was. She followed him to a side porch and there it was, set among the mops and brooms. It looked like he'd tossed it out of the wagon.

"I should have brought it in," he mumbled.

She found the key deep in a pocket of her skirt and opened it. It contained two more dresses in dark, boring colors, and a long nightgown that was as sexy as a rock.

She looked up at Max, her face showing her disappointment. She pulled out a dress of mud brown and held it up. "It exactly matches the color of the streets of Garrett."

He gave a little laugh, then motioned for her to follow him. In the kitchen, he opened a cabinet door. Hanging inside was a big key. He took it out, then nodded for her to follow him upstairs.

He went to the locked door and opened it.

Inside was like a time capsule. It was as though someone got out of bed, left the room, and locked the door. The bed hadn't been made, a hairbrush was on a chair, a single shoe was on the floor. What was unusual was that everything was covered in dust, with spiderwebs collecting more.

She looked at him.

"My mother's room. We just closed it." He shrugged as though he had no reason why. He went to the big mahogany wardrobe and opened the door. "You may have anything you want."

"That's very kind of you."

"You can stay in here tonight if you'd like. Or downstairs near Alice. A room was set up for you there." He hesitated. "I could bring up some hot water."

"I would love that," she said, and he left. For a moment she looked at the closed door. "'Downstairs near Alice,'" she quoted him. It looked like he'd never planned on his marriage being a real one, with a shared bed.

She didn't have time to think about that. The lawyer would be here soon. Alice's future husband!

Inside the wardrobe were a dozen dresses hanging from pegs. "Tomorrow I invent coat hangers." The clothes looked like they would fit her. "Of course," she said. "It's my dream so I made them for me." There was a dress of lilac silk that she quite liked, and she pulled it out.

So now the question was how to get undressed and redressed. The clothes weren't exactly slip on and off. And there was the corset. *Shame on me for complaining about underwire bras.*

She was struggling with her arms at the back when there was a knock on the door, and she opened it. Max was holding a wooden bucket full of steaming hot water. *One bucket,* she thought. *And I want a tub full.*

She motioned for him to come in. He set the bucket down and looked around. "I think Alice and I wanted to forget this room." For a moment he watched Etta struggle with the dress. "I'll leave you to it."

"I need a knife to cut myself out of this thing. You couldn't help me, could you?"

"I guess."

She turned her back to him. When he did nothing, she twisted around to look at him. He was frowning, puzzled. It felt good that he didn't know how to undress a woman. "Freddy still here?"

"I sent her home. I don't want her being a distraction to the lawyer."

"Right. His attention is to be on Alice."

Max put his hands on her back and began loosening the hooks on the dress.

With each one, Etta felt relief from pressure. When the last one was undone, she shimmied out of the dress, letting it puddle on the floor. "That's heaven!" She turned to him.

He was staring at her. To Etta, she was fully clothed. A T-shirt and jeans was a lot less clothing than the yards of cotton she was wearing. She even had on *stockings*!

But Max didn't seem to think she was covered. Maybe it was the way he'd said that Freddy was "fun" or maybe it was his reference to Etta's age, but a devil seemed to enter her. She batted her lashes at him. "Could you help with this thing?" She meant her corset. "It's cutting into me something awful."

He bent as though he was going to kiss her, but then stepped back. "Not what I can do," he said quickly. "I'll send Esmeralda." With that, he left the room with the speed of a tiger with its tail on fire.

"What the hell?" she said aloud. "It's probably the only wedding night I'll ever have, and I don't even get *kissed*." She rolled her eyes skyward. "This is *my* dream and I want control of it. Got that, whoever is in charge of this thing?"

Esmeralda didn't show up so Etta had to figure out corset laces by herself. It was harder than making croissants by hand.

Twenty minutes later, she had washed as best she could and

dressed in the heavy, but beautiful, dress. She went downstairs to the kitchen to check on everything. On the table was a basket of early strawberries. The sight of them took away some of her annoyance.

Alice came into the room and she looked divine, like a vision in a dream should look. Etta told her so, then asked where the strawberries came from.

"We left them in the wagon. They were a gift from the man I told the girl she should marry."

"How nice."

"Yes and no. He included some hard little green fruits and a bottle of something that was bad. It had a worm in the bottom."

Etta's eyes widened. "Where is it?"

"I put it in the pantry. I'll pour it out later."

Etta nearly leaped to the pantry. Well, as much as the weight of her clothing allowed. Hidden in a corner near six bags of beans, she found it. Limes and a bottle of tequila. She took them into the kitchen.

"Etta," Alice said in horror. "You can't use that. It has a *worm* in it!"

"I'm going to make strawberry margaritas. My kingdom for a blender."

"But—"

Etta cut her off. "Do you have any pretty drinking glasses? Crystal, maybe?"

"Mother had a set. I know where they are." Alice left the kitchen.

Etta began making a pitcher full of the drinks. She had an idea that Max would be angry that she fed spirits to his precious sister, but tequila generally helped any party.

When it was close to seven, Alice went to her room to check her hair and clothes. She was so nervous she was shaking.

Max came into the kitchen. She hadn't seen him since she'd

been standing before him in her underwear. He didn't seem to want to meet her eyes.

"One of the men saw the lawyer. He's almost here. What's that?"

"Heaven in a glass." She poured some into one of the Irish crystal glasses that Alice had found.

He took a drink. "Nice. What's in it?"

"A drunken worm." She poured herself half a glass and drank it all. She needed strength for this dinner. "I want to see him. Is he worthy of our Alice?"

The affection in her voice pleased him. "Come on."

He led her to a window at the back of the house. Feeling the warming effects of the drink, she looked out. A tall man was on a horse. She'd expected to see Phillip, Alicia's husband, but that wasn't him.

"That's Ben," she said in shock. "Henry's son."

"He's the lawyer. Name of Bertram. I think he's called Bert."

"No, no, no! That man belongs to Caroline. To Cornelia." She tried to think what to do. "This is bad. Very, very bad." She looked at him. "You have to go get Cornelia and bring her here."

Max turned away and left the room, walking quickly. "Not on my life," he said over his shoulder.

She ran after him. "It's for Alice. You have to trust me on this. If she marries Ben she'll be miserable." Etta stopped for a moment. She didn't know that for sure, but at the same time she instinctively did know. Caroline and Ben went together. That's how it was supposed to be. *Had* to be. Maybe they'd eventually produce Henry's ancestor, who would produce Henry.

She looked at the back of Max. "If you don't go get her, I will." There was steel in her voice. "I'll tell her that you want to sell all your land to her father. Even the homestead. She'll come running. On a stallion."

Halting, he turned to her. "That's blackmail."

"Yes, it is. You *must* go."

He took a moment to contemplate what she was saying, and his face softened. "It's all right. There's nothing between Cornelia and me."

Etta gritted her teeth. "I am *not* jealous. This is more serious than female ownership of some man. Alice likes the lawyer, but he belongs to Cornelia." She saw that her words were having no effect on him. "Do you want Cornelia off your back or not?"

He hesitated.

"Do you think that she'll let up on you just because you got married? She's a woman scorned. She will never forgive or forget. Your only hope is to put her with another man." She could see that she was making headway in persuading him. "Please," she said. "Trust me."

After what seemed like forever, he nodded. He'd do it. "He'll be at the door soon."

"Get one of the men to keep him busy, then you get on the fastest horse and go get her."

"It'll take an hour or more."

"I need two hundred horses now," she said. "Just go as fast as you can. I'll distract Alice."

With a look that all this was ridiculous, he grabbed his hat and left the house. Etta waited, expecting the lawyer to knock on the door, but he didn't. She peeked out a window and saw two men practically dragging the lawyer into the barn. Poor man was gesturing that he was supposed to go into the house. He was barely out of sight when Max went tearing past on a horse at full speed.

"Oh my," Etta said. He certainly did look good!

"Where's Max going?" Alice said from behind her.

"To the grocery," she said before she thought. "I mean, there was an accident. He'll be back soon." When Alice turned away, Etta put her foot firmly down on one of her petticoats that was just visible under the silk. It ripped.

"I'm so sorry. Esmeralda will have to fix that."

"But he'll be here soon. I'll just pin it."

"He might see that and think you're a slovenly person," Etta said seriously.

"You're right. Esmeralda!" Alice shouted. "I need you."

Alice was hardly out of the room when Etta heard a sound that was becoming familiar. A wagon was driving in. *Now what?* she thought. *Drop-in visitors?*

To her disbelief, she saw Max driving a silver-and-black buggy that didn't take any historical knowledge to know that it was the Mercedes of the day. Beside him was the elegant, the beautiful, the eternally bad-tempered Cornelia.

"Why did I think inviting her was a good idea?" Etta mumbled.

Max seemed to know she was watching as he turned angry, glaring eyes on her. Etta stepped out of sight. "Okay, so now I can wake up."

Nothing happened.

An angry Max got out of the elegant buggy and started to go around to help Cornelia down. But the handsome Hank beat him to it.

Max gave a look of disgust and went to the house and straight to Etta.

"She was on her way here," he said, his jaw clenched. "Her father sent her back to finish the job she failed at today."

"What job?"

"Of getting me to annul our marriage and marry her. Or her father's going to sue me."

"Oh," Etta said. "Can you afford that?"

"Not at all."

"Then help me marry Corny to Ben–Bert."

"Ben what? And Corny? I dare you to call her that to her face."

Etta was thinking. "It would be better if you weren't so friendly to me. I don't want to set her off."

"What gave you the idea that I was friendly? And she knows it's over between her and me."

"You say that because you won the fight. That poor girl has a narcissistic, power-hungry father who is demanding that she do whatever he wants. She is not going to give up." She raised an eyebrow at him. "Today? You saw her today? You didn't tell me that. When?"

His eyes said he was getting her back for her threats to him. "She showed up between the preacher and the lawyer. She pulled me into the shade and kissed me. She said she wanted to marry me."

That he'd kissed another woman but not her, made Etta angry. "Maybe you *should* marry her since you like her kisses so damned much. And just so you know, I'm better at kissing than I am at cooking." She did a spin on her heel and turned away from him.

In the next moment she was in his arms and he was kissing her.

It wasn't an ordinary kiss. There was no awkwardness to it, no strangeness. It was as though they knew each other. And now, in spite of time and distance, they were at last together.

It was Max who broke away, then he held her close to his chest. She could feel his heart pounding under her cheek.

"Who are you?" he whispered. "Where have you come from?"

"I don't know," she said honestly.

When they heard voices, they broke apart. For a moment they stood there looking at each other, hearts pounding hard and fast.

Then the doors to hell seemed to open up. Alice came out from her side of the house. The lawyer came in the front door, and the divine Miss Cornelia entered the house from the back.

In the middle were Max and Etta. For a second their fingertips touched. "The war begins," he said, then he stepped forward.

★ ★ ★

At dinner, Etta couldn't bear to look at Alice. What she was feeling was so clear she might as well be wearing a sign. *Why have you done this to me?*

Max sat at one end of the table and Etta at the other end. She'd meant for the lawyer and Alice to sit across from each other. They did, but Cornelia sat herself next to Bert. She even moved her chair closer to him. Her actions were understandable after having been dumped by Max.

Etta didn't know Ben and Caroline in the twenty-first century, but if their attraction to each other was as quick as between Cornelia and the lawyer, it's a wonder they didn't elope on the first day.

"I met your father," Bert said to Cornelia after the introductions. "And I saw you with him." He didn't need to say that "him" was Max.

"A goodbye. That's all," Cornelia said, sounding wistfully sad. "He insisted."

When Max started to contradict her, Etta glared at him. Wisely, he didn't speak. She nodded at the big chunk of Kansas beef that she'd roasted. He was to slice it. "Tell us about your job," she said to Bert.

"It's good," he mumbled. He couldn't take his eyes off Cornelia.

"I heard you were moving to Wichita," Max said.

"Just a rumor spread by Mrs. Ellis."

"So you like our little town?" Cornelia asked demurely.

Etta and Max exchanged looks. This wasn't the woman they'd seen earlier, the one wielding a riding crop.

"I'm thinking of building a house here."

Etta remembered the photos of Garrett in the book of Kansas ghost towns. It was bare land. Not one building had survived. "No!" she said too loudly, and they all looked at her. "I mean,

Garrett depends on the railroad, doesn't it? If the rail connection is moved to, say Wichita, Garrett might disappear."

They were staring at her. She had told too much, but she couldn't stop. "Kansas City," she said. "It has trains and cows both." She knew that from all the movies she'd watched with her father. They were still staring at her in a way that made her uncomfortable. "And Cornelia can design a house for you."

To Etta's great relief, they looked at Cornelia.

"Can you do that?" Bert asked.

"I believe I can." She was beautifully modest.

Etta took a bite. "Italianate. Two stories, round-topped windows, porch across the front and to one side. Simple, not gaudy. Timeless." Of course she was describing Henry's family home.

Yet again, everyone looked at Etta as though she was a freak.

Max saved her. "So how do you like your food? Etta cooked everything."

Etta braced herself for Cornelia to say something about "old and plain" women, but she said nothing.

Max also waited, seeming to expect Cornelia's comment. When there was nothing, he said, "Here! Have one of these."

In all the turmoil, Etta had forgotten the pitcher of margaritas. Strawberries, lime juice, and tequila. Delicious and lethal. Max filled the glasses. He hesitated at giving one to Alice, but Etta gave him a look to not leave his sister out. Alice had had enough of being excluded.

The drinks on their relatively empty stomachs took away the tension. Alice frequently cut looks at Max and Etta as though they were traitors, but she made a funny story out of her and Freddy's trip to get vegetables.

Bert was the first to understand. "You mean Freida from the Red Dog?"

"Yes. I hired her to work for us."

"You did what?" Max sounded threatening.

Cornelia said, "Don't you dare use that tone with her! Alice is my friend and you took her away from me." In her anger, she was coming out of her seat.

Even though he'd just met her, Bert put a hand on Cornelia's wrist. It was like he'd applied a tranquilizer to her, and she sat back down.

It's funny, Etta thought. *Two people can say the same things, yet one enrages you and the other one soothes you.* "You are always welcome here," she said to Cornelia. "I know Alice misses you very much."

Cornelia turned to her. "Thank you." She paused a moment. "I'm sorry about today. I..." She didn't finish.

"Forgiven," Etta said, and everyone except Alice smiled.

The rest of the meal was pleasant. Bert practically hired Cornelia to design a home for him. Anything to get to see her again. Max kept smiling at Etta with thanks and relief. Cornelia acted like a vestal virgin for Bert, but she also pulled Alice into every conversation. Etta got the idea that being deprived of her girlfriend was half the reason she'd been so angry at Max. After all, there was an unwritten law that boyfriends couldn't interfere with girlfriends.

After dinner, they sat in the pretty parlor to listen to Sally sing. "Isn't she—" Bert looked at Max.

"From the Red Dog."

Bert gave a quick glance at Etta, then Sally. "You may have stopped going there, but you seem to have brought them home with you." He walked away before Max could reply.

Throughout the performance, Bert and Cornelia sat close and looked at each other often.

It was late when they left, and Bert insisted on driving Cornelia home. He tied his horse to her buggy and they left. Max, Etta, and Alice waved goodbye to them.

"Kisses in the moonlight," Etta said to Max, and he smiled. She had just solved the biggest problem of his life.

When Alice sniffed, they turned to her.

"I hate both of you," Alice said, then ran back into the house, slamming the door behind her.

It was dark but Etta could see Max's expression. *How are you going to fix this?* was what he was asking.

Suddenly, she felt dizzy. "I don't know," she said softly. "I don't even know if I'll be here." Yet again, she fainted.

9

When Etta woke, she didn't open her eyes. She saw light through her eyelids, but did it come from Ben's window or was she still in Max's house?

She wasn't ready to know. She thought about what had happened in the dream. She'd united Ben-Bert with Caroline-Cornelia, and she hoped she'd changed Freddy's life, and maybe Sally's. She may have ensured that Henry's house in Kansas City got built. Alice might have made some new friends, and she and Cornelia were again BFFs.

All of that was probably enough to make her wake up in Henry's house. It was just that logic had nothing to do with how she felt. She ran her hand over the bed. Was it Ben's or Max's?

"Please be Max," she whispered. "I don't want to leave."

Squinting, she slowly opened one eye. It seemed to take forever to focus. "Max!" she said. She was still in her dream. Still with all of them.

She flung back the covers and started to stand up, then flopped back down. She was sore all over. Yes, she'd solved some problems, but yesterday had been long and exhausting.

As she looked around, she realized she was not only in Max's house, she was in his bed. She lifted up on one arm. The pillow next to her was dented, as was that side of the bed.

Well, well, well, she thought. It looked like she'd been moved from a room downstairs up to Max's bedroom. Was it her reward for freeing him from his violent girlfriend? Or, maybe the bedroom honor wasn't for Etta herself but because she'd removed a problem. Who was she to look a gift horse in the mouth?

She made a second, more vigorous, attempt at getting up and she succeeded. She had on the voluminous nightgown that had been in her trunk. And no corset.

She gave a one-sided grin. Did Max undress her? It was a nice thought.

As soon as she was standing, she again wished for a modern bathroom. Now she'd have to dress before going outside to that smelly old building. Yuck.

She opened the bedroom door. No one was in the hall. She went to Max's mother's room. The beautiful silk dress she'd worn at dinner was on the bed, as was her corset and the cotton undergarments. Etta rummaged through the wardrobe to see what was in there. Heaven be praised but she found a white cotton blouse and one of those skirts that was actually a pair of pants. As long as no one asked her to ride a horse, she'd be fine. In a drawer at the bottom she found an abbreviated corset that laced in the front. She was falling in love with Max's mother.

By the time Etta was dressed, she ran to the outhouse. The only one she knew of was Alice's private one, but she wasn't yet ready to see someone who'd said, "I hate you." Etta went around the house to reach it.

At last relieved, she went back into the house, hoping Max would be there.

Instead, she almost ran into her father. She was so glad to see him that it was difficult not to throw her arms around him. "We meet again," she said.

From his look, he didn't remember her.

"Max's wife," she said. "Do you want me to show you to the office?"

He gave a silent nod, but then her father was always wary of strangers.

She led him to Max's office and again she looked at the big desk. It was just like Henry's but, with no carving on the front, maybe it wasn't his after all.

"Well?" he said.

"This desk should have something on the front of it, but then, it would have cost a lot and Henry couldn't afford it." He was looking at her as though she was crazy. She got herself under control and opened two drawers before she found the account book. It was a mess. Numbers had been repeatedly inked out. She knew her father would hate that disorder. She shut the book. "You won't like this."

There was a file cabinet in the corner, and she opened the drawers. In the bottom were new, clean ledgers. She put one on the desk, then rummaged until she found ink and a steel pen. She set them to the upper right of the ledger, the way her father liked it. She stepped back. "There you go."

He was looking at her with the expression that was beginning to be familiar. She was odd, strange, even a freak. This time, she didn't let it bother her. "Have a seat and I'll make you an omelet."

"A what?"

She waved her hand. "Trust me, you'll love it." She left the room. "Since you eat it and only it seven days a week," she said under her breath.

She still wasn't used to the big range that burned wood, but she managed. When the Denver omelet was done, she took it and a cup of strong black coffee to her father. He was looking at Max's account books and shaking his head in disbelief. Etta knew better than to talk to him. Small talk was not allowed when Thomas Wilmont, aka Preacher Tobias, was working.

In the kitchen she grabbed a leftover biscuit and some cold bacon and made herself a sandwich. "I just invented McDonald's. I'm a millionaire," she muttered as she went back upstairs.

Foremost in her mind was that she had to find Phillip or his Old West equivalent. In one way, last night's dinner had been a great success, but the hurt in Alice's eyes haunted her.

How do I do it? she wondered. Max was gone, probably up to his ears in men and cows, so how did she do this with no car, no phone, no anything?

Once she was in Max's mother's bedroom, she caught sight of herself in the old mirror over the dresser. She gasped in shock. Maybe she should have woken up in Henry's house. She needed a long shower and a triple hair wash. Cooking grease wasn't exactly hair conditioner.

She opened a drawer, looking for something that could help, and pulled out a bar of soap. Not the square, homemade lye thing that was in the kitchen, but soft, French milled soap.

She clutched it to her bosom. "I love you," she whispered.

A vision of Max, sparkling clean as he entered the kitchen, came to her. He'd bathed in the river. The only river she knew of was at the homestead.

Etta knew that before she went anywhere, she had to make herself look presentable. Her mind spun with a plan of how to do it.

There was a little desk in the corner, and she found ivory sheets of paper in a drawer. "Thank you," she whispered to Max's mother. She didn't have time to figure out where towels were so she pulled a sheet off the bed. Dust went up and she coughed, but she rolled it up like a bedroll and tucked it under her arm.

Downstairs, she went directly to Max's office and opened the door without knocking. Of course her father glowered at being disturbed, but this was an emergency. Alice's future was at stake. Etta knew that her father loved maps. He even liked to draw them. "Do you know where the old Lawton homestead is? The sod house?"

"I do."

She put the paper in front of him. "Then draw me a map of how to get there."

He didn't hesitate but started drawing. "You seem to know a great deal about me."

"A bit. You'll be hungry at one. There's beef and biscuits in the kitchen. And if you see Alice, talk to her. You two like each other." She took the map and started to leave, then looked back. "Have you ever heard of Wyatt Earp?"

"No."

It was too early for the man to be well-known. "You should keep a diary of your life now. You're good at writing." She smiled at his familiar look. He was trying to figure out what she was up to.

As Etta left the house, she saw Alice who gave her a look of *You are dead to me*, then went back inside.

"This is very bad," Etta said as she went to the stables. She was glad to see Rufus. When he smiled, she saw that he needed a dentist. "I need to go somewhere. Could you give me your most gentle, easy to ride horse?"

"Tulip is good. You want the sidesaddle?"

Etta knew that meant throwing her leg around a big post and trying to stay on. All in a belief that women shouldn't part their legs wide—except when creating and delivering babies, that is. "No, thanks. I'll take the wide angle version. I need the balance."

He seemed ready to protest but since the cook-off, he was a fan of hers. He saddled a big, lazy looking mare and made no comment as he strapped the rolled bed sheet on the back. He put a wooden box down for her to climb up.

Except for pony rides when she was a child, Etta had never been on a horse. It was tall and wide. Very wide. No gym abductor machine had prepared her legs to be spread that far apart.

When she groaned, Rufus looked at her in concern.

"So how do I make this critter back up?"

He looked ill. "I'll get the buggy."

"No! Just give me some lessons and I'll be fine. And do not tell Max that I know nothing about horses. Or riding."

Rufus looked like a man facing execution. "He won't like this."

"Please," she said as sweetly as she could manage. "It's a surprise for my new husband."

Rufus seemed to fight himself for a moment, but then he said things about pulling reins and using her heels and not trying to run. It all merged into one incomprehensible lecture.

In the end, he led the horse outside and gave it a rump smack to get it going. Etta pulled the map out of her pocket and followed it. The horse ambled along and after a while Etta relaxed. There were few turns, and the Kansas landscape was beautiful. She wondered if this area would someday be full of roads and buildings.

When she got to the homestead, she was almost sad for the journey to end. Tulip went straight to the water, then Etta had the task of getting down. She threw her leg around and slid to the ground.

Pain shot through her inner thighs. "Oh for bucket seats of Corinthian leather."

She tied the horse reins—she'd seen that on TV—looked around to make sure she was alone, then stripped naked. The water was cold but she didn't care. She soaped every inch of her body, swam a bit to rinse, then soaped again. About a pint of grease came out of her hair. *Wonder how many fish I smothered?* she thought. *But they're Kansas fish so maybe I delighted them. Beef rules!*

When she finally got out, she felt much better. She ran her fingers through her hair, wishing she'd brought a comb. Bar soap wasn't good as a shampoo.

She wrapped the sheet around herself, tucking it over her breasts, her arms bare, then sat down and leaned against a cottonwood tree. She didn't think that she'd ever in her life been as contentedly happy as she was at that moment.

When Tulip nudged her shoulder, she patted its nose. "Thanks for letting me ride you," she said.

The horse snuffled, then stepped back. There was some new spring grass nearby.

When Tulip moved, Etta saw Max standing there holding two open cans of peaches. She wasn't surprised. "Rufus ratted on me."

"He is sure he sent you to your death. You may have to give him the worm." She laughed, knowing he meant the tequila worm.

He handed her a can of peaches and a spoon. "I figured you'd be hungry after that." He motioned to the river.

"Did you see it all?" she asked.

"See what?"

She wasn't sure if he was telling the truth, but his eyes were twinkling.

He sat down beside her, their backs against the tree, sides touching, and for a moment they ate peaches in silence.

Max spoke first. "How do you know things? And don't lie to me about my sister's letters."

She took her time before answering. "I dream them."

He nodded at that. "I dreamed of my mother right after she died. She made me swear to take care of Alice. But you've dreamed about everyone."

"Not really. Just a few people. Cornelia and Bert. Freddy and Sally. And Alice."

"Is that all?"

"Actually, there was Martha, the woman you nearly ran over. She's with Henry, but I haven't seen him. And Tobias goes with Lily." Etta swallowed at the mention of her mother. "But I don't think she's here."

"Any dreams about me?"

"No. You're completely new to me. I've never seen you in a dream, or outside of one. I first saw you in the church." She smiled at him. "You're something I made up for myself. My dream man. I'm not sure you're real."

He lifted her hand in his and laced their fingers together. "I'm very real," he said softly, then kissed the back of her hand. It wasn't one of those little pecks, but his full, lush lips were pressed on the back of her hand.

She turned to him, ready for anything. Her sheet slipped down a little.

But Max turned away. "I think you have things you must do. It's like a quest in the olden days."

With a sigh, she leaned back against the tree. He was right.

"You seem to be afraid you won't have enough time." Again, he was right.

"So what do we do next?" he asked.

Etta was pleased by his "we," but part of her wanted to forget all that and spend hours making love under the cottonwood trees.

"Alice," she said at last. "I know the man she's supposed to be with. I just have to find him."

"Tell me about him. What does he look like? Maybe I know him. If I do, I'll run to get him. My horse will have wings. After I find him, I'll return to rip that sheet off of you."

Etta's laugh sounded like she was giddy. "That's a deal! Phillip is a mechanic. He's good with machines. And he's a health nut. He lives on kale and protein powder. He hits the weights hard."

"I don't know what any of that means. Health nut? Is that walnuts? Hits the weights? With his fists? Is that a sport?"

She twisted around to face him. "Phillip has muscles. Biceps, pecs, glutes, quads. He looks like a bodybuilder."

Max still looked blank.

She held out her arm and flexed a biceps. "Like this. He trains my sister and me. Name a muscle and he knows how to make it stronger and bigger. His physicality works with Alicia's brains."

"And what about you? What works with you?"

Etta's eyes widened because Max was unbuttoning his shirt. "I thought I'd wash off," he said.

She didn't say anything as he slipped his shirt off. His upper body was bare. He was ripped! Cut. He didn't have the giant, gym-created muscles that Phillip did, but Max had had a life-time of heavy work. And there wasn't even one tattoo on him. Made for a nice change!

She leaned back against the tree and watched him as he doused his upper body in the cold water. His chest, his arms, his clearly defined abs were glorious.

When he finished, he sat down beside her, still wet, still half nude. "When your quest is done, we'll go on a honeymoon to anywhere you want. Paris maybe. I'm not a poor man."

Etta didn't say that there was a place in Kansas City that she'd like to see. She'd have to make sure that Cornelia and Bert put their house in the right place. If she could remember how to get there.

He saw her glazed look. "I want you when I'm sure that I have your full attention. I don't want to be one of many people. I want to be the only person you see."

"That's why you're willing to help me? To speed things up?" His smile was his answer and she laughed. "You have a deal."

Max got up first. He picked up his shirt and put it on, but

when he started to button it, she pushed his hands away. She did the buttons. Slowly.

When she finished, she looked into his eyes. "Sure you want to leave?" She was saying that she was willing to stay there. They'd make love beside the river.

His eyes were blazing but he said, "There are things that need to be done. My sister isn't speaking to me. Her unhappiness would distract me." He didn't wait for Etta's reply, but gave a glance at her sheet-clad body. "I'll wait for you." He nodded toward the house in the hillside, then walked away.

Etta dressed with lightning speed, pulling the corset strings tight. If her waist wasn't the size of an ant's, she wouldn't be able to buckle the belt. And besides, an hourglass figure made her feel very attractive.

Max returned when she was dressed, and he lifted her so she could get onto Tulip's saddle. "I hear you're an expert horsewoman. Would you like to gallop?"

"Very funny. I'd like a seat belt and an automatic transmission."

Laughing, he easily mounted his big horse, who touched noses with hers. "Tulip is his mother."

She grimaced. "That makes us two old women together."

Max gave her a look of such heat that her hair stood on end. "Not old and far from plain. Follow me."

"Anywhere," she said. "To the ends of the earth, I will follow you and—" She cut off because sweet Tulip started running after her son. Etta held on.

Etta was sitting beside Max in a buggy, and the town of Garrett was in front of them. She could smell it. "My nose could find this place."

He smiled at that, glad she liked his home better than town. "Where do we look?"

"I have no idea. Phillip works on airplanes. There's no airport here."

He gave her a look of confusion.

"I guess we just walk around. Maybe we should buy a gift for Alice. Something expensive. Maybe diamonds."

"I agree, but I still don't think they'd make her forgive us."

She put her arm through his. "When a girl wants a man, she wants a man. Not even diamonds will compensate."

He chuckled. "If we have to turn this place upside down, we'll find him. Soon."

She smiled warmly at him. Once the man was found for Alice, they could turn their attention to each other.

Max drove through the town slowly, and Etta looked hard at every saloon, stable, and store, but she didn't see anyone who looked like her brother-in-law. She tried to concentrate on the faces in case Old West Phillip had a different body than the one she was used to.

She saw no man who was even close to him.

Max stopped the buggy near the train station. Etta hadn't seen it, but she'd supposedly arrived there. At least her body did. *Whose mind and body did I overtake?* she wondered.

To her, the hastily built station was sad. She knew the connection would be moved, and the entire town of Garrett would disappear.

There was a sort-of restaurant nearby. It wasn't clean, and it was too small for so many people.

"We can get something to eat," Max said.

"Salmonella in the making," Etta said under her breath.

As they were about to enter the food hall, she saw someone who looked familiar. It took her a moment to realize that she'd seen his photo and knew who he was. She slipped through the people to stand beside the man and spoke loudly. "Wouldn't it be great if someone opened a real restaurant at each of these train stations? They'd be clean and serve good food. The waitresses could be girls from the east. I bet they'd marry local men and set up schools and churches. They'd stop the violence in the Wild West. Whoever did that would make an absolute fortune."

The man was looking at Etta in surprise. Why was she saying all this to a stranger?

She smiled at him. "Think about it, Mr. Harvey. Harvey Girls could change the whole country." With that, she slipped back into the crowd.

Max was waiting for her. "Another part of your quest?"

"Maybe. I need to go to the, you know."

He nodded toward a door in the back.

As a child, Etta had seen two-hole outhouses when her parents took her to historical sites, but she'd never really thought about them. By comparison, Alice's private toilet was a palace. This one had four holes. Two were being used, and the smell of the place made her gag. She wanted to leave, but she needed to go. She soon found out the advantage of skirts. They lifted and kept you covered. Etta's gaucho pants had to be slipped down and exposed a person. "Sorry," she muttered when she was frowned at. She'd broken outhouse etiquette.

She reassembled her clothes, again thinking about the joys of elastic, and left the hideous place.

Just a few feet away, rapidly crossing the street, was an older version of her niece, Nola. Her hair was in braids, and she was wearing a dress of blue-and-white stripes. Like always, she was bent on going somewhere and letting no one stop her.

Etta glanced at the door into the train building. She should go tell Max what she'd seen. But if she did, she'd lose Nola. She ran after her niece, but she seemed to have disappeared. Feeling frantic, Etta looked around for her, then saw the skirt disappear through a door. The sign said Garrett Emporium.

Etta hurried after her. Inside, the store was long and narrow. Nola was in the far back where there were bolts of fabric. Etta didn't know how to approach her. "Hi, my name is Etta. Where is your father?" That wouldn't go over in any era. It hit her that in this life, Phillip could be married. *Please no*, she thought.

The storekeeper, in a white apron, was handing canned goods to a boy on a ladder. Fully packed shelves went from floor to ceiling.

She leaned over the counter and said quietly, "Do you know who that girl is?"

The man looked at Etta, didn't recognize her, and turned away. "Don't know."

"I'm trying to find her father."

The man shrugged. "Lots of other men in this town."

Obviously, he wasn't going to give her any information. So did she stalk the girl? Maybe she could lie to Nola, say she was a teacher and gain her confidence. *Or I could use Max*, she thought. "I'm Max Lawton's wife," she said loudly.

Immediately, the shopkeeper set the cans down and went to her. "What can I help you with, Mrs. Lawton?"

"I need a dozen cans of peaches. I assume my husband has an account here."

"Yes, ma'am, he does."

"I'll send someone to pick them up along with other necessities."

He smiled at her.

Pointedly, she looked at Nola, then back at him.

The shopkeeper leaned toward her. "She's the new blacksmith's daughter. Been here only a few months."

A blacksmith made sense. "Wife?"

"He's a widower. There are a dozen women trying for him. Mr. Lawton need some work done?"

"What kind of work does he do besides horseshoes?"

The man went around the counter to the opposite side of the store and picked up a bar of twisted iron. "He makes barley twists."

"Just what I need," Etta said. "Where is he?"

"Down Back Alley Lane beside the Cantrell Stable."

Etta figured Max could find the place. She was about to turn away when she saw a wooden box on the top shelf. "What is that?"

"A paint box. I ordered it for a painter that comes through here, but he never picked it up."

"I'd like to see it," Etta said. Nola had always loved to draw and paint.

The shopkeeper nodded to the boy who hurried up the ladder, got the box down, and wiped the dust off. WINSOR & NEWTON it said. Inside were squares of watercolors, brushes, a ceramic palette, and a tablet in the back.

"I'll take it."

"Certainly," the man said. "I'll wrap it for you."

The girl was leaving the store, and Etta wanted to follow her. "No, thank you. I'll take it with me. Charge it."

With the box tucked under her arm, she followed Nola down the main street. Twice she barely missed piles of fresh horse manure. Her only thought was that they smelled better than the outhouse.

Nola went between buildings, then came out into the sunlight near a big stable.

When Etta heard the unmistakable sound of iron banging against iron, she followed it. To one side was a blacksmith's shop. There was a big brick fireplace with a fire blazing, a foot-powered bellows beside it. In front a man with a hammer was hitting a red-hot piece of metal.

He was Phillip. Same face; same body.

Etta let out a sigh of relief so deep the man heard her over his hammering.

For a moment he seemed to recognize her, but then decided he didn't. "Need some help?"

It was Phillip's voice. Etta smiled broadly. "I need some sesame sticks. Could you come to my house today and start making them?"

He looked totally blank.

"Those twisty things I saw at the emporium. It's for my husband, Max Lawton. We need—"

He untied his leather apron. "Yes, ma'am. I'm ready. Whatever Mr. Lawton wants."

Wow, Etta thought. *This is what it's like to be married to the second biggest landowner in the area. Wonder what they do when John Kecklin shows up? Lay down for him to walk on them?*

"I just need to bank the fire."

"Take your time," Etta said. She saw Nola in the back. "Is this your daughter?"

"Yes. Nellie, come out here and say hello to Mrs. Lawton."

"She can come too," Etta said. "My sister-in-law would like to meet her." That seemed to surprise them both, and they stared at her in silence.

"I have to go," Etta said. "My husband is waiting for me. We'll be back to pick you up." She hurried away, her smile so big her face was cracking.

Now she just had to tell Max about delivering Phillip to his sister. After this was done, maybe they could spend the afternoon at the river. She smiled at the thought.

10

"A what?" Max practically yelled. "My sweet, innocent sister with a brute like that? I've seen him! He's a monster." They were standing by the buggy. Etta had put the paint box in the back and told him they were to pick up the blacksmith and his daughter. And oh yeah, Alice was going to marry the man.

"Phillip is a very nice person. He can fix anything. People like him."

Max was glaring at her. "So what are you going to do? Invite him to dinner? He'll eat with a wrought-iron fork. Or his hands." His lips tightened. "You are *not* going to marry my sister off to a blacksmith."

"You're a snob. An arrogant, judgmental snob. Just because you own a few acres, you have no right to think you're better than he is. Phillip is a good man."

"He's not right for my sister."

"He is exactly right for her. Phillip is a sociable person. He has a zillion friends. Alice needs someone like that."

"No." Max seemed to think that ended the matter. He turned away from her.

But Etta put herself in front of him. "You just don't want a virile hunk like him touching your little sister. You want her with a quiet, brainy guy like Bert, don't you?" She suddenly realized what the real problem was. She took a step back. "If Alice marries an actual man, she'll move out and you don't want that, do you? That's utterly selfish!"

He cocked his head at her. "And I'm different from you? Your sister and her husband and their kid and your father lived in a house that *you* ruled. And now that your family is broken up, you dream up ways to put them back together. Why don't you live your own life and not other people's?"

Etta was too angry to reply to that. She walked away from him. This whole thing was a dream.

Her dream so she didn't have to put up with someone yelling at her.

"Wake up, wake up," she said. "Go back to Henry and *stay* there." Or maybe Henry was a dream too. Maybe she'd wake up and be at home with her whole family. She'd be cooking for all of them, getting Nola ready for school, and reminding everyone of their appointments and schedules.

Suddenly, she stopped walking. She was standing near one of Garrett's saloons, and she could hear laughter from inside. "I *am* an old maid," she said. "I *am* living other people's lives." *Even in her dreams, she took over other people's lives.*

When she turned and looked back, Max was standing exactly where she'd left him, waiting for her to decide what she was going to do.

She suddenly realized that she didn't care if this was a dream or reality. It was here and now and she was going to take it for as long as it lasted. She ran to him and he opened his arms to her.

He pulled her to him, then moved them both to privacy in the shadows of a building.

"I'm sorry," she said. Her arms were so tight around him she could almost hear his ribs crack. "Forget the blacksmith. It doesn't matter."

"It does matter." His face was buried in her clean hair. "You're trying to help. And you're right. Alice and I have always been together. She is all the family I have left."

"And you were right about me." Etta started talking fast. "When my sister got married, I was a mess. It's because of me that they moved into our big house. It was wonderful, but then she got a job in California and Dad and I were alone. I was going to see them this summer to try to get them to move back. But my flight was canceled and..." She was crying.

Max stroked her hair and held her. "You and I will have to make our own family. We'll have a dozen children. If you still can, that is."

Instantly, her tears stopped and she pulled back to look at him. "Are you asking if I'm too old to have children?" Anger was rising in her. "In my world, I'm the perfect age. I can—" She saw the laughter in his eyes. He was teasing her. "With all the horse riding you do, I'm not sure you're capable of stud service."

He looked shocked, offended. "I'll have you know that—" He stopped, then laughed. "Now that's my Etta." He gave her a quick kiss on the lips, then pulled away. She was leaning toward him. "I suggest we turn everything over to a higher power." He released her and started walking.

Etta was close behind him. "You mean...?"

"Yes. Alice. My little sister who loves to look at men in wet shirts."

"Wait till you see Phillip in a wet shirt. He is a sight to behold. He—" Max stopped and looked at her without a hint of humor.

"Sorry," Etta said, but when he turned away, she grinned. She'd never had a boyfriend who was jealous. Modern men were into "freedom," which seemed to mean that they were free to do whatever they wanted. With whomever.

Max lifted her into the buggy seat.

"Someday I'll have to figure out how to get into this by my-self."

"Before or after you learn how to sit in a saddle?" He got in beside her.

"I think I did very well today."

"Sore?" He raised his eyebrows.

"More like excruciating pain."

Smiling, he flipped the reins and the horse pulled the buggy forward.

"You know where his shop is?" she asked.

"With the size of him, I can see him through the buildings. What am I supposed to give him to do?"

"Twisty sticks. How about a staircase with those things hold-ing up the banister?"

"He'll have to come back here to work on them," Max said.

"That's not enough time for them to be together. You'll have to build a forge at your home so he can spend days there."

"*Our* home," he said, and they smiled at each other.

Etta was glad the buggy wasn't a little two seater like Cor-nelia's hot rod, but had a long back seat so they could take the blacksmith and his daughter with them.

In spite of Max's agreement, when they got to the forge, he wasn't welcoming. He gave Etta a look of annoyance that the man had his daughter with him. Max stayed in the driver's seat, leaving it up to them to get in by themselves.

Etta had other plans. She slid down to the ground, then mo-tioned for the blacksmith to get into the front next to Max.

"I'll sit in the back," he said.

It was so good to hear Phillip's voice! Etta told him she wanted to sit by Nellie so she'd take the back. Neither man looked pleased at that, but in the next second, he lifted her off the ground and set her into the buggy. When Max glowered, Etta smiled at him.

The ride back to the house wasn't long, but the silence of everyone made it uncomfortable. Etta stared at the back of the two men. Max was taller, but the blacksmith was wider. They barely spoke.

She tried to make conversation. She learned that the blacksmith's name was Patrick "Pat" Adams and his wife died in childbirth. Nellie had never had a mother. *That's because she's hiding in a glass room*, Etta thought.

When the house came into view, Etta breathed a sigh of relief. She hoped that adding Alice to the group would lighten the mood.

But suddenly, Max snapped the reins and made the horse race. Pat extended a big arm toward his daughter. "Hold on. Something's wrong."

Instinctively, Etta put her arms around Nellie. After all, she'd been taking care of the child since the day she was born.

The buggy hit rocks and potholes and one time nearly turned over, but Max didn't slow down.

Etta tried to see what was going on, but she was bent over Nellie in protection.

Max drove past the house and jumped out before the vehicle stopped. Pat grabbed the reins, got the excited horse to stop, then jumped down. Etta knew him well so she yelled, "Pat!" then fell forward. He caught her easily, set her on the ground, then caught his daughter in the same way.

"Go into the house," Etta said to Nellie in the tone she used when her niece's safety was in jeopardy. The child obeyed.

At the entrance to the stables, a half dozen cowboys were gathered, all of them looking down at something. She could see Max's head in the middle.

Etta pushed her way through them to stand by her husband.

Rufus was on the ground. His left pant leg was ripped and soaked in blood. There was a deep cut in his thigh, and someone had tied a tourniquet above it. He was pale from loss of blood. The expressions all the men wore were horrible to see. It was as though Rufus was a dead man.

When one of the men drove up in the buckboard, Etta said, "You're taking him to a doctor?"

Max put his arm around her shoulders and led her out of the crowd. "Rufus is going to lose his leg. If he lives at all." He said it as a fact, not a possibility.

"But—"

"The only doctor around here is an old army surgeon. Cut your finger and he'll saw off your arm. There's no other choice."

"Take him to Martha," Etta said.

"Martha Garrett?"

"Yes!" She put her hands on his arm. "Please trust me. She'll know what to do. Does she live far away?"

"She's closer than town."

Behind them, the crowd parted and Pat came out, carrying Rufus like he was a child. He gently laid him in the back of the buckboard, then Hank jumped in beside him. Another man took over the reins.

Max climbed onto the seat beside the driver. "We're taking him to Martha Garrett."

"But the doc's in town," the driver said. At Max's look, he nodded, then drove away at breakneck speed.

Etta stood there for a moment, thinking of the dangers of nineteenth century life. No emergency services, no quick communication, a doctor who sawed off limbs no matter what the injury.

The men were looking miserable and she understood. Rufus was liked by everyone. His long-winded stories entertained them. None of them seemed to have any hope that they'd ever again see him alive.

Etta didn't know where Pat was, but Nellie was in the house. She went through three rooms before she found her. Nellie and Tobias were sitting together on a hard horsehair-covered sofa. She was eating one of the biscuits Etta had made, and Tobias was telling her about the accounts he was doing.

"This is the number of calves that were produced last year, and this is how much it cost to feed them. This number is the important one. It's the profits. Not bad, is it? Maxwell is a good manager."

As Etta leaned against the door frame, she blinked back tears. She was seeing her father with his beloved granddaughter. He'd never believed in reading fairy tales to children. "Useless things," he said. "The price of the glass slipper was more important than whose foot it fit."

Whatever his reasoning, Nola was exceptional at mathematics.

Tobias looked up and saw Etta. Startled, he stood up. "I was just..." He didn't seem to know how to explain what he was doing.

Etta stepped forward. "Thank you. There was an accident and it was upsetting." She held out her hand to Nellie, who took it, and they left the room.

"You enjoyed that?"

"Yes. He's a nice man, but the town doesn't like him."

"Right," Etta said. "Preaching. I think he likes numbers better than sermons. What do you think?"

"I think he likes anything better than sermons."

Etta laughed. "I have a gift for you and something for us to do." They were walking through the kitchen on the way to the back door. She'd left the paint set in the buggy, but Etta was glad to see that someone had put it on the kitchen table. *Good*, she thought. She didn't want to expose Nellie to the gloom of the men or see it herself.

She handed the pretty box to Nellie and she opened it.

"What is it?"

"Watercolors. Come with me." In the main parlor there were three framed landscapes and Etta had an idea that Alice had done them. "Like them?"

Nellie nodded.

"I thought you might try your hand at doing something like them. Would you like some lessons?"

Nellie's eyes widened and she nodded again.

"Then come on, I want to introduce you to someone."

Etta led the way back to Alice's private glass room. The door was shut. *Bolted?* she wondered. Tentatively, she knocked. There was no answer. "Alice?" she said. "I have someone here who wants to meet you."

There still was no answer.

"She's an orphan," Etta said with more force. She knew that her sister could never resist anyone who needed help. "Nellie's father is here to work and she has no one. Her mother died when she was born so Nellie is all alone. She—"

Alice opened the door. Her eyes were cold as she glanced at Etta. But when she looked at Nellie, she blinked rapidly.

As for Nellie, she looked at Alice as though she knew her.

Thank you, Etta thought. *By all that's holy, thank you.*

Alice put her hand out to Nellie to lead her inside the room.

But Etta stepped between them. She wasn't going to allow the two of them to isolate themselves in Alice's hideaway. "We're going to the homestead. Nellie's father has some work to do there." *Great whopping lie.* She smiled at Alice, silently conveying the message that if she wanted this child, she had to come out of hiding.

Alice frowned, debating what to do.

"Max stored food in the old sod house. I thought I'd cook while you show Nellie how to paint. Her father is a hero. He just saved Rufus's life. We all owe him a great deal." *Are lies told for a good cause acceptable?* she wondered.

"I can stay here," Nellie said. "My dad won't mind."

"You don't want a picnic by the river?" Etta asked innocently. "It would be so much better than that stinky old town you live in. And I'm sure your father would appreciate some time away. But if my sister-in-law doesn't want you to enjoy—"

Alice gave her a look to stop. "I'll go," she said to Nellie, doing her best to ignore Etta's existence on earth.

Alice took Nellie's hand and they walked out, leaving Etta behind.

Smiling, Etta watched them go. She'd completed two parts of her task. No, her quest, as Max called it. Now all she needed was to add Pat and see if he and Alice were a good match the way Phillip and Alicia were.

With fingers crossed, she followed them out.

Etta was in the sod house and using water she'd taken from the river to clean up. She was thinking of all the health codes she was breaking, but this was 150 years earlier. The water was clean. Well, maybe cows were using it, not to mention all the other critters. And who knew what the early settlers had done to it?

She stepped outside to wring out her rag. There was no sink with a handy drain. Sitting on the riverbank, under the cottonwoods, Alice and Pat were talking and laughing. To say they'd hit it off was an understatement. It had been an instant attraction.

Pat had driven them all to the homestead. On the way there, Nellie and Etta had sat in the back, their eyes in fierce concentration as they watched the couple in front. It wasn't difficult to see that Nellie wanted them together as much as Etta did.

When Pat said something to Alice in a low voice and she giggled like an adolescent, Etta and Nellie smiled at each other. Etta taught her how to do a high five. Triumph!

Now it was hours later, and Etta was glad to see that their fascination with each other appeared to be alive and well. Alice and Pat were so hidden under the trees she could hardly see them.

As for Nellie, she was farther down in the shade, bent over her watercolor set, and absorbed by it.

It was close to sunset, and Etta knew they would need to leave soon. She went back into the house and straightened things that were fine as they were. She wanted to give all of them privacy.

When she heard a horse—a sound that was becoming familiar to her—she looked up. Max was standing in the doorway. The setting sun was shining behind him, and he was a glorious sight.

Reading her lustful thoughts, he stepped inside and twirled her in his arms. "Miss me?" He was nuzzling her neck.

"More than I can say. Every minute of every hour."

He moved as though he meant to kiss her but then pulled away and set her down. "Time for that later. Is there any food?"

She laughed. "A true man. As it happens, I did save you a bit." There was a plate heaped full, a cloth over it, and she handed it to him.

"Trout?"

"Pat likes to fish," she said, then quickly asked, "How is Rufus?"

"He's doing well." Max was eating fast, obviously ravenous. "He's already had visitors." He looked at her. "He wants to see you to thank you. And by the way, my men may light candles at your feet. Between cooking and saving Rufus, they think you're from heaven."

"Yeah? I like that. Tell me what happened."

"Martha was great. It took me a while to get past her complaining, but I told her to stop it and fix Rufus."

"And she knew what to do?"

"She did." He was scraping his plate. "You were right about her. She was a nurse in the war."

"But she was probably really a doctor. She just wasn't given credit for all that she did."

He shook his head. "Always my Etta. I'm sure that's true. I saw nurses do incredible things. Anyway, she sewed him up."

"That's it? She just grabbed a needle and thread and went at it?"

"She doused his leg in whiskey and bawled us out for being so dirty. She told us we were useless and worth nothing." He shrugged. "It was Martha being Martha."

"But she did save him. And his leg."

"She did. She wouldn't let us move him out of her bed. I stayed there until he woke up. He looks good." He handed her his empty plate.

"Why are your hands bleeding?" she asked.

"You think Martha was going to let us men sit there and do nothing? She put two of us to work on fences. She made Hank clean the stalls." Max smiled at that. "Come here." He held out his arms to her.

Without hesitation, she went to him and slid her arms around his neck. But before their lips touched, the sound of Alice's laughter reached them.

Max moved his head away. "My sister is here?"

"Let's shut the door and lock it."

Max gave her a look that showed he knew she was hiding something. He went to the doorway and looked out. Alice and Pat had moved from under the trees and were by the water's edge. "I'm going to kill him."

She knew what he meant. Alice was barefoot and Pat was shirtless. His giant muscles shimmered in the fading light. Etta did a leap a gymnast would envy and put herself in front of Max, her hands on his chest. "You will not! Don't freak out about this! He had her take off her shoe so he could see her foot. He's going to make a brace for her leg. It won't fix it, but she'll walk more easily."

Max narrowed his eyes at her. "He did it shirtless?"

"His shirt was bloody, remember? He carried Rufus out. Alice told him to take it off so she could wash it."

Max looked at her in disbelief. "My sister never washed anything in her life." He stepped around Etta, his head down like a bulldog, and started toward the river.

Etta spoke loudly. "I'm sure Alice will be happy about this. She will have lost two men in two days. One of them was given to *your* former girlfriend and now this one is being tossed out because *you* don't like what he does for a living. Alice will surely understand and thank you."

Max had his back to her, but she didn't need to see his face to know his expression. He was *not* happy.

"Are you going to send Dad and me away?" came a small voice.

Etta turned and saw Nellie standing there, her new watercolor set in her hands. Her chin was trembling.

Max had stopped walking but he hadn't turned around.

"I don't know," Etta said. "It's up to my husband, the master of us all. The man who makes all the rules and pity on anyone who disagrees with him. He—"

Turning, Max glared at her.

"This is Nellie," Etta said. "Remember her? Pat's daughter? She and Alice like each other a lot."

Max was still glaring at Etta. He seemed to be trying to figure out what to do.

"How's your painting coming?" Etta asked the child.

"It's not easy." She held out the tablet to show her. It was a simple landscape of the river and trees.

Max, still frowning, took the pad from her. "You need some variety." Nellie was holding the wooden box open. There was a little cup full of water. He picked up the smallest brush and whirled it around on the damp square of green paint. With a dozen little flicks, he inserted dark green marks on the trees, taking them from a monocolor to looking like they had actual leaves. He went over the brown square to add lines to the bark.

Etta and Nellie were watching him in awe. Seeming to be unaware of them, Max rinsed his brush and in a few strokes, he put two people in the picture. One was a slim woman while the man…well, he looked like a hairless ape leaning over her in a predatory way.

Through this, Max never lost his frown. It was as though he had no idea what he was doing. He thrust the pad back to Etta. It was only then that he saw the way they were looking at him. "What is it?" he snapped.

Etta held the pad up in front of her face. "Where did you learn how to do this?"

He came out of his trance and looked at the painting. "I never did." He seemed to be as astonished as they were.

"Will you teach me how to do that?" Nellie asked. "Please?"

For a moment Max looked back and forth from Etta to the couple under the trees.

"It's late," Etta said. "I think we should all go home. Go tell your dad." Nellie ran off. Etta looked at Max. "I'm sorry. I've never meant to disrupt anything. I just want people to be happy."

Max didn't say anything, just went to his horse, got on it, and looked around. "What did you call this place? My man cave? Might as well be Kansas City now." He reined his horse away and left.

What was that saying about winning the battle but losing the war? Etta thought.

When they got home, Max wasn't there. Etta felt some happiness that Alice, Pat, and Nellie seemed to have bonded, but she thought, *What about me?* Even if all this was a dream, she still wanted…

I want what? she wondered. That home and family that Henry had asked her about? For years, that's what she'd had. She'd been happy with all of it: her job, her home, the people she lived with.

She'd felt needed and wanted.

But then Alicia and Phillip left, taking Nola with them, and her father had buried himself in his books and studies.

Was I lonely and didn't know it? she wondered.

That time, and whatever her life was then, seemed less real with every passing moment. Right now she wanted something for herself.

Max, she thought. That's what she wanted. She really, really liked him. Liked his home, his family, even his workmen.

"Please don't let him send me back to wherever I came from in this life," she whispered.

She went upstairs, hoping Max was there. He wasn't in his bedroom or the storage room. She took a breath before opening the door to his mother's bedroom. It was empty and clean. The cobwebs and dust were gone; the sheets were fresh.

On the dresser was a note. "Thank you" it said, and appeared to have been laboriously written. She knew the men had done it. *At least someone appreciates me*, she thought.

As she looked in the mirror, she thought she'd do her best to make it up to Max. But how?

Besides what she'd done to Alice, Etta had taken away his man cave. Invaded his private space. Unforgivable sins!

She stripped down to her underwear, unlaced the hated corset, and took some deep breaths. She'd love to take a hot shower and wash her hair, but she couldn't. The best she could do was try to clean up and put on a pretty dress.

She smiled. Maybe she'd coax Max into having that wedding night. "If I'm not too old and plain," she said with a grimace.

She opened the wardrobe door. What could she wear to entice him?

As she began to look, she felt that dizzy sensation. "No, no, no!" she said. "I can't leave now. It's my turn now. For *me!*"

But she couldn't escape the overpowering feeling. She fell crosswise on the bed and went to sleep.

11

When Etta woke, tears filled her eyes before she even opened them. She squeezed them tight. "Please don't let me be at Henry's house," she whispered.

She wiped away the tears then slowly opened her eyes. The first thing she saw was Max's mother's wardrobe.

A surge of energy and pure happiness exploded through her. "I'm still here!" she said, then leaped out of bed. Yet again, she had on a big cotton nightgown. "I've *got* to find out who keeps undressing and dressing me!"

Over the chair was a pretty cotton dress. It wasn't something made for cooking and riding horses. Beside it was a note written in an elegant hand. "Pat is taking us to church this morning." Written by Alice.

Etta clutched the note to her chest. She was so glad to still be there that she didn't mind that she'd spent yet another night away from her husband. Was Max still angry with her? Would he be joining them for church?

She dressed quickly. "I'm getting good at this." She ran down the stairs to make the necessary trip outside. When she got back, she heard voices.

Pat and Alice were sitting side by side in the big parlor. They moved apart when they saw Etta. She sat down, smiling warmly at them. She'd *done* it!

"There is no church today," Alice said. "The pastor is indisposed."

Etta fell back against the chair. Her father, who loved numbers and hated sermons. She remembered what Max had told her about him. "Drunk?"

Pat nodded.

"Nellie wants to stay here with her paints," Alice said.

Etta's eyes widened. "I have an idea of what we can do. It's something rather, well, unconventional. Is everything ready so we can leave?" It wasn't like they could just get in the car and go. Hitching horses took time.

Alice and Pat looked at her for a moment, then he stood up. "Mrs. Lawton, I will say that I love your ideas. Whatever you want, I will do it." He held out his hand to Alice, and she stood up beside him.

"I agree with him." Her eyes were telling Etta that she was no longer angry about the lawyer.

"Then let's go. We need to stop at the Red Dog."

Pat's eyes widened for a moment but then he nodded. "To the gates of hell if that's what you want. Alice, you should stay here and—"

The expressions of the two women said they would refuse to remain behind.

"My apologies," he said. "We'll all go."

Etta got in the back of the two seater and held on as Pat drove rapidly. It was like the ride after her wedding, but this time she wasn't about to fall out. *What a marshmallow I was*, she thought.

Pat stopped in front of the saloon but made no offer to help either woman get down. He had limits.

"Get Sally," Etta said. "Tell her to put on her prettiest dress and come with us."

Pat didn't question her but went into the saloon.

Alice turned to her sister-in-law. "You're going to have her sing, aren't you?"

"Oh yes."

"Her singing is better than the pastor's sermons. Not that I've heard them."

Alice's words reminded Etta of how she'd first seen her. Alice didn't even leave her glass prison to go to church. But now here she was, waiting for a man who had a daughter. A ready-made family.

Minutes later, Sally came out ahead of Pat and climbed in beside Etta. He drove them to the church.

Etta remembered Henry talking about Sophie's stage fright, but she also remembered that he said she sang in church. "Make us proud," Etta said when they were at the door. "Start off with 'Just a Closer Walk with Thee.'"

"How do you know that one?" Sally asked. "It's from my people."

"Trust me on this, that song will last through the centuries."

Pat and Alice went into the church to sit down, but Etta stayed outside. When Sally's beautiful voice began, people on the street stopped and listened.

Etta thought about a world where music was a rarity. She waved her arms for them to come inside and listen, and they did. Within twenty minutes, there was only standing room.

Bert the lawyer came up the steps and stopped by her. "Cornelia and I... I think we're a match. I—" He waved his hand. He couldn't explain. "Thank you."

"I've been hearing that a lot."

"You should. The gossip is rampant. Matchmaking, saving legs, cooking sublimely. People are beginning to say you're an angel."

"If only my husband thought that," Etta muttered.

"Max? But he can't take his eyes off you."

"Maybe that means something different in 1870, but in my day—" She cut off. She'd said too much.

"You met him last year?"

"No. This is—" She looked at him. "What is today's date?"

"The thirtieth of April 1871."

"Seventy-*one*?" she said. "Oh no. It can't be. That's… I have to go." She hurried down the steps. Her father had told her that the third of May 1871 was when Wyatt Earp escaped jail.

Wyatt Earp. The man no one except her remembered. Was *this* why she was having this very long dream? Was this thing real enough that she was to change something in the past? Not love matches or even saving a cowboy's life, but to put Wyatt Earp back into the twenty-first century's log of stories and movies? Was the man that important?

She stopped walking, the mud and manure of the street sucking at her shoes.

How do I do this? she thought. Through Max, of course. But he was angry at her for interfering in the lives of people. She'd done it again this morning. Maybe Sally wasn't supposed to sing in a church.

Etta stepped back when a man on a horse nearly ran over her. No doubt Max had had enough of her manipulations. She'd have to do this on her own.

Thanks to her father's obsession with the marshal, she did know details of the escape. It didn't happen in Garrett. It wasn't even in Kansas.

The question was: How would she get to him? By train, of course. Visions of trains in Old West movies came to her: cows on the tracks, derailings, attacks by men with guns. In movies, there were endless ways for delay. However, she did get to Garrett by herself. She came from... She didn't know where she was supposed to have come from. That she didn't remember didn't matter. The point was that she could do it! She just wished she could remember *how* she did it.

Did they have sleeping cars? What about food? Where did she get cash? She'd have to get someone to tell her what to do. But who? Alice? She barely ever left her house. Sally? Freddy? One of the cowboys? If only Henry would appear in her dream. He'd know how to do everything.

Etta was thinking so hard that when Max grabbed her about the waist and pulled her out the way of a heavily loaded buckboard, she wasn't concerned. Maybe getting run over would solve her problem. She was failing at her quest. Max was so close she could smell his breath.

"You've been drinking beer." She narrowed her eyes at him. "Were you at the local, uh... Where Freddy works?"

"Yes."

"Without me?"

"I didn't spend the night, if that's what you mean." It was, but she wasn't going to say that.

"Why are you standing in the street?"

She needed courage to tell him what she had to do next. "I could use a beer. Or a few shots of tequila."

"You can't go to the Red Dog. It's not for— Oh hell. Come on, I'll take you."

It took them several minutes to slog their way to the saloon. For all that he was speaking to her, she could tell that things weren't good between them. After all, she'd told him that she'd done all she needed to do. That she'd forgotten the biggest task, probably the most important, certainly the most difficult one, wasn't going to be easy to explain.

He had every right to refuse to participate.

The inside of the saloon didn't look like a place of sin. It looked tired and empty. It didn't take much to realize that it wasn't open to the public on Sunday morning, but for Max Lawton, it was.

He went behind the empty bar, got a couple of beers, and took them to a table.

It was silly of her and she had no right, but it annoyed her that he was so familiar with the place that he served himself.

She sat down at a table and took a drink. Warm beer. Yuck. *So how to begin to tell him something he was going to hate hearing?* she wondered. *Lead into it slowly.* "Everyone is enjoying Sally's singing. I think she was part of my quest. By the way, that was smart of you to call it that. Very imaginative."

"Why are you pouring sugar on me?" He gave her a hard look. "You have something else to do, don't you?"

"Just one more thing, and it may be the true reason why I'm here."

"What does that mean?"

How to lie without lying? "It's what I need to do. What I must do. I have to rescue a man who is in deep trouble."

"From what?" His eyes widened. "Please tell me it's not from hanging."

"Certainly not! I need to save him from what would probably be five years hard labor for horse thievery."

"No," Max said. "Absolutely not. I might help you save a murderer, yes. There're always two sides to that, but not a horse thief."

She didn't know if he was serious or not, or how to proceed with her plea.

"Where is he?" Max asked.

"Van Buren, Arkansas. I have to get there during daylight on the third of May." His silence made Etta know he'd reached his limit. "I guess I can take the train."

"What happens when you get there?" he asked.

"I have to get him out through a hole in the roof of the jail."

"A hole in the roof? A hole that no one has noticed? Even in the rain? Then you throw down a rope and pull him up? Little man, is he?"

"Not as big as you but close."

Max looked at his beer and said nothing.

Etta stood up. "I guess I'll go get a train ticket. I've discovered that if I say your name, I don't have to produce any money." She waited for him to reply but he didn't. "I guess I'll see you when I get back." *If I do return*, she thought. She turned away.

"There is no train."

She turned back. "What?"

"Van Buren is directly south of here. The train goes west, then south. You can't get there in less than a week."

"Maybe that's all right. It probably won't matter if he escapes on a different date."

"I heard that the Van Buren court is being moved to Fort Smith. A week from now your friend will probably be moved there."

Etta sat back down. "*Fort* Smith? You mean a place with soldiers? With rifles?"

He nodded.

"I don't know how to do that." She drained her glass of beer. "With no train and no car, how do I get there?"

"I guess you mean a carriage. You have to go by horseback. It's about two hundred miles, so it'll have to be fifty miles a day."

Etta's thighs and backside ached at the thought. Even if she could do that, there was the matter of direction. Did she use a compass? There'd be rivers to cross, and she'd meet men with guns. In the movies, when a woman alone encountered men, it never ended well. And there were snakes and creatures that bit. She looked at him. "Maybe I can hire a guide. Some bad-tempered old man who'll protect me. I hope I don't lose an arm." She mumbled the last as she remembered *True Grit*, one of her father's favorite movies.

Max was looking at his beer and saying nothing.

"I guess I'll ask Pat or Bert. Maybe they know someone who could be my guide."

"Who else?" he asked.

"Who else what?"

He looked at her. "What other lives are you going to take over? There's my sister and the blacksmith and his kid. Cornelia and her lawyer. Martha is now being called a healer. Freddy would rather dig in the dirt and Sally might become the first woman preacher in the world."

"I'm not a historian but I doubt that. Maybe Joan of Arc would qualify."

"So who else are you planning to change, manipulate, and generally rip apart?"

"Sorry," she mumbled. "I haven't meant anything bad. I just needed to…" She couldn't explain. "I think I better go try to find a guide. Sorry for making you pay for it, but I don't seem to have any money of my own."

"If I take you on a hell-bent trip to Van Buren, does that mean I get you to myself for four whole days?"

Her expression showed her surprise. "I guess so."

"You wouldn't suddenly tell me that I have to make a detour to, say, Wichita, because there's somebody there you need to save?"

A bit of hope came to her. "There's no one else. Even if I saw Henry, I'd just tell him to go to Martha. He can get there by himself."

"So you and I would have four days alone?"

She smiled. "Yes, we would."

"There might be a few hotels along the way, but they won't be nice places. People have to share beds."

"Really?"

"Or we'd have to sleep outside. Kansas wind is bad. Cold."

She tried to keep from grinning. "For warmth we should, uh, stay close together. That would fit in with my dream."

"Fifty miles a day to someone who hardly knows what a horse *is* might think it's a nightmare."

"I'll take my chances."

"You have to do the cooking. Ever skin a jackrabbit?"

"My boss, Lester, made me skin *cows*. He said I couldn't appreciate meat if I didn't know where it came from." She paused. "Can we leave now?"

"We need to get supplies. And I have to see to my sister."

"Leave her with Pat and Nellie."

He looked shocked.

"Oh right. Double standards are alive and thriving. You have to protect her."

"You don't need protection? Not even from the veterans roaming about? Some of them haven't recovered."

"PTSD," she said.

He didn't say any more, just looked at her.

"I would really, really like for you to take me to Van Buren. I would especially love spending time with you. Just you." She reached out to touch his hand, her fingertips against his. A touch of promises.

The look he gave her made her start to sweat. He stood up. "How soon can you get ready?"

She stood up. "Lightning is slower than me."

He gave a little smile then went to the door with such long, quick strides that Etta had trouble keeping up with him.

When they got outside, Max didn't bother with the buggy. Etta thought maybe it was the first time in his life that he didn't think of his little sister first. He didn't say so, but Etta knew he was leaving his sister to find her own way home. *Was he turning her over to Pat?*

Max got on his horse, then reached down to Etta and pulled her up behind him. He rode so fast that she would have fallen off if she hadn't held on to him tightly. *Very* tightly.

When they reached the house, he held her arm to let her down. "Wear the riding clothes and pack a clean set. I'll take care of the rest. Hurry. If we're to get there by Wednesday, we need to leave now." He raised an eyebrow. "This man is your...?"

She knew what he was asking. Former lover? "I've never met him."

Smiling, he reined his horse away and Etta ran up the stairs to his mother's bedroom. To her delight, spread on the bed, was the riding outfit. It had been washed and hung out to dry. It smelled of Kansas sunshine. Her fairy godmother who put her in and out of nightgowns seemed to have struck again.

She packed as fast as she cooked. She shoved a set of under-wear, which was the size of a modern ball grown, into a canvas bag she found in the back of the wardrobe, then added a clean blouse. There was only one set of gaucho skirt-pants.

"Oh for jeans and T-shirts," she muttered.

She ran down the stairs to the kitchen, planning what food to take.

Alice was there. "Esmeralda already put things together. She's happy that she can go home."

"Because you now have Pat and Nellie?"

Alice's pretty face blushed. "I guess."

"She was the one who put me in the nightgowns?"

"Yes."

Etta put her hands on Alice's shoulders and kissed her cheeks. "We'll be back as soon as possible. By train, I hope."

Alice just nodded, not asking where she was going or why.

I guess I'm too weird for them to understand, Etta thought. *And I agree!* She grabbed a couple of apples and two cans of peaches. Alice took them, and Etta ran out the back door then halted.

Max was there with two saddled horses that were loaded with bags of supplies. In front of him was a row of people, all of them waiting for Etta.

Cornelia stepped forward, holding out a beautiful leather jacket. "Kansas gets cold at night."

Etta took the jacket. "Thank you."

Cornelia stepped back and slipped her hand into Bert's.

Martha handed Etta a bag of food. "If you get hungry." She looked embarrassed.

Rufus, propped up on crutches, hobbled forward. He held out a knife in a sheath. "I hope you don't need it." There were tears in his eyes. "Thank you," he whispered.

Sally and Freddy gave her a blouse that had been embroidered with little blue birds. Their eyes told of their gratitude. Etta had changed their lives.

Preacher Tobias stepped forward. He was smiling broadly. "The town fired me. No more church. I'm doing accounts for the Red Dog as well as here." He pressed something into her hand. It was a symbol, probably Celtic, made of silver, and on a rawhide string. She put it around her neck. He whispered, "Thank you," then stepped back.

Nellie and Pat came forward. The child gave her a little bear made of iron. "My dad made it and it's for good luck," she said, then went back to him.

Esmeralda was the last one. Etta hadn't talked to her, hadn't done anything directly for her, but her life had been altered. She'd felt an obligation to Alice, who she'd helped raise, but now she was free to retire to her own family. She gave Etta a little bag of chili powder.

"Thank you for taking such good care of me," Etta said. Esmeralda nodded and stepped back.

All of them parted as Max came forward on his horse and leading another one. It wasn't sweet-tempered Tulip. He seemed to know what she was thinking. "This is her daughter, Daisy. Not old and not plain." His eyes were twinkling.

It was Cornelia who laughed, then the others joined in. It looked like they'd all heard the story of what she'd called Etta. Best was that their laughter said it wasn't true.

Pat gave Etta a boost into the saddle, and the mare followed Max as they rode out.

"Happy honeymoon," Cornelia called out, then threw a handful of rice at them.

Etta turned in the saddle and looked at the line of people. She'd come to love them all. She watched until they were out of sight, then she turned to Max. "I'm afraid I'm never going to see them again." There were tears in her eyes and her voice shook.

"If this trip is too much for you, let me know. I'll get you a rocking chair and you can sit on the porch."

"If you think that I—" At that moment Daisy decided to start prancing and Etta nearly fell off. "How do I stop this?"

"Pretend she's one of the humans you boss around. That should put her in line."

Etta would have made a retort but instead, she jerked the reins and said, "Stop it!" The mare obeyed.

"Just what I said." Max gave his horse a nudge and started moving quickly. Etta was right behind him.

12

About three hours into the journey, Etta was ready to stop. *No wonder we need to go to the gym in modern times,* she thought. *Everything in our lives is so easy.*

She had no idea how Max knew which way to go, but he seemed to be sure of it. A few times she saw in the distance towns about the size of Garrett, but Max avoided them. "There's no need to look for trouble," he said.

"What kind of trouble?" she asked.

His eyes twinkled. "I meant a delay."

"You mean the lure of saloons?" she retorted, and he laughed.

She followed him as closely as possible. A few times, he pointed to things. There was a flock of wild turkeys, grouse flew up, and she saw stands of wild plums. Lester had always loved dealing with game, and sometimes they had specials with them. Maybe on the return trip she could do some cooking.

They went at a steady pace, not a run but not a walk either. Her inner thighs gradually adjusted and fell into place in the big saddle. She hoped they'd stop for lunch. But no. Max pulled fried meat pies from the bag Martha had given them, handed her one, and they kept on going.

Etta thought, *Is Wyatt Earp worth all this? What exactly did he achieve?* But she knew it was her aching joints that were talking. She had a quest and she needed to complete it.

In the late afternoon, it started to rain. Etta began looking right and left for one of the little towns where they could stop. At the first sight of one, she yelled, "Max!"

He didn't turn, just put up his hand, then waved for her to keep going. They weren't stopping.

"Right," she muttered. "Fifty miles a day or bust."

One thing Etta knew about Kansas was why it produced so much fabulous food. Sunshine and rain. They were great when you could sit in a window seat and read Jane Austen for the thousandth time, but being outside, in the rain and sun, was not so pleasant.

Etta had on one of Max's mother's hats. It was really pretty: a fine quality Italian straw, wide brimmed, trimmed with a blue ribbon. It leaked. Rain drizzled down her face, onto her neck, and into her shirt. But that didn't matter since the sweet, fertile, life-giving Kansas rain was drenching every inch of her body.

She tried sending silent mind messages to Max. *Please stop. Please.*

He didn't hear her. Twice, he twisted to look back at her, seemed satisfied that she was still alive, then nudged his horse forward.

Between clouds full of the glory of Kansas liquid sunshine and the evening sky, Etta couldn't see anything. She put her head down and let her mare follow Max's horse.

When Max finally did stop, Etta was too wet and cold to appreciate it. He put his hand on her thigh and she opened her eyes. He held up his arms, she fell forward, and he caught her. Her legs gave way under her, and he pulled her up. He was laughing at her, but she didn't care.

He swung her up into his arms and carried her into what appeared to be a house. *Warmth*, she thought. *Dry!*

But no. It was a stone shell of a house with no roof. He set her down in a corner. At least the walls blocked a bit of the glorious Kansas wind.

She stood there, trying to stay upright as Max led the horses inside to the opposite end of the house, then removed the saddles. The animals shivered in relief and seemed to go to sleep instantly. She envied them.

He came to her, and for a moment he held her in his arms. She didn't know how it was possible, but his body was warm. She snuggled her cheek against his wet shirt and sighed in relief.

Too soon, he stepped away, went to the heap of saddles, and pulled out a blanket and a big black cloth. He spread the blanket on the stone floor close to a wall. "This is the driest place," he yelled over the rain that was impregnating the fertile Kansas soil. She thought corn might start growing in her hair.

When Max started unbuttoning his shirt, she understood his meaning. *Get out of the wet clothes.* Hallelujah! She felt no shyness, just a desire to rid herself of her wet garments.

Max also undressed.

Seeing him disrobe and seeing his strong, muscular and oh so masculine body made the rain seem less strong, less cold.

She beat him in getting undressed. *I've become a corset wizard,* she thought. Naked, she lay down on the blanket, then pulled the black cloth over her. By all the glories above, it was some kind of rain cloth. The pelting drops hit it but didn't penetrate it.

Max lifted one side and got in beside her.

Her cold, wet body found his warm one. He wrapped his arms around her and in seconds, he entered her. They'd had days of wanting each other, and they could not postpone any longer.

It lasted only minutes for both of them, but that was all right. The desire of fire filled them.

Afterward, she put her head on his chest and his arms went around her. He pulled the magic rain cloth over their heads. It was intimate under it: dark and warm, the rain hitting them but not touching them.

"You did well today," he said.

"I had a good guide." Smiling, she fell asleep in his arms. Her only thought was how perfectly their bodies fit together.

When she woke, she was aware of the aches in her body. She was on a blanket on a stone floor. The rain had stopped, and there was a bit of moonlight. In the silvery darkness, she could see Max with the horses. He hadn't a stitch of clothing on, and he looked like a Greek god of old. No fat on him, all lean muscle.

He seemed to feel her watching and he turned. His smile was of lust and happiness. She returned it.

He spent a few more minutes with the animals, then he returned to her. She moved the cover back in welcome.

They made love more slowly, exploring each other's bodies, touching, caressing, kissing. They fell asleep before dawn, clasping tightly to each other.

Etta woke to the smell of bacon, and for a moment she felt panic. At Henry's house she had awakened to bacon frying. When her eyes flew open, she was relieved to see that she was still in the stone shell of a house. It had window and door openings, but no roof. There was a fireplace, but it was full of fallen stones.

The horses and saddles and her clothes were gone, as was Max, but she could hear sounds outside. She wrapped the damp blanket around her nude body and went outside. Max, fully dressed, was cooking bacon over a fire. The horses were munching on the rich Kansas grass.

"Good morning," he said as he stood up.

He seemed cautious, as though he didn't know how to approach her.

Etta went to him and put her arms around his neck. As they kissed, her blanket fell to the ground. "A very good morning to you," she whispered.

For a moment they held each other, and she felt the way he clung to her. She suddenly saw his loneliness from over the years. So much responsibility was dumped on him at a young age. He had a mother and a sister to take care of. The next-door neighbor was demanding that Max marry his daughter.

He pulled back to look at her. "As much as I hate to cover up such beauty, we need to go."

Reluctantly, she released him. He started to look away from her nakedness but then seemed to remember that they were married, and he unabashedly watched her get dressed. During the night, when the rain stopped, he had wrung out their clothes and laid them out. At dawn, he hung them near the fire. They weren't dry but they were better.

In spite of the rush, Etta took her time dressing. This wasn't a modern man who'd been watching internet porn since he was a teenager. Max wasn't jaded and blasé about what he saw. As she put on the corset, she was glad for the thing. It was sex personified.

Max put out the fire. "That was worth all this bother."

She laughed. She'd never felt so desirable in her life! "What is this place?" As she slipped the knife Rufus had given her onto the belt, she was looking at the roofless, doorless house.

"It's one of the houses the government built for the Kanzas."

She looked at him in question.

"The Kanza tribe, also called Kaw? Kansas is named for them." He could see that she'd never heard of them. "They're a nomadic tribe, not farmers, but our government thought they could change them. The government built stone houses, gave them to the Kanzas, and told them to start planting crops." He nodded to the house. "The Kanzas thought the houses were horrible, dirty things. They took off the wood to use for fires, put their ponies inside, and lived in their nice, clean lodges. Then they went back to hunting buffalo, just as they'd done for centuries."

Etta drew in her breath. "But when the buffalo are gone, what do they do?"

"The government will feed them and take away what they are." He nodded in agreement at Etta's look of horror. "We need to go."

When Max helped her into the saddle, Etta groaned.

"Want to call this off?" he asked. "We could go to Kansas City and stay in the best hotel for a week. I'll buy you clothes, and we'll eat the finest beef in the world. And we'll make love from early to late."

Etta sighed. "Oh yes! I mean no. I mean afterward, yes."

"Promise?"

"With all my heart." She meant it. As Max mounted his horse, she whispered, "I hate you, Wyatt Earp. Deeply and truly *hate* you."

The morning ride seemed to go on forever. Max led them around a prairie dog village. She knew that if a horse stepped in one of the holes, a leg would be broken, but what she didn't know was that rattlesnakes loved the warmth of the holes. Max took the reins from her and led her past the danger.

The sight of him riding in front of her became familiar. She liked knowing he was close. That he'd agreed to do this for her, with her, still amazed her.

The sex they'd had was good, but there was something else and she wasn't sure what it was.

Max turned to look at her. "Are you all right?"

She smiled. "I'm doing quite well."

Minutes later, he stopped by a wide stream. "We need a rest."

His eyes were telling her that he wanted more than "rest." That was fine with her!

He helped her down and she limped to the stream. She wanted to strip off and go skinny-dipping. The other half of the glorious fertility of Kansas sunshine was making her sweat.

But she knew they didn't have time to dally. As soon as she sat down beside him, they began kissing.

When the earth rumbled beneath her, she pulled back. "What in the world is that? An earthquake?"

Max put his hand on her chin and moved her face back to his. "Just buffalo." He kissed her.

She pulled away. "Buffalo? They're making the earth tremble?"

"Sure." He started to kiss her again.

But Etta leaned away. "How many are there?"

"Ten or twelve, I guess." He bent toward her.

She leaned way back. "How big are those things that ten or twelve of them can do that?" She put her hand to the ground. "I can feel them."

He laughed. "Thousand. There are ten or twelve *thousand* of them. Maybe more."

Etta's face drained of color. "I have to see them." She stood up. "I must, *must* see them. Like life, I have to. See. Them. Now. Let's go!"

They were becoming so familiar with each other that she expected his usual hesitation. She liked that he thought things through before agreeing to do them.

But this time, he didn't hesitate. "I'd like to see them too." They ran to the horses, and he pulled off her hat and shoved it into a saddlebag. "You don't want to lose that."

Etta groaned as she threw her leg over the saddle, but pain didn't stop her. The ground was rumbling even more. It was vibrating. Quivering.

As always, Max seemed to know where to go. When he

urged his horse into a run, Etta said, "Go, Daisy! Follow your brother," and the mare flat out ran.

The wind in her hair felt glorious, and the excitement of what was ahead filled her. Daisy seemed as anxious to go as Etta was.

Max halted at the top of a hill, dismounted, and went to her.

She got down and stood beside him. Below them was a great, moving, solid mass. Buffalo. Thousands of them. They could hear them, feel them, even smell them. They weren't running, just sauntering along, denuding the prairie grass as they went. The beginning or end of the massive herd wasn't visible. On the side, sometimes a buffalo would lie down and wriggle around to form a huge hole. "It's a buffalo wallow," Max said.

She wanted to be closer. Below them was a flat area, a sort of cup in the land. She pointed to it and he understood.

He frowned a bit but then he nodded. They tied the horses, went down the hill and stretched out on their stomachs. The sound was louder, and she felt the danger of being so close but it was also exciting.

Etta was the first to see the man on the wiry pony. A young man wearing only a breechcloth, a fabulously beaded head-dress, and—her heart nearly stopped at the sight—with a bow and arrow. She was seeing what no human alive in her time had ever seen!

She nudged Max to look. "Tell me what's going on."

"The Kanza like bows and arrows because they're silent. They can get closer to the animal." He pointed. "The bulls are on the outside as protection, with the cows and calves in the mid-dle. The cows have the best meat, and the skins are used for clothes and housing. But you have to sneak past the bulls to get to them."

"And the bulls are unwanted?"

"Their pelts are stronger, and very valuable, but they're dan-gerous to get. If your arrow doesn't hit in the right place, a bull will attack and you're a dead man. A rifle is better. But you have to get it with the first shot or it'll be your last."

"What's that?" She was looking at a flash of light in the distance. When Max saw it, he glowered. "Stay here."

She watched as he hurried back up the hill to the horses. He pulled a spyglass from his saddlebag, then took his time staring through it in all directions. He returned to her.

"What's wrong?"

He got close to her so she could hear, and he nodded toward the young man on the horse. Now there were two more men. "Others are on the way here." He sounded angry.

"Who?" she asked.

"It's probably Cheyenne from the west, and buffalo hunters are coming from the south. They'll run the little Kanza tribe off, and they won't be allowed to take even a slice of meat away with them." He looked back at the herd. "If it's a good buffalo hunt, the Kanza will eat this winter. If it's bad, they'll starve. Have you ever seen people starve to death?"

"No," she said. "And I don't want to!"

Below them, she saw women arriving. On the edge of the land was a cow that had been taken down by one of the men. A young woman, dressed in a cotton blouse, a thick skirt with leggings below it, slid off a pony and went to the cow, her knife drawn. There were other women, but they were older, slower.

Etta looked at the hill she and Max were on. It was steep, but she was sure she could get down to level ground.

Max's head was turned away, the glass to his eye. "I think they'll have time. The Cheyenne and the hunters are still far away. They—"

Etta didn't hear any more because she was halfway down the hill. When she got to the bottom, the young woman had half the buffalo skin off. When she saw Etta, she halted, knife raised in threat.

Etta didn't have time for the niceties of introduction. She

pulled out the knife Rufus had given her and set to doing what Lester had taught her. As always, she moved fast. As Lester said, "Hungry people are waiting. Don't think, *do*!"

Skinning something as big as a buffalo wasn't easy, and Etta strained every muscle she had.

The woman, probably no more than eighteen or nineteen, didn't waste time. When Etta started to divide the meat the contemporary way, the woman stopped her. It was to be cut differently.

Etta caught on quickly. Two older women took the pieces and loaded them onto ponies. At one point, Etta stopped and pointed west. "Cheyenne." She pointed south. "Hunters." She pantomimed firing a rifle. They understood. There was great urgency in what they were doing.

When the women started going into the herd, Etta refused to let her modern day fears stop her from following them. The men had taken down two cows. Buffalo were big. Huge. Monster-sized. Scary as all hell.

But Etta kept her mind on the task. She didn't allow herself to think about the dangers.

They were on their fourth cow when one of the women shouted to Etta. She looked up. In the distance was Max. He had pulled off his clothes and had on only a breechcloth. His upper body was bare. His legs, strong from a life on a horse, were naked up to his waist. His long hair had been tied back and a single feather inserted. He was on one of the strong, fast ponies, no saddle, and he held his rifle.

As she watched, he leaned over so far he almost fell off. He was after a bull! He fired. For seconds, Etta couldn't see what happened. The bull stayed upright, and Max wasn't visible. The bull moved, but there was still no sight of Max.

After what seemed like an eternity, he came back up on the pony and the bull went down. Etta breathed again, her heart in her throat.

When she looked back, all the women were watching her.

Etta reacted in an age-old way. She grinned in pride and patted her heart. Her gesture said, "He's mine!"

The women laughed. They fully understood. They went back to preparing food for the tribe.

It was a while later when she heard Max's voice. He was shouting at her. She stood up, her hand to her aching lower back, and smiled at him. He looked really, really good. She made a gesture to indicate herself. She couldn't imagine how bad she looked. She was covered in blood and tallow and hair.

"Go! Go!" Max was yelling and riding toward her.

"Not yet," she shouted back, but a buffalo walked in front of him, and he turned to avoid running into it. She went back to work. Who cared about rescuing Wyatt Earp when feeding people was involved? She couldn't leave yet.

In the next second, she was picked up. Not nicely, not painlessly, but by her hair and her shoulder, and she was slammed across the spine of a horse. She got a mouthful of dirty horsehair.

The animal didn't slow down for minutes, then she was pushed off and landed hard on her backside in dirt that had been churned up by thousands of buffalo.

She assumed it was Max. "What the hell are you doing?" she said, then looked up at the man towering above her on a horse. The face was so very familiar! "Lester," she whispered.

Sometimes you met strangers and felt you knew them. This was the case. He also recognized her. Not as Henrietta Wilmont from the future, but as a spiritual connection. Kindred souls. He looked great! Resplendent. He had on buckskin, beads, feathers, and best of all, face paint.

His face had been divided diagonally, half of it painted a very dark brown.

They were staring at each other in silent recognition when Max rode up, dirt and manure flying. "You were almost killed!"

he yelled as he jumped down before the pony stopped. "I told you to move but you didn't obey. You *never* obey."

Etta looked around him and up at Lester. She knew his sense of humor. He'd say that a man yelling at a woman out of fear was true love. She stepped away from Max, removed the Celtic symbol from around her neck, and handed it up to Lester.

He took it, then removed a beaded necklace, and handed it down to her.

She smiled at him, he nodded, then he rode away. He looked downright majestic.

"What the hell was that?" Max demanded. He sounded jealous.

"Spiritual bonding? I have to finish this."

"You are the only woman still working. We have to go. The others are nearly here."

She knew he meant the Cheyenne and the hunters. She tried to orient herself. With no GPS it wasn't easy to figure out directions, but she thought she was facing north. "Who are they?"

Max looked in that direction. There were more painted men on horseback. "Pawnee." His voice was quiet and deadly. "We will be caught in a war. And we are the enemy of all of them." In the next minute, they were bareback on the pony. It was smaller and leaner than Max's well-fed horses.

"Stay down," he said as he led them to the side, as out of sight as he could manage.

It took a while but he got them back to their horses, still tied at the top of the hill, munching away, and quite peacefully happy.

13

After being bareback on a skinny pony, sitting atop Daisy and a saddle felt like being on a lounge recliner. Why had she ever complained about it?

As they rode through the warm Kansas night, Etta finally relaxed. Her weary muscles quit aching, her head fell forward, and she went to asleep. She woke once to see that Max was leading her horse. She smiled. He always took care of her.

The next time she woke, he was pulling her off the horse. She snuggled in his arms. He was bare chested. Lovely! She closed her eyes.

"No, you don't," he said. "You have to have a bath. You smell so bad I think wolves are following us."

"I just want to sleep."

"So do they with their bellies full of careless people. Get undressed."

"That sounds nice." She leaned against a tree and went back to sleep.

Again, Max woke her. "Here. Drink this. It'll help you for a while." He held a flask to her lips. She took a big swallow, then coughed. "That is truly nasty."

"Red Dog's finest. Come on, get that off."

She woke up enough to see that they were at a pool of water by a stream. "A hot tub," she said dreamily. "Steaming warmth."

"You'll wish it was." When she fumbled at her buttons, he brushed her hands away and began undressing her.

"You were wonderful today," she said.

"You think so?"

"I think—no, I *know*—that you're the most beautiful man I've ever seen." She slipped out of her filthy shirt.

"That whiskey went to your head."

"It hit another part of me," she said suggestively.

He laughed as she held on to his shoulders, and she stepped out of her gaucho pants.

"Where did you learn to ride like that? To shoot? Did you keep those G-string panties?"

"The what?" She didn't answer. "I spent some time with the Kanzas when I was a kid. Anything to escape my father. You were the surprise. It was like you knew the chief."

She was in her underwear. Not that it should be called that as it covered her like winter clothes. "Chief? Oh. You mean Lester. He looked good, didn't he? I should have guessed who he really was."

Max pulled her away from the tree and led her to the water.

As soon as her foot touched it, she turned back. "It's too cold. I really need to sleep."

He pulled her back, then guided her into waist deep water. "You walked straight through those buffalo but a little cool water scares you?"

Her teeth were chattering.

Max turned her around. He had some sort of soap, and he began washing her hair.

"That feels wonderful."

As his soapy hand moved downward, he slipped off her big cotton underwear and threw it on the bank.

With her eyes closed, she felt his hands run over her body. Her breasts, between her legs. Every inch of her. When he lifted his head, she put her arms around his neck.

He pulled her to him. He was naked and she wrapped her legs about his waist, her breasts against his warm, bare chest.

He held her tightly as they made love in the water.

She collapsed against him. "I think I need to be washed again."

"If I must," he whispered against her neck.

They held each other for a while.

"Let's get some sleep," he said.

She didn't release him. He carried her out of the water, then stood her on the ground. She was cold again. Max went to the saddles and pulled out a pair of trousers. He took clean under-clothes out of the bag she'd packed and handed them to her. As she dressed, she was shivering.

Max handed her the leather jacket Cornelia had given her. "Put this on."

It was nicely warm. "Beautiful Cornelia, my competition."

Max gave her a quick kiss. "If it was a contest, that means I'm the prize. I can assure you that you won."

Etta smiled. "That's like winning an Olympic gold medal in every sport."

He rolled out a blanket on the ground. "Not sure what that means, but I like it. Get in bed."

She readily obeyed, then looked up at Max. Moonlight glowed around him. "Come to me."

"In a minute," he said.

She heard no more as she went to sleep.

★ ★ ★

Yet again, she woke to the smell of bacon frying. For the first time, she didn't feel terror that she was back at Henry's house. She could smell the pure, cool air of Kansas. It was early, and the birds were beginning to chirp.

Slowly, she opened her eyes. Max, in clean clothes, his hair damp as though he'd taken an early morning swim, was at a campfire. A skillet full of bacon was sizzling.

"Good morning," he said.

She came up on her elbows with a groan. She was sore. "Did you sleep at all?"

"Enough. We need to go. Today will be hard."

"As opposed to the ease of yesterday?"

He smiled. "That was all your doing. I just watched."

The image of him on horseback, barely dressed, made her lie back down. Smiling. She had lascivious thoughts.

"No time for that now."

"But it's our honeymoon," she said.

He stood over her, looking down at her. "I think we can make it to a real town tonight. If we do, we can stay in a hotel."

She looked up at him with interest.

"There'll be a bed with clean sheets. We can go to a bath-house where they have tubs full of hot water."

She lifted up. "How hot?"

"Like you're a piece of Kansas beef on a grill. They'll have a laundry service, and everything can be washed."

She sat up. "What about flush toilets?"

He gave her a blank look.

With a sigh, Etta raised her hand for him to help her up. "It was worth a try. What's for breakfast?"

"Tortillas and bacon."

"And three leafy greens," she muttered, but she was still smiling. Memory of what they'd done the day before was coming to her. "Did they get away?"

He knew who she meant. "Yes. And with your help, they took a lot of meat." He nodded to the pendant around her neck. "That's for a chief's family."

She looked at the necklace Lester had given her. It was round, decorated with a combination of metal and glass beads. Quite beautiful. Her hand closed around it. "His family. That's appropriate." She knew he was waiting for her to tell more, but she didn't know how to explain how she knew Lester. "Where are my clothes?"

He looked at a wide rock by the pool. Her gaucho pants, the only pair she had, were stretched out there. He had washed them and set them out to dry. He must have done it last night after she went to sleep.

She picked them up. Like before, they weren't fully dry but they were wearable. "You did this for me," she said softly. She couldn't help it but tears gathered in her eyes.

Max pulled her into his arms. "What's this about? It's just a pair of pants, and they smelled so bad I wouldn't be able to stand you today." He leaned away to look at her. "Come on now, it's all right."

Etta put her head back on his shoulder. "No one has done so much for me in my whole life. I'm the one who takes care of people. My mother when she was alive, my little sister, my father. They all depend on *me*. Always."

He slipped his hand into her hair. "Then it's time for someone to look after you." Pulling away, he kissed her forehead. "Let's get out of here before the Cheyenne and the Pawnee find us. And the Kanza might kidnap you to keep. I'm not letting anyone take you away from me."

She smiled. "I won't let them or anyone else take me from you."

"Not even the horse thief you want me to save?"

When she laughed, he wiped away her tears with his thumbs, then kissed her. "Is that bacon burning?"

Etta leaped away and saved their bacon.

★ ★ ★

They rode for hours. Etta didn't know how Max knew the way to Arkansas, but he certainly seemed to.

When the sun was high and hot, he at last stopped. "The horses need rest," he said.

"Poor things." Etta achingly dismounted. "Too bad they're not humans and can go without stopping."

Max gave a grunt of laughter and pulled some hard little sticks from a bag and handed her a couple.

"Beef jerky. My favorite." She nearly fell to the ground. She hurt all over.

However, when Max stretched out beside her and began kissing her neck, she forgot about muscle aches. When she fumbled at her clothes, trying to get the wide split pants down, he said, "Dresses are better."

"This is my armor. Makes you work for the prize."

His kisses deepened, and they made love on the grass in the shade of an elm tree. Minutes later, he was helping her back onto her horse.

"You are the best lunch date I've ever had," she said. Smiling, he handed her the jerky she hadn't finished eating.

When the sun was dropping in the sky and Etta was dozing in the saddle, with Max leading the reins, he turned off the trail and they entered a little town.

Sleepily, Etta said, "What is this place?"

"I have no idea. It'll probably be gone tomorrow."

He's more right than he knows, she thought. She followed him to the stables and watched, her eyes barely open, as he talked to a man and handed over money. Max helped her down, removed their supplies from their saddles, and slung them over his shoulders.

"There's a hotel," he said. "Can you stay awake for it?"

"For clean sheets I could climb a mountain."

They left the stables and walked through the usual dirt to a building with a double front door.

Max opened one and let her go in first.

It was a simple room, but along the edge were some tables and chairs. She assumed they were for playing cards, like at the Red Dog. But then she got a whiff of… Her eyes widened. "Is that *food*?" she asked Max. "Real food?"

"Yes. Stay here." He dropped the bags at her feet and went to a tall desk to talk to a man.

Again, the aroma of cooking came to her. Etta closed her eyes. She felt like a cartoon character and she just might float away, buoyed by the smell.

"Come on." Max picked up the bags. "Food first or the hot bath?"

"Food!" She nearly shouted.

"Thought so. I ordered for us. There's a choice of beef or beef or some beef."

"I love Kansas," Etta said. She followed him to the back, to a table for two. He dropped the bags by his chair, and they sat down. Bowls were set before them. It was beef stew with carrots and potatoes. A basket of bread, still warm from the oven, and a crock of freshly churned butter was put on the table. Big mugs were filled with foamy beer.

Etta grabbed the mug, gulped down a lot, then looked at it in wonder. "It's an artisan beer."

"I don't know what that means, but the owner said his wife makes it."

"She is from heaven."

Max had his mouth full and nodded in agreement.

They ate ravenously. Etta slathered bread chunks in butter, keeping them both supplied. They doused the stew in salt, replenishing what they'd lost in sweat.

"This is the best meal I've ever had in my life," she said. She ate two bowls of stew and what had to be half a loaf of bread.

The waiter kept their mugs full of the home-brewed beer. It tasted of sage. "Wild Prairie Sage Beer," Etta said to the waiter. "That should be its name."

She made a run to the outhouse. Funny how after days of having to look out for rattlesnakes, the safety of an outhouse seemed downright luxurious.

When she went back inside, Max was still eating. She leaned back in her chair, enjoying watching him. She felt much better after the food, more awake. She looked forward to a bath. But then she saw the heaviness of his eyelids.

Invincible, indefatigable Max was worn out. She thought about the last few days and how little he'd slept. While she dozed in the saddle, he took over. While she slept at night, he washed her clothes. He went to bed after she did, got up before she did.

He really needed to sleep! But she knew him well enough to know that if she suggested that they skip baths and go to bed, he'd balk. He'd promised her a hot bath and no matter what, he'd make sure she got it.

It was time for her to be the caretaker. "I want to wear my new shirt, the one Freddy and Sally gave me."

"Sure. You can put it on after we take baths. They have peach cobbler here."

"I hope it's with cream."

It was. She ate only half of hers, then pushed the rest to him. Max ate it all.

"Can we get my shirt now?"

"I guess. Which bag is it in?" He looked down at the pile on the floor.

"I don't know. Let's take everything to our room and I'll search for it." When he hesitated, she said, "Please?"

He led the way up a flight of stairs, then down a short hall to open the door to a sparsely furnished room.

Afternoon sun shone through the window, highlighting the bed. To Etta, the clean white sheets and the soft mattress were like a golden throne. If angels started singing a hallelujah chorus, she wouldn't have been surprised.

Max dropped the bags to the floor but didn't move.

"You better sit down while I search for my shirt."

He headed toward the hard wooden chair against the wall. "Use the bed," she said. "I need the chair."

He didn't speak, just sat down on the side of the bed. Unlike the ground, the mattress sunk down, sweetly closing around him. He shut his eyes.

Etta waited a few moments, then went to him and pushed on his chest. He fell back like an overstuffed duffel bag. He was sound asleep.

She stood there for a while looking at him. He had days of beard growth, and his eyes were sunken in fatigue. She thought of him as a boy, having to take care of the women in his life. And running away to ride ponies with his native friends. And through it all, he'd had to deal with the bad temper of his father.

Max's feet were still off the bed. It wasn't easy to lift them, but when he turned on his side, that helped. She pulled off his boots. He had on socks and one had a hole in the toe. *I'll have to darn it*, she thought.

When she massaged his tired feet, he relaxed more, his wide shoulders dropping down.

Somehow, the massage, the thought of repairing his socks, and watching him sleep were more intimate than sex.

For the first time, Etta felt like she was really and truly his wife. Not girlfriend, not lover, not even friend. His *wife*.

She removed her clothes. The corset was stained and smelled so much of buffalo that she smiled in memory. When they got back, she'd have great stories to tell Alice and Pat and Nellie. Rufus and the men would love to hear them too.

When she was down to her underwear, not clean but not covered in buffalo fat, she lay down beside him. Instinctively, he pulled her to him like a teddy bear and she fell asleep in his arms.

★ ★ ★

"Time to get up," she heard Max say.

"Go away." There was a pillow. What an incredible, divine luxury. A pillow! She put it over her head. "I want to sleep."

"Remember the bath I promised you? It's here. Only now it's cold. If you don't get up, I'll pour it on you."

"You wouldn't! I'll—" She turned over to look at him.

Max was standing with one foot on the floor and the other one on the bed. The only clothing he had on was the buckskin breechcloth. His legs were bare. The sides of his glorious behind were exposed. His chest and arms were naked. A streak of early morning sunlight came through the window and hit him. Time for another hallelujah chorus!

Etta swallowed.

"What did you call this?" He flipped up the front of the teeny tiny breechcloth.

She tried to speak but nothing came out.

He put his leg down, walked across the room, then held up the shirt with the birds on it. "This what you were looking for? It was on top. Odd that you couldn't find it."

When he moved, she could see the muscles in his body. They undulated, rippled, moved in a lazy, easy way that made her mouth dry.

"How soon can you be ready to go?" he asked with feigned innocence.

"Do shut up." She opened her arms to him.

She discovered that a breechcloth came off *very* easily.

14

Compared to Garrett, Kansas, Van Buren, Arkansas, was New York City. There were stores, hotels, and of course saloons. The air was full of the sound of hammers and handsaws. There was lots of building going on.

They stopped near a very handsome courthouse. It was the kind of building Etta liked, not flashy but beautiful in a simple way. There was an impressive clock tower.

"I bet Cornelia could design something like this for Garrett." *And maybe it wouldn't be torn down*, she thought. She was so absorbed in the building that she hadn't noticed that they were surrounded by pigs. At first she was startled, but then realized it made nineteenth century sense. Why waste a good feeding area like the courthouse lawn?

Max had dismounted and was holding up his arms to help her down, but there was a pig nuzzling her foot. He looked at it. "If you knew what she does to creatures like you, you'd run for your life."

As though the animal understood, it ran away, squealing loudly in fear.

"You are so not funny," she said as she slid down into his arms.

"But honest."

He led them straight to a stone building with a high roof. There was a man sitting nearby, under a shade tree, a rifle over his shoulder. They kept walking.

"How did you know where the jail was?" she asked Max.

"I asked Rufus. He had an interesting youth, so I figured he'd know where the Van Buren jail was."

They got to the far end of the jail by going around a couple of other buildings. Along the side was a little window, but it was higher than Etta's head. Max muscled a full rain barrel to under the window, then lifted her up. She had to stand with her legs wide apart, her feet on the rims. It was a precarious balance, but Max put a steadying hand on her ankle.

As soon as she was up to the window level, she drew back. The smell was awful! She knew that ten men were locked inside one cell, with a bucket in the corner. Seemed that it hadn't been emptied in a while.

"Mr. Earp," she said as loudly as she dared. It was dark in the cell, and it took moments for her eyes to adjust. A man's face appeared at her level, so he must have been standing on the bed frame.

Etta tried to stay calm, but she knew she was looking at Wyatt Earp. Legendary man. Movies, TV, books would be written about him. He was a handsome young man, but she knew from photos that he would look better as he aged. *Is that fair?* she wondered.

"Who are you?"

Nice voice! Etta thought fast. "I'm Urilla's cousin." Urilla was his late wife, Etta's almost namesake. "And I want to say that I love ice cream too." A man was standing behind Mr. Earp. She lowered her voice. "Is that John Shown? The man who is blaming you for everything?"

"It is." He cocked his head to one side. "You seem to know a lot about my business."

She kept her voice low. "I don't think you stole those horses. His wife lied about you. On the stand. Under oath!"

Wyatt leaned forward. "Anna and I didn't exactly tell him the truth about some other things, so maybe I deserved it."

What he said wasn't at all the modern philosophy of blaming others for any bad that happened. It was so good to hear and she smiled broadly. "I'm here to help you escape. Go to the corner and pry off the ceiling, then hoist yourself up. Crawl across the rafters in the attic until you come to a small window. Max and I will be there to help you get down."

"Who is Max?"

"My husband."

He nodded toward her shirt. "And here I thought those birds flew you down from heaven."

"What a nice thing to say. Actually, I'm— Ewww."

Max had abruptly pulled her down to the ground. His look said what he was thinking: *Keep it to business.* When he took off walking, she ran to keep up with him. They stopped at the back of the building.

High up was a small window. "I guess that's it," she said.

"You mean the one with the bars across it? The one no adult could get through?"

"Yes. We have to remove some stones to widen the space. The question is how do we get up on the roof?" She looked at the building next to them. "We can go up that way. I think we can make it if we step on the windowsills. It won't be easy, but we can do it. Then we can leap across to the roof. We can—"

Max was gone. Her first thought was, *He was so jealous that he left me? Or was he just fed up with all my difficulties?* She didn't blame him if he had walked out. He could—

Max came around the corner with a tall ladder and two ropes coiled around his shoulders. "Or we can climb up. With all the construction around here, I figured one had to be close."

On impulse, she grabbed him and kissed him.

He stroked her hair. "You didn't think I'd abandoned you, did you?"

"Well, I did think…"

He pushed her away with a grimace. "Go!"

She scurried up the ladder.

As soon as Max was on the roof, he went to the chimney and gave it a good kick. When it didn't fall apart, he tied a rope around it.

Then, to Etta's horror, with one end of the rope he started tying what looked like a hangman's noose. "You aren't going to…to…?"

Max looked at her with angry eyes. "What have I done to deserve this?" He held up the rope then slipped his foot in the looped end. "After all the things I've done for you, you still mistrust me."

"Sorry. I apologize." She kissed his cheek.

"That's better." He yanked on the rope, then walked backward and began lowering himself down. When his face was at the roofline, he said, "And just so you know, I think you look really pretty in that shirt. And out of it."

"Thank you."

He slipped down out of sight. Etta stretched out on her stomach and looked over the side of the building. Max was standing with one foot in the rope loop in front of the little barred window. Out of the back of his shirt he pulled one of those decorative iron sticks that Pat had made. It looked like he'd brought it with him. She watched as Max pried out a stone from around the window. It fell down.

Unfortunately, it hit one of the curious pigs and it ran away squealing, and that set off the other pigs.

Etta made a frantic gesture for Max to come back up. That much noise might alert someone.

But Max stayed where he was.

As she'd feared, the guard they'd seen sitting under the tree came to see what the noise was about. All he had to do was look up and he'd see Max.

"Get the hell out of here," he yelled at the pigs and began kicking out at them. One of the big boars didn't like that, so he rammed the man in the back of his legs.

Etta's eyes widened. She'd heard too many stories of men falling into pigpens. They didn't get out.

But this man didn't fall. Instead, he chased the big boar, yelling that he was going to kill it.

When it was quiet again, Etta looked back at Max. He was removing more stones. Minutes later, she heard Wyatt Earp's voice.

"Who are you?"

"Urilla's cousin's husband. We're practically family."

"Reckon so," Wyatt said.

Max slipped the coiled rope from around his shoulder and pushed it through the bars. "Can you tie this up and get yourself down?"

"I can. I sure want to thank you for this. And I especially want to thank your wife."

Max smiled. "Not if you want to keep living."

"That I do." There was humor in Wyatt's voice.

Max pulled himself up, using the rope to climb in a way that a gymnast would envy. At the top, he stretched out on his stomach beside Etta to watch the men escape.

Wyatt came out first. When he got to the ground, he turned back to look up at the two of them peering over the roof. He put his hand to his mouth, kissed it vigorously, then threw the kiss to Etta.

She lifted her arm, caught it, and started to put her hand to her mouth. But Max's look made her put her hand to her cheek.

On the ground, they heard Wyatt's laughter as he ran away.

Max was looking at Etta in disgust, but she just shrugged. "So sue me."

He looked back at the ground. There were several men coming down the rope. "Who are they?"

"I don't know which is which but that one is John Shown, whose—"

"Yeah, got it. His wife played with your man, then she lied on the stand to protect her marriage."

"You're very clever to have figured that out."

"I wasn't even smart until I married a mystery woman. Since then I've spent my life trying to figure out what is going on and what I'm doing. I gave up thinking about the why."

Etta suppressed her laughter as they looked at the men going down the rope. "Two of them are the Perry brothers, in for counterfeiting and attempting to murder a deputy marshal. The other two were supposed to hang for murder."

"So you *did* want me to help you save murderers."

"I'm sure that now they'll become upstanding citizens and be productive members of society."

"Or politicians, which is one step up from murderers." He got up. "We better get out of here. When they find that rope, they'll know someone helped them."

"Oh! The blankets. They were supposed to use a rope made of blankets to escape. This will change things. They'll—"

"Oh hell!"

To her surprise, Max went down the rope again. As she watched, she was very nervous. This wasn't part of the story. What if a guard saw that seven of the ten men in the hideous cell were gone? They could find Max! They could—

He came back up. His second rope, the one the men had rappelled down, was coiled about his shoulder. "They'll just have to guess how the men got out."

She couldn't help throwing her arms around his chest. She was so relieved that he was all right.

"Come on," he said softly as he peeled her arms away. "Let's get out of here before some hog decides that ladder is good to eat. I don't want to have to jump across a building."

She knew he was referring to her original plan.

"Remember that hot bath I promised you? I bet we can find it in this big city. And let's get you some new clothes so I don't have to wash them every night."

"You are so good to me. You take such good care of me. You—"

He half set her on the top rung of the ladder. She quit talking and climbed down.

Etta was standing on the train platform waiting for Max to meet her. At her feet were four suitcases—or portmanteaus as someone called them. She was wearing a green dress so fashionable that Alice was going to be impressed.

As always, Max had taken care of everything. After they left the jail, he checked them into the finest hotel Van Buren had to offer. The quality was a great deal better than their previous hotel. This one was decorated in Victorian garish: red flocked wallpaper, heavy, dark furniture, gas lit glass fixtures on the walls.

As a bellman carried their saddlebags and canvas sacks up to their lovely room, Etta whispered, "I like the other hotel better."

"Me too," Max replied.

When they were alone, she turned to him. "Now what? Some poor overworked, underprivileged serf carries up our bath water?"

"I, uh..." He hesitated.

She sensed that he had something serious to say.

He took a breath. "I have things to do and we're going back on the train."

She had to translate that in her mind. "Things to do? You're dumping me here on my own, aren't you?" She wasn't a good enough actress to sound convincing. She wasn't actually angry. She understood work.

His eyes sparkled. "I am. I found a place with lots of Freddys."

Etta didn't smile.

Max pulled her into his arms. "Since I met you I haven't done two minutes of work. There are things I can do here. The hotel manager gave me the name of a Miss Louise. You're going to see her."

She pulled back to look at him. "For what?"

"A bath, then getting some new clothes."

"You could come too."

He shivered. "I'd rather fight a hundred rattlers than go shopping. I'll meet you at the station at six." He released her, went to the door, and opened it. A beautifully dressed, pretty young woman was standing there. "She's going to take care of you, then she'll deliver you to the station on time."

He started to leave but then closed the door halfway. Out of sight of the young woman, he mimicked Wyatt Earp's gesture of kissing his hand and sending the kiss to her.

Smiling broadly, she caught it and put it to her lips.

With a nod of satisfaction, he left the room.

The young woman was looking at Etta with a forced smile, as though she was facing an impossible task.

Some things never change, Etta thought. There was nothing more intimidating than the disparaging look that a saleswoman could give you. "I am yours," she said, and they left together.

That had been hours ago and Etta had been washed, shampooed, manicured, and finally dressed.

Miss Louise—a formidable woman—had held Etta's half corset between thumb and finger. "We shall burn everything."

"No!" Etta said. "Please just clean them."

Miss Louise obviously disapproved, but she had one of her many young workers take the clothes away.

Wonder how much Max paid for all this? she thought. When they got home, her father—correction, Tobias—wouldn't like how much money they spent. He was a frugal man.

Now it was nearly six and the train was there, ready to leave. But there was no sign of Max.

Sometimes it seemed hard to believe that this was all just a dream. She was acutely aware that it could disappear in a flash.

When Max kissed her on the neck, she almost fainted in relief. She clung to him.

"It's all right. I'm here." He lifted her chin. "Don't look so worried."

"You almost missed the train. It—" She broke off to step away and look at him. "You're still dirty." She sucked in her breath. "You're not going back, are you?"

"I am but I can't go on the train. There's no place for the horses." He put out his hand to her but she stepped back.

"You said *we* are going on the train. Us. Both of us."

"I lied. I'm sorry. I didn't want you to fret. I wanted you to enjoy yourself. By the way, you look mighty nice." He paused. "The horses can't take another trip like the last one. It would kill them. I'll take them back slowly."

"You really mean that *I* can't take the trip back. I was a nuisance to you, wasn't I? Buffaloes and you washing my clothes and…and…everything."

Through her whole tirade, he'd not lost his smile. "You know that none of that is true," he said softly. "You want to see what I did this afternoon?"

Etta was afraid that if she said more, she'd start bawling. She didn't want to be parted from him. No, the truth was that she was afraid of their being separated. Forever.

He handed her a little wooden case. It was about the size of a playing card.

She just stared at it.

"Go on, open it."

Inside was a miniature painting of the two of them. He was looking forward, while Etta was in profile, her eyes gazing up at him with love. "How? Who?" she whispered.

"When we rode in I saw the old painter. I met him when I was a kid. I couldn't believe he was still alive. Anyway, I got him to do it. I described you to him and I think he got you, didn't he?"

"Sir," a porter said. "The train is about to leave." He took away her cases.

Max's hand closed over hers, the portrait between them. "I sent a telegram, and Alice will meet you when you get there. Everything has been arranged. I'll arrive not long afterward. If the Cheyenne don't get me first, that is."

She didn't smile at his joke.

"Come on, get on the train."

Etta's mind suddenly seemed to come alert. She gave the portrait back to him. "I can't take it with me." There was urgency in her voice. "You must hide it in your big desk. Don't just put it in a drawer but build a secret place that no one will see for over a hundred years."

Max took her arm and led her to the train. "No one will steal it."

"No, no! That's not the problem. Please hide it. You don't understand. I *need* it and that's the only way."

"All right." He lifted her onto the train step.

She turned to him as the train started to move. "Promise me. Swear it."

"Yes, I will do it."

The train started and he walked beside it. "I'll be there soon." As the train sped up, he stopped walking. Then he again did the blowing kiss.

Etta caught it and put it to her lips. She watched until he was out of sight, then she went into the train and sat down. "I will not cry. I will not cry," she chanted to herself.

She sat there, looking out the window. The porter asked if he could get her anything. No, there was nothing she wanted. He told her that Max had paid him well to look after her so if there was anything she needed, he'd get it for her.

"I'd like to live in my dream forever," she said.

"That's what we all want." Laughing, he left.

The first stop wasn't far away. Etta was so forlorn that she didn't look out the window until the train was ready to start again.

And that's when she saw Henry. He was standing on the platform, and at his feet was the paraphernalia of an artist. There was a folded easel and a wooden box with a handle. It was stained with paint.

Etta had her nose almost to the glass, but when Henry looked toward the train, she fell back against the seat so he wouldn't see her. She stayed there until the carriage was far down the tracks.

When the porter came by, she stopped him. "There was a man on the platform. I think maybe he's an artist."

"That's Mr. Henry. He travels all over and paints things." Etta looked at him, waiting for more.

"There's a sad story about him. I don't know if it's true or not, but people say that when he was young he built a big house for his beautiful wife. But she died right away. They say Henry shut the door to the house and never went back. He's traveled ever since."

It was the story Max had told her. He'd met Henry, as had Alice.

"He painted a picture of my wife," the porter said.

"I'd like to see it sometime."

"I'm never without it." He reached into his pocket, pulled out his watch, and opened it. Inside was a miniature of a very pretty woman.

When Etta saw it, she thought her heart might stop. She'd seen the picture in one of the books Henry had written. It hadn't been a photo of an old painting, but something created for the book. Who illustrated them? She'd never read the credits. Her focus had been on Henry as the author. She looked at the porter. "What's his full name?"

"Henry Fredericks."

Etta just nodded. H. F. Logan. Henry Fredericks Logan. "Thank you for showing me the picture. Your wife is lovely."

"Married twenty-one years, three girls," he said proudly. There was a noise at the other end of the carriage. "Excuse me, ma'am."

"Yes, of course."

As Etta watched the country outside pass by, she felt a deep loneliness. As she'd ever known anything in her life, she knew it was over. Rescuing a legendary man, then seeing Henry. Those two things were what really mattered. And now they were finished.

When she and Max left home and everyone lined up to tell her goodbye, she'd had a premonition that she'd never see them again. All the friends she'd made, people she'd come to love. They would never return to her.

She leaned against the window. It was growing dark outside. "Max," she whispered. "Please come back to me."

She fought sleep as long as she could, but it overwhelmed her. Suddenly, she knew she was in Henry's house. The dream was over.

15

When Etta woke, she had no doubt of where she was, and she didn't hesitate in opening her eyes. The first thing she saw was a buffalo printed on the curtains in Ben's room.

In her arms was the lace snug she'd worn at her wedding. It was yellowed and smelled musty.

Her impulse was to curl into a ball and cry. All the people she'd come to love were gone. Or maybe they'd never even existed. Whichever, none of them were with her now. Worse, she'd probably never see them again.

With great effort, she swallowed the lump in her throat, then swung around and put her feet on the floor. She had on jeans and a long-sleeve T-shirt. It's what she'd been wearing the night she returned to Max for the second time. Since there was no dear Esmeralda to undress and redress her, Etta wasn't in her nightclothes.

As she sat there, looking about the room, she tried to think of what Alicia would tell her about dealing with how she was feeling. She'd say that right now, Etta had a choice of behavior. She could let misery and unhappiness overtake her. She could stay in bed and cry over what she couldn't have.

Or she could continue with life.

Etta knew that no amount of tears would bring back Alice or Freddy or Rufus or...or...

She took a breath, her eyes closed. Nothing she could do would bring Max back to her.

What happened after I was no longer there? she wondered. Did Alice and Phillip and Nellie go to the train to meet her and she wasn't there? Would they think she got off somewhere and ran away? They would be hurt and angry. Feel betrayed.

When Etta stood up, she was shaky, but she took a few deep breaths and walked to the bathroom. It was so big and shiny and clean that she looked at it in awe. She thought, *Is all this necessary?*

Her attitude almost made her smile. It was as though she was a time traveler coming forward and seeing modern conveniences as being too much.

When she removed her clothes, she glanced at herself in the mirror, then halted. Her body was different. Thanks to Phillip, she'd always kept in shape, but wagons and horses and a buffalo hunt had tightened her body. There was no longer any hint of "baby fat" on her.

Memories of what had caused her transformation almost crushed her, but she turned away, refusing to be taken down by what was in her mind.

She took a shower, using the gentle shampoo and the soft soap. But instead of enjoying it, she felt disgust at the waste. She much preferred a river.

And Max, she thought. *I want Max.*

She got out and dried herself with a towel of such softness that she looked at it in wonder.

Clean clothes were in the chest of drawers by the bed. She'd washed the few things she had with her after her attic visit. She made up the bed, straightened the room, and put Martha's cookbooks on a shelf. As Etta held them, she wondered if Martha's fried pie recipe was in one of them. Max had handed them out as they rode.

Dressed, Etta turned to go downstairs. Instead, she sat down on the edge of the bed. How was she going to play this with Henry? Did she tell him about this dream or not? Whereas the first one had been short and rather funny, there was little humor in the one she'd just experienced.

Well, maybe, the incident of Ben being mixed up with Phillip could be thought of as amusing. Alice's "I hate you" wasn't funny. But seen from the point of view of later, with a barefoot Alice and a shirtless Phillip beside the water, maybe it could elicit a laugh or two.

Etta leaned back on her arms and closed her eyes. The buffalo hunt and how important it was wasn't cause for laughter. When she inhaled, she could almost smell those animals, feel the rumbling earth under her body.

That hunt would be what Henry would most want to hear about. Dream or not, he would want her to tell him about everything from the grass to what Lester was wearing.

She stood up. She'd have to play this by ear. Henry had enjoyed her first dream, but this one... Was it so real that it would make her seem insane? Would Henry be so shocked that he'd call Ben to come throw Etta out of his house?

All in all, she thought the best thing to do was to tell only bits of the dream. The funny parts. Lighthearted. Frivolous.

She stopped at the staircase. She'd tell Henry that in this dream he was an artist. That was close to being a writer, wasn't it? Both were creative.

She started down the stairs. Remembering Henry as an artist

led her to the memory of Max giving her the miniature portrait of them. It had been so perfect. The two of them and—

At the foot of the stairs, Etta halted and her eyes glazed over, sightless. The portrait. She'd told Max to hide it in the desk. Did he do it? Was it in there? If it was, would that mean things were *real*?

"Good morning," Henry said. "Did you sleep well?"

She looked at him in wide-eyed silence.

"You had another dream, didn't you?" There was hope in his voice.

She nodded.

"Was it a good one? Was it longer? Who did you meet?"

When she spoke, it was a whisper. "He hid it inside the desk. I have to take your beautiful desk apart to find it. I'm sorry. I—"

"We'll take an ax to it." Henry started down the hall, his voice ringing over his shoulder. "We'll use a chain saw if need be, except that I don't have one. I'll get my toolbox. There's a short-handled sledgehammer somewhere. I'm sure I can still swing it."

Etta hadn't moved from the foot of the stairs. "It looks like Henry is going to get every word out of me," she said to no one. She started running. "Don't destroy anything. Max hid it. We just have to find it."

She ran into the library and stopped in front of the big desk in the alcove. The last time she'd seen it, her father had been sitting there. Before that, Max was using it, which made her remember the men showing off for pretty Alice. She smiled in memory.

Henry showed up at the doorway with a heavy red metal toolbox. She could see his heart was pounding, his face pale.

She took the box and led him to a chair by the window. "You direct and I'll search."

He was so out of breath he could only nod.

When she turned around, she gasped. The sides of the alcove were draped with heavy curtains, and she'd never stepped behind them. Along the far wall was an artist's tall, slanted table. Beside it was a cabinet with drawers. On top were cups of colored pens and pencils, and tubes of watercolors. They were Winsor & Newton, the brand she'd bought for Nellie.

Etta took a chair next to Henry. "You're an artist?"

He was breathing deeply, trying to calm his heart. "I illustrated all my books. I thought you knew that."

"No, I didn't." She looked at him. "Who is Wyatt Earp?"

"Legendary lawman. Didn't you say your father was writing a book about him?"

Etta had to work to keep from dissolving into tears. It appeared that she and Max had *done* it. Really and truly changed history. "He has movies? TV? Dodge City?"

"Yes," Henry said impatiently. "I've had that big desk for years, but I don't know of any secret compartment. Even when I carved it, I didn't see anything."

"Ah, right. You did the carving on the front."

"I did. I had to disassemble the desk to get the back panel out, then I carved on it." He was calmer now, and he turned to look at her. "This dream was different, wasn't it?"

"Yes."

He reached out and took her hand. "You don't have to tell me any of it. If you'd rather keep it private, I respect that. I can—"

"I went on a buffalo hunt. With the Kanzas."

Henry's face so drained of color that all that could be seen was his mustache and his eyebrows.

"If you pass out, I'll get so scared I won't tell you anything," she said sternly.

It was Henry's turn to repeatedly swallow. He looked at the toolbox, then the desk, then at Etta.

His meaning was clear. Start searching!

He asked her to describe the size of what she was looking for and what it was. He nodded in understanding. "I've done some paintings like that."

You did this one, she thought but didn't say. There would be time for that later.

First, she took out all the drawers and lined them up in front of him. There were seven of them, each one packed full of things no one had seen in years. Etta had some of her father's neatness gene, so she told Henry to sort it all out. She got his lap desk and a big trash bag, and one by one, handed him the contents of the drawers.

While he dealt with that, Etta went over every inch of the skeleton of the desk.

"You're different," Henry said as he tossed old receipts in the trash. "You're quieter and you're... How do I say this? Physically, you're..."

Etta was under the desk, knocking on parts to see if there were any hollow areas. "Not as soft? Now I'm leaner and meaner?"

"Exactly." Henry was looking astonished. "It defies the laws of nature that you could physically change overnight."

"This time I was gone for days. And I went through some rough times. You should see me on a horse."

"I think you should tell everything into a recording device."

She stood up. "Because my storytelling is so abysmal?"

Henry looked like he was trying to come up with a lie but couldn't. "Yes. But also, I want to hear about the hunt first—which is out of order." He looked back at the papers. "What was the first thing you saw at the hunt?"

She wasn't fooled by his seemingly innocent question. He was testing her. "The ground shook. Vibrated. I thought it was an earthquake but Max said no, it was ten or twelve buffalo."

Henry, a true historian, was so in awe, his jaw fell open. "Thousand," he whispered.

"Yup. As far as you could see, nothing but buffalo." She was looking at the desk and trying to keep sadness from overwhelming her. There was no hidden compartment, no miniature portrait. "It wasn't real," she whispered. "It really was a dream. I've had a lifetime of watching Old West movies so I made up a story, complete with buffalo and artisan beer. None of it really existed."

"Etta," Henry said softly.

"Maybe it's true that my own life is so empty that I—"

"Etta!" Henry shouted. "Look!"

She went around the desk to see where he was pointing. The seven drawers lined up on the floor were nearly empty. They varied in size but there was nothing else notable about them.

"Don't you see it? Look at the third drawer."

It took her a moment, but she finally saw that the interior of it was shorter than the others. It was as though a piece of wood had been nailed to the inside. She looked at Henry in shock.

"Pry it off," he said.

Etta's hands were shaking so hard she fumbled to get the toolbox open. She grabbed a screwdriver and a tack hammer, then sat down on the floor, the drawer in front of her. When she put the screwdriver into the seam behind the wooden block, she looked up at Henry.

He gave her a nod of encouragement.

It took her a while to widen the gap. She kept moving the screwdriver around, afraid of breaking through the block and hurting what it was covering.

When she got it about a half inch away, Henry handed her a little flashlight from the toolbox and she looked inside. There was something in there.

It seemed to take forever to get the wood off, then Etta just stared. Yes, it was the case containing the miniature portrait Max had given her.

"Take it out," Henry said gently.

As she held it in her hands, she thought of Max at the train station and saying goodbye to him. She remembered having the ominous feeling that everything was going to end.

Henry held out his hand and she put the little square into it. His hands were more steady than hers.

He opened it and stared at the picture for a full minute. "I have never seen you look so happy," he said softly. "And Max is a fine looking young man." He handed her the painting.

Until she saw the picture of Max, Etta had held it together. But seeing his beautiful face broke her. She collapsed, weightless, spiritless.

Henry did one of his leaps and caught her in his arms before her head hit the floor. Etta's deep tears of grief and misery came out in full force. Henry never let go of her.

When Etta woke, it was growing dark outside. She was stretched out on Henry's big couch in his library, and she could smell bacon. Her first impulse was to cry at the memory of being on the trail and waking to Max frying bacon.

But she didn't allow herself more tears. For the entire day, she'd cried, then cried some more.

Henry had been very kind, saying that since seeing the portrait, his attitude changed. After the first dream, he'd laughed and made jokes. This time, he didn't laugh. He believed her.

She got off the couch and made a quick trip to the marvelous thing called a bathroom, then went to the kitchen.

"I made us BLTs and fries," Henry said. "I'm not as fast or as good as you, but it's edible."

She gave a half smile. "I won over the cook. Rufus said it was the best meal he'd ever eaten. But then, Rufus may have had a less than a happy childhood, so what comparison did he have?"

Henry handed her a plate piled high, then opened his notebook to write down what she'd just said. He gave her a glass of iced tea. "How are you feeling?"

"Alive, but that's all."

Henry sat down by her with his food and drink. "I guess you won't want to, uh, remember things, will you?"

She started to say no, but then she stopped. "I don't know why all this has happened to me, and finding out it was *true* has twisted my brain around. How do I deal with that?"

"You did change history."

"My apologies to Mr. Earp, but I think there has to be something more important than that."

"I agree wholeheartedly," Henry said. "Maybe ghosts want to be remembered."

At that, Etta blinked back tears. It was 149 years later, and many of the people she loved were dead. If they were still around, it was as ghosts. She knew what Henry wanted. He was dying to hear the whole story, every second of it. He wanted to record it all.

And maybe he was right. Ghosts did want to be remembered.

She took a drink of her tea. "I guess I should start where the first dream ended. Alice made Max leave the room. I was so angry at him that I wouldn't open my eyes."

"You were sleeping?"

"No. When the first dream ended, I fainted. Max caught me and carried me to the couch." She paused. "He was always carrying me, catching me, lifting me. He takes care of people. He protects them."

"But that day you weren't happy with him."

"No," Etta said softly. "I wasn't."

"So what happened next?" Henry asked. His sandwich was forgotten as he held his pen poised over his notebook. What writer cared about food when there was a good story to be heard?

Three days! Etta dropped her head back against Henry's chair and thought, *Three whole days!*

That's how long she'd been under interrogation by Henry. She'd never talked so much in her life. Or typed so much. She talked; Henry recorded her; Etta typed it all. She was sick of the sound of her own voice. She'd had no idea that writing a book took so much organization and so many details. Endless details.

At first, Henry had been grateful for anything she could tell him. But by the second day, he wanted an outline in chronological order. Hour by hour.

"Did you meet Fred Harvey before or after the four holer?" was one of his questions and yes, he wanted to know all about outhouses. "Who were the witnesses at your wedding?"

"I don't know. I never saw them again. At least I don't think I did, but Max had lots of workmen. There were twenty or thirty of them the day I won the cooking contest."

"Ah, yes, the contest. How much did you win?"

"I didn't count it. I don't even remember what I did with the money. Knowing Max, he probably took care of it. Back then, men looked after their wives."

"Are you saying that you weren't allowed to handle your own money?"

"I wasn't saying anything even close to that. Do you have any tequila? I could use about three shots."

His response was to apologize then go back to his questions. He was relentless.

It was evening now, and Henry was absorbed in his many typed and handwritten pages. Trying not to be seen or heard, she tiptoed out of the room and went outside. Sophie's house was locked tight. There were no cars on the street as everyone stayed inside. Etta missed restaurants and people and stores.

Yesterday, she called Lester. It wasn't easy for her as the last time she'd seen him he was sitting on a pony and wearing a beaded headdress. Five minutes into the conversation, she couldn't resist saying that she'd dreamed about him. She used Henry's books to explain why she'd imagined being on a buffalo hunt. "You were the chief and you were magnificent." He listened to it all in such complete silence that she was afraid she was offending him.

But when she slowed down, he said, "It's always been my favorite animal. I have a buffalo tattoo in a place that you will never see."

"Really?" She was smiling wide. "Anything more to tell me?"

She said Henry was writing a novel set in 1871, and he was going to put in a buffalo hunt. "He illustrates all his books, so I'll get him to paint you as the chief."

"That would be an honor," Lester said.

They talked for thirty minutes more.

Etta called Alicia, Phillip and Nola, but they were busy and didn't have much time for chitchat. Alicia loved staying home, and Phillip was getting used to it. When he said he'd taken up welding in the garage, Etta nearly choked. As for Nola, Etta had Amazon deliver her a Winsor & Newton paint set. The whole world might be shut down, but Amazon was still doing overnight deliveries. "Can I send something to 1871 Kansas?" she muttered. "Max would love a big pickup truck. A blue one, like his eyes."

After the call, she thought, *And I believed that I could persuade them to return to living with Dad and me. How selfish of me!*

She went back into the house, preparing to answer more of Henry's questions, but he was reading and marking on every page in red. She said good-night and went upstairs to shower and go to bed.

One good thing about Henry's questions was that they kept her mind so occupied that she couldn't grieve.

But now and then, between questions, she asked herself *Why?* If she had gone back in time—and the portrait seemed to prove that she did—why did it happen? She'd searched through Henry's extensive library and had viewed hundreds of websites, but she'd found no mention of Max or Alice or Cornelia or Bert. The town of Garrett was only referenced in the ghost town book.

So why? she wondered. *Why did I go back?* She couldn't make herself believe it was all so she could get Wyatt Earp out of jail.

She went to sleep frowning. Why? Why? Why?

It was the morning of the fourth day since Etta returned. Henry had slowed down with his questions, and was now absorbed in putting the stories together.

She wasn't sure how she felt about the idea of her story being made into fiction, complete with illustrations. Lester had sent her three photos of himself so Henry could portray him accurately. In the last one, he'd used a light shade of makeup to partition his face on the diagonal. It looked the same but was the opposite of what Etta had seen.

"Did he do it correctly?" Henry asked.

"It's exactly like what I saw."

"Then part of him remembers." Henry said he believed that when a person was attracted to an era, it was because they'd lived during that time.

"You mean like how I don't like Viking stories but I love Elizabethan? And the Roaring Twenties bore me, but I'm fascinated by the 1940s?"

"That's just what I mean." He went back to putting the story in order.

Etta was left alone to entertain herself—which was bad. Without distractions, she thought too much. She was at the point where she could hardly bear to go into Ben's room. It reminded her too much of what she'd lost.

Early on the fourth morning, she was standing at the front window, looking out and hoping Freddy would show up. At least they could wave to each other. She wondered if in private Freddy liked to put on shoulder-baring dresses and apply gaudy makeup. That would fit Henry's theory of people remembering their past lives.

A big, sturdy-looking car, a Ford Bronco, slowly drove down the empty road. The name of the vehicle made her smile.

When it parked at the curb in front of the house, she was surprised. Was it someone coming to see about Henry?

The driver's door opened and out stepped a man. He walked around the vehicle, saw Etta at the window, and put up his hand in greeting.

She tried to smile at him, but couldn't. He was Rufus.

As she watched him walk to the house, she thought how alike they were, the same age, the same face. They moved in the same way. But it was as though he'd been put through some magic machine that had de-aged him. This Rufus had nice teeth, his skin wasn't damaged from a lifetime in the sun, and he was taller. Evolution at work.

She was in such a trance that he rang the doorbell twice before she got there and opened the door.

"Hello," he said.

It was Rufus's deep voice. *I will not throw myself on him and bawl my eyes out,* she told herself.

She managed to give a smile. "I'm Etta."

"You're the woman Ben hired?"

"No. I mean yes, I was hired, but Henry did it."

"That makes sense. He's always liked young, pretty females. Oh! Sorry. That's not PC of me."

"It's better than being called old and plain."

He chuckled. "I can't imagine that! I guess Henry's in his cave." He nodded down the hall.

"Of course. He'd live there if Sophie's singing didn't drag him out."

"Beautiful voice. I'm Zack Vaughn, Henry's research assistant. He probably told you about me."

Not a word, Etta thought. "Lots." She took a chance. "How's your leg?"

He smiled, glad to have been remembered. "It's good. It took some surgery, but it's nearly healed. I'll go see him."

"Sure." Etta was digesting this information. Rufus's leg was hurt in the past, and his reincarnation's leg was hurt in the present. Was that karma? Or fate?

She went to the kitchen and prepared a tray of lemonade and cookies to take the library. But Zack entered.

"He's in the zone and I don't dare disturb him."

"I understand. Would you like to sit outside?"

"Yes, I would."

As she suspected, he carried the tray. In 1871, men carried things. Unless the woman was, as she'd said to Max, "some poor overworked, underprivileged serf." The memory made her smile.

They sat at the little table and chairs in the side garden.

"How are you holding up in this isolation?" he asked. "I mean, Henry is good company, but..."

She laughed. "It's like living inside a book. Talk to me. Tell me all about yourself."

"Nothing interesting, really. I had a daughter when I was nineteen. Her mother and I couldn't stand each other, so she turned my daughter over to me and left the country." He grimaced. "My daughter now has a tall, skinny boyfriend and they live in Denmark. She translates books." He took a drink of his lemonade. "I had a farm until six years ago but I sold it to a rich guy, then I retired early. What about you?"

"No husband, no kids." Even to Etta that sounded sad. "But I'm in a serous relationship." It was a lie that wasn't a lie. "What do you do for Henry?"

"Whatever he can think up for me to do. We met at one of his book signings in Abilene. There weren't many people there so we talked. We discovered that he had too much to do and I didn't have enough, so we merged. I do any legwork that he needs. I drive him around, take photos, that sort of thing. Henry and I have been on half a dozen road trips together."

Like he used to do with Ben, she thought. "A road trip," she said dreamily. "That sounds wonderful."

"Getting stir crazy?"

"Yes, but it's more than that. There's a place I want to see. It's a town that disappeared when the train line moved to Wichita."

"There are a lot of those places. Now they're just empty land."

"I know, but I still want to see it. There's a town, a house, and a stream with cottonwood trees."

"That sounds like half of Kansas."

"There was a sod house cut into a hill near the stream."

"That's another quarter of Kansas."

"Then we'd only have to search a fourth of the state."

He laughed. "That's better than Henry's directives. One time he sent me nearly to Oklahoma just to look for one kind of a flower."

"Did you find it?"

"Of course."

"When do we leave?" She was joking but Zack didn't laugh.

"How about today?" he asked.

She could see that he was serious. "But this lockdown..."

"Henry and I only go on back roads. He says there's nothing historical on the superhighways. He doesn't even like pavement. And we'd stay away from people."

Etta was thinking hard. Could she leave Henry alone? On the other hand, would he notice if she wasn't there? Thanks to being so bored over the last days, she'd filled the fridge. "Do you know Freddy? Who delivers the vegetables?"

"Never met him."

"Her. I'll call her and see if she can stay with Henry. Can we do the trip in two days?"

"Depends on where it is."

"Have you ever heard of Garrett, Kansas?"

Zack's eyes widened. "Heard of it? That's my middle name. Ezekial Garrett Vaughn. My grandfather said we owe our lives to a Dr. Garrett because he saved the life of my great-great, et cetera, grandfather. Granddad said that to repay the doctor, every generation of our family has to name a kid after him. It's a ridiculous tradition and it needs to stop."

Etta wasn't in the least surprised at his revelation. "What's your daughter's name?"

Zack gave her a wide grin. "Evelyn Garrett Vaughn."

They laughed together.

She hesitated before saying what was on her mind, but if Henry was right and people did remember, then Zack would understand. "The doctor who saved your ancestor was a woman named Martha Garrett. Her husband founded the town." Etta didn't feel the need to tell him that Martha wasn't certified as a doctor or to add the part about her losing her husband and son. Besides, how could she explain how she knew all that?

"Interesting. I grew up near there. Granddad was the one who kept the family history alive." He tightened his jaw in anger. "The day after he died, his second wife sold everything. There were things that had been in our family for generations. She ran off with the money and we never saw her again."

"Did you tell Henry this story?"

"No. Should I have?"

"Probably." Etta didn't think it was her business to connect Henry's desk and trunk to Zack's story. If the men hadn't discovered that, maybe it was for a reason. "She held an auction," Etta said.

"She did." He was looking at her in curiosity. "I think you're a historian of Henry's caliber. No wonder he hired you."

"No one matches Henry. Are you serious about this trip?"

"Completely. When do you want to leave?"

"Now. Give me thirty minutes."

He smiled indulgently. "Women usually take a while to pack."

"You've been dealing with the wrong women," she shot back at him. "I have to call Freddy and—"

He stood. "I'll pick you up in an hour."

As they stood up, she thought about what she was doing. An overnight trip with a stranger. True, he was known to Henry, but still, there was room for concern. "I, uh..." she began but didn't finish.

He knew what she was trying to say. "Give me credit." He straightened his shoulders as though he was offended by her suggestion that he would try anything sexual.

She smiled in apology. Minutes later, Zack was gone and Etta called Freddy who said of course she'd stay with Henry. She'd be glad to since she was sick of the sight of her roommate. "I might move in with you."

"Lots of bedrooms here," Etta said. "And I'm sure Henry would love to have you stay."

"If I could move the garden, I'd take you up on that."

"You need a different roommate. Maybe a farmer."

Freddy laughed. "Great fantasy. The last guy I went out with couldn't tell a zucchini from a cucumber, and he said vegetables were for cows."

"When I get back, we'll talk. I have to go now. Zack will be here in minutes." She hung up, then went to tell Henry.

He was delighted about her trip. "Tell Zack to take the big Sony camera. I want hundreds of photos. See if you can find the place of the buffalo hunt."

Etta started to tell him she didn't know where that *was* much less where it *is*. But she just smiled and nodded. She'd do her best.

It was as she was throwing clothes into her carry-on that a thought occurred to her. *What if I meet* all *the people from the past in the present? What if Max is waiting for me in Garrett? I must find him!*

16

As Etta put her bag by the front door, she reminded herself that she needed to call the airport about the big suitcase she'd left behind. Sitting beside her carry-on was a box she'd packed with food and drinks. With most places closed, they'd have to take their own food. Zack returned an hour and ten minutes after he left.

"You're late," she said, and he grinned. He had a camera bag that looked like it weighed as much as a side of beef.

She kissed Henry goodbye, then Zack told him that, yes, he'd take many photos and yes, he'd make notes. Etta added that she'd record her impressions. After they'd answered all Henry's questions, they left.

Outside, at Zack's Bronco, he made the mistake of asking Etta if she needed help getting in. After all, it was high off the ground.

She gave him a look that made him step back, then she got in easily.

Zack knew the way and they traveled south. It was Kansas, so there was farmland interspersed with big homes shaded by huge trees. Sometimes they passed derelict barns and houses.

"If you were Henry, we'd stop and take photos of those," Zack said. "He's working on a book of pictures titled *Lost Kansas*."

"Sounds like a good project. When will it be done?"

"If Henry does half of what he's planned, he'll have to live to be a hundred and twenty. But then he'd come up with more things to do so he'd need to be immortal."

"That's all right with me," Etta said.

He smiled in agreement. "So tell me about yourself."

As they drove, she told him about her father, sister, brother-in-law and Nola.

"And you all lived together in one house?"

She started to say the usual about how wonderful it was, but she stopped. In her dreams she'd had a taste of having her own family, and she finally understood why Alicia had readily agreed to move away.

"Sorry," Zack said at her silence. "I didn't mean to stir up anything bad."

"You didn't. It's just that staying with Henry has made me think about things." She didn't add, *Not to mention that traveling back in time has turned everything in my life upside down.*

She wanted to change the subject. "Your ancestor who was saved by the doctor must have married."

"Yeah, sure."

"What was his wife's name?"

"I have no idea. I know he lived to be ninety-six years old, but— Wait! I think my father once told me his wife was named Fred. I was a kid, and I thought that was a funny name for a girl."

"Could it have been Freddy?"

"Like the girl you called to take care of Henry? That would be a big coincidence, wouldn't it?"

"Lately, my life has been nothing but coincidences." *I wonder if Freddy and Rufus were a match that I missed?* she thought. She'd always heard that ladies of the evening were sought after as wives back then, so maybe Rufus was looking for a bride. She wondered if they got together after she left. Freddy had been hired to work in the garden so she was there every day and so was Rufus. It made sense.

"You're looking very serious," Zack said. "Want to share?"

"I was thinking about the past. What did you have on your farm? Besides cows, that is?"

"No cows. I grew broccoli and corn and carrots. Lots of things."

Like Freddy does. Etta was smiling. "Do you miss it?"

"Sometimes. Are you planning to stay here in Kansas and get your own place?"

She started to reply, but Zack turned down a gravel road. "Are we near Garrett?"

"Yes."

Minutes later, he stopped the car and they got out. As the ghost town book said, there was nothing left. It was just flat, wind-whipped grassland.

Zack took out the camera and began snapping while Etta walked around. It was difficult to imagine what had once been there. Unlike Max, she didn't have a built-in gyroscope in her mind, so she couldn't orient herself. She looked for where the train rails had been, but Henry had told her that used train tracks were dug up and hauled away to be laid elsewhere. The buildings had all been thrown up quickly, so there were no remnants of stone foundations.

There seemed to be a bit of a dip in the ground, so maybe it was where the main road through town had been. If so, was the

Red Dog here? Was the Garrett Emporium, where she'd bought the paint set for Nellie, over there? Was the church at the end?

"You look like you're trying to find something," Zack said.

"Just imagining what it was probably like. It's hard to believe there isn't anything left."

"I bet if we used a metal detector we could find things. Coins and lost watches and wagon parts and— Are you all right? Maybe this place is getting to you."

"I'm fine," Etta said. "I think that if we head that way we'll find where the house was."

Zack had a map in his back pocket. "We'll have to go around. Will this be the river and the sod house?"

"No. They're somewhere else, but if I can find the house I could ride to the homestead."

"I'm not sure my car can go across the land."

"No," Etta said. "I mean I'd ride on a horse." She knew Zack was staring at her, but she didn't say any more as she went back to the car and got in.

He was excellent with direction, and he found where she thought the house had probably been. There was nothing left, just flat, grass-covered land.

"Not even any of Freddy's plants are left," she said softly.

"This is the woman taking care of Henry?"

"No. Not here, not now, but yes, it is her." She was trying to get her good mood back, but she couldn't. How could a town be totally wiped out? Stores, houses, even the railroad were completely gone. Erased. As if they'd never existed.

Zack turned to her. "I don't have a horse with me, but if you point the way, I'll try to find the old homestead. Sometimes those places have been preserved by a local historical society."

"Maybe so." There was no hope in her voice.

Zack took out the map and looked at it. "I don't know about you but I'm hungry."

"I brought food."

"I'd like something cold to drink and hot to eat. How about if we look around the area to find something that's open?"

Etta shrugged. It didn't matter to her.

"Let's see. The nearest town seems to be a place called Kecklin. It's not much but—"

"What?"

"Food," he said. "Lunch. We can—"

"No! The town. What's the name?"

"Kecklin."

"Kecklin," Etta whispered, then louder, "John Kecklin!" She looked at Zack. "Go. Hurry." She was frantically searching in her bag for her phone.

Zack drove back onto the road.

"It's here." Etta was looking at her phone. "There's a website for it. It's a tiny, unincorporated town. No mayor, no courthouse, no—" She halted. "It has a local museum." She could barely speak. "It's in a house built in 1876. The owner is Miss Bella Kecklin and her great-grand uncle, John Kecklin, built the house. She's spent her life collecting local history artifacts. She never married, never..." Etta trailed off. "I love this woman. Deeply and truly *love* her. Oh no!"

"What is it?"

"The museum is closed due to the lockdown." Etta's eyes widened. "Maybe we can find a window and get in through there. Or the roof might have—"

"Call Henry," Zack said loudly. "Right now, call him. He knows everyone in Kansas who's involved in anything historical."

She pulled up Henry's number and called.

"Just so you know," Zack said, "I do *not* break into houses no matter what's inside."

"Okay, but sometimes there are things that you must do. They're necessary. They—" Henry answered his phone. She didn't bother with formalities. "John Kecklin. Remember him?"

"Cornelia's father. Wants to own Kansas, right?" he answered.

"Yes. There's a Kecklin, Kansas, and they have a museum in an old house. But it's closed for this lockdown!"

Henry didn't hesitate. "I'll see what I can do. I know people." He clicked off.

Etta looked at Zack. *Go!* her eyes said.

Kecklin was very cute, with a main street lined with old houses under huge shade trees. There were a few stores, all tastefully inserted into old buildings. Unlike many historic towns, the old places hadn't been flattened in the sixties and rebuilt in ugliness. It was a charming little Kansas town.

Only the filling station with a convenience store was open, and Zack pulled up to a pump. "I'd better fill up while I can."

"I'll pay for the gas," she said. His look told her no. For the first time, he pulled a mask out of a box and put it on. As she watched him enter the little store, she thought how much she liked Kansas and its residents. Sane, sensible people with their feet on the ground. She hadn't thought of it before Zack mentioned it, but she could imagine living there.

He returned with a bag full of cold drinks and hot sandwiches. While he gassed the car, she spread the food out. He got in, drove to the shade, and they ate.

"How much aren't you telling me?" he asked.

There was too much for her to say and besides, it was all unbelievable. A man Henry's age and with his imagination was one thing, but Zack would be full of disbelief. "It's just the story Henry is writing. It's quite complex."

"And you're so involved in it that when you see where some town used to be, it makes you look like your dog died?"

Etta filled her mouth with food. "More or less." She could see that Zack knew she wasn't telling him everything, but she couldn't risk blabbing.

He'd bought chocolate oatmeal bars for dessert, and as they

were opening them, Etta's phone rang. It was Henry. "Yes… Yes," she said. "Thank you… Yes, he'll take photos… Yes, certainly." She put the phone down. "The door has been unlocked, and we can stay as long as we want."

"Great," Zack said. "Now we just need to find it."

The house was at the far end of the town. It was big and gaudily Victorian, with a huge tower in the middle. There was a large round, stained-glass window at the top, the only thing of beauty in the outlandish house. It was a house made to impress, not for beauty. Zack parked in front of it.

"Cornelia didn't design this," Etta said. "She has more taste."

"And who is Cornelia?"

"John Kecklin's daughter. I hope she and Bert moved to Kansas City." Etta quickly got out and shut the door. She practically ran away from Zack's coming questions of who and how. No wonder he and Henry got along so well as they were both insatiably curious. Of course it didn't help that Etta kept saying odd things.

Inside the house was the usual heavy, dark Victorian furniture. As with nearly all museums, it had no feeling of being lived in. Alice sometimes left her shoes in the living room. Max would toss his hat wherever he went. There was no Kansas mud, and the rug had no worn spots. And there were no smells anywhere.

Etta picked up a foldout history from a table next to a donation box. She put a twenty in the box. The brochure glorified John Kecklin. It said he was a saint of a man, a philanthropist, an all-round good and pure man who bettered the entire world.

Zack was reading a brochure. "Wow! No wonder Henry's writing about him. He sounds like a great guy."

"He was a megalomaniac who bullied his daughter mercilessly. But then if he hadn't, I wouldn't have…" She stopped.

"Wouldn't have what?"

Married Max, she didn't say. "Wouldn't have found him so interesting," she lied.

"Here's the Cornelia you mentioned." He looked at her. "She married a lawyer named Bertram Lloyd, and they moved to Kansas City." He looked back at the brochure. "It says Cornelia designed several houses in KC. Wait a minute. Did they build Henry's house?"

"Yes." Etta was glad to have a reason for Henry's interest. It sure beat saying "time travel."

"Now I'm beginning to understand his latest obsession."

Etta put the brochure in her pocket. "Henry wants photos."

"Sure." Zack pulled out his big camera.

Etta left him behind as she began to explore. It was great to be in a museum alone. She went to the kitchen and opened cabinets, picked up things and put them down. Everything was so sterile and clean, not like what she'd experienced at Max's house. The absence of abundant water certainly did change hygiene.

Leading out of the kitchen was a steep, narrow staircase for the servants. She'd never met John Kecklin, but she'd formed an opinion of him. He wasn't a man who'd want the help to be in his sight.

She went up the stairs to a long hallway. There were several closed doors. One of them was toward the front of the house. Kecklin would probably demand that his bedroom oversee what was going on in the town.

She opened the door, then gasped. On a mannequin was Cornelia's riding outfit. The green wool had faded, but it was still beautiful. A little placard said that Cornelia Kecklin had worn it to a speech given by her father in 1874.

"She wouldn't have worn her riding dress to a speech!" Etta muttered. "And where's her mean little whip?"

Her voice echoed in the room. She wanted to rewrite the placard. By 1874, surely Cornelia and Bert had left town. But which town did she leave? Garrett or this one Etta had never heard of? She wondered what John Kecklin had taken from Garrett to build this town that was named after him.

And why had this town survived but Garrett hadn't? *After I left, what did Max and Alice do?* she wondered. Alice probably went away with Pat and Nellie, so Max would have been left alone. Did he sell his empty house and move somewhere else?

She didn't want to think about that. She wanted to believe that she'd added to people's lives, not taken from them. And maybe she had. But not with Max. He was a quiet man, and his feelings ran deep. If Etta disappeared, never arrived on the train, he wouldn't recover from that.

"Hey!" Zack said from the doorway. "You look like you're in a trance."

"Just thinking. Be sure to photograph this outfit. Have you seen a riding crop around here?"

"Actually, I did. It's hanging on the wall of the little bedroom."

"I'm going to go see." She hurried out of the room. She opened three doors before she found the small bedroom at the end. It didn't have a bed but was filled with old things. She knew that half of them wouldn't have been used in 1871, but what did that matter? "They could put in a desktop telephone and kids today would think it was from the eighteenth century," she said, then shook head. "Etta, you are getting *old.*"

She slowly walked around the room, looking at the objects. By the door was a sign: Cornelia Kecklin Lloyd. Below it were things that had belonged to her. As Zack said, the riding crop was on the wall.

There was a glass case and in it was the beautiful parasol that Alice had made for Etta. It was opened to show that one of the panels had been cut and never repaired.

There was a card beside it: Property of Miss Cornelia Kecklin. Given to her by her illustrious father, John Kecklin. The cut is believed to have happened when Miss Cornelia fell at a town picnic put on by her father. A young lawyer, Bertram Lloyd, saved her from striking her head. This heroic act eventually led to their marriage.

Etta let out a snort of derision. "And novelists think they create fiction!" Part of her wanted to take the parasol. It belonged to *her*, not to Cornelia! She also wanted to put the riding crop with the green dress.

But Etta did neither. She was a guest and had no right to change anything. She found Zack and told him to photograph everything in the last bedroom. "Especially the parasol. Henry will want to see that." She went down the wide front stairs and left the house. She couldn't bear any more of the twisted glorification of John Kecklin.

Zack came out later. "I took photos of every inch of the place. I'll do the outside if you don't mind waiting."

"Go ahead." There were chairs on the porch, and she sat down in one. Only one car drove by, and she thought of the changes during this lockdown. But if she hadn't been caught in it, she wouldn't have met Henry. And she wouldn't have met Max.

When Zack returned, they went to his car and got in. "Where to now?"

"I'd like to see the homestead, but I don't know how to get there."

"Except on a horse," he said. "We know approximately where the house was, so close your eyes and describe how to go on a horse. I'll follow you on a map and see what I can find."

She did as he said, then opened her eyes and he was grinning broadly. "You have led us to a place called Garrett Creek."

She returned his smile. "Let's go!"

He started the car and pulled out. Minutes later, he stopped. The road had ended, but before them she could see the place she knew so well. She flung open the door and started running, Zack close behind her.

"Nature hasn't changed," she said. "The rocks are the same.

The water is less, but it's here. The trees are nearly the same. This is where—" She didn't say more than that.

Zack was looking at a nearby hill. "The sod house was over there?"

"Yes." They walked together to it, but there was no sign of what had been there. The roof and walls had long ago collapsed, and Kansas rain and abundant plant life had filled it in.

"Give me a backhoe and I bet we would find lots of stuff inside. Cans of peaches."

She turned away to look back at the stream. It hadn't been long ago that Alice and Pat had been there. Nellie was to the side with her new paint set. When Max got there, he'd expertly finished the painting. He'd been so angry about Alice and Pat, and—

"You're hypnotized again," Zack said. "We have drinks in the car. How about I get them and we sit by the water."

"That would be nice." He left, and she went to the place where Alice and Pat had sat and laughed. She couldn't help scanning the area to see if anything had been left behind. *Alice's shoes?* she thought, and smiled.

Zack handed her a drink and sat down on a rock. "It's quiet here. I can see why you like it. It seems to be a local make-out spot." He nodded to a tree where initials had been carved. "I better take pictures of that or Henry will beat me up."

Etta smiled. She felt like she never wanted to leave.

Zack walked around, taking many photos. He moved branches and weeds. When a pile of rocks fell, he jumped back, then snapped a photo of the pile. "Etta?" he said softly. "Look."

She turned toward the rocks. In the place that had been hidden, she saw that some letters had been chiseled into the stone.

"That says Etta," Zack said.

"No, it doesn't." She stood up and looked at it from another angle. It was worn and faded, but it did seem to be her name.

She clawed away rocks and plants. Below the name was an arrow pointing downward.

Zack was beside her. "There are two more letters, an *N* and an *A*."

"Nellie Adams." Etta sat back on the ground and stared at it.

"I'll be right back." Zack put down the camera bag, ran to the car, and returned with a small hand shovel. He held it up. "Once a farmer, always a farmer. Step back. I'm gonna dig."

He dug down about half a foot before he found anything. He held the shovel out, full of dirt and gravel. Something was sticking up.

When Etta saw it, she knew what it was. It was the little iron bear that Pat had made. He and Nellie gave it to her when she and Max left for their journey. "It's… It's…" she said.

"Do not cry," Zack said. "Please don't cry. I'm not good with women in tears."

Etta swallowed, blinked a lot, and took the bear out of the dirt on his shovel. She washed it in the stream. It had holes of deterioration and it was rusty, but Etta thought it was beautiful. She clutched it to her heart.

"Looks like it was buried there for you," he said. "Buried a long, long time ago." His expression was of astonishment mixed with some anger. He was realizing what he'd suspected. There were things he hadn't been told and lies that he had been told.

They sat in silence for a while. When Zack stood up, Etta realized that it was getting dark.

"We can try to find a motel that's open or we can drive back to Henry and KC. It'll take hours."

Her eyes answered him. She wanted to go home. To Henry. To wherever the connection to Max was. Maybe tonight she'd dream of him. Maybe she'd return to her long-ago family.

In the car, with the dark outside and quiet inside, too many memories were coming back to her. She looked at Zack. "Tell me things you and Henry have done together. Where did you go on the road trips?"

As in the past, Zack was a good storyteller. Best of all, he distracted her from her memories.

The next morning, Etta was last to get up. The door to the bedroom Zack had used was open, and the room was empty. Downstairs, on the table in the hall, was a box of vegetables. It looked like Freddy was also up. *Did she and Zack find each other?* Etta thought, smiling.

She found Henry in the library, his notebook open on his lap. "How far along are you?" She and Henry rarely indulged in small talk.

He grinned. "Wyatt Earp was just rescued. Tell me again how handsome he was."

"Not nearly as good-looking as Max. Shorter, shoulders more narrow, neck kind of scrawny, eyes that were—" She broke off. Henry's eyes were twinkling. "Brat. You have anything for me to type?"

"Some, not much."

She looked toward the open door. "Did you send them away? I don't hear anything."

"Last I saw, they were outside, staring at each other over tall drinks. Their eyes were full of stars. Seems that Henrietta has yet again shot the love arrow."

She laughed. "Cynic. I assume you know that he's Rufus, and she's the local..." Etta waved her hand.

"Max's go-to girl?"

"That's something we don't speak of. Have you been fed and watered?"

"Actually, no. Those two looked at each other and I no longer existed." He gave a melodramatic sigh.

"You poor thing." She stood up. "Anything new from Ben and Caroline? How's the baby?"

"I'll bring up my email. You'll have breakfast done by the time the internet engages."

She started out of the room. "Very funny. I can't wait to hear the connection shaking hands through your thirty-year-old router." Smiling, she went to the kitchen to make breakfast. She could see Zack and Freddy sitting outside. They did indeed seem fascinated with each other.

Etta made good ole Southern biscuits, then took some with butter and jam out to them. She didn't say a word as she set the plate on the table. But then, they didn't notice her.

She took eggs, bacon, and biscuits to the library to share with Henry.

"Thank you," he said.

They settled down to what had become normal—spending the day together in the library. After the road trip, her restlessness was gone. She was going through Zack's photos, and Henry was writing and editing. He was content.

When Zack and Freddy came to say they were leaving to go see her garden, Henry cleared his throat in a way that made Etta cut a look at him.

"Have fun," Etta told them. When they left, she looked at Henry. "You are a dirty old man."

"Hearing about you and Max is leading me astray. Breech-cloths hold all new meaning for me."

She shook her head in despair of him, but she was laughing.

By afternoon they'd received baby photos and Caroline wrote that she thought Henry's new story was the best thing he'd ever written.

Your heroine and her knife are magnificent. You should have carved *her* on the old desk.

Etta grinned in pride, while Henry looked at her in that way that said he was thinking hard.

"No, you can't tear out the back of the desk and redo it. It's beautiful as it is," Etta said. The truth was, she didn't think he was steady enough to safely handle chisels. She worried that he seemed to be getting weaker and less active each day.

At four, when she brought in tea with cold biscuits and jam, to her horror Henry was using a little screwdriver on the portrait of her and Max. She nearly screamed. "What are you doing?"

"I want to see something. Don't worry. I know how to do this. Aha! I was right." He held out the flat painting to her, with no surrounding frame. "See it?"

She was glad he hadn't damaged it with his tool.

"Bottom right. The signature."

There was a symbol at the bottom, an H.F. "Those are the artist's initials."

On the coffee table were some books written by Henry. He opened one to a watercolor of a cowboy on a bucking horse. In the lower right corner was the same H.F. signature.

"But your last name is Logan. Where's the *L*?"

He shrugged. "I came up with that mark when I was quite young. I thought the H.F. was cool, and I never changed it."

She was staring at him. "Henry, have *you* dreamed of that time? Were *you* there?"

"No," he said. "Not like you. But I think I must have been. On some level, Zack is reuniting with his past love, and I seem to remember things too."

"I want to go back," she said. "Like I want to live, I want to return to Max and Alice and all of them. I want to have babies and cook and...and do all those things. I want—" She quit talking and went to sit on the floor by Henry. She needed to be close to someone who knew and understood.

"I think you will return," he said. "There's a reason behind all of this, and I don't think it's finished."

"Yeah?" She had hope in her voice. "But when?"

"When you find out that reason, I think you'll go back."

They both looked at Henry's bookcases. Was the answer in there? Did those books hold the key that would open the past again? Was something in them that would take her back? "Where do I begin?"

"Look at people. Marshal Earp was the catalyst the last time, so find someone else who's missing."

"That will be my quest." The use of Max's word almost made her cry, but she didn't allow herself to break. She grabbed a book at random and began to read.

It was late on the third search day, and she and Henry were reading. When she saw him grow pale, she jumped up. "What do you need?"

"I'm fine. How about some gin and tonics?"

"That's a joke, right?"

"No gin for me but lots for you. You're so jumpy I can't concentrate."

"Sorry," she said, and a drink did sound good. In the kitchen, squeezing the limes made her remember the dinner party with Bert and Cornelia and Alice and— She made herself stop. Henry would say she was being impatient, but she was losing hope of ever seeing Max again. She'd started having flashes of *What am I going to do with my life?* Before Max she'd been happy. Well, maybe a little lonely after Alicia, Phillip and Nola moved out, but she wasn't unhappy. She had a good job and friends and her father and… Everything.

Now all she saw was what was missing in her life.

She took the drinks in to Henry and they sipped them slowly. Etta was reading yet another book about Old West bad guys and gals, and people who'd done things that formed the country. It was frustrating that she couldn't find anything or anyone who was missing.

When her drink was finished and she was relaxed, Henry handed her a book opened to chapter twelve. He'd stuck a marker at a paragraph about the Cheyenne Raid of 1868. It said that the battle was considered so insignificant that it was rarely mentioned in any history book. The Cheyenne had declared that they were going to "clean out the Kaws." About a hundred warriors, a third of them Arapahos, paraded through Council Grove in full, glorious regalia, on their way to the attack. Some accounts said the nearby settlers hid in fear, and some said they watched from a distance. Whichever, there was a magnificent display of horsemanship accompanied by war cries and volleys of bullets and arrows. After four hours, the Cheyenne took a few Kanza horses and the local merchants gave out sugar and coffee, then everyone went home.

In the end, two warriors, one Kanza, one Cheyenne, were wounded, but no one was killed.

She handed the book back, and looked hard at him. His face was solemn. "What else do you want me to see?"

He handed her another book, again with a passage flagged. There was an almost verbatim repeat of the 1868 conflict, but this one added another incident to it. It said that the Cheyenne were angry that the Kaws had taken too many buffalo on their last hunt. On Sunday, May 14, 1871, they returned to finish the job of "cleaning them out." But this time, they were success- ful. They killed all the Kanza in that one camp, including the chief and his family. Afterward, the Kanzas, already depleted by smallpox, pneumonia, and lack of food and medicine, were on their way to extinction. The 1871 massacre almost eradi- cated the entire tribe.

She looked at the cover of the book, then at Henry. "That wasn't in there before. I read this whole book and scanned through it yesterday. There was no mention of a massacre in 1871."

"It's only a few sentences. It's easy to miss." He gave her a hard stare. "It's history. It doesn't change."

Etta stood up. "I have proven that history is liquid. It can be changed. *I* changed it by putting Wyatt Earp back into the world."

When Henry hesitated in replying, Etta's lips tightened. "You don't believe me because you don't remember telling me that you'd never heard of the marshal. But you *did* say it. And my father told me the same thing. He texted me even though it's gone now." Her eyes widened. "*Google* had never heard of him."

"In that case it has to be true."

She glared at him. "You're laughing at me."

"I can assure you that I'm not."

"Don't you see how horrible this is? I changed history in a bad way. Me and the knife Rufus gave me made this happen. *I* did it."

Henry said, "Perhaps…"

Etta gritted her teeth. "Perhaps what?"

"If this wasn't in the book when you read it before, maybe that means time is passing. Think about it. You're not there now, so maybe time is going forward without you."

"That would mean Max and Alice are alone. They'd think I left them. It's what I've feared so much." Her head came up. "Wait a minute. If this has already happened and I wasn't there, then…"

"Then even if you went back, you couldn't change it. It's not like the lawman. That hadn't happened so you could rewrite history."

"But not now."

"You don't know what happened after you left or how long it's been. Or what date you'd arrive next time. You could show up in 1902 for all we know. We have no control over this thing."

She dropped down onto the chair. "This horror was all my fault. I helped with the buffalo. I must change it back. It's my responsibility."

"You mean you'd return and not help with the buffalo? How would that be possible?"

She put her hands over her face. "I don't know what I mean."

"Maybe it was fate. Kismet. Maybe you couldn't prevent it whether you're there or not."

"That's not right," she said. "There has to be something I could do. I'd warn Lester. Whatever I had to do, I'd *do* it."

"Unless it has already happened," Henry said softly. He looked at her in sympathy. "Sometimes I forget the energy and the beliefs of the power of youth. Maybe you could have changed things. I think it would be great if you could."

She looked at him. "I'm very tired. I think I'll go to bed. What about you?"

"Soon. I want to read a bit more."

He gave her such a look of tenderness that she went to sit on the edge of the couch and put her head on his chest. "Henry..."

He stroked her hair. "Yes, I know. You're the daughter I never had." He kissed her forehead. "Go to bed and dream of your dear Max. I think it's time that you found him."

"So do I." She kissed his cheek, then stood up. "I'll see you in the morning."

"I will always be with you," he said. "Remember that. Always."

They smiled at each other.

Upstairs, Etta took a long, hot shower and washed her hair. When she got into Ben's childhood bed, she held the little iron bear tightly in her hand, and went to sleep.

Right away, she heard the clickety-clack of a train on the tracks.

Etta gave a smile of such happiness that it went down to her very soul.

17

It was raining hard as Zack made his way to the door of Henry's small house in the back. Zack hadn't been asleep for a day and a half, not since Henry sent him a PDF of the book he was writing.

When Zack started it, he thought it was nice of Henry to use the names of real people. It was interesting to see how the people were portrayed, both past and present.

He wasn't sure when he began to think the story was *real*. Was it when he read of the blacksmith and the bear? Of the initials of the daughter's name? They were connected to what Zack had found buried by the stream. And Etta had said the sod house would be full of canned peaches. Like Max in the story ate.

It was late afternoon when Zack finished the book. There was something deep in his brain that was trying to find its way out, but he couldn't quite remember it.

He made himself a sandwich and tried to forget what he'd

read. It was too fantastic, too outrageous. If he thought it was true, he'd have to believe he was the reincarnation of his ancestor, Rufus. That they both had leg injuries was just a coincidence.

And then there was Freddy. True, he'd just met her and he did feel like he'd known her forever. But that happened to a lot of people. It was *not* some cock-and-bull story of reincarnation. And it was ridiculous that a nice girl like Freddy had worked in the Red Dog saloon as a…as a…

As he poured himself a beer, he tried to clear his mind. Writers wrote about what they knew, didn't they? That's what Henry and Etta had done. Henry was an expert historian and Etta could cook. It all worked.

It was as Zack started to sit down that he remembered what was bothering him. There was a book written by a family member. He'd read it when he was a kid. Why was he remembering it now?

What was in it that had made him think of it?

He called his father and asked about the book. Yes, his dad remembered it and knew where it was.

"I'll be there in about thirty minutes," Zack said and hung up.

That had been hours ago and now he was outside Henry's door, waiting to show him the book.

Henry was still dressed and looked like he hadn't been to bed. He stepped back and Zack went inside. He pulled a plastic-wrapped package from under his raincoat. "I went to Ottawa and got this from my dad." He held up a thin black book. "It was written and self-published by my great-grand uncle in 1923. The front says that only twenty copies were printed, and they were given to family and friends. I haven't looked at it in years. I came straight here because there's something in it… I'm not sure what. It's just a vague memory."

He handed the book to Henry, who flipped through it quickly, then abruptly halted. As he read, his eyes widened, then he collapsed into a chair.

"Are you okay?" Zack asked, and Henry nodded. "What does it say?"

When Henry looked up, he seemed to have aged. "We can't let her go back."

Zack snatched the book from him and read.

I was told there was a failed attempt to prevent the massacre of the Kanzas in 1871. It wasn't reported at the time, but a white woman was among those killed. She was the wife of a prominent landowner, and her body was taken away before the cavalry and the press arrived. I've never read any accounts that said she was there. I only know what my ninety-three-year-old grandfather, Rufus, told me. His memory was usually quite accurate, but it may have been off about this.

"We can't let her return," Henry said again.

Zack saw his worry. "I'm not sure that what you wrote about Etta's dreams is true, but if she's killed in the past, wouldn't she just wake up here? Alive and well?"

Henry frowned. "I'm afraid I'm not an expert on time travel. You know anyone we can call and ask?"

Zack knew when he was being told off. "You're right. The best thing is if we don't let her go back. She's in the house, upstairs, right? We'll just explain things, then she'll stay here."

Henry heaved himself up out of the chair. "I haven't known Etta long, but I can assure you that if she reads this it will make her even more determined to return. And I've seen the bruises her so-called dreams did to her body. A death in 1871 just might play forward. I don't want to risk it."

Zack thought about what Henry said. "So let's do what we must to keep her here."

"This should be easy," Henry said with sarcasm.

They went into the big house together, then, against Zack's protests, Henry went up the stairs with him.

Etta was curled up on the bed, sleeping.

"Etta?" Zack said. "You need to wake up."

There was no response from her.

He took her shoulders and lifted her. Her head fell back, but she didn't wake. He yelled, but there was no response. "We should call an ambulance."

"No," Henry said. "She'll sleep wherever she is. I'll stay here with her and monitor her breathing. If it slows down, we'll call." He saw that Zack was hesitating. "In her state and with that virus in the air, I don't want to risk it."

Zack didn't seem to know what to do. "She looks happy."

"I think she's probably very happy. She's with Max."

"For a while. Then she will…" The men looked at each other.

"Why don't you go get us something to eat?" Henry said. "Etta filled the fridge."

"Okay." When Zack got downstairs, he saw the little black book. Henry had brought it into the house and left it on the table. When Zack picked it up, it fell open to the back. The first thing he saw was a footnote.

Grandpa Rufus said the published date of the 1871 massacre was off by days. He said the wrong date was printed. Everyone quoted it as the fourteenth, but it really happened on the nineteenth. Grandpa said that's why the woman's attempt to prevent it failed, and why she was killed. I didn't include this in my account because it makes no sense. A wrong date given after the event wouldn't matter. But, as I said, Grandpa was very old.

Zack bounded up the stairs two at a time and thrust the book at Henry.

When he finished reading it, he was shaking. He was in a

chair by Etta's bedside. "She went on the date the newspaper said it took place," Henry said in disgust. "But it didn't. Not on Sunday, but on the following Friday."

"Somehow, Etta found out when it was really about to happen," Zack said.

"And she went alone," Henry said. "She wasn't able to prevent the tragedy, and she was killed along with everyone else." He took her hand in both of his. "Etta!" he said loudly. "Do not go alone. Take Max with you. Not alone! Do you hear me?"

"Yeah, Max," Zack said. He pulled a chair to the other side of the bed and took Etta's hand in his. "Take Max. He'll protect you."

"And maybe he'll talk some sense into you," Henry said in disgust.

"Yeah, that too," Zack added.

Henry squeezed her hand. "Do not go alone. Do you understand? Not alone!"

They didn't leave Etta's side.

18

When Etta woke, she didn't open her eyes. She was afraid she'd see Ben's curtains. The fact that she could hardly breathe could be due to covers wrapped around her.

Or it could be a corset.

She crossed her fingers in hope. She would have crossed her toes, but they were jammed into shoes that were way too tight. Were they the dress shoes the woman in Van Buren said were what all the fashionable ladies were wearing?

Cautiously, Etta opened her eyes a tiny bit. She was on a train.

She squeezed them closed again. Was it too much to hope that she was on the train Max had put her on? Or maybe it was like Henry said and it was 1902 or 1950s New York? Somewhere else in time and place?

"It looks like you're feeling better."

She finally opened her eyes to see the porter. He was the

same man who'd helped her when she left Max, and he was waiting for a reply.

"What is today's date?" she asked.

"The seventh of May, the year of our Lord, 1871. You must be hungry after all the sleeping you've been doing."

Etta's mind nearly clogged with flashing bits of all she'd done since she'd seen this man. Henry, Zack, Freddy, the flattened town of Garrett, the glorification of John Kecklin, the massacre of 1871. It jumbled together like a two-minute recap of a twenty episode TV series. "I, uh…" she managed to say.

"You just stay there and rest. You'll be home in minutes."

His look said, *And then you'll be someone else's responsibility.* He hurried down the aisle.

Etta saw that she had on a different dress from the one she'd been wearing when she boarded, so she'd changed. She wondered what she'd been like during the days she was on the train. According to the porter, she hadn't been well. *I was a zombie,* she thought. *No soul, just a body.*

As the train began to slow, she looked out the window. Sitting on a buckboard, his muscles covered by a big shirt, was her brother-in-law, Phillip, reincarnated as Pat, the blacksmith.

I will not cry in joy, she thought, then in her mind, she yelled, *Henry, I'm here!*

She'd meant her thought as fun, but she frowned. It was almost as though she could hear Henry. He was saying that he was alone. "I'm sorry," she whispered. "I'll—" She started to say that she'd return, but she knew she didn't want to go back. Not ever.

She waved at Pat and he raised his hand in greeting.

Out of habit, Etta looked about for her luggage, but no, it wasn't the twenty-first century. This was a time when women were thought to be weak and helpless and needed to be taken care of. The thought made her smile. "So much for female empowerment," she said and kept smiling.

Pat's big hands encased her newly small waist, and he swung her down to the wooden platform of dear little Garrett, Kansas.

"Is he back yet?" she asked.

Pat gave a smile of knowing who she meant. "No. Give him another couple of days." He picked up her big leather bag and she saw another one being put on the wagon. Pat helped her up to the seat.

When he sat by her and took the reins, she said, "Anything new with you?"

They looked at each other and laughed. They didn't need to say that his life and his daughter's and Alice's had changed completely.

"Tell me everything," she said. She knew Phillip had never been much of a talker except to people he knew and liked. That this version of him talked with her at ease felt like an honor.

Pat told her that Nellie was staying in a bedroom on the ground floor of Max's house. "The room near Alice's." The way he said her name made Etta smile broadly. "I don't know what Mr. Lawton will say to that."

"Max will be fine with it. So when's the wedding?"

Pat stopped smiling. "I can't ask her that. I'm not up to her level. I couldn't..." He trailed off. "Miss Alice is teaching Nellie. It's kind of her to do it. She may open a school."

Etta knew her sister didn't have the patience to be a schoolteacher. Alicia liked grownups and all their complexities. Etta turned her attention back to Pat. "You're right. Alice needs a less physical man than you. She's such a delicate little flower. Let's find her a dandy who tiptoes around."

As she'd hoped, Pat smiled at that image. Alice was not "delicate." And she was a very "physical" person. It looked like Pat had discovered that aspect of her.

Again, they laughed together.

"I need to get some supplies," he said. "Do you mind waiting?"

"I would love to just sit and look at this town."

He stopped in front of the mercantile, tied the horses, and went inside.

Etta looked around the town at the buildings. There were a couple of alleys but mostly things were slammed together tightly. How could every inch of this town have disappeared so completely? When she and Zack visited, she hadn't seen so much as a piece of iron. It had been just flat land.

The yelling of a man made her turn toward the sound. Down the street, three men were on top of a house. It was larger than the other houses, and the roof was steep. The men were holding ropes, and they appeared to be pulling something up.

Pat returned with two fifty-pound bags of flour, one on each shoulder. He was a living display of masculinity at its finest. If she had her phone, she would have made a video of Pat carrying the sacks then unloading them into the back of the wagon. *I'd show it to Alice*, she thought, but then she grinned. *Ha! I'd put it on TikTok and share it with the world.*

Pat looked at her, seeming to ask what was in her mind.

"What's going on over there?"

"While you were gone, we got a new doctor," he said proudly. "Came in from the East with his wife and two daughters. He bought the Oldham house and added on a story. He says that fancy window is his wife's dowry. She wouldn't come unless he brought it with them. You want something from the store?"

"Peaches." After he left, Etta looked at what the men were dragging up to the new second story.

When it was turned around, she drew in her breath. The stained-glass window was about two feet in diameter, a Victorian abstract of greens with bits of blue and pink. It was quite beautiful, and it was the window she'd seen at the top of John Kecklin's house. Did he steal it when he built the town he named after himself?

Etta looked around the town like she was on a scavenger

hunt. She tried to remember everything she'd seen in Kecklin. Were there other things that came from Garrett? There was a carved post on one of the saloons. Didn't she see that some-where else? A saloon was called the French Quarter, and it had a pretty iron railing on the upstairs balcony. Etta was sure she'd seen that in Kecklin.

Down the road was the church where she'd been married. It was a rough building, but the door had a round top. Wasn't that also on a building in Kecklin?

Her hair seemed to stand on end as she felt someone staring at her. A man in his sixties was sitting on a large black horse, and he was glaring at Etta. She'd never seen him in person, but there had been enough pictures of him in the museum to know he was John Kecklin.

As though he owned the world, he reined his horse toward her and stopped just a few feet away.

He was a man of normal height, but his horse was very tall so he looked down at her. *Compensating much?* she thought.

She didn't flinch at his glare, which was obviously meant to intimidate her. "You look just like my daughter said."

The "old and plain" hit. That was a slap in the face! Etta didn't let him know she was affected by his words. She smiled sweetly at him. "You'll have to come to dinner. My get-togethers are very productive." She was reminding him of how she'd taken away his dream of uniting Max's land with his.

A darkness went across his face. "Be careful of the fire you play with. Sometimes people get burned." He didn't wait for her reply but jerked the reins and left.

Pat came around the wagon. "You all right?"

Her heart was beating hard. "That man is a nasty piece of work. Poor Cornelia. No wonder she tried so hard to get Max. Anything to get that monster off her back." Etta let out her breath. "How are Cornelia and Bert getting along?"

"They're a good match, and from what I've seen, the lawyer holds his own with Kecklin."

"Good," Etta said.

It took Pat another half hour to fill the wagon with supplies, and Etta stayed on the seat and waited. She wanted time to accustom herself to living in the past again.

How long? she thought. *How long will it last this time? And what am I supposed to do while I'm here?* It was days before the Cheyenne would show up. She knew that Max would help her with that. But then, he always did help her.

She twisted about on the seat and looked at the town. The first time she'd seen it, she'd thought of all that was wrong with it. Too many saloons, too much manure, not enough bathing of the inhabitants.

But now all she could see was good. The town had played a part in building a great state, and a great nation.

Pat climbed up to the seat beside her. "Ready to go home?"

"Very much so." As he pulled out onto the muddy, smelly, beloved road, she said, "Tell me every word about everyone. I feel like I've been away for a lifetime. How is Rufus's leg? Have you seen Martha Garrett? Oh! Have you seen Henry the painter? Is he—"

Etta broke off because she saw a woman leave the dressmaker's shop, turn the corner, and disappear out of sight. "Who is she?" Etta whispered.

Pat was dealing with the horses. "Who? I didn't see anyone new."

Etta turned back in the seat. She knew it was no use badgering Pat, but Etta thought it was possible that she'd just seen her mother. Her dear mother who'd died so many years ago.

"Well," Pat said. "Let's see. Rufus is fine. Cantankerous as usual. And he seems to—"

"Like Freddy," Etta said absently.

"How'd you know that? You haven't even been here."

She was staring at the corner of the building where the woman had been. "Long story." She looked back at Pat. "What about Martha?"

Pat answered Etta's questions all the way home.

Three days! Etta thought. Three whole days of waiting. *Just like with Henry.* But this time, the problem wasn't boredom. The fourteenth of May, the day the massacre was to happen, was drawing near. With each hour Etta was becoming more anxious, and she could tell no one what her problem was. What could she say? That she'd had a premonition that people were going to be killed? She even knew the date. She'd be laughed at. Or thought to be crazy.

Max was the only person who listened to her and believed her. But he wasn't *here*!

In 1869, the Cheyenne had paraded through town, letting everyone know of their intentions. But now they were angry about the success of the buffalo hunt so maybe this time, they'd sneak in.

She'd done her best to keep busy. She didn't want to give herself time to think about what could happen. She'd put Rufus and Freddy together half a dozen times. She'd started regularly buying produce from the Mexicans. She wanted to introduce something besides beef and beans to the diet of Max's men. She'd come up with things for Pat to make so he wasn't forced to return to town. And she showed him how to hide the portrait in a drawer in the desk when he got it. When he asked why, she mumbled, "Just in case," but didn't elaborate. She spent time with her father, aka Tobias, and had managed to coerce three more saloons into hiring him to do their bookkeeping.

She'd talked to Alice about opening a school in town—where teachers could be hired. The brace Pat made for her foot worked so well that she was at last going out in public.

Etta was glad to see that Sally was still singing at the church services. She cajoled her into adding a short sermon to her songs. "Whatever is needed to get them in here."

Cornelia came by twice, both times with Bert. Other than Alice, Cornelia had never had many women friends. "Too rich, too beautiful," Etta muttered.

Bert heard her and added, "And too much of her father in her. I want to take her away from here and from him."

"Kansas City will welcome you."

"Or Wichita," he said. "We haven't decided which city we'll go to."

Etta replied, "How about another margarita and let's talk about it." She wasn't going to let Henry down so his house ended up being built in another city.

She'd kept busy to the point where everyone in town knew who she was. She liked being called Mrs. Lawton. The fact that some of the saloon owners vanished when she saw them didn't bother her. They were afraid she'd steal their best girls or bully them into hiring Tobias, then he'd see the truth about their finances. Who wanted their money overseen by a preacher?

What Etta hadn't been able to do was find Henry the painter or the woman she'd seen leaving the dressmaker's shop. Alice and Etta visited the dressmaker when they went to get Freddy some new outfits for around the house. Her regular attire was causing too much distraction for the men. She'd asked, but the dressmaker had no idea who she meant.

Etta had asked around town about the painter, but people said, "He comes and he goes." No one knew much about Henry.

She rode to Martha's farm but didn't see her.

What she didn't do was visit the homestead. She too vividly remembered when she'd seen it as grassland. And besides, that was her private place to be with Max.

It was at the night of the third day, as she got into Max's big, empty bed, that Etta thought maybe she was overstepping the rules of her time there. She could deal with anything old, but new things, like Henry, Martha, and the woman she'd seen, had to wait for Max to be with her.

"Max is everything," she said as she hugged his pillow. "It all revolves around him."

On the morning of the fourth day, Saturday, she was so nervous she was jumping at every little sound. Max still wasn't there. So what was she going to do to prevent what she knew was coming? Whatever she decided, it looked like she'd have to do it alone. Would going to Lester and warning him be enough? Or would he ignore her, a woman?

She was sitting high up on the seat of the buckboard. Rufus was driving, and Freddy, in her new, modest calico dress, was between them. Etta's plan was to gather and buy enough food that this afternoon she could go to the Kanza with gifts. Then what? Blackmail them into leaving? *You get the food if you pack up and leave?* Or would hiding be enough? What if they all went to town for the day? Or visited Max's house?

She wasn't prepared for when she heard the voice she most wanted to hear.

"Any room for me?"

She twisted around so hard and so fast that Freddy grabbed Etta's arm to keep her from falling out.

It wasn't necessary because when Etta saw Max, she just plain fell onto him. She was a foot above him when she let go.

He gave a grunt when her full body hit him and he staggered back a few steps as he fought for balance.

As for Etta, she was like a baby monkey. Her legs wrapped around his waist, her arms around his neck, her face buried in his flesh.

The people who'd seen it were at first too astonished to react, but then they repressed their laughter.

Rufus flicked the reins and drove away, and the men around them quickly left the area.

Max and Etta were alone.

"Miss me?" He was laughing.

She didn't lift her head, just nodded.

"So you sat around and waited for me?"

"Busy," she said, her lips on his sweaty neck.

"That's what I heard. I rode through town and I was told that you are the worst and the best. Some people want you to be mayor, but others want me to run you out of town."

Etta kept her head down and shrugged. It couldn't be helped.

"I heard you met John Kecklin."

"He stole a window."

"What?" Max was still holding her full weight, and he shifted her a bit. "Window. He stole it to use for his house in Kecklin."

He pulled back to look at her. "He set up a town while I was gone?"

Again she shrugged.

"How about we go to the homestead and you can tell me everything? And we can go swimming."

Instantly, Etta dropped her legs, stood, and started toward the barn to get a horse.

He caught her hand. "Did you forget something?"

She put her arms around his neck and they kissed. In it was all the loneliness and fear she'd felt while she was away from him. It wasn't a kiss of passion but of loss and tears.

He broke away, frowning, and stroked her hair. "Something bad happened, didn't it? On the train? Did someone in Garrett do something to you?"

She wanted to say, *I was taken away from you*, but she didn't. She cuddled against his chest, his big arms enveloping her. She hadn't been safe in so long that she almost didn't remember how it felt. "No, no one. I was worried about you. You took a long time to get here. I was afraid I'd never see you again."

"I had a flooded river and I ran into some trappers. All the usual things. Daisy missed you. She got used to the way you pull the reins then let them go too loose, then pull some more. We had a long talk about you."

She didn't move. She never wanted to leave the comfort of his arms.

"So no swimming? Too bad as I need someone to dry my back."

"If I must," she said, and they smiled in anticipation.

19

A saddled horse had magically appeared near them. It looked like everyone knew where Max and Etta were going.

There was only one horse with one saddle, and it was all they needed. Max lifted Etta into place. She moved forward, and he climbed on behind her.

For a moment she closed her eyes in the ecstasy of being so close to him.

They didn't speak as they rode to the homestead. Their vibrating bodies said all that was needed.

He stopped in front of the dugout, and Etta felt joy in seeing it whole and intact.

When he got down, he held up his arms to her. She didn't fall but gave herself over to the strength of him as he set her on the ground. He took her hand and they went inside.

There was the urge to rip and tear at their clothes, but there was also the desire to make it all last. As they undressed, hurriedly but not frantically, their eyes were locked.

Naked, Etta lay down on the narrow bed. She saw that Max was ready for her. In one movement, he was on her and inside her. Their pent-up wanting and needing of each other made them hold on tight.

He had days of sweat and grime on him. Was there anything more masculine than a man covered in the product of *work*? Not paper shuffling, but lifting and hauling and doing physical labor. The smell of him, the taste of his skin, was as exciting as feeling him inside her. The sheer strength of him made her feel that she might pass out from the deep pleasure of it.

It was only moments later that they came together, unable to prolong what they both wanted so much.

She tried to hold him inside her. That closeness of being linked, conjoined, of being one person, made her legs tighten, her arms holding him to her.

But he did slip out. He moved so her head was on his arm. For all that the bed was narrow, at the moment they could have been on a single iron track and it would have been enough room.

Etta's hands were on him, her legs clasped about him. When she tightened her body, she realized she was willing his precious seed to stay inside her. She wanted it to travel upward.

Baby Lust, she thought. Her psychologist sister had spoken of it. "It's primal!" she'd said. "It's ancient and very, very strong. When it overtakes a woman, it's all-consuming."

All Etta knew was that more than anything in the world, she wanted Max's baby. Maybe if she were carrying it, she'd never leave. And if she were taken away, the unborn child might stay with her. Her body changed from her time with him so why not change it forever?

As though he knew her thought, his hand went to her belly, and she clasped both of hers over his, holding his hand there.

His fingertips curled slightly, as though he was helping her keep him inside her.

They stayed still for minutes, not speaking in words but saying everything. They were sharing the essence of themselves with each other.

After long minutes, he readjusted her body so she was facing him. She was glued to him, their legs together as almost one.

"You are different," he said.

Fatter, she thought, and remembered sitting in Zack's car and eating a huge bread roll filled with meat and cheese and grilled vegetables. That one sandwich was more than she ate in a day in Max's time. On their long journey it was more than the two of them ate in days. "When you're not around, I eat too much."

"It's more than that. You are..." He hesitated. "You don't seem like a wild horse fighting to get back to open land."

His perception made her smile. "Even after I nearly knocked you down?"

"Especially then."

"I've come to appreciate what I have at this moment. Here. Now. Not the past. And certainly not the future."

He pulled back to look at her. "You have no impossible tasks to do? No one to save? No marriages to plan?"

She laughed. "Well, actually, I did have a dream that the Cheyenne rode through the town before they attacked the Kanzas on the fourteenth of May. Tomorrow. Sunday." She was holding her breath, her eyes begging him to believe her.

He looked at her for a moment, then gave a smile. "Then we'll visit them. Many of us will go. With rifles."

She released some of her fear. "But the next day they might show up."

"I'll warn the agent and he'll warn me. Forewarned is forearmed."

"Thank you." The rest of her fear left her. She'd known that Max would know what to do. Yet again, he was the savior.

"What else?" he asked.

She didn't want to start listing things she felt needed to be done. She looked at the familiar interior of the sod house. Max's childhood home. How could it disappear so completely?

"Well?" he asked. "What more do you plan to fix? *Who* else?"

"I did think of Henry."

He looked blank.

"The painter?"

Max leaned over, picked up his trousers off the floor, and withdrew the miniature portrait and opened it. "What was it you told me to do? Hide it in the desk?" He was amused.

She tried not to remember how she'd awakened in Henry's house and how she'd searched for the portrait. Or how miserable she'd been when she found it. She was glad she'd shown Pat where to hide it.

"You've gone off again. What about the painter?"

"I want to invite him to dinner. I want him to meet Martha Garrett."

Max gave a scoff of disbelief. "That's not good. Henry is a gentle, quiet man. I've seen him walk into half a dozen prancing, nervous horses and they calmed down. But Martha…"

"She walks into a pack of sheep and they start fighting?"

"Worse. She'd probably pick Henry up, break him into pieces, and throw him to the hogs. I don't think putting them together is a good idea."

"I agree with whatever you think we should do."

He rolled over to look at her with wide eyes. "Did you just say that I might be *right*?" He put his hand to his ear. "Tell me again. I want to remember it always."

She repressed a smile. "With the law of averages, you're bound to be right at least once."

With a groan, he rolled off of her, but she stretched out on top of him, touching nothing but him. "It would just be a dinner party. We'll see what happens."

"Your last dinner party made Alice say she hated me."

"And look how that turned out. Cornelia no longer tries to cut your ears off, and Alice is madly, passionately in love."

"With an oversized blacksmith. I'm afraid he's going to fall on her and crush her."

Etta was serious. "Beautiful naked men on top of you are weightless."

Max clenched his teeth.

"Too soon?"

He blinked at the unfamiliar term. "You say the oddest things."

"And you *do* the oddest things. Where did you learn about watercolors? You were brilliant with Nellie."

"That was the first time I ever picked up a paintbrush." He paused. "That's all? Just Henry and Martha?"

"Well… Your sister wants to open a school."

That absurdity made him laugh so deeply she could feel it in his stomach.

"That's just what I thought too, but I saw a woman in town who might be able to run a school."

"Who is she?"

"No idea. She was leaving the dressmaker, but she didn't know who the woman was. I'd know her if I saw her again, so—"

"You and I have to go searching. Like finding your blacksmith. I hope the woman is smaller. No matchmaking?"

"I, uh, think Tobias and the woman might be a pair."

"He'll like that. What else?"

"That's all."

"Sure?"

"I think so, but then Rufus and Freddy caught me by surprise."

He looked at her as though trying to figure out something. He lifted her off of him, got out of bed, pulled on his trousers, then turned back to her. "Since I met you so many strange things have happened. I thought about it all as I came back." He looked at her nude body stretched out on the bed. "I think better when you're not there to distract me." He gave her a serious look. "Do you think that what is between us is...?" He didn't finish.

"Normal?" she asked. "Is this what other people feel?"

He nodded. Yes, that's what he meant.

"I don't know about other people," she said, "but I do know that I've come a very long way to find you. Not even time has been able to keep me away from you." She swallowed as tears were coming to her. "This time, I want to stay. With all my heart and soul, I want to be with you forever."

"Why wouldn't you be? Barring death, we'll be together."

"Death. That's the easy one. I worry about the end of dreams, and worse, of never dreaming again." She looked at him. "I fear not seeing you. There'll be a time when all of this—" she waved her hand about "—all of this will be gone. As though it never existed. Places and people will be forgotten. I—"

He took her hand and pulled her out of bed. "You're only allowed to cry in happiness. Let's go get in the water and wash off." He cocked an eyebrow at her. "Usually, you're mincing about over this." He raised his hand with finger and thumb extended, as though holding something smelly. His face had a look of disgust. "This isn't clean," he said in a high, mocking tone. "How can I touch this if it isn't cleaner than Kansas sunshine?"

"I don't sound like that!"

"Ha! I'm surprised you touched *me*. I must smell like a horse."

She was serious. "And that's why I tolerate you. You wouldn't mind putting on your shirt and pouring water over yourself, would you?"

"So I look like my men?" He sounded shocked.

She shrugged. "You could do worse."

He grabbed her to him and kissed her, then held her head

against his bare chest. "You make me laugh." He stroked her hair. "Before I met you, I thought my life was complete, that I needed no one else."

"Me too. I thought I had everything."

They held each other for a long moment, then she pulled away. "You do stink. I better give you a bath. What body part should I start with?"

"Your choice," Max said, grinning. "Just so you get every piece."

"I will do my absolute best."

Laughing, they ran to the stream.

It was the morning of the fourteenth of May, *the* day, and Etta was sitting in church beside Alice and Nellie. Pat wasn't there. But then, the only man in the church was John Kecklin. She'd never seen him there before, but today he was making a point to Etta.

Yesterday, she and Max had a rip-roaring, blistering argument.

Actually, the anger had all come from her. Max had been so calm it was like arguing with a mountain made of granite. In fiction, a strong, silent man sounded good, but in real life, it was infuriating.

When they returned home from their day of laughter and love at the homestead, Etta had done what she was good at. She'd started organizing things. First, she told the men what food was to be taken to the Kanzas the next day.

Max had come up behind her and said, "I'll take care of this."

"Thank you," she said. "We'll leave early in the morning. I don't know when—"

"Go to the house," he said in a tone she'd never heard before.

But it was a voice the men recognized because they instantly disappeared. Poof. Max the boss was there, and they obeyed him without question.

She whirled around to face him. "Why did you do that? I need them to help me prepare for tomorrow."

He didn't smile. "This is my territory, and I will deal with it. Go into the house."

"And be the little wifey?" she snapped at him. "Keep to the stove where I belong?" She saw his eyes flicker at her words since he'd never before heard feminist rhetoric. "I am a person first and I—"

"If you don't leave, I will carry you inside. I don't think you want anyone to see that."

Her eyes blinked rapidly, then she softened and put her hand on his chest. "Max," she said sweetly. "I have things to do. I must…" His eyes didn't change, and she knew he'd carry out his threat. She gritted her teeth. "We'll talk about this later." With as much dignity as she could muster, she went into the house.

Inside, she chopped onions and cooked beef even faster than usual. She was furious! How dare he treat her like that? He had no right.

When Max came into the house, he sat down at the table, and Etta plopped a plate heaped with food in front of him.

"I don't like being treated like that," she said. "When we get to the Kanzas tomorrow, you can't—"

He didn't look at her. "You aren't going. You're staying here."

"No, I'm not."

He didn't reply, just kept eating.

She sat down beside him. "Max, I must go. Lester, the chief, knows me. He trusts me. He'll listen to me."

"You are not going," he said calmly, firmly. It was his rock voice.

Over the next hour, Etta talked and Max listened in silence.

She reasoned with him. She spoke of women's rights and of centuries of being held down by men. She emphasized that she knew about events and people, things he didn't know.

Max didn't so much as bend. The only answer she got from him was, "No." She was *not* going with him to the Kanzas.

When they went upstairs to their bedroom, Etta burst into tears. She *had* to go.

For the first time, he responded more fully. "Then you will go without me and my men. You have two choices—with men and guns, or with women with your hat pins. The choices will not be combined. If there is to be a battle, women will not be present."

Etta put her hands on her hips. "Women can fight. We can—" When she looked at his face, she knew she wasn't going to win. She sat down on the bed beside him. "I can help. Please let me go."

"No," he said.

It was obvious that twenty-first century ideas of womanpower didn't work with a nineteenth-century man.

He stood up. "Are you done now?"

She nodded. She was truly exhausted. The mountain had won.

After he left the room, she got undressed, put on a nightgown, and got into bed. She did *not* like fighting with him.

When he returned, she pretended to be asleep. He got in with her, and she held her breath.

How angry was he?

But Max pulled her into his arms, and they clung to each other. "I hate it when you cry," he said.

They didn't make love, but fell asleep wrapped about each other.

In the morning when she woke, he was gone. Feeling very bad, she got out of bed.

Alice threw the bedroom door open so hard it slammed against the wardrobe. "Pat and Max are gone." Her voice was accusatory. What she was really saying was, *What the hell have you done now?*

"They're with the Kanzas. There's a rumor that they're going to be attacked today."

"The men said it was because you killed so many buffalo." Alice was very angry.

"I didn't—" Etta began, then stopped. "Whatever the reason, I agree that it's all my fault. If anyone is hurt, it's because of me."

Alice gave a snort of derision. "There's nothing I hate more than self-pity."

Etta turned to her. Alice not only looked like Etta's little sister but sounded like her. Sisters took no prisoners. "Said by a woman who wouldn't leave the house because her twisted foot wasn't pretty."

Alice, who had never had a sister, looked shocked. Then she almost smiled. One warrior to another. She calmed somewhat. "Pat told Nellie that we're to go to the church."

"And men must be obeyed," Etta muttered.

"When it suits us, yes."

The change in tone was familiar. For all the times she and her sister had fought, they had often bonded against whatever decree their father had made. "Have you heard anything from them?"

"Nothing. I don't like this."

"Nor do I," Etta said. "Help me with the corset. Does Rufus have the buggy ready?"

"He's gone. All the men went with Pat and Max."

Etta sighed. "He said he'd take them. Can you drive a buggy?"

"No, but Nellie can."

Etta thought how much male and female *needed* each other. *Not like in my time*, she thought.

As they drove through town, they saw that there were no men. Saloonkeepers, lawyers, criminals, cowboys, shopkeepers were missing. All the men were gone.

The women who were left behind stood along the street and glared at Etta. Even the ones who'd liked her now let her know of their anger. Because of her, the men had left to go to a possible war. Again. It hadn't been long since they'd returned from the War Between the States.

Nellie was driving the buggy with Alice and Etta squashed in beside her.

"I take it back," Alice said as she looked at the angry women lining the street. "You *should* pity yourself."

Etta did her best to keep her chin up and her eyes straight ahead. "If anything happens to me, would you please embroider my name on the parasol you gave me? I want everyone to know it's mine."

Alice gave her a wide-eyed look then nodded.

Nellie stopped at the church and the women got out.

"No men to help us down," Alice muttered and shot a look of fire at Etta. "So help me, if anything happens to Pat, I'll… I'll…"

Etta felt the same way. She locked arms with her sister-in-law, and they went up the stairs and into the church.

She and Alice sat with Nellie in the front pew on the left. Across the aisle from them was John Kecklin and Cornelia. The females from in town and the nearby countryside, young and old, filled up the seats behind them. There were farmer's wives beside girls from the saloon. *At least people are united*, Etta thought. *I just wish they weren't joined together against* me.

Now, everyone was silent as Sally read passages from the Bible. When she sang, they stood up and joined her.

The church service went on for a long time. No one seemed to want to leave the sanctity of the little building. When Sally finally closed her Bible, the congregation silently exited.

Alice, Nellie, and Etta stayed in place, looking straight ahead until the church emptied. Etta squeezed Alice's hand in thanks for staying with her, then they got up and left.

She should have known that John Kecklin would be waiting outside for her. Alice tried to pull her away, but Etta held her ground. Let the man say whatever he wanted to. Words couldn't hurt more than her fear.

Kecklin was smirking. "After today's scare, the women will throw you out and so will Lawton. Or maybe you'll be a widow. I'll give a good price for your land." He laughed. "But then, maybe you made it all up."

With that, he left, his hands in his pockets and whistling. He believed he'd won the war.

Behind him was Cornelia. She looked as frightened as Etta was. "Bert went with them. I hope all this *is* a lie." She started to walk away but stopped. "I know I owe you, but I can fight only one battle at a time against him." She hurried after her father.

Etta knew what she meant. It was a fight with her father to get the man she loved. Cornelia didn't have the strength or energy to fight for Etta too.

As Nellie drove them home, they were silent. Etta was almost glad she didn't know exactly where the men were, or she'd go to them. What was happening? The lack of communication was tearing her apart. Oh for a mobile phone and a text saying they were all right. She had visions of riots and fire and men screaming in pain.

At home after lunch, they sat in the living room. Alice had her embroidery frame out and was working on a replacement panel for the parasol. This one bore Etta's name.

Nellie was painting, while Etta tried to read one of Max's mother's books about eighteenth-century gardening. So far, she'd managed about ten words. She was twitchy, restless, and her body kept shaking. Pure, unadulterated *fear*.

At four, they'd still had no information about anything. No wounded, bleeding man had returned to them with bad news. Or good news.

Alice left the room and made a big pot of tea. "Drink it," she said to Etta.

"I don't want anything. I—"

"Drink!" Alice commanded, and she sounded exactly like her brother.

Reluctantly, Etta obeyed. After she finished the second cup, she felt very sleepy.

"Why don't you go upstairs and take a nap?" Alice said.

"No. I want to be here if anyone comes with news."

"I'll wake you if I hear anything."

Etta heaved herself up and went to the bedroom she shared with Max. She fell onto the bed and was asleep instantly.

She began to dream and she knew she was. *I'm in a dream inside a dream*, she thought. She saw Henry. Not the painter but Henry in Kansas City. He had on his old green cardigan and he was talking, but she couldn't hear him. *Alone*, he was mouthing.

"I know," she said. "If I return, I will be alone." He picked up something, and at first she didn't know what it was. It was a war bonnet, a glorious thing with lots of feathers. When Etta had spent days researching, she'd read that the Cheyenne were one of the few tribes that actually wore the huge headdresses that modern people knew about.

She seemed to be floating, her arms and legs spread out like a weightless astronaut. Her eyes were on Henry. He was holding the beautiful war bonnet and saying over and over, "Alone. Not alone. Alone." She didn't understand what he was trying to tell her.

He held out his hand to her, wanting her to take it.

She shook her head no. If she touched him, he might pull her back with him. "Max," she said. "I want to stay with Max. Forever."

Henry was reaching out and trying to get her to take his hand.

Etta flailed her arms to get away from him. "Go away! I want Max."

"Please," Henry said. "Not alone."

"No!" she shouted, and kicked out so hard she sent her body tumbling away.

"Etta! Wake up."

She opened her eyes, afraid of what she'd see. But it was Alice. She was still in the past. Safe.

"You were shouting."

Etta tried to sit up, but she fell back onto the bed. "The men," she whispered. "Max."

"They're all fine. They're here. No warriors showed up. There was no battle. Absolutely nothing happened. Everyone is laughing at Max about it all."

Etta could only blink at her.

"Come on and get up. It's morning. You've slept for hours."

She looked at Max's side of the bed and it was indented. He'd slept there but he hadn't waked her. But why would he? Because of her, he was being laughed at.

Etta raised up on her arms. "Yes, I'll get up." She put her hand to her forehead. "What was in that tea you made?"

Alice got to the door in two quick steps. "You needed to relax," she said defensively. "I'll see you downstairs." She scurried out of the room.

Etta took her time dressing as her mind was so full it might explode. What was most vivid was her dream of Henry trying to pull her back. She didn't want to leave. She didn't want to return to what she now saw as her empty, lonely life.

She dawdled as much as she could. She didn't want to face anyone. Would Max be angry at her? She had humiliated him in front of the whole town. Everyone knew it was Max's mail order wife who'd sent him off to a war that didn't happen. Of course they'd ridicule him.

In last night's dream, was Henry's appearance her way out? So she wouldn't have to face Max's anger? Wouldn't have to endure the whole town's sneers?

When she was dressed, Etta sat down. She needed to think about where to go from here.

She'd thought that this time she was sent back to stop the massacre. That was over and done with, but she was still here. So that wasn't the reason for this trip into the past. That meant there was something else to happen, some trigger that would send her away. After releasing Wyatt Earp, she'd been sent back immediately.

She stood up and began to pace. *What else is there?* Martha and Henry needed to be introduced to each other. But why? Max said they'd never get along. As for the woman who might be the reincarnation of her mother, Etta thought it would be better not to meet her. If she was forced to return, she didn't want to relive the grief of losing her mother. As for Tobias, he seemed happy enough just being away from preaching.

As she'd gone through Henry's books, Etta thought that maybe her job was to make sure Henry the Painter's work was remembered. She hated that there was no modern record of all he'd done. To last forever, he'd have to be published, and she'd thought about encouraging him to do that.

What if I don't do any of those things? she thought. *If I quit ordering everyone about, I won't make any of those things happen.*

"And if I don't do them, maybe I'll stay here," she said. That meant she'd have Max and Alice, Pat and Nellie, and— She took a breath. And maybe a baby or two.

She imagined a life of home and family, and she liked it very much.

I just have to avoid certain things, she thought. If she realized someone was missing, she wouldn't try to find him or her. The twenty-first century would just have to do without that person. The best thing to do was to just plain mind her own business.

"I've done enough," she said. "Now all I have to do is avoid the pitfalls of seeing too much. Of comparing now to then.

Most of all, I have to conquer my own nature of trying to fix everyone and everything."

The thoughts made her smile. *Stay calm*, she told herself. *Keep your nose out of trouble and you won't be taken away.*

With her shoulders back, she left the room.

20

Max was frowning. He was driving the buggy, Alice beside him, Nellie in the back, and his mind was in turmoil. *What the hell was wrong with Etta?*

He and the men got back late on Sunday, and she was asleep. He couldn't help making noise, but she didn't wake up. Since he didn't feel like explaining his actions of the day, he was glad she stayed asleep.

When he got up the next morning, he was concerned that she was still hard asleep, but Alice said Etta was exhausted. Almost as though she was guilty of something, Alice had hurried out of the room.

Max spent the day outside, catching up on work. When he got back that night, Etta was...well, different.

"Max!" Alice said. "Stop here."

He came back to the present. "Oh, right." He was to let

them off at the dressmaker. Alice was buying new clothes for Nellie.

"What are you going to do?" she asked.

"Get supplies."

"No," she said in exaggerated patience. "Pat did that and anyway, there's no room in the buggy. Please tell me you aren't going to spend two hours drinking beer."

He gave her a look that in the past would have made her back down. But now that she had what Etta called a significant other and the care of Nellie, Alice was not so respectful of her brother. Max looked away. "I have to see Bert about some contracts."

"Good! Maybe he'll cheer you up."

"I don't need—" He didn't finish, just got out and helped them down.

Alice kissed his cheek. "Please try to be happier."

As he watched her and Nellie hurry away, he marveled at how she walked now. She hardly even limped. *Changes*, he thought. All due to Etta. She had turned their lives upside down.

"I just wish she didn't hate me," he muttered.

He left the buggy where it was and walked to the Red Dog. For a moment he thought about going in and drinking. After a couple of hours, he'd feel better.

But he didn't do it. He went up the stairs to Bert's law office, and to his good luck, Mrs. Ellis wasn't there. Max didn't knock, just opened Bert's door, sat down, and stared at the lawyer across the desk.

Bert leaned back in his chair, seeming to be glad to stop reading papers. "Are you all right?"

"Physically, yes, but my wife hates me."

"That's bad. Did she tell you why? I mean besides about Sunday."

"She hasn't said a word about that."

Bert's mouth dropped open. "Cornelia has not stopped bawling me out. In two days, she's said more words than I read in all of law school. To make her shut up, I proposed and gave her a ring."

"Congratulations." Max didn't sound happy. "I wish Etta would yell at me."

"Does she sulk in silence?"

"No. She's cheerful and happy and never wants us to get out of bed."

"That's scary," Bert said.

"Yeah, it is."

"But you did tell her about Sunday, didn't you?"

"Lord, no! Never. But then, she never asked anything. She's been absolutely perfect. She's been working with the cook to make better meals for the men. And she and Freddy are putting in a garden."

"Sounds like she's bossing people around. Cornelia says Etta's good at that. She said Etta is worse than her father."

Max gave a one-sided grin. "Two rattlers in a pit."

The men looked at each other in understanding. On Sunday they'd spent a lot of time together, and they'd become friends. One of the things that bonded them was the ferocity of their women. They both liked that about them.

"It all sounds good," Bert said.

"Not really. Etta won't leave home. She doesn't want to see anyone. She just wants to cook and…" He raised his eyebrows, silently saying that Etta was insatiable in bed.

Bert was obviously not understanding Max's problem.

Max looked at his friend. "Etta is different from other people. She seems to have things she has to do."

Bert nodded. "Like putting me with Cornelia, and Alice with the blacksmith?"

"Yes."

Bert used his lawyer brain of figuring things out. "She has things she needs to do, but she's not doing them. Is that what you're worried about?"

Max nodded. "Since Sunday, it's like she's afraid of something. I asked her about it, but she won't tell me what it is. She says she's not angry, but maybe she is. I don't know what's wrong, but she is not doing the things she said she wanted to do."

"Did she tell you what they were?"

"More or less." Max laughed. "You know Henry, the painter who comes through here every few years?"

"No. Never met him."

"He's a nice old man. Etta wants him to meet Martha Garrett."

Bert grimaced. "I do know her. She chased me off her property with a shotgun."

"That's Martha. Etta wanted to invite her to dinner. With Henry."

"You'd have to set up an armed guard."

"Exactly," Max said. "It's a silly idea."

Bert was looking at Max as though he were a client. Sometimes he had to work to understand what they really wanted. "What else?"

"Alice has the idea of opening a school."

"That sounds good."

"You don't know my sister. She'd lose interest in a month. But Etta said she'd seen a woman in town who could run it, but that's all. My wife refuses to come to town."

Bert leaned forward. "Sometimes with a woman, you just have to put your foot down. I told Cornelia we are going to move to Kansas City, and she's going to create a house for us."

"You mean you're going where Etta told you to go and do what she said you had to?"

Bert blinked a few times. "Yeah, that's right. My point is that maybe *you* can do what Etta wanted to do."

"What does that mean?"

"Invite them all to dinner. You do it."

Max raised an eyebrow. "Do I shake out the lace tablecloth? Get out the good glasses?"

Bert waved his hand. "Cornelia would love doing all that. She says she owes Etta in a big way."

Max scoffed. "For getting *you*?"

"I'm the prize bull. Awarded to the winner." The men laughed.

"I have to go to KC on Friday," Bert said. "I'm going to buy a piece of land. This is Wednesday, so I guess dinner will be tomorrow?"

Max stood up. "I don't even know where the painter is, and Martha won't come. And who is the schoolmarm Etta saw leaving the dressmaker?"

Bert lifted his hands in surrender. "All that's beyond me. Get Alice and Cornelia together. They'll solve it." He stood up. "I'm not an expert on women, but it sounds to me like Etta may be nesting."

"Like a buffalo wallow?"

"Like a bird," Bert said. "Making a nest. To lay eggs. For baby birds."

Max's eyes widened. "Oh. Right." He smiled. "Yeah." He turned to the door. "I'll go talk to Alice now. Tomorrow we'll have dinner."

Bert was grinning. "You'll be the best man at my wedding?"

"Of course." Max put on his hat. "Thanks."

"Anytime," Bert said.

When Max was driving home, he was feeling no pain. Alice was chattering so fast he could hardly understand her. It had been an interesting afternoon. After Max told his sister about putting on a dinner for Etta, and who was to be invited, Alice did everything. She'd found Cornelia at a shop down the street, and the two of them bullied the dressmaker into telling them who the woman was who'd been seen leaving her shop.

As the women suspected, she was a seamstress. The dress-maker was afraid Etta would take her business away, so she'd lied. They then planned to search for the painter.

Yet again, Max was struck by the changes in his life since he'd married Etta. Cornelia was no longer demanding things from Max. Part of him wanted to ask her how she was dealing with her father now that he knew he wasn't going to get Max's land. But the larger part of him was too cowardly to hear the answer.

The women told Max to go away while they worked. Both women knew he'd go to the Red Dog. "Just you!" Cornelia said and narrowed her eyes at him. "If you try to corrupt Bert, I'll make you sorry."

Max looked serious. "I'll leave him as virginal as I found him."

Cornelia glared at him, trying to decide if he was being honest or playing her for a fool.

Max went to the saloon and in defiance, he sent a girl upstairs to tell Bert. The lawyer delighted in escaping Mrs. Ellis and joined Max. They enjoyed themselves very much. The only snag came when Cornelia marched in, Alice trailing behind her.

"She won't come," Cornelia said to the two men who were smiling happily.

"Who?" Bert asked.

"That woman! Lillian Oates. She refuses to come to the dinner."

Alice was looking around. "This is where Freddy worked? What are the towels for?" They were hanging down from the long bar.

"Wiping their mouths from their filthy tobacco spitting," Cornelia snapped. She was staring at Max, waiting for him to solve the problem.

"I don't know what to do. She—" His head came up. "Etta said she and the preacher were a pair." He was pleased he remembered that.

"That doesn't make sense," Cornelia said. "Lillian is young and pretty. Tobias is neither of those."

"Like you and ole Bert here?" Max said.

Cornelia started to protest, but it was such a nice compliment that she agreed.

Alice spoke up. "We'll get the preacher to talk to her about starting a school. In the church."

Cornelia smiled at her. "That's an excellent idea." She looked back at the men. "Please don't get drunk. There are things that need to be done. We want to make Etta proud of us."

"That is our goal in life," Bert said seriously, and the women left.

The two men drank until Alice came to tell Max that it was time to leave.

All in all, he was glad the horse was well trained because he was half-asleep.

Thursday dawned sunny and bright, and Max found he was genuinely excited about the surprise dinner that was coming. He and Alice had managed to keep all of it secret from Etta.

Unfortunately, that had been too easy. The "new Etta" asked no questions. The woman he'd come to know asked who, what, and where about everything. And she was never without an opinion. But now she just went about preparing meals and seeing to laundry and, well, to bed pleasures. It was as though they were the only things in life that mattered to her.

She didn't seem to notice the preparations that were underway.

In the afternoon, one of Kecklin's men arrived in a wagon. In the back were pots of food that had been prepared for the evening. Cookie was to see to them for the dinner.

"Etta's food is better," the man said, his upper lip in a sneer.

"She can't cook for her own surprise, now can she?" Max snapped at him.

Cookie was unperturbed. "I'm just saying that she won't like this." He carried a big iron pot away.

Alice came to him and said, "Pat doesn't want to come."

"Let him eat with a pitchfork and he'll be fine."

Her glare made Max sigh in defeat. "Tell him I'll be drinking beer and there will be lots of beef."

"And *you* will be nice."

"Always am," he muttered, then said, "I promise."

With the food, the Kecklin man gave Max a note from Cornelia. It was on her blue vellum stationery that she ordered from London. It said that she'd found the painter, Henry Fredericks, and he was glad to come to dinner. Cornelia also wrote that she'd offered Martha Garrett six heifers if she'd be there, and she'd agreed.

The last bit made Max smile. The question about Cornelia and her father was answered. To get John Kecklin to part with six cows Cornelia must have had to bully and berate him. It looked like she was doing well with the man. Maybe keeping his daughter's respect was more important than buying all of Kansas.

Two hours before people were to arrive, Rufus brought Etta back from where she'd been loading up on her beloved vegetables. He'd had to endure three lectures on the value of a "plant based diet." When he said cows ate plants, she hadn't even smiled.

"Could we go upstairs?" Max asked.

Her eyes lit up. "Gladly." She hurried into the house and up the stairs ahead of him.

Max followed. He dreaded what was coming because he didn't know how she'd react. He closed the door behind him, and she put her arms around his neck. He disentangled them. "I have something to tell you."

She stepped back. "I'm sorry. Really and truly sorry. I shouldn't have done it. I know you can never forgive me but please let me stay here."

He had no idea what she was talking about. "Sorry for what?"

"Sunday. I didn't mean to humiliate you. I know everyone was laughing at you. Kecklin said I was the kid who cried wolf. The women hated me. It was horrible." She sat down on the bed. "I'm so very sorry. I've been trying to keep my nose out of things." She looked up at him, her eyes full of tears. "I never meant to hurt your feelings. I truly believed there was danger." She put her hands over her face.

Max was so stunned it took him a while before he could speak. "You've been dragging around here because you thought you had—what was it you said? Hurt my feelings? That is great. I can't wait to tell Bert."

She looked up at him. "Bert? What does he have to do with this?"

"He tried to help me figure out what was wrong with you." He sat down beside her and took her hands in his. "It's true that everyone laughed at me. Like they did at our wedding, remember?" He kissed her hands. "Nobody teases and laughs at a man to his face if they don't like him. And respect him. You think anybody ever made fun of Kecklin in front of him?" Max stood up. "I should have told you the truth about Sunday, but I was embarrassed."

"About what I did to you? Everyone knew it was *me*!"

He took a breath. "That day I went to the Kanzas, we had a very good time. I had beer delivered. And a hog. I was supposed to be some sort of rescuer, but I was a…a…"

She was blinking at him. "You were a drunken lout?"

"Pretty much."

"But I asked people what happened that day. Rufus and Pat ran away and wouldn't answer my questions. I thought it was because everything was so awful. Are you saying that no one would tell me about it not because I'd made a fool of my husband, but because my husband had made a fool of himself?"

"That's not exactly how I'd put it, but yes."

She stood up. "It was a boys' night out? Was there gambling?"
He nodded.

"Dancing?"

"Quite a lot."

"Did you...?" She motioned to her face to indicate painting it.

"I did. I had to stop at the homestead to scrub down. I didn't
want you to see what I'd done. I was afraid you'd think less of
me."

Etta was trying to soak this in. "Before you went, did my ar-
guments persuade you in the least?"

"No. Not at all. Your safety is important to me."

It was as though life was coming back to her. "Safety? You
had a drunken party!"

He smiled. "That's true, but we didn't know if the Cheyenne
were going to show up."

"And join you? Did you have enough food and beer for them?"

"We did."

"You're a horrible person," she said.

He didn't smile. "Maybe I am, because I've done something
else."

Etta was so happy that Max wasn't angry at her that she felt
he could do no wrong.

"I invited people to dinner tonight."

She stood up. "I'll start cooking."

"No. That's all done. The woman who works for Kecklin sent
over some food." He gave a half smile. "I sure couldn't leave it
up to Cornelia and Alice to cook."

Etta took a step back. "Who did you invite?"

"The people you wanted," he said happily. "Cornelia and
Alice found out who the woman at the dressmaker was. Lillian
Oates. And they found the painter, and Martha is coming." His
eyes were sparkling. "We did it all in secret."

"And they're coming here tonight?" Etta's voice was a whisper.

"Yes." He was smiling proudly.

Etta sat back down on the bed. "Then it's over. The massacre was averted and now Henry and Martha are here." She could hardly speak. "And Lily is coming. It's all done."

Max looked at her in confusion. "I thought you'd be pleased."

"To see her again," Etta said. "She was so very sick." She looked back at Max. "To see her now, then go back to her not being there. I don't know if I can do it."

Max had no idea what she was talking about, but he could see that his surprise was a failure. "You don't have to be there." He turned to the door. "We'll send a plate up to you." He looked back at Etta. "If the 'her' you're talking about is the seamstress, she won't be here. She won't come. I don't know why. Maybe she's afraid of losing her job." He opened the door.

"So only the painter is coming?"

Max didn't look at her. "Yeah. And Martha will be here. I'm going to put a shotgun under the table in case she gets too feisty."

In one leap, Etta got up and slammed the door shut. "Then it's not complete. It's not done. Not finished."

"What does that mean?"

"Nothing. You have to help me get dressed. That long corset takes two hands. I bet Cornelia will be wearing something from Paris. Where's Sephora when I need them? And my hair is awful. Go get your mother's brush. I have work to do. When will they be here?"

Max hadn't moved an inch and his face showed complete bewilderment. "I'll send Alice," he said and quickly left the room.

21

At dinner, Etta was in such a good mood that she felt like a spotlight had been turned on inside her. First of all, no one had ever done for her what Max did. It was as though the world was divided into two categories. There were those who did the work and those who sat on silk cushions and were waited on. At home, her father and Alicia worked, but it was for their own businesses. Anything outside that was "get Etta to do it."

By default, the same dynamic had been set up in the Lawton household. Esmeralda had gone back to her family, and everything had been turned over to Etta.

But not tonight. Food, guests, even the table settings were all done by other people.

When Etta saw Henry, it was all she could do not to throw her arms around him. He was so very familiar to her. She wanted to ask him about Ben and Caroline and how the baby was doing.

She wanted to tell him how Max had averted the massacre. Her punchline would be, "The Cheyenne didn't even show up!"

But she couldn't do any of that. She just praised Cornelia's utterly divine dress, asked her where she got her earrings—from New York—and smiled at Bert.

When Martha arrived, Etta held her breath. Would calm Henry like fiery Martha in this life? Etta practically pushed Cornelia out of the room so Henry and Martha could have time alone.

Cornelia knew what she was doing. "That's like leaving a rattler with a baby mouse and hoping they'll become friends."

Etta didn't retreat.

In the dining room, they all took their places, but the two seats along the side were empty.

Henry and Martha were still in the entryway.

"She's killed him by now," Max said and started to get up.

Etta looked down the table and gave him a glare to stay seated. They sat in silence for minutes.

"No gunshots so far," Max said.

"Too bad," Bert said. "I've always wanted to do a murder trial."

Pat spoke up. "I should see about them."

"No!" Etta said, and he sat back down.

A minute later, Henry and Martha came into the dining room, and they were smiling as they took their seats.

The grinning smirk that Etta directed to the others was of triumph and I told you so.

Max ducked his head toward her as though in a salute. Cornelia, Bert, Alice, and Pat looked at her in astonishment.

Even though Etta hadn't been in charge of planning the meal, she took over as they all expected her to do.

"My worry is that the little town of Garrett will disappear," she said, and they all blinked at her. It was an odd beginning to the dinner conversation. "If the railroad moves, this town will vanish. No one will remember it." She passed a bowl of potatoes to Henry and looked hard at him. "Instead of wandering all over the country and making pictures that aren't related to each other, why don't you make a portfolio of drawings and paintings about one town? About Garrett?" That Etta was saying this to a man she didn't know stopped them all in place. Even Max halted, fork to mouth.

Henry just smiled. "I don't stay in one place for long."

"But you could. You could rent a room from Martha."

Even Henry was taken aback by this. "I can't... I don't..." He didn't seem to know what to say.

Etta looked at Martha. "Since this is your town, you know more about it than anyone. You could tell the history and Alice can write it down."

"Me?" Alice said. "I don't know how to write."

"Of course you do," Etta said. She looked back at Henry. "You should go to New York and get your book *published*. Like George Catlin did. You can't just leave your work behind. It'll be lost forever. It won't survive unless it's published."

Everyone was looking at Etta is astonishment. She was being very aggressive. Rude, even.

Cornelia broke the silence. "I think that's a good idea." She looked at Henry. "Your art is excellent. You could—"

Etta cut her off, giving Cornelia an intense look. "You need to design a building, something so beautiful that it will last forever. A church, maybe. Make it of stone so it won't burn down. Pat will help build it. He's a true artist. And get your father to pay for it. He wants his name to live forever, so tell him the church will do that. He doesn't need a whole town, just one glorious building."

They were staring at Etta in what could only be described as shock. She was bossing all of them around. Planning their entire lives.

Alice was the one who broke into their silence. She laughed

loudly. "I'm next," she said cheerfully. "What plan do you have for me?"

"Schools that will draw settlers here. Families, not just saloons." She glanced at Max and Bert. "As much as they're liked, they won't last."

"Freddy will design a garden for Cornelia's church," Alice said.

"Yes, of course," Cornelia said. "This chicken is delicious."

With relief, everyone turned their attention to the food, and they avoided looking at Etta.

She knew she'd overstepped, but she couldn't tell them what she knew. A windswept plain was all that was left where the house stood now, and it had devoured the town. Worse was that there would be nothing left to remember any of these people. How could they so completely disappear?

She didn't say much for the rest of the meal, and no one spoke of building houses, or stone churches, or schools. Nor did they mention how Etta had warned of a Cheyenne attack that never came. It seemed all right for her to instigate love matches, but she was to stay out of the rest of it.

When everyone started to leave, they were subdued, rather formal.

At the door, Henry said, "I will think about what you said."

Martha looked at Etta and shook her head. "You are a strange woman," she said, then left the house.

Cornelia took Etta's hand in hers. "I've never had anyone believe in me as much as you do. Thank you."

"That means a lot to me."

"Come over tomorrow and I'll give you some chickens."

"I'd like that."

Cornelia kissed her cheek and left.

Bert shook Etta's hand. "I like your idea. I think Cornelia should do it."

"So do I," Etta said. He'd made her feel better.

Pat paused at the door. "Thank you for believing that I can make something besides horseshoes."

"I just told the truth," Etta said.

Alice hugged her. "I think I'll try writing about our family." She hurried to her room. They all knew she would slip out the back and meet Pat in private.

Alone, Max turned to Etta. "Let's go to bed."

"I need to clean up."

"That will be taken care of." When they were alone in their bedroom, he turned to her.

"I put my foot into it," she said. "I was too bossy."

"I was glad to see you back to being yourself, but…"

"But what?"

"You didn't give *me* anything to do."

It hadn't occurred to her, but he was right. "You're the leader of everyone. You'll have to oversee whatever is done. Henry will have to be pushed and Cornelia needs constant praise, and Alice will need you to remind her of what living in a sod house was like."

He was still looking at her, not satisfied with what she was saying. He began to undress. "I guess if Preacher Tobias had been here, you would have told him he was to do the accounting for everyone."

"Yes. I'd give him his orders tomorrow, but I think I should keep quiet."

"I doubt if he'll be here." Max turned away to put his shirt on the hook in the wardrobe.

"Has something happened to him?" she asked in alarm.

"Not anything bad. Alice and Cornelia sent the woman Lillian to him. You said they're a pair."

When Etta was silent, he looked back at her.

All the blood seemed to have drained from her. Her legs began to wobble, and she collapsed to sit on the side of the bed.

Max sat down and pulled her into his arms. "Tonight wasn't

that bad. I'm sure they'll all laugh about what you said. Imagine John Kecklin paying to build a church! And Cornelia and Bert are going to move to KC. *You* did that."

"It's finished," Etta whispered. "It's done."

He pulled back to look at her. "What is done?"

"My mission. Why I'm here. That was the last one. My parents are together."

"Your parents are here? Why didn't you tell me?"

She took his face in her hands. "Max, I love you. With all my heart and soul, I love you. I want to stay with you forever."

He pulled her to him and held her tight. "It's all right. Don't cry. I know you love me." He stroked her hair. "Did you know that I've loved you since our wedding day?"

Her face was buried in his neck, and she shook her head no.

"Any woman who could be calm in the midst of one of Cornelia's tantrums had my heart. And you were so appreciative of Alice's gift. I was a goner."

"But later, you got mad at me," she whispered.

"I expected you to feel the same way about me, but you didn't."

"I hurt your feelings?"

He laughed. "That you did. But you repaired the damage." He moved back to look at her. "I love you, Henrietta. With everything I have inside me, I love you." He kissed her tear-damp eyelids.

"I'm afraid I'll be taken from you."

He didn't ask what that meant, but then, he was growing used to the odd things she said. "If you are, then you'll just have to find me. I'll wait for you forever."

She didn't answer, just held on to him tightly.

He pulled back. "In the meantime, you want to try to make a baby?"

"Oh yes. Yes and yes!" was all Etta could say as she pulled him down onto the bed and on top of her.

22

It was in the wee hours of the morning that they were awakened by men shouting. Etta was groggy, but Max was already out of bed and half-dressed.

"Go back to sleep," he said.

"What is it?"

"There's a grass fire. We're all going. I'll be back when I can." He leaned over to kiss her goodbye, but Etta was getting out of bed.

"You'll need food. Give me an hour and send a wagon back for it." The look of love Max shot her warmed her. "Go on," she said, but he took time to kiss her thoroughly before he ran down the stairs. Etta was close behind him.

Etta had put bread on to rise before daylight and by eight they were slicing it. By midmorning, she and Cookie had filled two wagons.

Every hour, a dirty, soot-covered man returned with news and to get fresh horses. By ten, the fire was under control.

"Kecklin sent men and water barrels," Rufus said. "But then he's worried the fire will spread onto his land."

At eleven, a sooty young man Etta didn't know, who worked for John Kecklin, rode up to the house and asked if he could have something to eat. Etta gave him a plate of beef and ratatouille—something he'd never eaten before.

"How's it going?" she asked.

"It's almost out. I've heard about you."

Etta groaned.

"No, it's all been good. Or mostly good anyway. Mr. Kecklin laughed hard about the Cheyenne not showing up, but I heard your husband gave a fine party."

"That's what I was told too."

"I guess he'd give one today if it weren't for the fire."

"I think that was the last one."

The young man handed Etta his empty plate. "Too bad as the Cheyenne missed out last time. Maybe that's why they came today." He turned toward his horse.

"Today? What do you mean?"

"They're parading through town in full dress. Feathers, beads, and war paint. They're a sight to see. Well, thank you. I need to get back."

"Stop!" Etta said. "You need to find Max and tell him about the Cheyenne. He can meet me at the Kanzas."

"Ma'am," he said in a patronizing way, "I don't think people will come out a second time to fight for nothing."

Etta put her face nearly nose to nose with him. "Find Max! Now! Tell him I'm going to meet Lester. If you don't get my husband, your life won't be worth much."

"Yes, ma'am," he said, then quickly mounted and rode off.

Etta put her hands to her temples. What was she to do? Fourteen. Nineteen. The dates. Were they misprinted in the book she'd read and today was the massacre?

She looked around. There was no one about. All the men had gone to fight the fire. *I'll have to go alone*, she thought, then halted. Is this what her dream with Henry had been about? He was warning her? *Not alone*, he'd told her. She wasn't to go alone?

"I don't have a choice," she said aloud and ran into the house. The first thing was to find out where the Kanzas were. As before, she'd get her father to draw a map. She hadn't checked but she assumed Tobias was in Max's office, his nose buried in the account books.

She was glad she was wearing Max's mother's riding outfit, the one she'd worn when they went to Arkansas. She threw open the office door and, as she'd hoped, Tobias was sitting at the desk.

"I need a map," she said. "I have to go to—"

Sitting to the side, her lap covered by a half-made dress, was her mother. It had been years since Etta had seen her, and back then she'd been emaciated and sick. This woman was younger and healthy. "Mom," Etta whispered, staring.

"A map to where?" Tobias asked impatiently.

Etta couldn't pull her eyes away from her mother.

Lillian stood up. "You're Henrietta?"

Etta swallowed. Her mother always used her full name.

In that moment, Etta remembered how her mother had always been the one to take care of them. "You'll take on my job," she'd said days before she died. "I hope they don't dump it all on you, but they will." She'd taken Etta's hand. "Find your own life, my darling daughter. That's my wish for you."

Lillian stopped in front of Etta. They were the same height, had the same bone structure, but then Etta had always looked like her mother. "Where do you want to go? What do you need?"

"To the…" Etta cleared her throat. "Where the Kanzas are."

Lillian nodded. "I know where that is. Come on." She led the way out of the house.

As though she were a child, Etta followed, then stood back while Lillian took over. Max had ordered that horses be kept ready in case they were needed, so they were saddled.

Lillian climbed onto one, then motioned for Etta to mount a big black horse that was prancing about. Maybe it smelled the smoke that could be seen in the distance.

"I can't," Etta said. "I can't ride this animal."

"Get on!" It was her mother's voice, the woman who never let Etta admit defeat. She obeyed.

Lillian was a good horsewoman, and Etta worked to keep up with her. She struggled to hold on while her mind ran with thoughts. *Henry!* She tried to mentally connect with him. *Get Max. Tell him to come.*

It didn't take long to reach the little village. As Etta feared, the tribes were facing each other, bows and rifles at the ready.

Max was almost to the house when he saw one of the kids from Kecklin riding toward him. "Did you get fed?"

"Yes, sir, I did."

"Good. Go help fill the barrels."

The young man turned away but then looked back. "Mr. Lawton?"

"Yeah?"

"Sorry to say this, sir, but your wife said she was going to go see Lester."

"Why?" Max asked.

"I don't know." The young man looked almost scared, but that was a frequent expression of people who worked for John Kecklin. Max was still staring at him. "I asked her if there was going to be another party, and she said to tell you that she was going to go see Lester. Maybe she wants to see the Cheyenne."

"They're here?"

"Yes, sir. They rode through town this morning. They're a fine looking bunch of—" He didn't finish because Max had kicked his horse into a run.

Etta and Lillian sat on the horses, side by side. They were an equal distance between the two tribes. The Cheyenne were in full, glorious battle gear, while the Kanzas were in everyday clothing. Quite the contrast.

"We'll stay here," Lillian said, and she pulled on the reins so her horse stepped back.

But Etta dismounted. She was going to do whatever was necessary to stop this from happening.

She faced the Cheyenne. "This is my fault," she said loudly. "I'm the one who helped with the buffalo. I'm the one to blame."

From the back, one of the young Cheyenne men, a teenager, lifted his bow and arrow and took aim. Etta didn't see him but she felt the tension in the air. The Kanzas were behind her, and the Cheyenne in front, all of them nervous in anticipation. To her right, she saw a movement. It was Lester, the chief, a man she knew to be knowledgeable and calm no matter what. She turned to look at him, glad he was there.

In that instant, Max arrived at full speed. He saw what no one else did: the boy in the back, ready and aiming at Etta.

Max leaped down from his horse while it was still running, and he launched himself in front of Etta.

The arrow flew through the air.

"Max!" Etta yelled, overjoyed to see him. Between him and Lester, everything would be solved. Peace would be obtained. No one would be hurt.

When Max collapsed at her feet, she didn't understand. She just stood there, staring down at him.

A hush fell over everyone. Not a person or animal, not even

birds, made a sound. Lester stopped a few feet away and didn't move. Lillian sat on her horse, utterly still.

"Max?" Etta said. "What happened? Did you trip?" She just blinked down at him.

Lillian came to her and put her arm around Etta's shoulders.

Etta shrugged the arm away, then knelt beside Max. His eyes were closed. "Max?" she cried, but he didn't move.

"Henrietta," Lillian said, "I'm so sorry."

Etta saw the arrow sticking out of Max's chest. Blood was at the base. "No, this isn't right." She sat down on the ground and pulled at Max's shoulders.

It was Lester who lifted Max's inert body so his head was in her lap.

She stroked his hair. "Please wake up. We have so much to do. You promised me a trip to Paris, remember?"

Behind her, the Kanza began to sing a song of mourning.

"Max, please," Etta whispered. "Please."

Lillian sat down beside her.

"Mom," Etta whispered. "Mom, I can't bear this. I can't do it."

"I know. I know too well."

"Etta," came a voice she recognized, and she looked up. The sun was bright and she wasn't sure what she was seeing, but they all seemed to be there. Alice, Nellie, and Pat. Tobias was behind Lillian. Cornelia and Bert were looking down at her.

At the end was Martha and beside her was Henry in his suit with the string tie. But as Etta looked at him, his clothing changed to a plaid shirt and khaki trousers. He held out his hand to her.

Etta shook her head no, her arms around Max in her lap. "No," she whispered.

Henry leaned forward, his hand closer to her.

"Etta!" she heard. It was Zack's voice. "Etta! Wake up. Henry is leaving."

But Henry was there, beckoning to her.

She reached up and her fingertips touched his.

In the next second, Etta knew she was in Henry's house in Kansas City, and the people she'd come to love were far away in distance and in time.

And Max was...

Etta wouldn't open her eyes.

23

Etta lay still, her eyes closed. *This one is different*, she thought. The other times after her dream ended, she'd felt a strong need to return. She knew there was more she had to do. But not this time. Now she knew it was over. Done. Her task had been completed.

She waited a while, not moving, and she could feel the past being "put away." It was like it was going to another part of her mind, like tucking away a love letter in a box of memories.

She refused to think about—to remember—the very last of her dream. She didn't want to see Max lying on the ground. Didn't want to recall the looks on the faces of the people around them. Had everyone really been there or had she imagined that?

Gradually, she opened her eyes. Ben's room was as she remembered it. Nothing had changed. Actually, there were two chairs beside the bed, one on each side. Had someone been watching her as she slept?

When she tried to move she was weak and shaky, but she lifted herself up. On the pillow beside her was the little bear that Pat had made and Nellie had given her. She picked it up, her hand closing around it. "Give me strength," she whispered.

She dreaded going downstairs and facing people. From the light through the curtains, it appeared to be morning. Would she find Henry frying bacon? Was Zack here? Freddy?

Henry would want her to tell him all that had happened in this last dream. How could she do that? This time she'd been too fearful to do what she was sure she was supposed to do. Max had done it all. He'd invited people and put them together. Henry and Martha. Lillian and Tobias.

Etta closed her eyes. Her mother! Seeing her again, talking to her, and best of all, relying on her, had been glorious. But remembering it might break her heart.

Turning, Etta put her feet on the floor, then cocked her head and listened. There were no sounds. With the lockdown, there was no traffic noise, and inside, it was eerily silent. No matter how quiet people tried to be, they made noise. But not now.

Henry must be in the library, she thought as she got up to go to the bathroom.

Inside the spotless, shiny room, she didn't take time to marvel at it. She didn't feel like half of her was in the past, or even that the past was pulling her away. No. She was fully here and now. She would never again dream of a town and people who no longer existed.

She showered and dressed, and tried to brace herself to face Henry and his umpteen questions. Who? Where? When? "What *exactly* did he say?" There were never enough details to satisfy Henry. And this time, she'd need to talk about Martha. Should she tell him what Max said about Martha cutting Henry up and feeding him to the hogs?

For a moment she put her hands on the counter and looked into the mirror. Today she didn't feel "old and plain," but "old and empty." She felt drained, as though her life had been taken from her.

She stepped back. "It's showtime," she said, quoting one of her favorite movies. It was time to face Henry and his questions.

Slowly, she went down the stairs, then glanced in Henry's library. He wasn't there. Nor was he in the kitchen. She remembered Zack's voice saying Henry was leaving. But he was too ill to go anywhere. She went outside to his house and knocked. No answer. The door was unlocked and she went in. No one was inside.

She got her phone and called Zack. It went to voice mail. "I'm up and Henry isn't here." She started to add more but couldn't think of anything.

She made herself a breakfast of scrambled eggs and toast and ate in the kitchen. She knew what was facing her, but she didn't want to do it. After the second dream, it had been fun to see that she and Max had saved Wyatt Earp and he was back in the history books. But right now she didn't think anything in her life would ever be "fun" again.

She finished her meal, cleaned up, took a very deep breath, and went into Henry's library.

The first book she picked up was the one that had told about the 1871 massacre. She knew that account hadn't been in the book the first time she read it. She quickly flipped the pages. The Cheyenne attack of 1869 was there, but there was nothing in 1871.

"Looks like you stopped it," she said aloud. She meant Max. At the cost of his life, the violence had been prevented. The memory made her sit down heavily on Henry's big leather couch. Usually, he was stretched out on it, writing in his notebooks.

On the coffee table was a large book she'd never seen before. It was one of those editions that cost hundreds of dollars and was sold only to libraries and avid collectors.

The title and author were printed in small type on the beau-

tiful linen cover. There was no flashy font meant to attract customers. *A Study of a Town*, by Henry Fredericks.

She opened the book to the title page.

A Study of a Town, Garrett, Kansas, in 1871.

As seen through the eyes of an artist and the residents.

Drawings and paintings by Henry Fredericks.

Stories by the people of Garrett.

On the next page, it said, *I dedicate this book with love to my
wife, Martha Garrett Fredericks.*

Etta's heart jumped a bit at seeing that. She was glad they'd
found each other.

The next page was a watercolor of the main street of the
town, and it looked just as she remembered. The painting was
so vivid she could almost smell it.

She turned the page. There was a portrait of Pat, muscles
bulging, wearing trousers and a leather apron, hammer raised
over an anvil. Behind him, a fire blazed in a forge.

Etta shut the book. Seeing someone she loved and would
never see again was too much to bear.

She curled up on Henry's sofa. Her eyes were dry, and she
wished she could cry. Maybe tears would be a release.

She was very tired. In theory, she'd been asleep during the
long dream, but her body didn't seem to think so. She pulled
Henry's lap blanket over her and went to sleep.

Etta's phone was ringing.

At first, she didn't know what the sound was. It was hard to
wake up. Her body was stiff and sore. Her cell phone was on
the table next to "that book," the thing that proved that what
she loved was gone.

She fumbled for the phone and almost dropped it. For a second she couldn't remember how to answer it. Oh yeah. Accept.
"Hello," she said groggily.

"Etta!" Zack said. "You're awake. Finally! Are you okay?"

"Yes," she said, but it didn't sound like she believed it. "Henry's not here. Is he with you?"

"He is, and we're on our way to Denver."

"Good. Wait! Henry's not well. He can't travel."

"I know that but I couldn't stop him. Did you see the big book on the coffee table?"

"Yes. It's beautiful." She didn't want to tell him her true feelings about it.

"I don't know where it came from. Henry and I were sitting vigil over you. I tried to wake you up but I couldn't. I wanted to call an ambulance but Henry said no. Anyway, I went down to get food and saw the book and took it up to him. He looked through it for a few minutes, then he went crazy. I thought he was going to have a heart attack. He said he was going to drive himself to Denver."

"He can't do that!"

"That's why I'm driving him there. I called Freddy to come look after you but I couldn't tell her you were in some sort of coma, so she felt it was safe to leave you alone while you were sleeping."

"It's okay. I'm fine. Did Henry tell you why he had to go to Denver?"

"Not really. He just mumbled, 'If it happened then, it will happen now.'"

"Oh," Etta said. "He must be worried about Ben and Caro and the baby."

"Maybe," Zack said. "But I think it was something he read in the book."

Etta didn't respond to that. "Where are you now?"

"At a big service plaza just outside Denver. Henry's inside and taking his time. I guess you saw in the book that Garrett is now a Kansas Historical Site. They reenact gunfights there."

"There weren't any gunfights. Their boots would have stuck in the mud and manure."

300

"You're too realistic," he said. "What happened to Max in your story?"

She took a breath. "He was shot with an arrow."

"Fatally?"

"Yes."

"I think that's what's freaking Henry out. This is none of my business, but true story or not, I think you two need to change the names of the characters."

"Change the names? Why?"

"Because you're the author and your name is Etta and well, Max is Max."

"What does that mean?" she asked.

"I thought it was odd that you and Henry used Max's name. And Ben's. And your sister's real name. You need to fictionalize the whole book."

"I'm confused." Etta's voice was rising. "What do the names matter?"

"I have to go. Henry's coming. I don't know why, but he doesn't want me to talk to you. Not now, anyway. Do what you want, but naming the main character after Henry's son is strange."

"Ben is Henry's son."

"Okay, if you want to nitpick. Technically, Max is Martha's kid but Henry legally adopted him. I have to go." He clicked off.

Etta put the phone down on top of the big book. It was afternoon, so she knew she'd been asleep for hours. She was hungry, but she didn't want to eat. More importantly, she didn't want to *think*.

For some unknown reason, Henry had ignored his ill health and was now going to Denver. *To see his grandchild*, she told herself. That made sense.

What made no sense was what Zack had said about Max being Henry's son.

But compared to all she'd seen and done in the last weeks, a confusing phone call was nothing. She was at the point where if Zack had said Big Foot was Henry's cousin, she would have nodded in agreement.

She got up, went to the kitchen, and made herself a sandwich. As she looked around at Henry's beautiful house, she thought, *I should leave.* When she was taking care of the owner of the house, she had a reason to be there, but with him gone, she was a stranger in someone else's house. A trespasser. She'd get on the internet and find a place to stay.

She went back to the library to get her phone. She didn't look at it, but instead, she sat down on the couch. Yes, she should pack her suitcase and leave. Never again did she want to see Henry or his house. Or risk dreaming of a time when she fell in love then was crushed, destroyed. She just wanted to go home to her father and Lester and the safe world of fast meals and modern plumbing.

She looked at the cover of the big book that contained paintings of a time that no longer existed.

She'd seen Pat's portrait. Who else was in there? Nellie? Cornelia? Her mother?

Was Max in there? But no. When Henry made those paintings, Max was already "gone."

Slowly, Etta stood up. Yes, she should leave. But as she got to the door of the library, she looked back. She didn't know what it was, but something was different.

She scanned the beautiful room. Except for the book on the table, it seemed to be the same. It was on the second sweep that she halted at the desk in the alcove. To the left of it was Henry's tall, slanted art table, the one she was sure wasn't there before her second dream.

It took her a moment to see what was different. There was no carving on the front of the desk. The relief of the man on the horse, the one Henry had carved, wasn't there. There was just a blank piece of wood.

Why would that have disappeared? she wondered. That had been done in this century by modern Henry. It was the desk he and Ben had bought at the auction. Later, Henry had taken it apart and chiseled the beautiful relief into it.

Now it was gone. Why?

Beside the desk was Henry's toolbox. It hadn't been put away after they'd looked for the portrait hidden in the back of the drawer.

A quick glance showed her that the portrait in its little frame was on top of the desk. That made no sense as Max still had it when Etta got off the train. But she'd shown Pat where to hide it. By all that was logical, the portrait should still be hidden.

"Logic!" she said. That was something that no longer applied to her life.

Right now all she knew for sure was that she *had* to see what was on the back of the front panel of that desk.

She went to Henry's toolbox and opened it. She wasn't a carpenter, but she'd had some dealings with old furniture. She got out a flat pry bar, turned on the flashlight of her phone, then crawled under the desk. Right away, she saw that she wasn't the first person to take out the back panel. Had Henry removed it then tacked the desk back together?

It didn't take much to loosen it and the thick piece of wood fell out. She picked it up, scooted backward, and put it on the desktop.

This panel had also been carved, but not by twenty-first century Henry. It had been done by Henry the Painter. It was of the buffalo hunt. There was Etta, wearing Max's mother's culottes, her knife to a buffalo on the ground. In the background was Max with his rifle and wearing only the tiny breechcloth.

Etta collapsed onto Henry's chair, staring at the wooden artwork.

It wasn't difficult to put the story together. The old carving had been hidden so the desk wouldn't be sold to a museum or a collector or some art dealer. It was saved so Henry would find it many years later.

He'd found the carved panel but he'd put it back in place. Re-hidden it. Why? So Etta would find it? That couldn't be. Henry would have to have known that Etta was coming.

She took a photo of the panel with her phone, then texted it to Zack and asked him to show it to Henry. She didn't have to wait long for a reply.

I am sorry. Please look under the stairs. The code is Max. For-give me. Henry.

If there was anything in life that Etta did *not* want to see, it was whatever was under the stairs. She'd had all she could take of Henry and his ancestors and the dreams that tore her apart.

As she got up, she told herself she was doing the right thing. On the desk was the portrait of her and Max. The faces were hidden inside the cover and she thought about having one last look, or maybe of taking the portrait with her. But she didn't do either. She was going to make a clean break. With her shoulders straight, she left the room.

She got all the way to the foot of the stairs before she halted. She'd cleaned the house thoroughly, from the attic on down. Had she missed the place under the stairs? No. It had been full of storage boxes. She'd pulled everything out and dusted them.

Now she remembered that Henry had made a rare excursion out of his library to tell her to put it all back. He'd been frown-ing. "It's just research materials. I'll get to them someday."

She'd thought he was worried that she'd mess up his old files. It was the same with her father. She'd given a quick swipe at the dust, then shoved everything back inside and closed the door.

So what was he hiding in there? Maybe Henry wanted her to know that it actually was him in her dream.

But Etta instinctively knew what was hidden there.

She didn't want to do it, but she went to the door, braced herself, then opened it. She pulled out the boxes, then looked around inside. At the tall end was a curtain. It was the same fabric that was in Ben's room, with plains animals. She flung it open to expose a door with a cylinder lock with three dials.

She swirled them to spell MAX and the lock fell away. She opened the door.

The shallow shelves inside contained things that she was sure had been taken from around the house. Framed pictures filled the bottom half of the space. She pulled out one. It was a photo of two little boys laughing, seeming to be swatting at each other. One of them was a young Max. The Max from her dreams. Even as a child, she knew it was her Max. Henry's adopted son.

There were several more pictures. She looked hard at one of Martha with Max. In her dream, she hadn't noticed the likeness between them. They had the same square jaw. But then, they were mother and son.

There were photos of Henry with both boys as they grew up, showing the things they did together. They were at Mount Rushmore, Dodge City, by tents in a forest. Martha didn't seem to be with them very often. When she was in the picture, it was in their house. She was often in hospital scrubs and smiling fondly at all of them.

On an upper shelf, there was a stack of letters written by Max while he was in college. Veterinarian school. Yes, her Max had loved animals. He wouldn't allow his horses to be subjected to a second arduous journey to get home. As she held the letters, she knew that Henry would want written accounts of his son's life.

On the top shelf were wire-bound sketchbooks that were stacked by age. She pulled out the bottom one. The cover said, MAXWELL LOGAN, EIGHT YEARS OLD. The first page was a drawing of a dog with a ball in its mouth. It was signed with ML. Just like Henry's H.F.

The sketchbooks got better with Max's age. There were portraits of people and animals. The people were mainly family members, with sweet ones of Martha. By the time Max was twenty-six, the drawings were professional quality. There were a lot of Henry, and Ben was a favorite subject. It was sad that Martha was missing from the more recent books.

Etta leaned back against the wall, her lap full of pictures and books and packets of letters. She was holding the photo she'd found the first night. Now she knew the tall young man in the picture was Max. When she woke on the first morning, she hadn't noticed that the photo was gone from the bedside table. Had Henry hauled himself up the stairs to take it away? Had he been afraid she'd ask who was in the picture?

These thoughts led to the main question: *Why?* Why had Henry done this? And when? On the first day she'd entered the house, she'd noticed the many framed pictures that were in the rooms. Henry was a stranger, and she'd wanted to establish him as a family man. Not some loner who lured women into his house.

She was absolutely sure there had been no photos of Max. No group portraits included him. He had been wiped out of the family. It was as though he'd done something horrible and had been disowned, removed forever.

But from what Zack said, that wasn't the case. He seemed to know Max.

As Etta sat there, she wondered what it all meant. Her dreams had been of such vividness that they were real to her. She put her head back against the wall and closed her eyes. Had it all actually *happened*? And how much did Henry really know?

She looked at the shelves beside her. Obviously, he knew much more than he'd confided in her. She thought of all his interrogations, his questions about every detail of what she'd dreamed—or maybe experienced—yet he'd been keeping secrets.

He *knew* the Max in her dreams was his son. Martha's son! Yet in all of Henry's stories about his life, he'd never mentioned his other son. Why?

Etta started to put the things back onto the shelves. She'd lock them away, out of sight.

But then something struck her, and it took her seconds to realize that it was anger. Fury was probably the only emotion that could override grief.

Anger seemed to start in her heart and flow outward until it reached her fingers and toes. She grabbed a box and turned it upside down to empty out Henry's file folders. Papers came out, mixing them up, and she was glad of it. It would take him a long time to reorganize them.

She put all the things about Max into the box, then left the low room under the stairs and stepped into the hall. She took her time placing pictures of Max around the house. She made sure they were prominent. She put his sketchbooks on the side tables and on the mantels of the fireplaces.

There was a pretty wooden box in Henry's library that was full of his precious pens. She dumped the pens onto the floor, then put Max's letters into the box. She set the box on the big desk, the front of which was now open, so Etta leaned the old carving up against the hole. She wanted everything in plain sight.

When she finished, she felt better. When Henry returned, he'd see what she'd done and he'd understand how angry she was at him.

She went upstairs to the bedroom she was using. Her small suitcase was in a corner and she rolled it out and put it on the bed, ready to pack.

But her phone rang. *If that's Henry or Zack*, she thought, *I'm not going to answer it.*

It was Alicia. Her dear sister. A member of her *real* family.

"I was going to call you," Etta said quickly. "I'm going to get to you as soon as is humanly possible. I'll fly, take a train, or whatever. There has to be some transportation available." She sat down on the bed. "I just want to go *home*, so maybe I should go to Dad. And Lester. I can run the food truck by myself until he's well, and I can help Dad with his book, and—"

"Etta!" Alicia said loudly and with force. "You can't go home again. You can't go back to what used to be because it's gone. It's no longer there."

"I know that you guys moved, but Dad is—"

"No!" Alicia nearly yelled, then she gave a groan. "Dad told me *I* had to tell you what he's done. He's too cowardly to do it himself."

"What do you mean?"

"Dad sold the house. He's already packing up. For the last two years, Steve Hartman, with his five kids, has been begging Dad to sell the house to him. He finally said yes. Papers have been signed."

"Years? Dad has been thinking of this for years? But he never said a word to me."

"Of course not. We all protect you. And listen, there's more. Lester has decided to retire. He says he's had enough of working twelve-hour days. He's going back to his homeland."

"His homeland? But Lester was born in Tonga."

"Right. That's where he's going and his whole family is going with him, including his grandchildren."

Return to his tribe where he's the chief, Etta thought. It seemed that the home she wanted to return to was disappearing. "Where will Dad live?"

"Eventually, he hopes to travel to see the world."

In her whole life, Etta had never heard her father say anything about traveling. "But his books?" She was beginning to feel frantic. "What about Wyatt Earp?"

Alicia gave a bit of a laugh. "Dad said the world can do without yet another book about that man. What does some gunslinger matter in the scope of life?"

"Everything," Etta murmured. Her mind filled with visions of riding with Max day and night to get to the prison where Mr. Earp was being kept. Then flirting with him and Max being jealous.

"Etta? Are you there?"

"Yes, I'm here," she said quietly.

"I'm sorry for dumping all this on you. I told both those men they were yellow-bellied snakes for not telling you themselves, but they said they couldn't bear to break your heart."

It was Etta's turn to laugh. "It takes more than that to even crack my heart."

"What does that mean? Has something bad happened?"

"Other than my life being completely and totally destroyed?"

"Etta," Alicia said in her I'm-calming-down-a-patient voice, "you need to look on the bright side of this. You're no longer tied down. Try to look at all of this as freedom."

"Right. I've lost my family, my job, and my home. Does that sound like freedom to you? You have a gorgeous husband, a great job, and the best child in the world. If all that disappeared from your life, would you look at it as 'freedom'?"

Alicia was quiet for a moment. When she spoke, it was in her sister voice, not that of a therapist. "No, I wouldn't. Come here to us and we'll talk."

"You mean you'll protect poor old Aunt Etta?" She didn't give her sister time to answer. "I need to go. Believe it or not, I have things to do."

"Etta, please." Alicia sounded on the verge of tears.

"It's okay. I'm going to be fine. I may murder Henry but then I married a man who he knew was his son, so he owes me big time. He—"

"What?" Alicia yelled. "Married? You *married* somebody? I've never heard of this person so you must have just met him. You can't do that. Marriage is serious. You need to find out about his character. You—"

"Give me a break! You saw Phillip in the gym with sweat rolling off of him, and you nearly fainted with lust. And afterward you went to the gym in so little clothing that Dad and I were afraid you'd be arrested. So much for you giving a crap about his 'character.'"

Her therapist voice was back in full force. "I do admit that I was attracted to Phillip, but I—"

"Attracted, ha!" Etta said. "I have to go. Zack or Ben might be trying to call."

"Who are these people?" Alicia demanded. "Dad and I should meet them."

Etta grimaced. "And you've put yourself back into the role of caretaker for poor, sad Etta. Call me when you're ready to talk to me as a sister and not like I'm one of your crazy patients."

"They aren't all—"

Etta clicked off and immediately started shoving things into her suitcase. "I have nowhere to go," she mumbled, "and no way to get there, but I'm going. I'm the new Etta. The symbol of freedom."

She knew that if she let go of her anger, she would fall down in a heap of misery. Poor Etta. On her way to being a spinster. Like Martha of old. No family, no home, no job. No—

Her ringing phone broke into her self-pity. She picked it up, expecting it to be Alicia or her father. Would they apologize? Or dump more loving-and-caring pity on old and plain Etta?

The screen had a number and below it was, Denver, Colorado.

Maybe it's Henry, she thought and gave a malicious little smile. She would enjoy telling him what she thought of him.

"Hello? Is this Etta?" said a male voice.

It was Bert. No, she reminded herself. In this life, it was Ben.

"Yes, I'm Etta."

"Would you mind doing FaceTime?"

"Not at all." She pushed the tabs and Ben came into view. She didn't know him, but she did. There were dark circles under his eyes. His baby, his wife, his father, all of them had recently been in jeopardy. He'd been through a lot in the last days.

"Dad told me to call you. He's worried about you."

He should be, she thought, but said, "How is he?"

"It's good. We finally got him to agree to surgery. They're putting in a couple of stents. We've been trying to get him to do it for the last year. But he wouldn't. And he refused to come to Denver with us. He kept saying that he had something he had to do so he couldn't leave Kansas City."

Sit on his porch and lure me to him with cookies and lemonade? she thought, but said nothing.

"Max is here. He flew in from Africa. By the way, Caro and I were surprised that his name was used in your book."

She knew he was asking her opinion about that. "Yeah." She wasn't going to take the blame for what Henry had done. "Henry did that. And he gave my name to the woman. I wanted to name her something like Rowena, but Henry took over. May I talk to him? I'd like to tell him that I greatly appreciate the secret he kept. In fact, I can't wait to tell him exactly how I feel about everything."

"What secret?"

She couldn't tell Ben what was between her and Henry. She thought quickly. "About the carving on the back of the desk. The desk you and Henry bought at auction."

Ben smiled. "That wasn't me. That was Max. I was home with

Mom with the chicken pox. Max and Dad went to an auction, and they came back with a truckload of things. Mom wanted to skin him. Dad had to get rid of furniture to make room for that monster desk."

When Ben paused, she could see that he had something else to say. "Etta, I don't know you so this will seem strange, but Dad made me promise to tell you how he met Max. I don't understand why he never told you as he says it's his favorite story. Do you have a few minutes?"

"I have all the time in the world, and I would love to hear the story."

"I'm not a good storyteller like Dad is, but I'll try. Mom was a great doctor, but her personality was… How do I describe her?"

"Not a woman who gushed with sentiment?"

Ben gave a half smile like she'd seen Bert do. "Yeah. I think Dad gave the fictional Martha Mom's character. Anyway, she was widowed and left with a young son, Max, to take care of. She put him in the day care run by the hospital. But one day, Max escaped and they had to call Mom. Maybe I shouldn't tell this, but they were fearful of her temper."

Etta was putting together what Henry had told her about his life. He hadn't lied, just skipped big chunks. "Henry has always been a storyteller."

"Yes!" Ben's face lit in happy memory. "That's what he was doing. Dad was in the pediatric ward, surrounded by kids, and Max was glued to his side. When Mom told Max to leave, he refused, which was unusual for him. Max said, 'He found me.' To my big brother, that meant it was a done deal. He was going to keep Henry forever."

"I can understand that feeling. Henry is like a human magnet."

Ben laughed. "He is. That day Mom was due in surgery and

Henry was well-known to the staff, so she let Max stay with him."

"HEA," Etta said. At Ben's look, she said, "And that led to a happily-ever-after."

"Eventually, yes. Mom used to say that she married Dad because Max wanted him so very much. It started out as a marriage of convenience for them. Dad wanted a family and Mom needed help. Later, it became a love match. Mom was type A on steroids, while nothing ever flusters Dad."

Some things do, she thought. "And what about Max? Which parent is he like?"

Ben smiled. "He's Dad all over again, except that he can never seem to settle anywhere. My brother has been offered a job in Mason, Kansas, but no one believes he'll take it. He's a bit of a tumbleweed. Which brings me to what I was told that I must ask you. But feel free to say no."

"What is it?"

"Dad is fierce about finishing the last part of your novel. He said that by now you know the ending." Ben waited for her reply.

"I do," she said softly but didn't elaborate. She didn't want to repeat that memory in thoughts or words.

"Dad made me swear to ask a favor of you."

"What does he want?"

"He asked Max to drive down to KC and go on a road trip with you. Of course Max said yes. Dad wants to see what's been done to that little town, Garrett. Max is a good photographer and an even better artist. He's not as good as Dad but close."

She thought of Max with Nellie's watercolors and the sketchbooks. "I bet he had years of lessons from Henry."

"He did! So maybe you'll agree to go with Max to see the town? And maybe you'll make a recording of the last part of the story so Dad can transcribe it?"

"Yes, I'll do that." Etta could feel her heart in her throat. She was to go with Max.

"I think you two will get along, but be warned that my brother isn't the heroic man like in your story. And by the way, he's not read the story you and Dad are creating. Max is more—" Ben cut off as he looked to the side. "Speak of the devil, here he is. Max! Come here and talk to Etta."

To her shock, Max, *her* Max, took the phone. The last time she'd seen him…

"Hi," he said. "I've heard a lot about you."

It was Max's face. His voice. She looked at him as though drinking him in. Studying the face she loved. "Your ear is scarred," she managed to say.

Grinning, he put his fingers on his earlobe.

Max's fingers. Max's smile.

"Oh that," he said. "I caught it on barbed wire when I was a kid. Mom sewed it back on."

And Henry never said a word when he heard that in my story, she thought. *I'm going to kill him.*

"I hope you're okay about this. Dad conned me into doing work for him. Not that *you* are work, but…"

Etta was recovering. "I know Henry. It's always, 'Get the story done no matter what.' Sure, I'll do it. Come here whenever you can."

"Actually, I was thinking of leaving in about an hour. I'll get there late, so I'll see you in the morning. If that's okay with you. I'll be in Dad's little house. He said you chose my room to stay in."

She'd said it was Ben's room and Henry didn't correct her. "It was the buffalos on the curtains that did it."

"I've always loved animals. I better go. Caro has me on baby-sitting duty. I'll see you soon." He handed the phone back to his brother.

Ben said, "You're sure about this? It's not an imposition?"

"No, I look forward to it."

"Great! Dad knows the people who run the Garrett Historical Society. With this lockdown, the town is closed, but they said that for Henry, they'd let you visit. Every building will be open. You and Max will have the whole town to yourselves. Dad said you can even spend the night there in a hotel."

"Uh…" She didn't know what to say to that.

Ben grew serious. "You needn't worry about Max. He won't overstep. Uh-oh. The doctor's here, I have to go."

"Text me," Etta said quickly. "And send photos."

"Will do," Ben said, then ended the call.

Etta put her suitcase on the floor and went to bed early. It had been an exhausting day. Way too much information had been heaped onto her.

Part of her wanted to figure it all out but another part thought it was too much to comprehend. She was trying not to feel betrayed by Henry for not telling her about his other son, but she couldn't do it.

Then there was her father. As soon as Etta left the house, he sold it. Had he been hoping that she'd leave? And Lester. He hadn't even called to tell her his decision.

She got into bed and opened her laptop. There was something she wanted to check. She typed in Kecklin, Kansas. It came up empty. There was no such place and she was pleased.

She opened the only entry for Kecklin and saw that it was a bio for Miss Bella Kecklin. *The woman who made the museum,* Etta thought.

Miss Kecklin had married Ralph Pence, a prominent businessman, and they'd two children. The bio said that Mrs. Pence's ancestor was John Kecklin, who was known for contributing heavily to the beautiful church in Garrett, Kansas. Mrs. Pence had been involved in the restoration of the town and was now on its board of directors. "She is a highly valued woman," the article said.

Etta closed her computer. "At least we accomplished something," she said, then turned out the light and snuggled down. Tomorrow she would see the church and the town. And Max. She went to sleep.

24

Etta woke to the smell of coffee and to the feeling that the house was no longer empty. She got up, showered, dressed, and went downstairs. She glanced inside rooms but no one was there. In the kitchen, the coffeepot was full and there was an old canvas bag on the tall table.

Slowly, anticipating but also dreading what she'd see, she turned to look through the glass doors to the outside. Sitting on a chair, his feet propped on another one, was Max. He held a sketchbook and pencil and was drawing something.

Right away, she saw that although he looked like her Max, it wasn't him. He was a bit taller, heavier, and older than the man she loved. She'd never asked Max his age because she knew he was younger than she was. But this man was a bit older than she was. He was in profile, showing skin that had seen a lot of sun and wind, and probably some hardship. He was a handsome man, like a model you'd see in a travel brochure. *Come on safari with us*, it would say."

She glanced down at the bag on the counter. It was old and worn, like something in a Ralph Lauren ad. On top was a little red photo album. It was open to a picture of Max holding his newborn niece. He looked very happy.

She knew she shouldn't but she flipped the pages. The pictures were from all over the world. Max was with people and animals in India, China, Africa. There were two photos of a beautiful, tall, thin blonde young woman. One of them was signed, *With all my love, Mandy.*

She put the album back to the way it was. There were no signs that he'd cooked anything, so she whipped up a couple of breakfast platters, put them and drinks on a tray, and went to the door. Her hands were full, so she knocked on the glass with her elbow.

Max looked up, smiled, stood, and opened the door for her. "This is a treat," he said.

It was her Max's voice. If they were standing side by side, they'd be considered brothers, with just age separating them.

But for all the resemblance, the eyes weren't the same. Maybe the two men were physically alike, but they looked at Etta differently. This man didn't have her Max's look, the one that said though he didn't know what to make of Etta, he was very interested.

Most important was that she felt no attraction to this man. She had no desire to throw her arms around him and certainly not to rip his clothes off. "I figured that if you're like your father, you're hungry."

He gave a little laugh, a sound she'd heard many times. They sat down across from each other and began to eat.

"Do you mind?" She nodded to his sketchbook.

"Not at all."

It was a black-and-white drawing of the corner of the house with roses on the wall. Quite sweet, but somehow a bit sad.

She looked at him in question. Though there was no sexual tension between them, she felt that she knew him. Like a brother she hadn't seen in a while. She knew he had intentionally made the drawing look like a memory.

He understood. "Caro has family outside Denver, so they want their kids to grow up near their grandparents."

"Henry is a grandfather." She sounded defensive.

"Yeah, but he's one. Caro has four grands and lots of cousins, aunts, and uncles. And they like the weather there better. Skiing at Wolf Creek, that sort of thing."

There wasn't anything she could say. He was telling her what Henry had worried about on the first day. No one wanted to live in his beautiful house.

"Dad won't leave here." He gave her a serious look. "We talked about it, and we really hope you'll stay here with him."

"I don't know if I can do that."

"Yeah, I guess not. I'm sure you have your own life. And old places need constant maintenance." They both knew he was talking about Henry as well as the house. "But just so you know, Ben and Caro and I would pay you the going rate, whatever that is. And there's free room and board." He was looking at her with *please* in his eyes.

She shrugged. "My life is upside down right now."

"You and me both." He took a bite of his omelet. "This is very good. If you need more to do, you could open a restaurant."

"Or I could take the job offered to you in Mason. I'd have to learn some, but there are no pet elephants around here so maybe I could do it."

Again, he laughed. "I see why Dad speaks so highly of you." He cocked his head to one side. "I feel like I know you. I don't mean to be overly familiar, but there's something about you that

I seem to…to remember. But that makes no sense. We haven't met before, have we?"

She was glad he hadn't read the book where the main characters were named Max and Etta. That would be embarrassing. She shook her head no, that they hadn't met, then looked away. "I know what you mean. Henry and I bonded quickly. I'm sure he's disappointed that you're not taking the job here in Kansas."

"Dad's the one who found it. The man who owns the clinic lives in a house that belonged to an ancestor of his."

"Henry Frederick, the itinerant painter. He built the house for his beautiful bride, but she died young. It's said that he shut the door to the house and never went back. He traveled for the rest of his life."

Max was looking at her. "Dad never told me that story."

A porter on a train back in 1871 told me and so did your doppelganger, she thought but didn't say. "Just a few weeks around your father and I've become obsessed with the past. There's a book in the library by the painter."

Max looked shocked. "I've never seen it."

What could she say? That the book was published in the nineteenth century but had just appeared now? And that something in it had greatly upset Henry? Or maybe she should tell him that she feared if she read it, she might go into a downward spiral with no return.

Max was staring at her as though he was going to start a barrage of questions. *Like father, like son*, she thought. *The interrogators.* She glanced at his empty plate. "I'd like to show you something."

When he hesitated, she figured it was because he wanted them to leave on their road trip soon.

"It'll only take minutes, then we can go. I imagine you want to get back to Henry."

"You're very perceptive, and yes, I'd like to go back, but I have a favor to ask of you."

"Anything," she said sincerely.

"Would you drive? It was an eight-hour trip here and I haven't slept. I thought I might take a nap in the car on the way to this place."

"I wouldn't mind at all, but I have no car here."

"That's right. Dad picked you up off the street."

She laughed. "He did."

"I have Zack's car."

"Of course you do. The Bronco. I bet you two are friends."

Again, he gave her that cocked head look, just as her Max did. "We are. Dad has a way of finding people we feel good with."

She turned away. *Freddy, Sally, Bert, Cornelia.* The list was long, with doubles of everybody. If this man ever met her family, he'd like them too. Especially Alicia. Were they all some karmic family that kept choosing to live their lives together? If so, this time sucked.

She led the way through Henry's library to the alcove. The old carved panel was leaning against the empty place in the front of the desk.

"You found it!" Max picked up the heavy board. He sat down on the couch, studying the carving. "This is why Dad bought the desk."

"It was out in the open? I'd think that some collector would have paid a lot for it."

"It wasn't visible. Dad crawled under the desk. I don't know what made him suspicious, but he knows history. Anyway, he said there was something hidden in the back."

"So he bought the desk and took it out. But why did he hide it again?"

"Because of me. I was fascinated with this picture. I would sit on the floor and stare at it for hours. I said I wanted to be the man on the horse. I even tried to get Dad to buy me a breech-cloth."

All Etta could do was nod at what he was saying.

"One day Ben kicked a ball and hit it. See here? There's a tiny chip that Dad repaired. He was afraid Ben and I would hurt it, so he took the panel out. He said he put it in a safe-deposit box at the bank." Max shook his head. "But he just turned it around."

"I bet it was you who found the key and opened the trunk from the auction."

"You caught me. That was another obsession of mine. I kept on until I figured it out." He kept staring at the artwork. "Now, looking at this as an adult, it's not right. That woman isn't wearing the traditional indigenous dress. And the man on the horse has a rifle. That would scare the buffalo. It might make them stampede and kill people. Maybe—"

Etta took the panel out of his hands and put it on the desk top—over the closed portrait of her and Max. If he saw that, he'd ask too many questions. "Do you have a camera ready to take with us? Maybe you could print out the directions while I throw together some food. There aren't many places open now. Do you have the art supplies you'll need?"

He was looking up at her with the amused expression that she'd seen on her Max many times.

A feeling of such lust ran through her that her scalp spit out tiny beads of sweat.

His expression changed to surprise when he seemed to feel it too.

Etta nearly ran from the room. "Ten minutes," she called over her shoulder. Upstairs in her bedroom, she closed the door and leaned against it for a moment. "He is not my husband, and he never will be," she said aloud. She went to the bathroom and splashed her face with cold water.

Max started to get in the front passenger seat. "I can sleep anywhere," he said.

Etta didn't want him so close to her. Asleep, he might remind her even more of her Max. She opened the back door and told him to stretch out across the back seat.

As her Max had often done, he smiled at her bossiness. She handed him a pillow and Henry's lap robe, and he thanked her. She saw in the rearview mirror that he was asleep before she pulled out of the driveway.

She was glad of the drive as it gave her time to think. When she was in the past, she'd seen the life she wanted to live. Home and family. It's what she'd thought she had, but now it seemed that it was an illusion. Alicia had been craving her own home, and her father wanted to get away from responsibilities. He'd wanted the freedom to go and do. Etta seemed to be holding him back.

She knew that it was up to her to figure out what to do now. She'd had a good job offer. She could stay in KC and be Henry's assistant, his caretaker. But would she want to stay after she'd told him what happened the last time she'd seen Max?

When the word "last" came to her mind, it upset her so much that she almost ran off the road. It was good that there was no traffic and she was avoiding all the major highways. As Zack had done, she was going by farm roads.

By the time she saw a sign that said Garrett Historical Site, she'd made no decisions, no plans about her future.

She drove through a small town that in other circumstances would have been flourishing, but now there were no people on the streets. Even the little hospital on the outskirts looked empty. "That's good," she murmured and kept driving. A sign advertising Wild Prairie Sage Beer made her do a double take. Could it be the same one?

Finally, a sign sent her down a side road and through an open gate. Beyond it she could see the buildings of the town, her Garrett, Kansas. She started to wake Max and tell him but she didn't. He could see it later. Right now she wanted to look and say nothing.

The car rolled down the street, which was clean and had some modern surface on it. Not asphalt, not gravel, and certainly not horse manure.

The first thing she noticed was the absence of many of the saloons. It looked like the historians didn't want to admit that their ancestors' favorite pastime was getting drunk. *Rotgut whiskey was probably what created your great-great-grandfather,* she thought.

The Red Dog was one of the saloons that had been rebuilt. Etta doubted that this one was as dirty as the real one had been. She wondered if Freddy saw this place, would she remember it?

Not far away was the doctor's house, and she was glad to see that the window John Kecklin had stolen was there. The Garrett Emporium and the sheriff's office were in place, and to the far right was the train station. She knew Fred Harvey had set up his restaurants, and she wondered if her words had given him the idea. *I like to think I made a contribution.*

The town was one street so there were no alleyways, no forge for Phillip, no big stables where the horses were kept. And she didn't see any outhouses anywhere.

All in all, it was a clean, nonsmelly version of Garrett and she loved it.

She had reached the end of the street. What she had so carefully and studiously avoided looking at was the church.

She glanced back to Max. He was still sound asleep, so Etta allowed herself to look through the windshield at the church.

Where once had been a rustic, thrown-together structure, there was now a magnificent building. She knew enough about architecture to know it was Romanesque, simple, elegant, timelessly beautiful. Like Henry's house.

It was all brick. The center had a peaked roof, a round window in the apex, and an enormous, welcoming door. It was flanked by two towers with arched windows, a clock in each one, and topped by two very tall, pointed roofs. It was glorious. Stunning, really.

As Etta leaned on the steering wheel, she felt enormous pride. She knew Cornelia—her friend—had designed this.

The door was slightly open, and she wanted to see the inside. Opening the car door didn't so much as make Max stir, so she went up the stairs.

Inside, the church was long and narrow. At the far end was a domed ceiling that had been painted with angels. *Henry did that*, she thought.

There was a brochure on a table by the door. She put a twenty in the box, stuck the leaflet into her pocket, and walked down the aisle. There was an embroidered cloth near the pulpit. It was old and yellowed but exquisite. In the lower corner were the initials ALA. Alice Lawton Adams.

Etta turned back to look at the interior of the church, admiring its majesty as well as its beauty.

On the walls were plaques with names and dates. She walked along to read them, down one side, then up again. They were dedicated in memory of loved ones. World War I, World War II, the Korean War. Vietnam. One was to *"a loving mother and the best cook in the world."* Etta paused at a large plaque. *For John Kecklin, whose generosity built this church.*

"Well, Mr. Kecklin," she said, "looks like you got the remembrance you wanted so much." There was a small, rather insignificant plaque nearby. *Our eternal gratitude goes to Cornelia Kecklin Lloyd, who designed this church.*

Smiling, Etta kissed her fingertips and placed them on the bronze plate. Cornelia had used her talent in a way that benefited everyone.

When Etta reached the front, she saw a short red curtain on the wall. She wondered what was behind it and pulled the cord.

At the sight, she stepped backward.

On the wall was a big gray metal slab. It had the profiles of a man and woman on it, facing each other.

The portraits were of her and Max.

It said the church was dedicated to Henrietta and Maxwell Lawton. Below, in smaller letters, it said, *Max died saving others, and his beloved wife died minutes later. They leave behind many people who will love them forever.*

Etta staggered back as though she'd been hit. Turning, she ran down the long aisle, then out the door. Seeing that tribute made what happened too real. Until now, she'd been able to block it out, but the truth was finally hitting her.

She didn't know what would have happened if Max hadn't stepped out of the car. She didn't want him to see her in a state of panic, or in any deep emotion. Nor did she want to have to explain why she was near collapse.

Max was stretching and looking around at the town. "Cute," he said.

She didn't know if that was a compliment or a disparagement. She stepped away from the church and went down the stairs.

As he was opening the back of the car, he looked up at the church. "Now *that* is magnificent. Wonder why it was built in some two-bit cow town?"

"So the town and the people would be remembered forever," she said. "They succeeded." He was pulling out his camera equipment. "Do you mind doing that later?" she asked. "It's past lunch time, and I know a great picnic area."

Anything to give me a break from here, she thought.

He slid the case back into the car. "Great idea. Want me to drive?"

"I couldn't tell you how to get there. I'll just pretend this is a real bronco and follow its lead."

He looked at her in surprise, then said, "I like that idea."

She had no problem finding the stream, the place that had so many memories. But they were thoughts of peace and love, while the church held reminders of the end of life.

"This is great," he said as he got out. "Is that a sod house?"

Etta turned toward it. When she'd been there with Zack, the house had fallen in, but now it had been restored. Outside there were signs with pictures describing how it had been made. "Yes, it is."

"Dad will want photos of that!"

"Go," Etta said. "I'll set out lunch."

"You don't want to see it?"

To see where Max and I made love? No thanks! "Maybe later," she said.

"Sure." He got out his bag of photo equipment and left.

The first thing Etta did was check the rock by the stream where she and Zack had found the bear. Just as before, behind the plants was the name Etta and an arrow pointing downward. But she knew she still had the bear so it was no longer buried.

When she went back to the car, just as she reached for the picnic basket, her phone rang. It was a FaceTime call, and she was tempted to not answer it. But she did.

It was Henry. He was in a hospital bed and he looked like he'd aged in the last few days but then so had Etta.

"Do you hate me?" he asked, his eyes sad.

She wasn't going to give in to him. "Don't give me that puppy dog look," she snapped. "You did a rotten thing to me. You lied, scammed, and tricked me. And for what?"

Henry's face brightened. "No sympathy for poor old me? Are you sure? They're about to roll me into surgery."

"Which you should have had months ago. But no, you scared everyone by refusing to get the surgery, then you refused to leave Kansas, then you—"

"Etta!" he said loudly. "I want to tell you the truth."

"That would make for a change."

He gave her a little smile. "You did a lot for many people. You righted some wrongs, saved lives. You and I and Zack are the only ones who know the truth of all you accomplished."

She wished his flattery had no effect on her, but it did. Her anger calmed. "Max…" she whispered.

"Yes, I know. I read about it in the big art book."

"The one *you* wrote. The first Henry. Your Max is a lot like him. He can't stop moving around." She paused. "Are you going to tell me what freaked you out so much that you became the drama queen and demanded to go to Denver?"

With a laugh, he shook his head. "Sometimes you remind me of my beloved Martha. She never gave sympathy either."

"I'd take that as a compliment if I hadn't met her."

"It is the greatest of compliments. Okay, a couple of years ago, I had a dream. It was as vivid and as real as anything you experienced."

"I'm listening."

"It was a view into the future. I saw that my beloved Max would be killed in an accident. Something would hit him in the heart. I couldn't see what it was, but it was instantly fatal."

"That happened to *my* Max," she whispered. "Not yours."

"Maybe," he said. "But then, the dream changed and I saw a lovely young woman. You. I was made to know that *you* could save my son. I didn't know how, but I did know that I was to stay in my old house and wait for you."

"And that dream is why you refused to look after your heart?"

"Yes. Besides waiting for you, I knew that under no circumstances was I to ever mention Max to you. And that was it. I woke up and I knew what I had to do. I waited until you came down my street pulling that little case behind you. I was very afraid that you'd refuse the cookies and lemonade, but you didn't." He looked on the verge of tears. "I'm sorry I lied to you, but I would do anything for my children."

"So when you read about my Max in the big book…"

"I thought that tragedy might duplicate itself in my son. I had to see that he was all right."

"Then later, you contrived to send him here to me."

"Yes, I did." He sounded proud. "My wish is for him to find someone to share his life."

She knew he meant her, but that wasn't going to happen. "I think he has. He carries photos of a beautiful young woman named Mandy."

Henry looked like he was trying to figure out how to say something.

"What is it you're trying to tell me?"

"I know you were annoyed by all the questions I asked you, but I wanted to know things that I couldn't tell you about."

"Such as?"

"I wanted to know if your Max was like mine."

"Was he?"

"I think that at the beginning he was. But my Max has always had a deep streak of melancholy in him. He was like that even when I met him as a child. Maybe it was because his father died when Max was so young. Whatever it was, the emptiness has never left him, and he's searched the world trying to fill it."

"Maybe he has with Mandy."

"He hasn't seen her in months, and he doesn't miss her at all. I asked."

When Henry was silent, she said, "Max and Ben want me to stay on and look after you." She saw him smile. "That means I'd be stuck with going through that mess of files you have hidden under the stairs. Including the ones I dumped out."

"I hope you'll say yes. You are wonderful company and your food is divine."

"Your Max said I should open a restaurant."

"Ah," Henry said. "You two. Maybe you will—"

"No," she said firmly. "There is nothing between your Max and me, and there never will be. He looks at me differently than my Max did." Her eyes lightened. "But if I grew a trunk and had really long eyelashes, he might be interested."

Henry laughed. "Oh, Etta, I've grown to love you so much.

Please stay. If you want a boyfriend, I'll find you one. I have lots of friends."

"Some nerdy guy who never looks up from a book? I am spoiled by the sight of a buffalo hunter in a breechcloth."

Henry looked away from the phone, then back. "They've come to get me. What did you think of the church?"

She knew he was asking about the dedication. "It nearly broke my heart, but I'm glad that my friends are remembered."

"Me too," he said.

A woman's voice said, "You need to close that now."

"Please stay with me at least until I get the book done," he said quickly.

"Only if we change the names. I get to be Rowena with violet eyes and Max is—" She didn't finish as a hand took the phone away from Henry and cut off contact.

Etta turned her phone off and put it in the picnic basket. She didn't want to talk to any more people. She just wanted to enjoy where she was—and maybe think about where her life was headed.

When Max returned, she was by the water and she'd set the food out on a pretty cloth.

"How was it?" she asked.

"Unsettling. I was struck with strong déjà vu, like I'd been there before. I felt a mixture of misery and happiness." He gave a crooked grin. "And sex. That was there too. And love. I don't mean to sound too wimpy, but I felt an all-consuming, do-or-die love. I envy whoever lived there."

Again, Etta felt that tingle when looking at him. It was almost like her Max was somewhere deep inside him. She turned away.

Max shook his head as though trying to rid himself of his thoughts, then looked at the basket. "You made all this in the minutes before we left?"

"Yes."

He started piling meat and cheese onto bread. "I identify

with the owner of the place. There was a whole row of old-time canned peaches in there. My favorite fruit."

Something else Henry didn't remark on, she thought. "So. You became a veterinarian."

"I did. I wanted a job that would let me travel. There are animals everywhere."

She made herself a sandwich. "You weren't tempted to become a doctor like your mother?"

"Too much responsibility. When a patient died, Mom would get depressed."

"I never saw that in Martha. I guess she hid it." When Max was silent, she realized her error. "Sorry. I've read and heard so much about this place that I feel like I know the people."

"Ben said you and Dad were writing a novel, a piece of fiction. He's never done that before. You two work well together."

She didn't want the conversation to be about her. "I guess you know that he wants you to stay here."

"Oh yeah. Like Ben. Marriage and kids and a mortgage." When he looked at her, his eyes were sparkling. "I'm willing, but she hasn't found me."

Etta remembered what she'd been told, but she wanted to hear his side. "What do you mean?"

"When I was a teenager and saying I wanted to travel forever, Dad said that some girl would find me."

"Like Henry found you."

He gave a little laugh. "You know as much about my family as I do. Anyway, Dad said this girl would find me no matter where I was in the world. Even if she had to travel from the moon. She hasn't found me yet, so I must keep wandering."

"Maybe she'll go in the other direction. If you were in, say, 1871, maybe she would appear out of nowhere. She'd suddenly be standing in a church wearing a lace jacket and her father would be conducting a marriage ceremony."

Max laughed. "Ben said your book was good. I see how vivid your imagination is. I really hope you'll stay with Dad."

"So you can leave?" There was a wave of something that crossed his eyes. A sadness, a longing, and it was painful to see. "What happens if she finds you?" she asked. "Would you trade the jungles of the world for a mortgage?"

He looked as though all humor had left him. "I'd trade my life for what my brother has."

For a moment their eyes locked, and it was like a bond passed between them. They understood each other. She saw what Henry called the "melancholy" and the emptiness that lived inside him. She had a feeling that her eyes looked exactly the same.

He was the one to turn away. "What's that?"

He was looking at the brochure she'd picked up at the church. She handed it to him.

He unfolded it and looked at the photos. "It's nice to see a forgotten town so well documented. 'Cornelia Kecklin Lloyd,'" he read out loud. "She seemed to have been the money behind it all. Wonder where it came from?"

"Her father, John Kecklin, tried to buy Kansas. Looks like his daughter talked him out of it. What does it say about her?" She handed him a chocolate-covered oat bar.

He began to read.

"'The small town of Garrett, Kansas, was frozen in time by the renowned artist, Henry Fredericks, in his book of drawings and paintings from 1871.

"Unfortunately, when the train moved to Wichita, the townspeople left. They abandoned their homes and businesses, often leaving their possessions behind.

"Over the years, only the church was kept in repair, while the town buildings were allowed to decay. In 1930, Mrs. Cornelia Kecklin Lloyd, the brilliant architect for the Church of Garrett, was eighty-six years old. She said that it was a 'loss of our heritage' that the town would eventually disappear.

"Mrs. Lloyd hired her son and her four grandchildren to rebuild the town, using Kecklin money. In the restoration, she gave many jobs to people during the Depression. It took years to rebuild the town, but Mrs. Lloyd lived long enough to see it restored to what it had been. At the ribbon cutting, she said, 'I cannot adequately describe what it means to me to see this dear little town brought back to life. To those of us who lived here, it wasn't just a town. It was where we made lifelong friends. To me and to the people I have lost, it is the most beautiful place on earth. I miss all of you and I will join you soon.'"

Etta was blinking quickly. Cornelia had lost her beloved Bert, but she'd had at least one child and multiple grandchildren.

"You okay?" Max asked.

"Fine. I'm glad she got to see the town restored."

He seemed about to say something, but instead he looked back at the brochure. "This is interesting. There's a plaque of dedication in the church. It was made by Henry Fredericks and has profiles of a man and a woman." He held up the photo to her, and she politely pretended to look at it, but she didn't. Seeing it once was enough.

"The man, Maxwell Lawton, was a rancher and it says he gave up his life to stop an attack." Max looked up. "An attack on what? Who?"

"If he prevented it, it wouldn't be in any of the history books so we wouldn't know about it."

"Good point." He looked back at the paper. "It says it wasn't known where his wife came from, but she helped with a buffalo hunt." He smiled at that, then frowned. "This is far-fetched, but I wonder if that relief on Dad's desk has anything to do with this?"

"There were lots of hunts," was all Etta could think to say.

"Where we got the desk, in Mason, is a long way from here. Although, that's where the Fredericks house is. Maybe—"

She interrupted him. "What else is in there?"

"Opening hours and how much children can learn from visiting the town. They stage gunfights. Gotta have violence." He refolded the pamphlet and looked at the back. "Here's a list of people who did the restoration. No, that's not right. It says that Mrs. Lloyd wanted the original people involved in building the church to be noted."

"Read it to me," Etta said softly.

"Okay. Here's an interesting fact. The first pastor of the new church was a black woman, Sally Roberts. It says she could sing."

"She could," Etta said. "Beautifully."

"During the week, the church was used as a school that was run by Lillian Wellman, whose husband was the accountant for the whole project."

Etta's throat closed and she couldn't speak. Her parents did marry.

"Needlework was done by Alice Lawton Adams, and her husband, Patrick, made the big bells in the towers. Mrs. Lloyd's husband Bertram was legal counsel." Max looked at Etta, but she was staring at the water and said nothing.

"It seems that there was a garden in the back. I wonder if it's still there," he said. "It was designed by—" The pamphlet slipped out of his hand, and he made a grab to get it.

"Freida Simmons," Etta said. "Is Rufus in there?"

"Yeah. You know your history. The garden was created by Freida and Rufus Voss."

Etta nodded. "Anything else?"

"In 1890, the care of the church was handed over to Miss Nellie Adams, who ran it for the rest of her life. I guess she's related to the other Adams."

"Pat's daughter," Etta said.

Max put the brochure in the basket, and Etta started straightening up. "Tell me how you know so much about this place."

She managed a smile. "Maybe someday. The next time you're

home I'll make margaritas and nachos, and I'll tell you the whole story."

He frowned but he saw that she wasn't going to say more. "That sounds like a deal. Etta?"

She looked at him.

"Thank you for coming into our lives. Ben and Caro and I have been in agony at leaving Dad alone, but…"

"You have to follow your own dreams. Henry knows that." She smiled. "I'm glad your father and I found each other. We both need things and…" She didn't finish that thought. "You ready to go take pictures of the town?"

"I am. I think I'll do some sketches of the church. You don't expect something like that to be on the plains. I wonder why Mrs. Lloyd put it here and not in KC or another city? And why in the world didn't Dad take us to visit it when we were kids?"

All because of me, she thought. *Because I said I hated to see the people and the town disappear as though they'd never existed. But that didn't happen. The people I loved didn't vanish without a trace. Each of them left a part of themselves behind. We were here, they seemed to say. And we contributed something beautiful to the world.*

Max was staring at her.

She couldn't tell him her thoughts. "I'm trying to remember all of your father's instructions. Did you get pictures of the stream?"

"No," he said and got out his camera.

She was glad she'd given him something to do while she packed the car.

25

As Etta drove them back to the town, Max's attention was on the buildings. "Planning your shots?" she asked.

"Yup. I think I'll set up a tripod. I brought an extra camera body. Would you like to take some interiors?"

She hesitated. She wasn't sure she wanted to see the place more closely. Comparisons of past and present might take too much out of her.

"Or not," Max said.

"I've never been good at photography but I'll try. I could—" She broke off at a sound. "What is that?"

Max put his window down. "It's a bell ringing."

Etta smiled at the heavy, methodical sound. "I bet your dad arranged that to welcome us."

"It's the kind of thing he'd do. Let's go see."

She parked the car some distance away from the church, and

they got out. Max went inside, but Etta couldn't bring herself to go in. As she waited for him to return, the sound of the bell grew so loud it was all that could be heard.

When Max came out of the church, he was frowning. "The door up to the tower is locked," he said loudly over the pealing. "I don't like this." He ran down the stairs, and Etta followed him.

He stepped back from the church and looked up. "It's coming from that tower. Someone is up there." He yelled, "Who are you?" There was no answer. He looked back at her. "I hope it's not kids. I bet there are usually caretakers here, so they're taking advantage of the place being empty."

Etta looked up to see that the big bell was swinging so hard that the side of it was coming out of the arched window. Whoever was doing it seemed to have a malicious streak. "Please don't hurt Pat's bell," she said.

"Go back to the car," Max said. "I'm going to get that door open and stop this."

He spoke in the voice of her Max. It was a command, and she nodded and turned away. In the next second, there was a boom, like cannon fire as seen in old movies.

Etta whipped around in time to see that the bell had come loose, and it was falling. From where she was standing, it was headed toward Max. He stood there, unmoving, as though he was paralyzed.

She ran faster than she'd ever run, and for the last feet, she made a flying leap.

When the huge bell came down, the bottom edge of it hit Max's chest just before Etta fell on him and knocked him to the ground. She landed facedown beside him while he was on his back. Terror flooded her. She couldn't move. She was sure he was dead.

It was a groan that made her lift up.

Max was staring at the sky. "That was close," he said.

She was so relieved that she grabbed his face and kissed him firmly on the mouth. "You're alive."

He grinned at her. "It appears that I am." He was looking up at the tower. "Did you see anyone leave?"

"No." She was still lying beside him, her arm across his chest. "Are you sure you're okay?"

He put his hand to his chest. "Yes." He started to sit up but had to pause when dizziness overtook him.

Etta grabbed his shirt and tore open the front of it. There was a red mark just over his heart. Not big and not bloody. Maybe it was her imagination, but it was exactly where the arrow had hit her Max.

"See?" he said. "It's just a bruise. I don't know what was wrong with me. I couldn't move." He started to get up but then put his hand to his forehead. "I think I'll sit here for a while."

Etta leaned back on her heels. "I want you to get into the car. I'm taking you to the emergency room."

"No," he said. "I'm fine. I still want to find out who was up there."

"No one was," she said. "Max!" She was stern. "You're going to get into the car and I'm taking you to the hospital. Do you understand me?"

"Sure." He smiled as though she was amusing. "If it'll make you feel better."

She had to help him up, and she kept her arm around his waist as they went to the car. She insisted that he lie down on the back seat.

"My home away from home," he joked as he got in.

As Etta got in the driver's seat, her hands were shaking.

"If I'd known being hit by a bell would get me kissed, I'd have done it sooner."

She was looking at him in the mirror, and she saw that he closed his eyes. She yelled his name twice, but he didn't respond. It looked like he had passed out.

Etta pushed the red triangle button on the car, making the emergency lights flash, then she sped down the street of Garrett. She was grateful there was no traffic, so when she hit the pavement, she went as fast as she could make the car go.

When she saw the hospital, she laid down on the horn. The staff seemed to know what to do because when she skidded to a stop under the portico, they were outside, a gurney ready.

They had Max out of the back seat and onto the gurney before Etta could cut the engine and get out. As she ran toward the entrance, a young man held out his hand and she tossed him the keys.

Inside, she was blocked from following Max to wherever they were taking him.

"We need some information," a woman said.

Etta looked at her blankly, not understanding what she was saying.

"I need his name and address," the woman said.

"I have to tell Henry," Etta whispered.

The man who'd taken her keys handed Etta her purse. She got her phone, and with shaking hands, she called Henry's number. It went to voice mail. She left no message. She called Ben and he answered. "Max has been hurt. I'm at..." Wild-eyed, she looked at the nurse.

The woman took the phone from her and gave Ben the necessary information. Another nurse led Etta to a chair and sat her down. The woman who had her phone came to Etta and said, "Ben will be here as soon as he can. Do you understand me?"

Etta nodded.

"I'm going to give you a sedative and when we know something, we'll tell you."

"Etta?" she heard someone say. "Etta?"

She was curled up in a chair in a hospital waiting room, and she'd been sleeping. She woke but she was groggy. Bert was leaning over her. "Is Cornelia all right? Where's Alice?"

"Etta!" Bert said. "You're dreaming of your book. Max is all right. Do you hear me? Thanks to your swift action, he's going to be fine."

Her mind was beginning to clear. "Ben?"

"Yeah. It's me."

"What time is it?"

"Two hours and twenty-two minutes after you called me. One of Caro's clients has a plane. He set it down on a road near here and I ran."

She sat up in the chair. "Max!"

Ben sat down in the chair beside her. "I told you. He's okay, but the doctor said that whatever hit him nearly broke his heart."

"Max is sad but—"

"No," Ben said, "not like that. I mean physical. If you hadn't got him here—" Ben broke off as he began to cry.

Etta put her arms around him and held him while he sobbed.

After a few minutes, he said, "I'm sorry," and pulled away. "To lose my brother is too much to think of. Thank you."

"How is Henry?" she asked.

"We haven't told him anything. His surgery went well. The doctor said there's no reason he won't live for another ten years. Dad said, 'Good! I have a book to finish.'"

Etta gave a semblance of a smile. "Have you seen Max?"

"Not yet, but he should wake up soon." Ben hesitated. "They're saying 'family only' can see him."

"I understand. As long as he's okay, I'm happy. When can he leave the hospital?"

"Not for days. They want to make sure he's all right. I thought about your book. I'm glad this isn't 1871 or Max wouldn't have made it."

She realized that Ben hadn't read the ending, but then Henry hadn't written it yet. She mumbled, "Yes, very glad." When she stood up, she was wobbly and caught the chair arm to steady herself.

"You don't need to leave."

"Henry said I could stay in one of the hotels in Garrett. But you don't have a car here."

Ben smiled. "Don't worry about me."

"I'll stay nearby so if either of you needs anything, let me know."

A doctor came to them. "He's awake," he said to Ben. "You can see him for a few minutes but he needs to rest." The doctor looked at Etta in question.

"I'm just a friend."

The doctor smiled. "From what I heard, you could drive at Daytona. I'm sure he'll want to thank you for saving him."

"I'm glad I could," Etta said. She picked up her handbag and looked at Ben.

"I have everything I need." He stood up and put his hands on her shoulders. "Etta, you will always have a family with us. We will be eternally grateful to you. Dad will..." Ben shook his head. "He's going to be a mess when he hears of Max's close call." Ben kissed her cheeks, then stepped away and started to go down the hall.

"No." A nurse had walked up, and she looked at the doctor. "He wants to see her. He's getting very agitated. He says he has to see Etta."

Ben was taken aback. "But I'm his brother."

The doctor spoke up. "He probably wants to thank the woman who saved him."

"But Ben should go first," Etta said. "I can see him tomorrow."

"Go," Ben said. "I don't care who he talks to first. I'm just glad he's talking."

The doctor said, "He may be a little confused, but that will probably wear off in a day or two. Physically, he's doing well."

Etta followed the nurse down the hall and went into Max's room.

The second she saw him, the hairs on the back of her neck stood up. Something about him was different.

"Etta," he said, then closed his eyes and gave a smile of contentment. He extended his hand to her and she took it. "What happened?" he asked, his eyes still closed.

"A bell fell on you."

He gave a little laugh then winced in pain. "Is that what you're calling an arrow?" His thumb was moving on her hand, rubbing it in affection.

"An arrow? Max?" she said softly. "Look at me."

He obviously had drugs in him, and he was struggling to stay awake. "There are so many things in my mind. I think I dreamed it all. My father is a good man, but he's ill. He needs me." Max started to sit up.

"It's all right. Henry is fine. He's well."

Max relaxed. "My mother is…" He smiled. "Martha. Can you imagine that?"

She was blinking rapidly. Had he read the book but told no one? Was that what he was remembering? "And Bert is actually your brother," she said.

"Yes. How did you know that?"

"Henry and I wrote it all down." She wondered how confused he really was. "What would you do if a horse had a bowel obstruction?" She'd heard that on TV.

"Electrolytes, fluids. Probably surgery." His eyes widened. "How do I know that?" He ran his hand over his face. "There are things in my mind that I don't understand. I've been places and done things. I like elephants and giraffes." He closed his eyes for a moment. "You're right. It wasn't an arrow. It was a bell. Did Alice's Pat make the thing? Did he throw it at me?"

Etta couldn't help laughing. He and Phillip were never going to be friends.

"Are you crying?"

"I think maybe I am."

"You're not going to go away again, are you? I don't think I can carry you up any stairs right now."

She shook her head no.

For a moment they looked at each other. "Things are different, aren't they?" he asked. "There's two of everything in my mind. Our home—yours and mine—is fading." Suddenly, he looked frightened. "Are you still my wife?"

She nodded, too choked up to speak.

"There's a voice in my head saying, 'She found me.' Do you know what that means?"

Again, she nodded.

He closed his eyes tight for a moment. "I have a job. With animals. And there's a house. Cornelia designed it." He smiled. "And Dad lives with us. You and he are friends." He paused. "There are people in my mind. They're the same but they're different. When I was a kid, I saw a wooden picture of you and me. I knew who we were but I didn't know. I—"

A nurse opened the door and looked at Etta. "You need to leave now. He has to rest." She closed the door.

Max tightened his grip on Etta's hand. "I think maybe I've traveled a very long way to get to you. I saw that arrow coming at me and I started praying. I said I wanted to go whenever you are. Not where but when. 'When' seemed to be your secret. Was I right?"

She kissed the back of his hand. "You are exactly right."

"You won't leave me again, will you?"

"No, never," she said. "I know for sure that throughout time, you and I will be together. Forever."

There were tears in Max's eyes as he held her hand. "I have a question. What's an emoji?"

She laughed and kissed him. "Tomorrow," she said. "I'll see you in the morning. We have a lot to talk about. And I promise that you can adjust to two worlds and duplicate people. I did."

His eyes were drooping with fatigue. "I look forward to it. Forever and always?"

"Yes," she said. "Always. Even time can't separate us." As she left the room, her smile was brighter than the hospital lights.

★ ★ ★ ★ ★